PENGUIN BOOKS

HANNAH'S GIFT

Thomas Eidson, whose work has been published in fifteen languages and in nineteen countries, is the author of four major works of fiction, all of which are published in Penguin. His parents and grandparents lived on farms and ranches in Oklahoma, Kansas and Southern Colorado, and it is out of oral family histories and storytelling that his books have grown. *St Agnes' Stand*, his first novel, was shortlisted for the 1994 *Sunday Express* Book of the Year Award and was winner of the 1995 W. H. Smith Thumping Good Read. It was followed by *The Last Ride, All God's Children* and *Hannah's Gift*. Thomas Eidson lives in the USA.

D1513716

BY THE SAME AUTHOR

St Agnes' Stand
The Last Ride
All God's Children

HANNAH'S GIFT

THOMAS EIDSON

PENGUIN BOOKS

PENGUIN BOOKS

Published by the Penguin Group
Penguin Books Ltd, 27 Wrights Lane, London w8 5tz, England
Penguin Putnam Inc., 375 Hudson Street, New York, New York 10014, USA
Penguin Books Australia Ltd, Ringwood, Victoria, Australia
Penguin Books Canada Ltd, 10 Alcorn Avenue, Toronto, Ontario, Canada m4v 3b2
Penguin Books (NZ) Ltd, Private Bag 102902, NSMC, Auckland, New Zealand

Penguin Books Ltd, Registered Offices: Harmondsworth, Middlesex, England

First published by Michael Joseph 1998
Published in Penguin Books 1999
1 3 5 7 9 10 8 6 4 2

Copyright © Thomas Eidson, 1998
All rights reserved

The moral right of the author has been asserted

Set in Monotype Baskerville
Printed in England by Clays Ltd, St Ives plc

Except in the United States of America, this book is sold subject
to the condition that it shall not, by way of trade or otherwise, be lent,
re-sold, hired out, or otherwise circulated without the publisher's
prior consent in any form of binding or cover other than that in
which it is published and without a similar condition including this
condition being imposed on the subsequent purchaser

For my friend,
David Wynne-Morgan

PROLOGUE

Los Angeles. 3 March 1997

The evening light from the windows had been filtered through rain clouds off the Pacific and was casting a shadowy grey wash over the small office. Father Richard Mulcahy sat behind his desk on the third floor of the archdiocese, his arthritic hands clasped around a cold mug of coffee, his eyes locked on a yellowed stack of manuscript paper. Father Mulcahy was tired but he couldn't rid himself of the sensation that he was not yet done with something. Something important. He moved in his chair, his legs shifting freely beneath his black cassock, then he raised a hand and touched absently at the Roman collar around his neck, as if he wanted to loosen it.

Father Roberto Cordova had been dead since early that morning, the rumour spreading quickly through the church bureaucracy that he had taken his own life. Mulcahy forced himself to look away from the manuscript, to let his gaze drift slowly over the desktop. It was cluttered with papers strewn helter-skelter around the computer that sat squarely in the centre. His life was just as jumbled, just as cluttered, he thought.

He reached and put a hand to the cold metal base of a crucifix that seemed to preside over the chaos of the desk, then glanced at the framed photograph beside it. It had been taken some twenty-five years before when he was a parish priest in East Los Angeles. He squinted harder, as if seeing something in it he didn't want to see. The man standing next to him in the photo was Father Cordova, his hair white, his body frail. He had been very old, Mulcahy realized, even then.

He took a deep breath and held it. Why had he done it? It seemed so against the old man's nature, so foreign to his love of life and God. It had been Father Cordova who had reasoned him out of quitting the church some thirty years before when his own faith had ground down with the daily priestly rituals of death, marriage and birth. Mulcahy closed his eyes and felt guilty that he had not spent more time with the old priest after he had retired. That he had abandoned him to a secular world. Was that what he had fled?

He could hear the sound of talking through the open doorway behind him, but it didn't hold his thoughts. Again, he was feeling that he was not done with something. But what? He had no idea. His eyes moved back to the yellowed stack of papers. He knew from talks with Father Cordova over many years what the manuscript meant to the old man. He'd never agreed with the priest regarding its authenticity or worth. And now, like some sort of boomerang of his disbelief hurtling back at him, it was his.

He rolled his shoulders to release the tension building in them. The yellowing pages had been found that morning near the old man's body with a note addressed to him. He re-read it, as he had been doing all day long: 'It is yours now.' That was all it said. There was something in the words that sounded like mockery, as if the old man hadn't written them, as if they'd been penned by someone laughing at the two of them.

He picked up the cold mug of morning coffee and took a sip and tried to remember back to when he had known the truth, or thought he had, about anything related to the faith. That had been a long time ago. The feeling was gone now, that headiness of being filled with boundless priestly joy and surety. He hadn't felt it in years. He wondered why. Was it simply part of the deadening journey from youth to old age? Or was it even more mundane than that? Had his heart medicine robbed him of the sensation? He didn't know. All he knew was that Father Cordova's faith had been anchored to the contents of the yellowed pages and now, suddenly, inexplicably, he'd taken his own life.

A sound drew his eyes to the window. He watched as a pigeon landed and balanced precariously on the thin concrete ledge, its wings battering against the glass as if it were frightened of something and trying desperately to get inside. Then suddenly the bird launched itself back into the air and flew across the parking lot to the large cross that towered in the centre of a small patch of green. Father Mulcahy tensed. No, his problem was more than lost youth or the side effects of medicine. His was a mortal sin. He had lost his faith. More frightening to him, he didn't know why. It was just gone. Gone as if it had been nothing more than a mystical fog burned away in the harsh light of reality. Once again, Father Mulcahy was gripped by the unsettling sense that there was something he must do. Whatever it was, he told himself, it would have to wait. He turned away from the window. It had been a long, trying day and he was tired. He stopped the movement of his swivel chair with his feet and sat staring at the neat stack of musty looking paper. He had been purposefully ignoring it since one of the priests who had been in Father Cordova's apartment had delivered it earlier that afternoon. He bit at the inside of his lip and continued to stare at the pages.

Father Cordova had always just called it 'the manuscript'. And he could see now that it was untitled. From their many talks, he knew that it had been written as a personal memoir

3

by a member of the diocese, Tucker Gibbens, the pages describing one week in Gibbens's life when he had served as a deputy sheriff for Los Angeles. That was it: one week. But seemingly the man had gone through fits for forty-some years trying to start and finish the work. The cover page said that he had begun writing in 1887, completing the work in 1928, the year of his death.

Mulcahy knew that Tucker Gibbens had been a member of Father Cordova's parish in Pasadena, California during the mid-twenties and that Cordova had helped the dying man finish the manuscript. For whatever reason, Gibbens and his story had left a deep and lasting mark on the young priest. One that had stayed with him almost until the very end. Almost to the end. Mulcahy shook his head. It was amazing what belief did to some.

He stood and walked to the window. The soft rustling sound of his cassock was reassuring in a funny way. Even with his lost faith he still knew who he was and what he had tried to accomplish during his sixty-seven years. Perhaps his religious beliefs had lost out to secular pragmatism, but he had still done good things. He had tried to live a decent life. To do what was honest and right in his own eyes and the eyes of the Church. To believe in the exalted goodness of mankind. To live simply and to love. Yes, he knew who he was and what he had done. That was more than most people could say about their lives.

Mulcahy stood staring out blindly at the glistening pools of water that had formed over the parking lot during the afternoon rain, listening to the growing silence of the archdiocese at evening time. Mass spoken in Spanish would begin in the first-floor chapel in fifteen minutes. And he needed to attend in Roberto's memory. Suddenly, he was feeling angry, his eyes locked on the manuscript.

4

He cleared his throat and picked it up, the sensation of work undone still gripping hard at the back of his neck like an invisible hand. He had loved the old priest like a father. So he would read Tucker Gibbens's story. He owed that to his friend. He sat down hard in his swivel chair and switched on his desk lamp . . .

CHAPTER ONE

El Paso, Texas. 17 July 1887

I was looking down the darkened alley-way past splashes of yellow light that pooled on the dirt beneath the cantina's windows and watching as the three men disappeared into the doorway. There was a piano playing somewhere and drunken laughter. The air was hot and the vault of black sky above was shot through with a blast of stars. I kept telling myself: it's almost over. It was coming to an end after three months and a thousand dirty miles of tracking. Ending in this hot, stinking little cluster of adobe hovels. I had promised myself that when I was done with these three – after I'd evened things – I would get on with it.

This last thought comforted me in some odd, sadistic way. It didn't matter what anybody thought about it. I had to do it. I'd decided to kill myself the night my wife died and I was just going through the motions of what was left of my life until somebody like these three did it for me, or I got tired enough to do it myself. I was getting close to being that tired now. Just finish this job, I told myself. I forced myself to study the front door of the cantina again.

I pushed my hat up and wiped sweat from my face with a handkerchief that had once been white but now more closely resembled the trail dust I'd been eating for weeks. It was then that I caught a brief glimpse of my face in a nearby window and wondered what my wife had ever seen in me.

Not short, not tall, well enough proportioned, dark haired, and in the eyes of some women who saw me, I guess, handsome. Still, I knew it was a hard kind of look that didn't give off much warmth. I was going to be thirty-three years old this next January, had been a lawman for eleven years . . . and tired of it for the past five. At my wife's urging, I'd enrolled in classes to study the one thing in this life that I loved best after her: butterflies.

I'd been a collector since a kid in Arizona but never figured there was any way to make a dollar at it. It was just something I loved, the way some men love gambling or women. She'd magically opened the door. Six months ago, I'd been offered a position as an assistant entomologist at the newly opened Museum of Natural History in Pasadena as soon as I took my degree. The pay wouldn't be much, but the job would be. But that was then. I shrugged the thought off and looked across the alley at the cantina again.

I might have guessed that the three men I'd tracked all the way from Los Angeles would end up in a misbegotten hole like this. They were foul souls. One, a Mexican, Altar Ramon, was a cutter, having knifed to death a number of California whores and more respectable citizens over the past five years. The other two were Americans – John Husker, big and fat and bald, and Wilbur Lessing, whose face had a sunkenness to it like it had been stomped by a boot. Those two were wanted on both sides of the border for various crimes, including killing women and kids. No better than pond scum. Well worth postponing things to finish off.

Somehow the three of them had tossed in together in Santa Barbara, drifted down to Los Angeles, played road bandits for a few weeks along El Camino Real, the old stage route that ran between Los Angeles and San Francisco, until I got a tip on their whereabouts from a padre at the San Fernando Mission. I was working as a deputy sheriff for the County of Los Angeles and, together with three other lawmen, surprised them one moonless night in a sheep-herder's shack in Sherman Oaks. That was three months back, a month after my wife's death. The memory caused the muscles across my shoulders to tighten.

I forced myself to focus back on the trap we'd set that night. Something had gone wrong. The men had killed the herder and one of the lawmen and high-tailed it into the dark on the backs of just two horses, riding into the Santa Monica mountains and losing themselves in the chaparral. They knew their way around in the sticks, I'll give them that. Like chasing smoke in the wind.

I had followed them into the brush-covered hills until my horse and I were cut up and bone-tired and I'd lost them good. It was then that I guessed they were headed for the Pacific Ocean; either to follow the coastline north toward their old stomping grounds, or south to San Diego or Mexico. Or maybe even to hire a boat to Santa Catalina or one of the Ventura coastal islands – though I didn't figure them the creative type. They were much more burp and scratch boys.

It didn't matter which way they went. Trying to find them on the beach would be a hell of a lot easier than doing it over sandstone hills. So after wasting a night and most of a day, I rode out of the brush and over Las Virgenes Pass to the ocean near Santa Monica. Then with nothing but a gut feeling to guide me, I'd turned my horse north along the sands, listening to the roaring surf and the screeching of the gulls, looking for fresh sign among the dead sand crabs and rotting seaweed. And remembering. I couldn't get my wife out of my mind. The sooner I caught up with these three, the sooner it would be over.

With two horses and three men, unless they were fools, they'd come down out of the hills and on to the beach at some point. Just to keep their horses from crapping out. Probably at night. Then they'd hug the shoreline. At least until they could find another horse to buy or steal. I was growing more and more convinced of the logic. I liked to reason things out. It was the best part of law work. While these three bums weren't logical, they were lazy. And that was something to bet on.

Standing in that El Paso alley, I remembered the ride along the sands, watching the sea birds rushing after the receding surf like they'd lost something valuable in it, the big-billed pelicans diving in the green waters beyond the breakers. It had been lonely. Damn lonely. My wife had loved the ocean, especially this desolate stretch of white sand that ran from Playa Del Rey some ninety miles north to Santa Barbara. We'd often used my days off to ride along it, camping at nights in the dunes. We would sit for hours listening to the steady rumbling of the big waves in the moonlight, watching the water surging to shore with a hissing sound, then rushing out again as if pursued by angry lovers. The salt and kelp smells over everything.

Yes, it had been a lonely trip. But I'd been right about the outlaws. Three days out, near Santa Cruz, I'd come upon the tracks of two horses trotting in wet sand where the tide had ebbed and not yet returned. One of the animals was riding heavy. Knowing the tides came every six hours, I guessed I was somewhere around five behind. I had the spoor in sight. And once on a decent trail, I rarely lost it. I'd kicked my horse into a slow lope.

That night I made camp in some sand dunes that would provide shelter from the sea breezes. I was no more than a couple of hours behind them now. I tossed some driftwood together and lit a small fire, and spent the night watching sparks climb like angry bees into the dark sky and thinking about my wife and similar fires, and our life together which had burned out like these sparks. I had loved her like I had loved no one else. I don't know what it was about her.

She'd been beautiful – tall and brown haired, blue eyed, thin and straight, strong in the shoulders and legs. But the best thing was she was always smiling. I loved that smile. She hadn't deserved to die at thirty, to lose her baby. But she had.

I pulled in a sharp breath and held it. When she and the child passed on, it took something out of my guts that was vital for me to keep on living. Now I didn't want to. Not if there was a chance I could exit this world and catch up with them across the black waters of time and space. If there was a god, I hated him for letting these two fall backwards into their graves and didn't give a damn what he thought about it.

The pounding of the night surf, eternal and abiding, white in the moonlight, dashing to and fro like ancient ghosts over a dark stage, slowly calmed me. My wife had loved it here, these sounds and misty sights. I would respect that: the memory of her intimacy with the starry ocean night, the black, restless waters and the shifting sands.

I gazed up at the field of yellow stars in the high night sky over the Pacific Ocean. 'Miss you,' I whispered, the words almost choking off my wind. Then I rolled myself in a saddle blanket and fought the moaning that welled in my breast. I dreamed about her that night, dreamed of what could have been, but never would be.

The next day at sun-up, the tracks of the two horses turned away from the shoreline and rode up the steep sandy slope toward a big white clapboard ranch house and prosperous looking barn that could be seen higher up in the green hills. These folks, the Ashwells, were friends of mine. My wife and I had often stayed with them during our coastal rides. They had two pretty daughters, Emily, fourteen, and Jane, sixteen. So I had put my horse into a canter, hoping that Leonard Ashwell had seen the men coming and that some of his hands had been around the house and barn.

I brought my thoughts back to this alley in El Paso. I had been thinking backwards a lot lately. And it hurt too much. I looked away from the yellow light of the cantina's doorway and broke open my shotgun, dropping two shells inside the heavy chambers and snapping the weapon closed again. With one hand I slipped the leather thong off the hammer of the revolver at my side, sliding the heavy weapon halfway up to make certain it would clear the holster without a hitch if I needed it. Finally, I checked to see that I had the two sets of hand manacles in the pocket of my suit coat, then patted the bulge under my vest, my four-shot belly gun.

I was ready. I would give the three men a couple of minutes more to get settled inside the cantina, then I'd spot them through the window, waiting to move through the door until I could get a clean drop on them. The rest would be easy. I'd manacle them together and march them off to the local jail. I didn't figure any of the locals would want to cut in on this dance. As for jail privileges, while I hadn't made the acquaintance of El Paso's sheriff, I had a legal California warrant for murder in my vest pocket and figured I'd have no trouble on that end of the game.

The alley remained empty. I leaned against a mud wall trying to look casual. My small-brimmed stetson and pin-striped business suit, filthy as they were, would look out of place in a dump like this, but I hadn't had time to change after the Ashwells. The thought of those people made me tense, my thoughts drifting back to their ranch house and that lovely stretch of Santa Cruz beach, the blue-green ocean stretching out behind the white breakers for miles to the distant horizon that looked like the end of the earth.

Leonard Ashwell had been shot in the back of his head while on his knees on the front porch of the house, like he had been begging for his life . . . but I knew that wasn't the way Leonard would go out. More than likely they had knocked him to his knees.

I had stepped over the body, cocked the shotgun, eased the front door open and moved slowly inside. It was quiet. The only sound was the ticking of the mantel clock over the fireplace. It was keeping me from hearing other sounds and so I crossed the room and put a hand to the pendulum. Silence fell hard on the place. I just stood and listened for a while, my mouth open slightly so that my breathing wouldn't interfere with my hearing. Nothing. Just the muffled sound of the wind rising off the beach. Then I heard a noise somewhere in the back of the house. Somebody was alive.

Though the day was bright with sunlight, the downstairs curtains were drawn and the rooms were shadowy. I waited until I was certain there was no one above me on the second floor. Whoever it was they were in the kitchen, the vague sounds continuing to drift through the quiet.

I eased the barrels of the scattergun through the open doorway and saw the Ashwells' two big dogs up on the table. I yelled at them and thought of shooting them, but they were just animals.

Mrs Ashwell was on her back, her dress up over her face, hands tied down to the table legs with cords. The cord had embedded deep in her flesh as she realized what they were going to do and panicked, then fought the horrible pain. Her ankles had been strapped down the same way. I figured the Mexican, Ramon, had done the work. The dogs had just been attracted by the smell.

I pulled the dress down to cover what was left of her body and cut the cords loose. In life Martha had been handsome. Now her face – rigid, smeared with her own blood, her lips pulled back over her teeth in a horrible grimacing smile – was a grotesque mask that stared up hideously at me. My chest went hollow and I froze for a moment. She'd been my friend – my wife's friend. I fought to control myself. When I could move again, I touched a hand to her matted hair and said, 'I'll get them, Martha.'

The sunlight out the back door of the kitchen hurt my eyes. I took a slow, careful walk around the big white barn, checking the sheds. Nothing.

I stood and ran my eyes along the windbreak of eucalyptus trees behind the corrals, smelling their pungent odour in the soft breeze. Usually the sight brought good thoughts because my wife and I had been saving to buy a ranch with a barn and eucalyptus trees and views of the ocean. No more.

The tender intimacy I'd once felt with my dreams was gone for ever. They only served to scare me now with glimpses of faces and snatches of soft words that drifted aimlessly in my thoughts. I forced my eyes around the grounds. No movement out of place. All the signs said the men weren't here. But that could be the way they wanted it. They weren't fools. Madmen, but not fools. I was hoping they'd try me. So we could finish it now.

Two horses were tied near a water trough – tied cruelly so they couldn't drink. Both were badly blown, their heads hanging, their sides covered with dried sweat. They'd never recover. I checked their hooves: they were same two the men had ridden in on. I'd never seen anybody ride horses this hard.

I pulled their halters off and turned back toward the barn. From the jumble of prints in the dirt, I calculated the men had taken four horses from Ashwell's stock and headed northeast, back up into the hills and back toward the San Fernando Valley. Four horses. It was a good bet the fourth was carrying provisions.

Standing there in the burning sunlight, staring up at the hot, dry hills, I wished to hell they'd taken five animals. Five might mean that Emily and Jane were with them. But they hadn't. And I knew the girls were inside – knew it as surely as if I'd already seen them.

I walked to a side door and stepped into the barn. The same sweet cloying scent that I'd smelled in the house was in the still, dark air. I'd smelled it too many times not to know what it meant. I took a shallow breath and held it, my eyes slowly adjusting to the dark shadows inside this cavernous structure.

Emily and Jane were both inside, their bodies dead white in the murky light and covered with flies. Emily had been hung on a meat hook and hoisted into the air. From the awful look of the wound, she'd been alive when they'd done that to her. Jane was lying on her back in a horse stall, her face so badly damaged that I almost couldn't recognize her.

I couldn't breathe right for a while, just stood looking at those two young girls, remembering them talking and laughing with my wife . . . the three of them collecting sea shells along the beach in the mornings. Seeing them now – twisted and broken – I knew I'd follow these men to the moon if that was what it took to get them. I also knew that for evermore my nights would be peopled with the faces of those who were dead. I would hear the soft murmuring of voices, the muffled sounds of footsteps . . . echoes of lives that would never be resurrected.

I found two of Ashwell's Mexican herders back up in the hills and had them help me bury the family. The young one fainted in the kitchen when he saw Mrs Ashwell. When we were done, I gave him five dollars to take a letter to my boss, Sheriff Eli

Matson, explaining where I was headed. Or thought I was headed. I then loaded up on ammunition I found in the house and took a nice bay Roman-nosed gelding from the barn, but no change of clothes.

Leonard had been a big man and I was five-ten. So nothing fit me and I rode after the men in my work suit. Three months later, I was still in my suit and a holy mess: filthy, sun-baked and shredded. The suit had once been dark blue in colour. I didn't know what the hell colour it was now. I didn't much care either.

I saw movement down the alley and tensed, watching as a cowboy and a woman came out of the cantina's doorway and turned away from where I stood. I pushed off from the wall figuring I had waited long enough. I was running on long hours now and didn't want to fall asleep where I stood. I cocked the exposed hammers on the shotgun, listening to both triggers snap into place with loud clear metallic clicks in the darkness. Satisfied I was as ready as a man ever gets at a time like this, I walked up next to one of the cantina's windows and tipped my head slightly and looked in.

There were about a dozen people inside, mostly Mexicans. But my Mexican was sitting at a table in the centre of the room with his back to the window; the fat, bald man, John Husker, was sitting opposite him. Both were nursing drinks. I scanned the room for Lessing but couldn't see him. Either he was upstairs with a bath or a whore. Or maybe just taking a piss. I decided to wait a minute and see if he came back. If not, I would take these two out quietly and then go looking for him.

The three men, I knew, were aware that I'd trailed them across the San Fernando Valley, because they had spotted me coming up on them near the Los Angeles river and spooked off at a wild run. I had varied my trail then to throw them off guard, riding south to pick up my two dogs where I'd left them with an old Mexican I knew in Sherman Oaks the night we'd tried to ambush the outlaws at the shack. I always took my dogs. And whenever I was making an arrest outside the city limits, I also took a pack horse loaded with supplies, knowing that things could go wrong, just like they had. The old man had my pack horse as well. I had shifted my things on to Ashwell's big bay, figuring it had more miles in its legs than my own animal. Knowing also that Ashwell would want me to take it and even things with these three.

This brief side trip concluded, I was right back after them, like a pit bull that had stopped momentarily in the middle of a fight to catch his breath before renewing the attack, tracking them out across the Mojave Desert, past the little road shacks of Palm Springs. I'd never liked losing criminals. It was pride with me. But these three had tortured and killed friends, so it was more than just simple pride. It was get-even time.

All the way across California, the three knew I was still behind them because I had tried to take them one night while they slept outside the crap town of Needles on the Arizona border. But they'd given me the slip in a windstorm after my horses and theirs had prematurely exchanged greetings. They might be outlaws and murderers . . . but they weren't stupid.

Stupid or not, since I hadn't tried them in over five hundred miles of dirt trails and ten-by-ten towns in what the Indians called the 'country of lost borders', I figured they must be thinking by now they had given this city-slicker lawman the slip. What they didn't know was they'd ridden into my backyard. I had grown up on the southern border of Arizona and New Mexico, the son of a Union sergeant turned cattle rancher. And for eight years after I'd left the ranch I had served as an Arizona ranger until my wife had said she wanted to go to Los Angeles.

I wondered if she'd known then that she was going to die. Probably. But she never let on.

All this territory out here wasn't worth a snap of the fingers. Just dust and heat and sand. It was hardest on women and children. So I had gone and done what she wanted . . . and watched her die happy in a little house on the palisades half a mile from the Santa Monica pier. The house wasn't much. But you could sit on your porch and see the ocean below the cliffs, then when the breeze shifted, smell orange blossoms and look north to snow-capped mountains. It was nice country. Picturesque and clean.

I rode the trolley into downtown Los Angeles at six every morning, a nice city of about 40,000 people, with electric street lights and elevators in buildings as tall as five storeys. The buildings would have been taller if it hadn't been for the earthquakes. And then each evening at five-thirty, unless I was on a case that wouldn't hold, I rode back out on the same trolley, down through the citrus groves and the fine houses to the beach and Ramond station, walking two tree-lined blocks to our little house. I liked California. At least when she was alive. Now I didn't like to think about it.

The only horse I rode was stabled on First Street across from the sheriff's office, and belonged to the County. A pretty looking four-year-old sorrel mare, maybe sixteen hands high, with a nice arched neck and broken tail, she'd held up well across the great stretches of the Big Lonely without much water and feed but with plenty of heat. The bay had done alright as well. They were tied up around the corner. Knowing good-looking animals wouldn't last long unattended in a town like this, I had left my dogs with them. The horses weren't going anywhere. Not with those dogs around. The only problem was I wished the dogs were backing me up. But this shouldn't be too hard an arrest.

Anyhow it didn't matter. If they killed me, they'd be doing me a favour. But I didn't want that to happen. I wanted these three put away or put down.

I felt the muscles across my shoulders suddenly tense. Lessing hadn't returned. But something that the fat man had just done made me instinctively understand that I had made a mistake. The worse mistake in my life as a lawman. I had been watching as Husker raised his glass to take a drink. Two things were wrong with the man's movements. One, his hand was shaking badly. Two, when the glass was up to his mouth, Husker's eyes had jumped nervously from the open door down the row of windows. They were waiting for me. They knew I was out here. How they knew didn't matter. What mattered was that Lessing hadn't gone upstairs or to the outhouse for a leak. He had slipped out the back of the cantina to come kill me.

I heard the soft crunching of boots on sand behind me and turned just in time to take the full charge of a shotgun chest-high at twenty yards. I was dead and knew it as I blew backwards from the concussion, smashing through the window into the yellow light of the cantina and the screams. All I could see as my eyes glazed was the clouded-over face of my wife. She was crying and I wanted to tell her to stop but the only thing I said was: 'Mother of God, help me! Sweet Mary . . .'. I mumbled the words out of reflex; my wife had taught them to me when she'd tried to convert me to religion. I wasn't a willing student – but at least I'd remembered them.

My shirt was wet.

Then the night air grew cold and I trembled hard, like something large had grabbed me. I quit moving . . .

CHAPTER TWO

When my eyes popped open I was no longer in the cantina. I was staring up at what looked like the ceiling of a small room, uncertain what I should think. Even if I could have thought clearly – which I couldn't because my head felt caved in – I wouldn't have known what to think. But I was trying: focusing on the ceiling and a glass lantern hanging there, and the rest of what I could see without turning my head. I'd never thought much about it, but I guessed I hadn't figured either place – heaven or hell – would look like this. I wondered how long I'd been dead. Maybe an hour. Maybe a day. Maybe a thousand years.

I slept.

When I awoke the second time, I rolled my head carefully to the side and, save for the throbbing in my brains, I seemed all right. Weak and dizzy, but basically OK. The little I could see of the room looked small and cheap. Poorly furnished and dusty like flop houses I'd hunted wanted men in. More flop house than I'd imagined either destination in the Great Beyond would be. Nothing wondrous about it. No golden veneers. No beautiful music. Nothing red hot and sulphureous. No sinners' screams. Nothing unusual at all. It was just like life. Maybe that's what happened. Maybe you just went on in the same kind of way in the same kind of places. But then, I wondered, what was the point?

Before I could come up with any kind of reasonable answer, the dizziness rolled over me and I was sliding under it, gasping for air and one last look.

That was when I saw her.

She was standing at the end of the room, tall and thin and graceful, wearing a high-collared blue dress that looked plain and simple, with long dark-auburn hair that seemed to catch and hold the sunlight. Handsome face, delicate bone structure. Thirty some years old. My first thought was that it was my wife . . . that there was a heaven.

Then she was fading in front of my eyes and I was floating in a sea of emptiness that felt warm and comforting like nothing I'd ever experienced. I could hear the woman praying. It wasn't my wife – but it was beautiful sounding, sure and confident about things. I was floating now.

The idea that I might be in a holding pen – like they put Los Angeles hard-timers in before they ran them up by rail to the state prison at Lompoc – drifted through my mind. That made some kind of sense . . . perhaps they were trying to figure out where I should go. That made even better sense. Then my brain shorted out completely.

When I awoke the woman was next to the bed staring down at me and chewing on an apple. She was beautiful, her focused gaze piercing me in a funny way. It wasn't imperious but there was something serious in it that kept me quiet for a time. Then I saw something in her eyes that made me want to smile. I didn't. I was too weak.

'Where am I?'

'My room,' she said, continuing to look down on me in her appraising way while she worked on the piece of fruit.

'Heaven or hell?' I asked, not joking.

'Sir?'

'Where did I end up?'

She studied my face carefully and then said, 'In my room in El Paso. I found you in an alley. You shouldn't talk too much.' Her voice was deep and filled with a mixture of strength and gentle consideration. A good match for her looks.

'Impossible,' I mumbled.

'It's not a great room. But it's not impossible,' she smiled. She had laugh lines around her eyes like my wife's.

'No. That I'm alive.'

I sat up too quickly and felt the pain clamp down on my head and swooned. The woman helped me back down on to the bed, the apple clinched in her teeth.

She pulled the apple out. 'You have a bad cut on your forehead. I had a doctor sew you up. You need rest.' She patted my hand in a reassuring way, then took another bite.

I reached my other hand under the bed sheet and touched tentatively at my bare chest, then dipped my chin and looked. The area was sore but that was all. The skin wasn't broken, wasn't even bruised. But that wasn't possible. I had taken two barrels from a shotgun at twenty feet. There should have been a hole the size of a dinner plate. But there wasn't. Not even a scratch. I had to be dead. It was the only thing that made sense.

'I'm dead,' I repeated.

'It's silly to talk like that,' she chided, mopping my brow with a cool damp cloth. 'You've hurt your head. That's all. In a day or two you'll be fine.' She placed the apple core down on top of a table. It had been chewed to the bitter end, but I wasn't thinking about apples at the moment.

I ran the tips of my fingers slowly over my sternum, my thoughts returning to the alley, the sound of footsteps, my turning, the volcanic flash as the shotgun ignited spewing flames and the awful hot blast of pellets that blew me backwards off my feet and through the window, the screams, my eyes glazing fast the way I had seen dying men's eyes cloud. I shuddered hard.

'You don't understand,' I mumbled. 'I was shot in an alley by a man with a shotgun. There's no way –' I stared at her for a long time.

The woman reached and took my hand and raised it until the tips of my fingers touched the long gash across my forehead. It hurt like hell. She moved my fingers along, counting the stitches for me: twenty-nine.

'I don't know about the shotgun – but you were hit hard across your forehead. The doctor thought you might be blind.'

'I'm not blind. I'm dead.' None of it made sense. I hadn't imagined what had happened. 'I was about to make an arrest,' I continued. 'One of the men came up behind me. And when I turned, he shot me.'

'Perhaps he hit you across the head and you only thought you'd been shot.'

'No, dammit!'

I realized I had sworn at her and I caught myself and said, 'Sorry.'

'I understand.'

She'd said the words softly, but something was smouldering deep in her eyes.

'I was shot,' I said. 'Point-blank.'

She shrugged and went and sat down in a rocking chair, took a pair of delicate gold-rimmed spectacles out of a leather case and put them on her fine nose, then she took to knitting something black. The tiny glasses did nothing to detract from her beauty. 'If that's true, then the man is a very bad aim,' she joked.

'This is serious.'

'Of course. I'm sorry. But obviously you're not dead.'

I frowned at her and then spent time examining her clean, natural face that didn't need anything to look good, and wondered what had happened to me. Again, I touched my fingers over my chest. Nothing. Nothing at all. Then I realized that I was stark naked and this woman must have undressed me and bathed me. I glanced across the room and caught her eyes still watching me over the quick movements of her knitting needles and I felt a little spasm of embarrassment and quickly went back to staring at the ceiling again.

I hadn't been naked with a woman since my wife. I hadn't wanted to. It didn't matter. At this moment, having just escaped death, I wasn't going to fret over it. She didn't appear concerned. That was fine with me.

Then one of the answers I was hunting came swimming out of the ether: my clothes! My shirt and vest would have a hole in them big enough to jump through. I sat up fast again, fighting off the pain.

'My clothes?'

She put her knitting down and looked ready to restrain me. 'Sir, you are not going anywhere.'

'I just want to look at them.'

She sat with her mouth open for a moment before she closed it and pulled her glasses down some and squinted her eyes at me, then said, 'Do you realize how dirty those clothes were?'

'They'll prove I was shot.'

'Maybe not.'

'What do you mean?'

'I took everything out of your pockets.'

'I don't care.'

'Well, you may care.'

I didn't like the sound of that. 'Why?'

'Because I had them burned,' she said.

'You what?'

'I had a man destroy them,' she repeated, nodding her head up and down to confirm she wasn't kidding. She frowned like my mother used to. 'When was the last time you washed them?'

I wasn't listening to her.

'Sir?'

'What?'

'When was the last time you washed them?'

'I'd been hunting these men.'

'Well they were filthy,' she said, sounding a little stiff.

For a moment I was mad that she had taken it upon herself to burn my clothes, especially when they would prove that I wasn't crazy. But I stopped short of being harsh with her. I didn't know why, there was just something about her – the way she looked and spoke, thoughtful and caring and laughing – that caused me to keep my anger to myself.

'Covered with blood, right?'

'Yes.' She pushed her glasses back into place and picked up her knitting and shook her head in a woman's disapproving way. 'Covered with blood and many other things,' she said slowly, her face squenching up as if she might still be able to smell the aroma.

'That proves it.'

She looked at me rather strangely. 'Proves what?'

'That I was shot. That I'm dead.'

She was biting at the inside of her cheek and shaking her head again. 'Proves nothing,' she said matter-of-factly. She had resumed her knitting. 'I used the money in your pocket to buy you some new clothes.' She paused. 'I hope that was alright. I didn't know the kind of things you liked. So I guessed.'

I nodded slowly.

'They're in the closet. But you need rest.'

I squinted at her. 'Who are you, lady?'

'My name is Hannah Morgan,' she said, continuing to knit, the rocker moving slowly.

I continued watching her for a while. Her dark beauty was burnished with a nice layer of what I guessed was dignity: the way she spoke, dressed, her carriage. But then there was that other layer – the funny layer – that almost didn't seem to fit.

Sunlight from the window poured over her and even its harsh glare didn't diminish her unadorned handsomeness. I looked around the cramped little room again. It was as dirty and dusty and cheap as I had first thought. I couldn't figure it: an uncommonly handsome woman in a room like this. They didn't fit together. And I liked things to fit. And what was she doing in a dangerous alley late at night? Or in this godforsaken heap of a town for that matter? None of it made sense. Absolutely none of it. Unless . . .

'You a prostitute ma'am?' It was the deputy sheriff in me talking.

Hannah Morgan looked up from her knitting and smiled a smile that seemed to say a lot of things . . . I just didn't know what. But I did know her smile was a good one.

'No,' she said.

'And this is your room?'

'For tonight. I mean it's not great. I'm just passing through. I'm not buying it,' she teased, laughter surfacing silently in her eyes.

'To meet your husband?'

'My husband is dead.'

'You're wearing a wedding ring.'

She smiled again. 'So are you.'

I squinted harder. 'How'd you know my wife was dead?'

'I didn't.' Her serious tone returning. 'I'm sorry.' The concern in her voice sounded genuine.

Neither of us said anything more for a while, Hannah Morgan just continued knitting while I studied the room and thought about what had happened. None of it made sense. Then my eyes stopped on a large pile of dirty dishes.

'Mine?'

Hannah Morgan looked up from her knitting. 'No.'

'You?' I said, amazed at the sheer number of dishes.

'Yes.'

She had returned to her knitting.

My thoughts returned to the shooting and I worried about it for a while. Then some sound caught my ear and I looked at her. She was sitting with her head back, her eyes rolled to white, her mouth slack. My first thought was that she'd had a stroke or was seized with the shaking palsy, tremors passing through her body, her arms rigid by her side, groaning words like they hurt her. I listened.

'I will go,' she moaned.

'Ma'am?'

'He is the one.'

'Ma'am?'

I started to crawl out of the bed, then couldn't move and felt myself slipping under the black wave again, drifting off into emptiness . . . this thing just beginning . . .

CHAPTER THREE

She was gone when I woke. The room was quiet and I could tell from the tint of reddish-gold light on the wall that it was late evening. My first thought was once again that I was dead . . . that there was no way the man could have missed with the shotgun. My second thought was my horses and dogs. They'd been tied to the hitching post too long. If they were still there, they were going crazy from thirst and hunger. I swung my legs over the edge of the bed and felt light-headed but not enough to fall down.

I made my way across the room to the closet, figuring the woman had taken my cash and left. But no – the money was on a small table with a receipt. Minus what she'd spent, it was all there. More than a hundred dollars. That surprised me. So did the three rows of apple cores – maybe twenty of them. I liked apples but this was crazy. Slowly, I continued on to the closet. The clothes were inside, including new boots and my old stetson. And in the corner: my shotgun, pistols and manacles. Everything neatly arranged on the shelves and hangers. This woman, whoever she was, had done a damn thorough job.

I began to dress.

I was surprised again. Everything fit passably well: the pants, belt, socks, boots. I stopped and looked around. Where was the shirt? Surely she hadn't forgotten a shirt. There was a cardboard box on the floor. I picked it up and opened it and couldn't believe what I saw. It was pink. Bright pink. I didn't even think you could buy a pink shirt in these parts. In El Paso? Maybe it was her idea of a joke. She had a humorous bent. At least she thought it was humorous. I pulled the shirt on and looked at myself in the mirror. Damn. I looked like one of those frozen ices they sold in drug stores.

I'd buy another as soon as possible. At least she was a good judge of sizes. Most people calculated I was larger than my five-ten frame, mainly because of my build. At 165 pounds, I rarely had much trouble handling men 200 or more pounds. I had a good grip and hand speed that gave me an edge in most encounters. Even so, I tried to avoid physical confrontations, figuring lawmen who rammed their heads into things were eventually going to come up holding a fist full of their own brains. And I never figured I had any to spare.

When I opened the door to the room and looked down the stairs that led into a small sandy yard, I got the next surprise: there at the bottom were my horses and dogs. The horses were hobbled and munching on a pile of hay that had been freshly forked for them, a large barrel of clean water within easy reach. The dogs were rushing up the stairs like they had never expected to see me alive again. They'd been right, of course.

Jack, the little brown and white rat terrier, reached me first, spun joyfully in a circle for a moment, then grabbed my pant leg in his familiar greeting, growling and tugging away. Then came Martha, the bull-mastiff, tawny brown in colour with a broad head and black muzzle, and weighing an easy 120 pounds of hard muscle and bone. She sat down at my feet and looked up at my face as if it was the most beautiful face in the world and barked once with enough velocity to almost topple me.

'Good dogs,' I said, patting their heads and wondering how

in the heck the woman had found the four in the first place, then how she had ever convinced Martha to let her unhitch the horses and bring them here. Getting Martha to go along with anything that countered one of my orders would have been no easy feat. I'd never seen anybody but my wife pull it off. Jack could be smooth talked . . . the little terrier was a sucker for women, good food and nice compliments. But not Martha. She was stubborn to the core, not easily swayed from her duty by force or sweet words. She understood orders and carried them out. She was serious minded and somewhat austere . . . and she loved me. Both dogs did. It was just that Jack got incredible urges to do wild things sometimes that made sense only to him, and therefore he wasn't as reliable. He was brave but he could also be crazy and free of reasonable cares.

Jack stopped yanking on my pant leg and started bouncing up and down in the air like a ball with hair. I knelt and let both of them make happy over me. When I'd had enough, I stood back up and stretched the pain out of my joints and did what I should have that first night. I led the horses to the livery and paid a man to watch them. Then I checked to see that the four animals were still in their stalls. Indeed. The stable owner told me he'd seen the men in a gambling house at the corner of El Paso and Overland.

I didn't wait outside this time. I was feeling dizzy and raw and I just walked in through the open doors, Jack and Martha at my heels, and took a seat at an empty card table in a corner. I laid the loaded shotgun on the table, setting my hat on top of the breech so that no one could see the hammers were cocked.

The room was cool and filling with evening shadows. I could use a beer. I was fighting two things in my head: what had happened to me in the alley . . . and my desire to kill these three. I sucked in a deep breath and held it, then blew it out and took a look around.

Some rough-looking men were playing billiards in the back and an old bartender was inventorying his whisky, writing things down on a pad of paper. Off to my right, there were two sets of card games. My three men were at the closest table, the Mexican with his back to me, Husker and Lessing facing me. None of them had done anything more than take a casual glance as I walked in. They'd never seen me up close in good light. And even if they had, the last thing they would've figured was ever seeing me again.

I forced myself to stop thinking about what had happened. Just be damn thankful you're alive, I told myself, so you can take care of these three. When that's done, it's a different story. I looked over at the card game. There were two fairly prosperous-looking men in the game. I was sure my three boys were cheating the hell out of them.

Martha was exhausted from guarding the horses all night and she walked under the table and flopped down with a groan, Jack hopping up on her large back. That was standard for the two of them: Martha didn't think much about basic comfort but Jack couldn't live without it. Since the little ratter didn't weigh more than twelve pounds, Martha tolerated him sleeping on her, unless it was very hot.

I felt better having the dogs along as backup. More than once, the big one had kept me from getting shot or losing a prisoner. And Jack had a genuine gift for knowing when things weren't right.

The dogs had been my wife's idea. She had worried about me working the bad sections of the city – Little Tokyo town and the filthy side streets and alleys of the old Mexican barrio – and she had gone to the public library in Santa Monica and checked out a book on dogs. The result was two puppies. The first came from a breed the book called 'the greatest protector of man that nature has ever provided'. Martha, the bull-mastiff.

On the day the pup arrived, my wife had just finished a book on Martha Washington and I made the mistake of joking that the mastiff had many of Martha's fine features. Big mistake. I tried to get her to change the name to Champ or Atlas or anything . . . but she wouldn't hear of it.

The second pup came from a local man who raised rat terriers. My wife's reasoning was that Martha could do the heavy work while Jack did the sneaking around investigations, slipping into sewers and through holes in walls. Again, she had hit on a pretty good combination. The only problem was Jack's devil-may-care attitude about crooks and life in general.

I ordered a beer from a pretty Mexican waitress in a long red skirt and yellow blouse who knelt down to make nice over the two dogs. And Jack, as usual, made a fool of himself jumping up and trying to smooch her face and whining like he had to go pee. I told him to knock it off, but it was too late.

The men at the table were looking at us. I moved a boot and nudged Martha and she came out from underneath like somebody had just played a bugle in her ear.

'Hold on, girl,' I said quietly, tipping my head toward the men in greeting to let her know who I was interested in. She sat and drilled them with her lowering gaze.

'Sombitch,' the one known as Lessing muttered, staring at Martha's bulk.

'That's some gawddamn dog,' Husker, the fat bald one, said.

'Likes her tortillas and beans,' I said, realizing as soon as the Mexican turned that I had said the wrong thing.

'You making fun of Mexicanos?'

'Just stating a fact.'

32

Ramon squinted at me, then whistled. 'Bonita rosado camisa,' he smirked. 'Pretty pink shirt.'

'Thanks.'

'You steal it from a whore?'

The others laughed and I forced a grin. The bastard was right, of course.

The Mexican waitress came back fast with my beer and stood between me and the men and caught my eye and made faces to warn me off Ramon. 'I know,' I mouthed softly. She nodded and returned to the bar. 'Steady,' I said to Martha.

The dog continued to sit as if frozen, staring across the room at the men without moving a muscle in her heavy body. But thin-skinned and more attuned to things like voices and gestures, Jack wasn't having it. He hadn't liked the threatening tone in Ramon's words and he raised a hind leg now to the table and pissed a yellow puddle, then scratched in the sawdust, kicking it backwards toward the men like he weighed 120 pounds instead of twelve. I knew that with Jack these were usually signs of something bigger and better about to happen. Something I definitely didn't want at the moment. 'Sit!' I hissed. The terrier did what he had been told, but he didn't look happy.

I took a pull on my beer, noticing over the rim that the Mexican was still watching me. 'Salud,' I said loudly, raising the glass to Altar Ramon, while under my breath I said, 'Gotcha.'

Ramon spit in my direction and said, 'Pinkee. Go someplace else.' The Mexican watched to see if I was going to get heated.

'After my beer,' I said, taking another drink.

'Now,' Ramon said, pulling his pistol and pointing it at Martha. 'Or I'll shoot your pero.'

I put my hands up like this was my first day at school, like I was surrendering or going to faint, and stood and tried to look nervous. The way I was feeling, it was a hard act. 'I'm heading out.' Martha had become intensely interested in the man as soon as he pulled the pistol and pointed it at her, and she leaned forward barely able to keep her haunches on the floor. 'Steady,' I whispered to her. 'Steady, girl.'

Ramon smiled a smile that could have peeled paint, put his pistol away and turned back to the card game. I picked up my shotgun and the stetson together in one hand to cover the cocked hammers and took a long swig of beer, Lessing watching me to make sure I wasn't going to turn brave and ugly all of a sudden. I then made a show of walking to the bar to pay my bill. The Mexican glanced at me, then back at his hand. Jack and Martha trotted at my heels, Jack grumbling deep in his small throat the way he did when he didn't like something.

'Knock it off,' I hissed, nudging his rump with the toe of my boot. The little dog stopped complaining, but was still peeling his lips back, exposing his white teeth like he was smiling. He wasn't.

After I slipped my change into my pocket and smiled at the Mexican waitress who was feeling bad for me, I started for the door, the route taking me directly behind the Mexican's chair. When I was almost where I wanted to be, Jack lost it completely and took a leap up on to the middle of the table and went for the Mexican. Surprised to have twelve pounds of snapping teeth in his face, Ramon swore and shoved backwards tipping himself and the chair over.

I was swearing as well as I brought the shotgun to play on the two American outlaws, the other men scattering for cover. Neither Lessing nor Husker looked ready to do much of anything beyond fouling their pants. But when I looked down toward the floor, I saw Ramon going for his pistol and I yanked the muzzle of the shotgun away from the Americans, just as Martha lunged and caught the Mexican by the throat, her weight knocking him back hard to the floor, his head slamming against the planking.

The big dog had a nasty grip on the man's throat. Jack was barking encouragement that needed no interpretation, and I was about to call the mastiff off when I caught a quick, furtive motion out the side of my eye. Lessing, the one who had shot me in the alley, was pulling a pistol. The outlaw fired under the table at me. The noise was deafening in the room, blue smoke immediately billowing out from the edges of the table. I was still on my feet and didn't feel anything. But that didn't mean a thing. What did mean something was the fact that I could hear Lessing cocking the pistol a second time under the table. So at the horribly short distance of eight feet, I cut loose on the man with the shotgun.

Maybe I'd killed half a dozen men who had resisted arrest or tried to kill me. But the instant that I pulled both triggers of the full-choked ten-guage I knew I would never forget killing Wilbur Lessing. Not in this world, or the next. The man's sunken face and skull just disappeared in front of me in a spray of blood, bone and brains. Stunned by the awful carnage, I stood staring for a moment at the decapitated body still sitting in the chair, blood pumping like a fountain from his neck, the hands now on the table, twitching. Then I heard Altar Ramon's deep gasping rattle and looked down to see the man's eyes rolling up to white, Martha shaking the limp neck back and forth.

'Martha!' I yelled, and the bull-mastiff immediately released the Mexican and backed away, staring down at the man. It was too late. Ramon had been asphyxiated by the dog's massive clamp on his throat.

Shocked by the devastating blast of the shotgun and the awful spray of blood over tables and chairs, both Husker and Jack had had enough. The outlaw sat with his trembling hands out in front of him on the table, mumbling, 'No, no, no . . .' over and over, while Jack was sitting on the floor next to my leg, shaking hard and looking alternately from the dead Mexican to the blood dripping down one of Lessing's elbows and pooling on the floor.

I couldn't move or say anything for a minute. Just stood and watched a fly buzzing slowly in the room's air, the fetid smell of death already adrift in the hot currents. Jack leaned hard into my leg for comfort. That was typical Jack: quick to start trouble, then just as quick to feel bad over it.

'Dammit, Jack. I ought to whip you for this.' The dog whined mournfully as if anticipating the punishment, even though I'd never laid an angry hand on him in his life.

Martha just sat watching the still body of the Mexican as if she wasn't convinced he was dead, and might make another play for his gun at any moment. To Martha this was business. The man had made a move to hurt me. And she had stopped him. No more, no less. She never got excited like Jack about such things. I reached and patted her head. 'No more throat holds. Grab the weapon.' The year before, she had almost killed a gambler in Los Angeles' Chinatown this same way. Since then, I had been trying to train her to attack the arm holding the weapon. As I looked down at Ramon's blue face, I could see she needed more work.

CHAPTER FOUR

El Paso's marshall, Jake Solomon, hadn't been any too pleased by my handing him two dead men – one killed by decapitation, the other by strangulation – but the fact that I had papers showing I was legally sworn in Los Angeles and carrying proper California murder warrants for the three men helped. The testimony of the bartender and the Mexican waitress was all that was needed to close officially.

Husker was in the El Paso jail now and Solomon had promised to hold him until I could get tickets for us on the next train to California. I wrote out a statement, then signed a document obligating the County of Los Angeles to pay for the dead men's burial, Husker's keep, and damages to the gambling parlour.

I felt better.

The sun had dropped behind the distant mountains laying a thick blanket of night over the town and cooling the desert air. I was crossing the dirt street, heading for the stable where my horses were waiting. I would check on them, leave the dogs to watch, get a hot bath and a stiff drink, then buy some train tickets. I stopped and looked up at the moon behind some white clouds. 'Martha Ashwell, it's done.'

I'd already telegraphed my boss, Sheriff Eli Matson. Matson had been worried about me since my wife's death and he cabled back: 'We're going for blue marlin off Point Dume.' We'd caught a 512-pound monster last summer, the huge fish taking both our efforts to land. I appreciated the gesture but knew I'd never go sport fishing again. I started walking.

The moon slipped out from behind the clouds. It was close to being full and yellow light splashed over the low adobe buildings that lined the sides of the street. I'd forgotten how bright and clean it made the desert look. El Paso even looked OK. Martha was trailing at my heels, Jack was following a few steps behind her, his head drooping and still looking crestfallen over the scolding I'd given him.

My thoughts returned to the night before in the alley and the woman. No matter how I came at the problem, it still added up the same. I'd been shot by Wilbur Lessing and, like Lessing, I should be dead. But I wasn't. And that was impossible.

Maybe the woman was right. Maybe I'd whirled around at the sound of Lessing's approach and been hit hard across the forehead. Maybe I'd only imagined the blast . . . expecting to be shot. It had to be something like that. Nothing else made sense.

I walked on, deep in thought until Jack barked once. Then again. I didn't break stride.

'Don't start. I'm in no mood.'

He stood looking alternately from the alley to me; Martha and I continued down the street. Making up his mind, Jack darted off into the darkness between the buildings. I didn't care. I cut the dogs plenty of rope to do the things they had to do. I made them mind when they were working but afterwards they were on their own.

I couldn't stop thinking about the woman. Something bothered me. Something about her looks and manners. They didn't fit with the dirty room, this town and travelling alone.

I was turning into the stable when I heard Jack running behind me. The dog barked. I frowned and turned back. The small terrier was straddling a bundle of some sort. He grabbed it and dragged it forward a few feet. Then he released it and barked again.

'I'm tired of you making trouble.'

He barked again. And as mad as I was at him, I knew when to listen and I walked over and took a look. Jack had brought me my old clothes.

With hands that were shaking so badly that I had to flex the muscles of my arms so I could control them, I untied the string that bound the garments, and, squatting on my haunches, rolled them out on the ground. Nothing now made sense at all. Maybe it never would again.

The clothes were stiff with dried blood. But that wasn't what bothered me. What bothered me was in the centre of the vest and shirt: a ragged hole the size of a Mexican cantalope. I wasn't crazy. Nor had I gotten knocked on the head and just thought that I'd been shot. I had been hit every bit as hard as the outlaw Lessing. The only difference was Lessing had been blown to smithereens while I was walking around admiring the moon.

I stopped and looked up at the stars. 'What the hell happened?' There was no answer save for the faint sound of an out-of-tune violin playing somewhere. Jack was whining and looking for praise and I patted him. 'Good dog,' I said, my voice distant-sounding. Jack spun in a small circle, feeling absolutely redeemed of all earlier sins. I stood in a daze in the middle of the street until a man in a wagon wanted to pass and I stumbled out of the way and leaned against a mesquite stick corral filled with a bunch of rough-looking Mexican bulls. I spread my bloody shirt out over the fence. It was blown to hell. It made absolutely no damn sense.

Ten minutes later, I was standing in the livery, getting ready to saddle the sorrel. I didn't have any more answers than before.

39

The man who ran the place was sitting on a chair eating a plate of beans that were hot enough to throw steam.

'You know a pretty woman in town?' I asked, picking straw from the saddle blanket I was holding over a raised knee.

'Know a lot of pretty women,' he grinned. One of his front teeth was missing and made him look like an idiot.

'Yeah. Well this one's tall, dark haired, maybe early thirties; wearing a long blue dress. Calls herself Hannah Morgan.' I tossed the blanket up on the mare's back and looked over my shoulder at him. 'You know that particular one?'

He'd been sopping bean juice with bread when I asked. He stopped and stared down at his feet.

'Good-looking woman?'

He didn't say anything.

'Hello?'

He looked up at me and sucked on his teeth. 'Yeah. I know that one. Sold her two horses this morning.' He paused and got a half-pained look on his face. 'Don't care for her much.' He shook his head and then went to staring down at his uneaten beans like he was wondering what they were for. 'Real high and mighty,' he mumbled.

Hearing that, I knew we were talking about the same woman. 'Two horses?'

'One for her. One for the girl.'

Suddenly he was grinning like he had gas.

'Daughter?'

He laughed, spitting bean fragments on to his pants, and shook his head. 'Shit no. She just walked into Elmira's bagnio on Main this morning and took a young gal out. Like she owned the place.'

'Lost me,' I said, throwing my saddle up.

He was grinning again. 'Elmira brought this gal from Mexico. Name was Lucia. "Juicy Lucy".'

'Prostitute?'

'Yep,' the man said, a finger up his nose. 'Elmira claimed eighteen.' He removed the finger. 'But hell – couldn't been fifteen.'

'Sheriff Solomon?'

'Didn't like it. But Elmira had this Mex certificate. And the girl was scared to say shit.'

I led the sorrel out of the stall, stopping in front of the man. He had a bad smell and I thought about him and the girl together and felt the thing start up in my chest. I forced it down.

'So?'

'Woman walked up the stairs to where the whore was locked in her room. Everybody asleep except a coloured. Nobody knows how she got the door open. Nigger didn't have a key.'

The man put his plate of beans on the ground and stamped his feet in moronic glee. 'Anyhow she walks out with Juicy Lucy.'

He was laughing so hard I thought he might puke up his beans so I stepped back. I had a temper about people being used. Especially kids. I swallowed it down and swung up into the saddle and sat thinking about the Morgan woman and how I'd seen her trembling and staring up at the ceiling of her room. She'd said: 'I will go.' I wondered now whether she'd meant this Mexican gal. I also wondered what she meant by, 'He is the one.' I hadn't liked the sound of that. Not then, not now.

Then I heard the livery man yell.

'Hey!'

'What?'

'Your gawddamn dog just ate everything on my plate.'

I glanced down at Jack as he licked the platter clean. 'Yeah, I see that.'

'Well?' he asked, as if I was going to make Jack give the beans back. When I didn't, he continued, 'What you got to say? – that meal cost me a quarter.' He was whining now.

I didn't answer him.

'You going to say something?' he whined again.

'Yeah.'

'What?'

'He best not get sick.'

'Him sick – hell! I ought to kill the little bastard.' The man was pulling at an old Navy Colt in a scuffed leather holster.

'Do it – I'll blow your feet off.'

The man studied my face and realized something. He put the gun away and mumbled an obscenity. I left him and rode out into the dark streets of town thinking about this woman. And what had happened to me.

The front door to the jail was locked, so I reined the sorrel around back and squinted into the small barred windows, hunting for John Husker.

'Husker?'

A black man came to the bars. 'Mister, get me out of here. I'll give you a thousand dollars.'

I ignored him and moved to the next window. 'John Husker.'

'Who is it?'

'Tucker Gibbens.'

'What the hell do you want?'

'To know something.'

'Go ask somebody else. Wilbur was my partner.'

I sat holding in the prancing sorrel. She'd been tied for the past forty-eight hours and was eager to stretch her legs. I cleared my throat. 'That mean you won't talk to me?'

'Brilliant.'

I waited a few moments longer, then in a lower voice said, 'The Ashwells were friends of mine.'

'Who the hell are the Ashwells?'

I stuck the twin barrels of the shotgun in through the window at the figure of the fat man sitting on the floor of the cell in a strip of moonlight. 'The family in that ranch house on Santa Cruz beach.' I cocked the hammers on the gun.

'What do you want to know?' Husker said quickly.

'The other night. The night you rode into town.'

'Yeah?'

'You went into a cantina that opened out on an alley. Lessing went in with you then went out the back, came around and shot a man out front. That happened, didn't it?'

There was silence in the cell. 'Yeah. Lessing did it.'

'Shot the man?'

'Yeah.'

'Killed him?'

'Blew him in through a window. Hell, you saw what happened to Lessing. He did the same thing to that fellow.'

'Then what?'

'Don't follow.'

'What happened to the man who was shot?'

'I got no idea. The three of us just made our way out the back in a hurry and went to our room.' He paused. 'I guess they tossed him outside. He was bleeding over everything. That's all I know.'

I didn't say anything, just fought the urge to pull the triggers, to finish it up for the Ashwells. But they wouldn't have wanted me to do that. I didn't think much of the idea myself and I yanked the shotgun out of the window.

'Why'd you want to know about that fella?' Husker asked.

I didn't answer. The man wouldn't have believed me anyway. And I was getting sick to my stomach hearing him talk, knowing what he'd done to my friends. I had to get away before I finished him.

*

I wrote Marshall Solomon a note and left it on top of his desk saying I would be back for Husker in a few days. Then I packed my things under a canvas on the back of the bay, and did some asking around about the woman. I was in a daze of sorts.

I forced myself to do the things I physically had to do with the pack, but my mind constantly focused on getting shot and waking up in that room. I wanted some answers. And not the kind the woman had fed me. I wanted real ones about what she had seen. I was certain she knew more than she was telling. I just didn't know what that could possibly be. It didn't matter. She was tied to all this somehow.

I wasn't big on believing in things beyond this life. I hoped my wife had gone to heaven – if there was such a place – so I could have a chance at seeing her again . . . if they'd ever let me in. But that was about all I'd given much thought to. I figured people were born, struggled, things happened, luck and stuff, we were either happy or sad, rich or poor, then we died and rotted into muck. That was about it. No hocus. No pocus. Nothing but sucking air until we couldn't suck any more.

Jack was barking now to be let up on the horse's rump. I rode slowly down the darkened alley-way. Martha was following close behind the bay's heels. Tired of listening to the little dog complaining, I stopped and held my toe out and let him use it to bound on to the mare's rump.

'Now shut up,' I said, still mad at him. Jack did what he was told, just glad to be riding.

The yellow pools of light that flowed out the windows of the cantina brought a shiver to me. I stopped the mare and sat looking at the broken glass. It was an eerie feeling, sitting there and looking at the place where you'd died. And knowing you hadn't . . .

CHAPTER FIVE

New Mexico Badlands. 19 July 1887

Crows were making a racket in the steep-walled canyon. I ignored them, feeling hot and thirsty. I figured from the thickets of tamarisk trees and stands of marsh reeds filled with red-winged black birds that there had to be water down here somewhere. I'd been tracking the woman and the girl for two days, pushing my animals harder than they were pushing theirs, and steadily closing on them, their tracks freshening by the hour. I was tired. I hadn't been sleeping at night, things kept popping up in my mind every time I dozed off. It was growing worrisome.

I pulled the mare to a stop and studied the canyon. The walls were red-coloured sandstone, the cracks and small cliffs edged with toadflax and Russian thistle and on the sandy floor a few stunted cottonwoods. It was nice enough looking. I guessed I was no more than a few miles behind them now. Or at least I hoped it was them. A man in El Paso said they'd ridden northwest out of town. And these were the only fresh tracks I'd found on the road. There was a distinctive cut in the metal of one of the horse's right front shoes that made them easy to follow.

I pushed my hat back and looked up at the sun. It was maybe two and relatively cool for these parts . . . I guessed 100 degrees, not much more. Lucky. It could easily rise to 115 or 120 on a bad day. I shook my head, wondering what the woman was thinking about coming out here with a young girl.

From the look of their tracks, the way she let her horse pick the trail and hunted shade during the worst of the day, she knew how to make it in the desert, and knew where she was headed. And I was guessing she'd come into this sandstone canyon with its soaring walls for the same reason I had: water. But even if she could ride and knew how to survive in this country, the livery man said that she didn't have canvas water bags, just a bedroll and saddlebags and a couple of canteens. She was crazy.

On a hot day in short-grass desert like this, a man needed three gallons of water just to replenish what was parched out of him by the sun and wind. After a few hours without it, he'd begin to get light-headed and tired and his temperature would rise to 101 or 102 degrees. If he got water then, he was OK. But if he didn't, he was in trouble. In another couple of hours his heart would begin to beat slower and slower, then suddenly his temperature would skyrocket.

At 106 degrees he'd slip into delirium and wouldn't be able to walk. At around 108 degrees, it was over. You could drop him in the middle of an ice-cold lake and it wouldn't save him. He was already dead, even if he was still moving. His brain, his muscles, his heart ... steamed to death. That's why I was hunting water in this canyon. And that's why I figured the woman was doing the same. She knew some things about staying alive in the desert. But maybe not enough.

Jack was sitting behind me on the mare's rump, half asleep. Martha and the bay horse trailed lazily along a few yards back, trying to conserve energy. Watching the bone-tired look of the two dogs, I didn't figure I had any trouble ahead. Half-asleep or not, Jack would catch the scent or sound of danger. The little terrier had a gift. I put my heels gently to the sorrel's flanks and she crow-hopped a couple of times, then moved ahead at a brisk walk. I hoped her eagerness was because she smelled water. My thoughts drifted back to Hannah Morgan.

The more I knew about her, the less she made any kind of real sense. We were somewhere in the middle of New Mexico territory, heading north, a good 100 miles northwest of El Paso, and riding in a direction that looked to me like it would take us up into southeastern Utah. Zion, the Mormons called it. All of this territory was nothing but desolate parched land. Part of the Big Lonesome. Good for raising blisters and not much else.

But at the moment it was more than hot desert that concerned me. The woman and the girl had clipped the northeastern tip of the San Carlos reservation. She had been headed comfortably north of it, then she'd taken a sharp turn southwest. By the time they turned north again they were moving across Apache land. And she was kicking hard. Mile after mile they rode at either a canter or a stiff trot that had to be taking a fierce toll on her, the kid and their horses. I wondered how long they could hold up moving this hard. And what the hell she was suddenly chasing after? There was nothing but dust devils and dry brush out here.

I scanned the canyon walls. Whites weren't supposed to be here. The federal government would arrest them. The Indians would do worse. They'd been whipped and stomped and spit on too long. They were done with it. I didn't blame them. I just didn't want old scores evened on my hide. I stopped again and studied the tracks . . . she was still moving at her mile-eating trot. I shook my head. I'd followed enough riders to know she wasn't wandering. Her trail was straight and while it had deviated, it had done so with purpose. What could possibly bring this woman down here in such a hurry? I guessed she didn't know much about Apaches. She didn't look the type who would.

The crows were raising hell again down the canyon and I tensed and checked to see that my weapons were loaded and that the dogs weren't concerned. They weren't. Still, I didn't like being on Jicarilla land. Having stolen the horse from the Spanish in the 1500s, a good fifty years before any other people in North America got their hands on them, they were every bit as skilled at riding as the Sioux and Comanche.

No more than fifteen years ago they'd been hunting buffalo on the plains of western Kansas and the panhandle of Texas, and raiding across the southwest on their little desert ponies. And while most of the tribe was 'pacified' on the reservation now, I knew that small bands of warriors simply used the place as a winter staging area for warm season raids through Arizona and New Mexico.

Hopefully most of them were out on a long ride, raising hell in other parts. The farther the better as far as I was concerned. Jack growled, his tiny lips curling. Here we go, I thought, pulling the shotgun and cocking it, then sitting and waiting, studying the rocks and cliffs that surrounded me, listening to the various sounds in the soft breeze.

Jack continued to pace around on the rump of the horse, grumbling. Something was bothering him. Martha looked alert as well, trotting out ahead of the sorrel a couple of yards and stopping, her ears perked. I guessed it didn't much matter whether I rode forward into the canyon or back out. If it was Apaches, they already had me. And I needed water, so I rode slowly on.

She had done a good job with the grave. The girl had helped, her smaller footprints evident in the dust. It had been hard work. The rocks were melon sized and piled up two feet over the body. There was a nice cross at the head of it fashioned from sticks of green cottonwood lashed together with a leather thong.

I studied the place for a few minutes and wondered who this was that had made the mistake of trying their luck in Apacheria. Whoever – they'd come up busted.

I could see the dark brown stain on the earth where the Indians had worked. It hadn't been a quick death. It rarely was with the Apache. Especially nowadays, when they got so few chances to ply their trade. They made the most of every opportunity. Jack had hopped down and he and Martha were nosing around the blood spill and the grave. Neither one had their backs up, so I figured whatever had happened here had happened a while ago, the attackers gone. There was an apple core on the ground nearby, neatly chewed to the bitter end like all the others. I shook my head. She surely loved her apples.

Jack found the depression in the ground, about three feet deep and four across, where the person had made their stand. It was up a rise of sandy ground, close against a towering sheet of sandstone that soared a good hundred feet high giving protection from the backside. The hole was filled with close to a hundred spent .45–70 cartridges. Whoever it was, they'd gone down pissing. Then I froze. Along with a man's footprints, there were footprints of two small children. My heart was banging against my ribs. What the hell was he doing with kids out here on Apache land?

I squatted next to the hole for a while and felt some of the desperation the man must have felt, knowing he was trapped with these kids and finished . . . going to run out of water and ammunition . . . and nobody was going to help them. As I was thinking this, I noticed a small piece of paper under the cartridges and I reached down and picked it up. There was writing on it. I scanned the words and felt bad.

Anybody who finds this:

I'm dead. But I've got my two kids. I pray they won't kill them. You got to find them. Please. They got nobody when I'm gone. Find decent folks for them. Tell them I loved them.

God, forgive my sins. I prayed to the Virgin but she has not come.

Robert Dunnet

I put the note away in my shirt pocket and stared out across the canyon for a while, thinking about losing my wife, knowing something of what this man must have felt at the last. Maybe I should just end it here. I forced myself to stand. No. I had to look for the kids. Perhaps they were hiding in the brush. They'd die in a day or two without help.

I searched for their tracks. Nothing. Maybe the man had carried them off and hidden them nearby and then covered the trail before the Apaches cornered him. I called out as loud as I thought reasonable with Apaches around. There was no answer. Then I took Jack and set him down and pointed a finger at the small tracks in the dirt and said, 'Find them.'

Jack did this kind of work all the time and understood immediately what I wanted. And he got interested. But he didn't leave the area of the pit. He made a couple of quick circuits around the hole, nose pressed hard to the ground. But each time he returned to the depression and took another careful whiff of the tracks as if to make certain he hadn't made a mistake.

After ten minutes of this, I knew the kids hadn't walked away and weren't hiding anywhere nearby. They'd been taken by the Apaches. What they'd do with them, I wasn't certain. If they were jumping the reservation to Mexico, they might take them as their own. Otherwise, they'd probably sell them as slaves to one of the haciendas south of the Rio. That trade had been brisk for the past twenty years. The Apaches hadn't invented it. Renegade whites and Mexicans had. The Apaches just saw the profit.

I turned and walked back down the sandy slope to the water, feeling bad for these kids. I hoped they hadn't seen what had happened to their pa. I could see Hannah Morgan's and the girl's footprints at the edge of a small pool bordered with cat-tails and bright green marsh grass. The thin blue sky was filled with birdsong and there were a few large tamarisk bushes and water grasses that provided shade and green and gave the place a nice look.

The female tracks were on top of the Apaches' deerskin teagus, soft knee-length boots they rolled down like socks when they weren't in the brush or cactus. Hannah Morgan had come rushing in here, but after the band had left. How long after, I had no idea. I just hoped she wouldn't ride into them on her way out. But she might. I was hoping she could read tracks.

I squatted and took a drink from my canteen and thought about the kids. I wanted nothing to do with Apaches. But taking time to find the US army wouldn't work. These braves would be long gone into the wastelands. Nope, I didn't have much choice.

I watched the sorrel and the bay sucking up water until I thought they'd burst. I let them. They were going to need it. Martha was wading around in the pool enjoying herself while Jack sat watching from the bank, worried about getting his feet muddy. He was careful about keeping clean, avoiding carrion, horse droppings and mud. I shook my head. For a rough little character he was fussy.

I stopped thinking about Jack and noticed the sky suddenly turning black, then a few minutes later lightning was flashing above the canyon. The terrier went scurrying under bushes while Martha waded out on to the beach and shook water from her coat, then stood enjoying the drops of summer rain that dried as soon as they hit. I just stood as well and let my clothes get wet, the lightning ferocious.

Ten minutes later it was done and the sky had a pretty bluish-pink look. I glanced back at the pile of stones and wondered if the dead man was the reason she'd made the turn down here? Her trail had been straight. But that was crazy. She had no way of knowing. I stopped and cogitated for a second. Unless she knew him. Unless she'd planned on meeting him. But if that was true, her route out of El Paso had been odd. She'd ridden forty miles out of her way before suddenly turning south. And if she'd planned on meeting him, the man would have mentioned it in his note.

After a long drink, I took my binoculars and climbed a narrow deer trail into the sandstone hills; climbed until I reached a high flat-topped mesa that gave me a good view of the terrain for five or six miles to the north. I squatted and began to pan the hot barren landscape. Nothing moved. Nothing looked alive. Nothing but a silence you could almost touch and the great mountains in the far distance and the wide expanse of desert in between. It was a land of basalt-lava flows, mirages and blistering sand. Malpais: the badlands.

I glassed for a long time but couldn't see anything and went back down the trail and mounted the mare and started. Two miles later, I found their tracks in a gully at the foot of the sandhills. Moving fast again. Where the heck was she going now?

The land here had started down in a slow slope toward the lonely stretch of desert. It was filled with good sized cracks in the earth that could catch and cripple a horse. But that wasn't what concerned me. What concerned me was seeing the hoof prints of unshod horses that had ridden out of the hills in front of the woman and the girl. The hooves of Hannah Morgan's horse showed clearly on top of the mounts of the Apaches. And they stayed on top through every twist and turn. If I had any doubts about her ability to read sign, they were gone.

Hannah Morgan hadn't stumbled on to these Indians – she was chasing them. When they turned, she turned, making a beeline after them like she was catching up with friends from the Sunday school picnic.

Having just buried the man, she had to know what they were capable of doing. The hair was rising over Jack's body. He could smell trouble with the best of them . . . and he had the scent now. I was certain this was the same crowd that had killed Dunnet. And this lady was hurrying after them like there was no tomorrow. Maybe there wasn't.

I glassed the desert in the direction they'd gone, but saw nothing. That wasn't unusual. Though the land looked board-flat, it was criss-crossed with gullies and depressions that could hide half the Mexican army. I kicked the sorrel hard in the flanks and she leaped forward into an easy gallop, Jack scrambling to stay balanced on her rump, the bay coming up alongside, while Martha brought up the rear in her lumbering run.

I'd figured this woman was a problem the moment I'd seen her in the room. Now she was proving it. Nothing she did made sense. She looked nice enough . . . but she had a knack for putting herself in the middle of things: my shooting – or whatever it was – stealing the girl, the man's death. Now she was hunting these Indians like she had the US cavalry backing her.

I pulled my hat down against the wind and tried to figure what she was thinking. Neither her nor the Mexican girl's tracks had been near the pit. Therefore she hadn't seen the note. So it followed she didn't know about the kids. Or did she? I told myself no. If she'd been planning on meeting them in that canyon, Dunnet would have mentioned it.

Half a mile out on to the flats I pulled the mare down hard, sliding to a stop in a stand of bloodweed and feeling a tingling over the back of my neck. She was stubborn and foolish. I could see where she'd finally caught them. From the hoof prints it was easy enough to reconstruct what had happened. The woman was crazy.

She and the girl had come trotting down the hard-sand trail right up to them, bold like. So bold, I could see that the Apaches had been surprised. They'd backed off as she rode into the middle of them. The girl had hung back. I didn't blame her. Then they'd closed around Hannah Morgan, the horses milling, the men climbing down.

Neither the woman nor the girl had dismounted. There were no signs of a struggle. They just stood around for a while . . . then they started off together. What did she think they were going to do: let her just say 'howdy' and trot off?

I shook my head, reset my hat and kicked the sorrel into a steady canter that would eat up the miles but save both horses and the big dog. I was figuring I was going to need all three when I finally caught up with this crowd. I rode this way for another fifteen minutes before the mare and I went sliding down a sharp slope of white sand-dune. At the bottom, I saw where the Indians had stopped again and stood around some more. Then the unshod horses had ridden south in the general direction of Mexico, while Hannah Morgan started off toward Utah with the girl's horse and a pony trailing pretty as sweet peas.

I pulled my hat off and wiped a handkerchief around the inside band. There was no question these were the same Indians who'd killed the man. Now, two hours later, they'd let this lone white woman and the young gal come tripping across their lands and talk their way out. And I had a funny feeling the pony was carrying the Dunnet kids.

54

A woman like Morgan would be worth a fortune in Mexico – the girl and the kids, a fat bonus. But instead they'd let them go, slick as spit on a brass doorknob. There wasn't a chance in hell of that happening. Not unless she knew them. That thought jarred me a little. Maybe she did. Maybe she was selling guns. Or buying stolen mules and horses. Maybe. I scratched my head and reworked the signs on the ground again. They came out the same. Crazy.

CHAPTER SIX

I caught up with Hannah Morgan after sundown, the land had gone dark and quiet, the air cooling fast. I reined in the sorrel and studied the woman's camp-site from a small sandy rise some seventy-five yards off in the night. She was sitting near the fire and didn't seem to know I was anywhere around. There was a pile of blankets a few yards away and I figured the girl and the Dunnet kids were under them. I continued watching the woman. She didn't appear to be mourning the death of the man. She was just singing and knitting.

I couldn't make out the words, but it was a nice melody. Definitely not mourning. Maybe she and Dunnet had just been business partners. Jack took to whining when he heard her. I hissed him and pushed my hat back and sat watching her. I couldn't believe it. Out here in the middle of nowhere singing like a canary.

The woman had made her camp in the middle of windswept flatland covered with nothing but rabbitbrush, bitterbrush and sagebrush. Lots of damn different brush. The country stretched north in the moonlight toward a good-sized range of purple mountains. But the location of her camp wasn't bothering me. The thing that bothered me was that she had a bonfire going that was big enough to be seen by a blindman in Peru.

It was like she was asking to be found. But by whom, I

wondered? More than likely it would be the Apaches again – and the next batch might be less sociable. Or maybe the Utes, or Mexicans up from the south. Or just low whites. No, it didn't pay for a lone woman to advertise. But maybe advertising was part of her business. Maybe she was selling like I'd thought. Not romance. She'd have stayed in town for that.

I rubbed the stubble on my chin and stretched in my saddle, feeling like a policeman again. It wasn't a bad feeling. I nudged the sorrel with my heels and started down the slope toward her. She hadn't seen me yet and the way she was singing, she certainly hadn't heard me. And if Jack would keep his trap shut, she wouldn't until I was ready. She had stopped knitting and was sitting with her arms around her knees, staring into the fire and singing.

As I rode, my gaze was drawn again to the large blaze. And again I shook my head. It sure wasn't for cooking or warmth. It definitely looked like a signal fire. But something kept telling me that she wasn't a contraband runner. Too stylish for that. But from my line of work I knew you couldn't tell anything by looking at a person. I'd seen preachers who were child killers and Mexican saints. I even knew a couple of Chinese I could trust.

I continued rocking side to side in the saddle as the sorrel moved down the sloping hill . . . figuring that none of what this woman was up to mattered to me. Not a bit. The only thing that mattered was what she knew about that alley. For what seemed like the thousandth time, my thoughts mulled over the events in El Paso. I was growing tired of worrying the bone.

When I was fifty yards from her camp, she started belting out a new song as if she were the main act in the Denver Opera House. I shook my head and turned the sorrel and made a wide circle to see if the dogs could pick up scent . . . or flush anybody waiting in ambush. I was still going to kill myself . . . but after El Paso nobody was going to do it for me. Not if I could stop them. There was nothing around that shouldn't be. As far as I could tell, the woman was alone with the kids and her singing. It wasn't half bad . . . I just wasn't listening.

Hannah Morgan had nerve. I'd give her that. She didn't jump like most ordinary people would when I suddenly rode out of the desert darkness and into the firelight. That surprised me. But then this woman was full of surprises. She just looked up and smiled at me, studying my face over her little glasses as if she'd been expecting me all along. She kept looking until she finally said, 'Hello, Mr Gibbens. How is your head?'

I found myself suddenly aware of how quiet it was without her singing . . . just the crackling of the fire. Her smile was natural and nice . . . beaming up at me as if I were the only person in the world she'd ever cared about. I squirmed and looked off at the dark horizon as if searching for something. I wasn't.

She was sitting on a blanket bathed in the golden light of the large pile of burning greasewood, her arms still wrapped around her knees and the long dress she wore. She was indeed a dark beauty, I thought, but without the brooding moodiness that often accompanied her kind of looks. Her personality – at least on the surface – was happy and open. Still, there was something deeply serious about her . . . so serious that it was unsettling. I could see that. Or maybe I just sensed it. Whichever, it was there beneath everything else . . . a levelling thing that seemed to weigh down even her moments of gaity. And there were plenty of those. I shook off these thoughts and cleared my throat.

'My head is fine. Thanks.'

She pressed her lips together and nodded and studied me in

a friendly manner – as if I'd done something wonderful just showing up – her dark eyes almost hidden by the happy creases around them. Hannah Morgan's hair in the fire's light was throwing off sparks of luminescence that made it look rich and thick. The only thing that didn't look like a painting about her were those eyes. They were beautiful enough. But they looked tired, sunk into her lovely face, darkened with fatigue. I watched them longer than I felt comfortable, then I turned away and scanned the camp again. The kids hadn't stirred. I looked back at the fire.

'Expecting company?'

She didn't answer, just continued staring up at me.

Her black gelding, the girl's bay and a small grey pony were tethered a few yards away on a decent patch of blue grama grass that grew next to a small, clear sand-bottomed pond. Always on the lookout, Martha walked over and inspected the animals. The woman's horse backed away and snorted at the big dog. The bay and the pony just looked bored and continued grazing. Jack was busy ogling the woman from the rump of my horse.

Seeing the way she'd used lead rope to tie a Spanish hobble on the forelegs of the horses, the thought again crossed my mind that she was no fool when it came to getting along in the wilderness. Again, it didn't seem to fit her. She looked like she belonged on a carousel horse, not a real one. But here she was and, except for the mistake of the fire, she was doing things pretty much right.

She knew when and where to ride, how to find water and feed for her animals . . . this camp was nicely tucked in against a high dune of sand that would provide a good enough windbreak if it started to blow. Nope, she was no tiptoeing pilgrim.

I leaned forward on my saddlehorn. 'Mrs Morgan.' I tipped

my head toward the fire. 'Expecting company?' I asked again.

'Well you've come,' she laughed, her tired eyes almost disappearing with the mirth.

I found myself staring at her wonderful features once more, watching the beautiful flash of white teeth in the full-lipped mouth and the soft wrinkling around her brown eyes, and not wanting to stop. That was rare for me. I often had a passing thought that a woman was pretty . . . but it was unusual for me to think or feel much more than that. Not after my wife. Jack, on the other hand, felt this way about every woman, and he was off the mare's rump now, dancing around and making a fool of himself in front of her.

'Knock it off,' I said, stepping down from the saddle.

'No,' she chuckled. 'Jack can kiss me all he wants.'

I stopped moving and turned slowly to face the woman. 'How did you know his name?'

She caught up the little terrier and hugged him while Jack twisted and turned trying madly to lick her face. She seemed to enjoy it immensely, nuzzling him back. Then she set the dog free and stood, straightening her clothes.

'When you were unconscious, you called his name. Your other dog is Martha.'

I continued to study her face for a moment, as if I didn't trust her completely. Then I said, 'Yeah, that's right.' I walked over and scooped sand on to the bonfire until it was nothing more than black smoke snaking into the night sky. The desert air was chilly but not cold. The moon and stars were hovering over these flat lands as if they hovered nowhere else on earth.

'I'd suggest you not light up the territory like that.'

She nodded.

I walked across the camp and squatted next to the bundle of blankets, gently lifting one corner and seeing the peaceful sleeping faces of two small negro kids, maybe five and seven. They looked so sweet that I felt a sad smile come across my face. They were alone now. It was hard enough when you were my age. These two were too young for it.

I moved around to the other corner of the blanket and took another look. She was cute in a boyish way – her black hair cut short and stylish, too old for her age. My guess was she wasn't much over thirteen. Then her eyes popped open and she was pulling back, staring at me like I was going to grab her.

'Lucia. Salvo – safe,' I said.

She continued to look scared, turning her head quickly until she saw Hannah and calmed down some.

'Policia,' I went on, pulling my badge and showing it to her. It didn't help much. I stood and turned back toward the woman. She was smiling at me and I thought for a second she was fighting tears. I had no idea why.

'That girl OK?' I asked when I got beside her.

'Just frightened of people.' The woman had turned and was staring into my face as if she had something to ask me. But she didn't ask it.

'She the reason you were in El Paso?'

Hannah Morgan nodded and continued to stare at me.

'Kin?'

'No.'

I hadn't come here to talk about the girl, and the woman's staring was making me uncomfortable, so I let it drop. 'I'll spend the night,' I said, 'in case you've lured any crazies out of their burrows.' As soon as I'd spoken the words, I was surprised at myself. I had planned on making a quick meal, asking a few questions, then heading back towards El Paso, to get on with what I had to do. Now, I was settling in like this was a permanent camp and I was a regular. Deputy sheriff to the rescue. I shrugged the thought off and rubbed my hands together over the hot coals of the fire.

'I'd enjoy your company,' Hannah said.

I liked the way she spoke: her voice strong and pleasing, with the soft hint of an accent that was maybe the eastern part of the country. Whatever it was, it sounded nice. She turned and pulled her small glasses off and looked out across the wide expanse of land, pale in the moonlight, neither of us saying anything for a while. Then she put the glasses back on her fine nose and returned to her knitting, her hands moving fast.

'What are you making?' I asked, not really caring but trying to make conversation, staring at the large black pile of knitted material that was spread over her lap and across the blanket.

'Nothing.'

'Nothing?'

'I just like to knit.'

I studied her face to see if she was kidding. She didn't look like it.

'Let me get this straight. You knit but don't make anything – you just like to do it? Row after row of those stitches.'

'That's it. You've grasped it completely.' She was smiling in jest at me.

I ignored her teasing. 'What do you do when that thing – whatever it is – gets too heavy to cart around?'

'I unravel it and start over again.'

I nodded. 'Maybe you should make something.'

'Why?'

'Isn't that the point of knitting? To make something?'

'Not for me. I just like to do it.'

'That's crazy. It's a waste of time. You should really make something.'

She looked up over her glasses, her needles still flashing, and said, 'Mr Gibbens, you don't have to beg. If you want me to make you something, just say it.'

I was suddenly feeling embarrassed. 'What? I'm not begging. I don't want anything.'

'A sweater maybe? Socks?'

I held up a hand. 'No. This shirt's plenty.'

'It looks nice on you.'

'It's pink.'

She sat as if she was seriously contemplating what I'd just said.

'I can't believe you bought pink.'

'I like pink.'

'But it wasn't for you. It was for me.'

'It was on sale, Mr Gibbens,' she said, as if that would explain everything to me.

'And I know why,' I said, sarcastically.

'I saved you a dollar.'

'Great,' I moaned. 'Saved me a dollar but almost got me killed,' I mumbled, thinking back to Altar Ramon.

'Must you always talk about getting killed? Mr Gibbens, it's not healthy.'

I could tell I wasn't going to get anywhere with her on the subject, so I stopped and made myself a cigarette. We didn't talk for a long time after that. I puffed on my smoke and felt surprised I'd gotten sidetracked – talking about silly things like knitting and pink shirts. I had serious things to ask this woman. She continued knitting.

'Did you know that man?'

'The one we buried?'

'Yes.'

Her face didn't change expression. 'No.'

'How'd you find him?'

'He was just in that canyon.'

'Yes. But how'd you know?' I paused. 'You turned from riding north, rushing down here. How'd you know?' I repeated.

She hesitated and in that instant I knew I had her.

'No idea?'

'Just a feeling.'

'A feeling?'

I could see her hesitating again, then she folded her hands in her lap and looked up into my face, waiting a moment before she cleared her throat and said, 'My voices told me, Mr Gibbens.'

I stopped and tried to figure if she was back pulling my leg again. She didn't appear to be.

'Your voices?'

'Yes.'

'What kind of voices?' I said, squinting at her.

She shrugged. 'Just normal voices.'

'Voices – but nobody around?'

'Yes.'

'Ma'am, those aren't normal.'

'Perhaps you're right.'

'Not perhaps. Voices out of the blue aren't normal.'

She nodded and then went back to her knitting. I stood watching her until my curiosity got the best of me.

'Where do they come from?'

'Sir?'

'These voices. Where do they come from?'

'God.'

'From God? God talks to you?'

'Not directly. He sends the voices.'

'And what do they say?'

'They let me know things.'

I thought about this for a long time because it wasn't every day somebody said something like this. The woman didn't look uncomfortable – just sort of nonchalant. Like maybe these kind of things happened to everybody.

'How do you know they're from God?'

She stopped knitting and looked up at me. 'Who else would they be from, sir?'

'Maybe nobody.'

'Nobody?'

'Perhaps you're just crazy. Maybe you just think you hear voices.'

She smiled and resumed her knitting. 'No, sir. The voices are from God.'

I sat nodding at her as if I understood – which I didn't – and pursing my lips, trying to figure what to say next. Finally, I decided to switch directions to see if I could trip her up. 'How'd you know he had kids?'

'Mr Gibbens?'

'Those coloured kids. How'd you know the man had them with him? They'd been taken by the Apaches by the time you got there. But you went straight after them.' I was rushing my words as if the truth might get away if I didn't hurry up and catch it.

Hannah stopped knitting and took her glasses off and put them away in a little carrying case, then she sat staring off across the dark landscape without speaking and I was aware again of how silent it was in this place. I liked the sound of silence. Always had. But I wanted answers now.

'Ma'am?'

'Yes?'

'How did you know about those two kids?'

She looked up at me. 'I've already told you.' She sounded a little stiff.

'The voices?'

'Yes.'

I tensed. 'They tell you to find me in that alley?'

'Yes.'

I stopped talking and thought about what she'd mumbled in the room when she'd gone into that trance: 'He is the one.' I shivered, then forced myself to ask the question.

'Why?'

'Sir?'

'Why'd they send you after me?' I said, not certain I wanted to hear.

'I don't know.'

'You don't know?'

'No.'

'That's it? These voices tell you to do things you don't understand. But you go ahead anyway.'

She sat staring down at her knitting for a few moments, then slowly she raised her head and looked at me. 'Wouldn't you, Mr Gibbens?'

'Wouldn't I what?'

'Do what your God asked you to do?'

I didn't answer. I just sat studying her face to see if she was joking again. She didn't look it.

'Let me see if I understand,' I continued in a tone that sounded like I was talking to a nut-case. 'You and the girl were riding north, minding your own sweet business, when suddenly a mysterious voice says: "Go to the canyon. There's a man in trouble there." That about it?' I could see from the look on her face that she didn't care for the scoffing.

She paused, still staring at me. 'I heard a voice. Yes, sir. But I wasn't riding, I was drinking from a stream when it came to me. It was evening and it was quiet. I'd just said my prayers for vespers. They come to me in the quiet. Always in the quiet.'

'What did this voice say?'

' "Find them there." And I saw the canyon in my mind and knew how to get there – it was all there inside my head.' She stopped talking and looked down at her knitting again. 'I don't expect you to understand.'

'You some sort of religious diviner?'

'No, sir.'

'No?'

'No.'

'You just get instructions from God. Complete with maps.'

'I see things. People and places. We all get messages, Mr Gibbens.'

There was something straightforward, some natural innocence about her that made her sound believable. Even so, I wanted to say, 'That's crazy,' but didn't. I'm not certain why I didn't, I just know that as I stood there looking down at this woman an old memory came to me.

I was eleven or twelve. I'd gone with my mother to spend a month with her parents in South Florida. On the day we were to start back to Arizona, I caught a rare female Cuban Devilliers Swallowtail that had somehow strayed from its island home across the Gulf. I put the beautiful little creature in a jar, determined to keep her alive until I could get to our ranch and my cyanide so I could dispatch her without fixing her muscles so rigidly that I couldn't properly mount her in my specimen box. She was a great prize for any collector. Doubly so for a kid from Arizona.

I noticed Hannah Morgan watching me, waiting for me to say something. I nodded. 'Yeah. Things sometimes happen,' I said.

She didn't say anything.

'When I was a boy,' I went on, 'I caught a rare Cuban butterfly in Florida and brought it back alive to our ranch for my collection.'

She was listening carefully.

'We arrived home late at night and I was tired and put the jar and the butterfly near the window in my bedroom, deciding I'd kill it in the morning.' I stopped talking and stared at her, wondering why I was telling this.

'And?'

'Nothing much,' I mumbled. I turned and looked off into the night.

'You haven't finished, Mr Gibbens.'

'Right. Well, this was a rare butterfly even for South Florida. They simply didn't exist in Arizona.'

She nodded. When I didn't continue, she said, 'Yes?'

'When I got up the next morning, there on my window, fluttering outside the glass where the female was held in the jar, I saw a male of the same species.' I paused. 'I still don't know how he got to Arizona . . . and having gotten there, how he found that one female of his kind. But he did.' I stood pondering the mystery of it all over again, then said, 'Somehow, I always figured, she must have called to him. But how, I'll never know.'

Hannah Morgan was still watching me. I moved a rock with the toe of my boot.

'I was surprised . . . so I let them go.'

Hannah tipped her head back and stared up at the sky for a while. 'I don't think so, Mr Gibbens.'

'Ma'am?'

'I don't think you let them go from surprise. I think you did it out of kindness.'

I cleared my throat. 'Whatever.' Suddenly I was feeling annoyed that I had gone drifting off down a side trail again.

'But I don't think that butterfly was delivering me some message, ma'am.'

She ignored the comment.

I changed direction again. 'Who were you expecting?'

'Where?'

'Here.'

'No one but you, sir.'

'Me? That's why you lit the fire? For me?'

'I just thought you might try and find me.'

Momentarily flustered, my mind leaped back to what she'd said in her room. 'He is the one.' I forced myself to slow down. She hadn't been talking about me. I cleared my throat and said, 'What made you think that?'

'Sir?'

'What made you think I'd try and find you.'

'Just a feeling,' she said brightly.

'Another one of your messages?'

She ignored me. 'I know you're confused about what happened in El Paso.'

It was my turn to ignore her. She was right but I suddenly wasn't ready to talk about it. I looked across the camp at the pile of blankets. 'How are those boys?'

'Fine, Mr Gibbens,' she said. A cool wind was whipping over the camp now and Hannah put her knitting down and walked to her saddle and picked up a red wool blanket, moving on to the children. She knelt and spread the blanket over them. I stood watching.

'They see what happened to their father?' I asked.

'No.'

'Good.' I reached behind me and put my hands on my lower back and stretched. This woman had been pushing all of us hard and I was feeling it. The kids were too from the looks of them.

'What are you going to do with them?' I asked, watching as she brushed sand from Lucia's cheek.

She didn't respond.

'The girl can go back to Mexico,' I said. 'I don't know where the boys go. Aren't many coloureds in these parts.' She hadn't turned, but I sensed she was listening.

She touched a hand softly to each of the children's heads. It was a gesture I'd seen mothers make before – a simple touch but one that carried a world of feeling.

'Lucia's family sold her.'

I knew now why the girl looked frightened. After a few moments, Hannah stood and returned to the fire.

'These children are together now,' she said softly. 'God wants that.'

That made no sense. It wasn't like they fit right – a mess of black and Mexican kids mixed up together.

Her gaze was moving slowly across the dense purple expanse, out toward the large mountains darker in the distance, staring as though she were trying to see something in the far reaches of the night. Maybe she was trying to hear her voices. I found myself listening. But there was nothing and I could see she'd gone to daydreaming again: her eyes closed, her lips moving as if in prayer.

'Ma'am?'

'Yes, Mr Gibbens?' she said, opening one eye to look at me.

She wasn't pleased by the interruption. I didn't particularly care.

'They don't fit together.'

'The children?' she asked.

'Yes. Two negroes and a Mexican. Nobody is going to take that combination on. Not in these parts.'

She didn't respond.

'Ma'am?'

'Yes?'

'Who's going to want to care for them?'

She shut her eye down tight. 'I, Mr Gibbens.'

I watched the side of her face for a moment before I said, 'Just because you found them – doesn't mean you have to take responsibility.'

Her eyes opened and she turned and stared into my face. 'It's a gift from God.'

I ignored that talk. I liked kids fine but her ideas were a little loopy. For a moment, she seemed to be drifting off into prayer or meditation again, then she caught herself and focused and looked at me and smiled.

'It's lovely here. Isn't it?'

'If you like dust and heat.'

'And you don't?'

'It's OK,' I repeated.

We didn't talk for a while after that until she reached and pulled a branch off a small plant and sniffed it, inhaling as if it were a breeze from heaven. 'What a wonderful smell.'

'Purple sage. Stinks up the whole territory.'

'It's magnificent.'

'For raising sheep and goats.'

'That's all it's fit for?'

I wanted to say: 'Cut the crap,' but surprised myself and said, 'Some folks make a tea from it that cures boils and stuff, and the Paiutes and Shoshones use it for baskets and sandals. Not much else.'

'You're from here?' she asked, beginning to knit and watching me as I worked some Mexican oil into my saddle leather.

'Few hundred miles southwest.'

'And now Los Angeles.'

71

I nodded. When she didn't continue, I said, 'Ma'am?'

'Yes?'

'You adopting these kids?' I was thinking the absurdity of the question would shake some sense into her.

She smiled. 'I wish,' her voice sounding far away.

I thought for a moment about my dead child and what it would have been like to have had a daughter. My chest was tightening when I spoke again. 'The girl's Mexican. The boys negro. You're white and heading in a direction where you aren't likely to find Mexicans or coloureds.' I paused, letting these facts sink into her – letting the silliness of her contemplations come clear in her head. 'Los Angeles has a nice place where they take care of kids. I'll wire some folks and get it done.'

Hannah Morgan faced me as if I'd said something bad. She just sat there looking at me, staring into my eyes – something hurt in her expression – as if I were an old friend and had forgotten a thing that was important to her. I just didn't know what.

'No, Mr Gibbens,' she said, looking down at her knitting.

'Probably best under the circumstances.'

'No,' she said firmly. She sat and poked at her yarn with the needles. After a time, she looked up and said, 'Mr Gibbens,' her tone so serious, so personal sounding, that it caused me to tense.

'Yes, ma'am?'

She started to say something, then stopped.

I waited a few moments, then nodded. But I wasn't certain what I was nodding about. I placed my saddle, candle down, on the ground and picked up my grub sack and took out some flour, bacon and a heavy chunk of raw goat cheese that I'd bought off an old Mexican woman outside a little town two days back, and began to make a fire hole.

The woman seemed to have returned to happy thoughts again, smiling at me whenever I glanced her way. I dug the hole some three feet deep in the sand. When I was finished I built a small cooking fire in the bottom that would be hard to see.

As I was doing this, Hannah stood, hands clasped behind her, and watched. Every so often she would cluck her tongue or say 'hmmmmm' as if she found my activities instructive. When I was done she said, 'Very interesting.' I had the funny feeling she was teasing. Her record wasn't real good on that score. So I ignored her.

'You and the kids eaten?'

'Oh, yes. We had a wonderful meal of Mexican black beans and rice and a tamale pie that Lucia made. It was absolutely delicious. Have you ever had tamale pie, Mr Gibbens?'

She asked the question like it was a rare dish instead of survival grub for every poor Mexican mucking a living in these parts. 'Yeah,' I said.

'Isn't it the best thing?'

'I don't care much for Mexican.'

She looked at me like I might be slightly off kilter. 'Ohhhh, you'd love Lucia's.'

She joined me now, dropping down on her knees in the sand and cutting the bacon into strips with my pocket knife. She was tall and lean, beautifully muscled beneath translucent white skin. Strong but not masculine. I noticed one other thing: no timidity. When she wanted to do a thing, she just did it. Straight out. No dancing. I liked that. My wife had been like that.

But still, for a reason I couldn't explain to myself, I remained confused about Hannah Morgan. And that bothered me. I'd always been able to figure women pretty fast. But I couldn't get a decent bead on this one.

'You know those Apaches?'

She didn't hesitate. 'Is that the kind of Indian they were?'

'Yes,' I said, not believing she didn't know.

'No.'

'How'd you get away?'

She laughed. 'You make it sound as if I made some daring escape. I merely told them that I would care for the children. Then I asked them where I could find the next water. And they told me.'

I squinted at her. 'Let me get this straight. Those Apaches – the ones who'd just killed the boys' father – see you trespassing on their reservation. You ask them for the kids and directions to the nearest waterhole. They hand them over and tell you – real polite, like big city gentlemen. That about it?'

'They behaved like gentlemen, Mr Gibbens. Yes. They gave me the children and told me where to find water.' She had sensed the change in me.

'You speak Apache?'

'A number of them spoke English quite well.'

Her tone was changing. She was no longer joking. That was fine with me. I watched her to see if she was telling lies. Something told me she wasn't.

'You talked quite a while. What about?'

Hannah pressed her lips together and looked at me for a time before she said, 'You don't really trust me much, do you, Mr Gibbens?' All humour was gone from her.

'Not much.'

'Why?'

'Because you lied in El Paso.'

She looked like she'd been slapped. When she spoke it was slowly and thoughtfully, but she almost seemed to change shape and content somehow before my eyes . . . from gentleness to a

74

deep, dangerous anger that was unsettling to witness. 'No, sir.' The words were low and bothered me in a way I can't explain easily. 'I did not lie.' She was hesitating, as if struggling mightily to control her emotions. 'And do not –' I sensed she'd caught herself before she said something she'd regret.

'Those Indians.'

She frowned and lowered her voice. 'Did you hear me, Mr Gibbens?'

'Yeah, I heard. Now about those Indians.'

She waited a few moments as if she were considering not answering me, then she continued in a quieter voice, 'They thought I was some sort of supernatural being who materialized from that storm. They said they had seen me ride out of the lightning. I tried to tell them no . . . but they wouldn't believe me.'

She started the bacon in the skillet. 'One old man kept putting his hands on my head like I was a magical being and calling me a thunder spirit.'

I stared at the wavering flames of the fire and thought. It was the first thing she'd said that made good sense. Apaches worshipped lightning. Ussen, their god, used it as arrows during the hunt.

I nodded at her. Having just slaked their thirst for killing on Dunnet, these warriors could have been surprised to see the woman riding across this desolate land. Seen her at the same time the storm hit. They certainly would have been impressed that she wasn't scared. Then perhaps some shaman made the claim she was one of the revered Thunder People. She had the looks of a goddess . . . Apache or white. That might have happened. If it had, she was damn lucky.

I nodded. 'They worship lightning.'

She patted Jack's admiring head and smiled up at me, some

of her good-naturedness returning. 'So there. You believe me now?'

I half-smiled. 'Could be.'

She laughed. 'What does "could be" mean? That maybe you believe me . . . or that those Indians let me go because they thought I was one of the thunder gods?'

I waited, then said, 'Both.'

'Good,' she said, turning her head back to the skillet.

Hannah Morgan could turn happy fast and she did so now. I relaxed some and watched her cook. While I badly wanted answers about El Paso, the food smells were getting to me. Questions could wait.

The meal – bread on a stick, bacon, beans and cheese – looked wonderful when she finally heaped it on to the plates. But as I was starting to take a bite, she clasped her hands together, closed her eyes and said, 'Would you, Mr Gibbens?'

'Would I?' I squirmed.

'Speak over the food.'

I lowered my head and tried to think, but couldn't, blood rushing to my face. 'Bless this meal,' I mumbled, hurriedly raising my fork.

'And bless these children,' she continued, her voice bright and cheerful.

I clamped my eyes shut again.

'Give them hearts of great courage and the calm of Your abiding peace, Dear Lord. And bless this good man, Tucker Gibbens. Strengthen his spirit for what he must face, bringing him into Your grace, Father. Do not let him falter or fail.'

I could feel moisture on my forehead. I cleared my throat. She heard me.

'Yes, Mr Gibbens?' she asked, picking up her fork and starting in on the food like she hadn't eaten in a year.

'What did you mean?'

'Sir?'

'Strengthen my spirit for what I must face.'

She swallowed and said, 'You worry too much, Mr Gibbens.'

I looked down at my plate, not as hungry as I'd been moments before. Hannah Morgan was watching me.

'You must have meant something.'

'It was just a simple prayer for you.'

I didn't say anything.

The food was good. She polished off half. Looking at her slender body, I wondered where she stuffed it. I was working now at trying to not get caught looking at her. But it was hard. I felt like a schoolboy. She didn't seem to mind. She just sat and talked, carrying on about my dogs and my life in California, directing most of the talk to me, giving away little about herself. The dogs watched her like she was the best thing they'd seen in a long while. Compared to me, they were right. But it still seemed odd.

I wondered what she'd done in El Paso to get Martha to let her move the horses. Anyone else would have lost an arm trying. It was part and parcel of this whole confusing thing. None of it made sense. Most confusing of all was this woman who claimed she heard voices from God and had been directed to find me in that alley. More than likely, she just had something loose in her head.

'Tell me again how you found me,' I said, standing and walking back to where I had dropped my pack after unhitching the bay.

'I already told you.'

'I'm curious.'

She sat watching me with a firm look on her face.

'Go on,' I said.

'You just want to see if I can tell the same story again. Don't you, Mr Gibbens?'

'Maybe,' I muttered, surprised she'd guessed what I was up to.

'No. Not maybe. Please be honest.'

I could feel my face turning a shade of red.

'I will if you will,' I countered, realizing that I was dangerously close to the line she'd told me not to cross . . . and wondering why I cared.

I watched her stiffen, then avoided her eyes and knelt and rolled out my blood-stained clothes on the ground, determined to have my say. 'You told me there weren't any holes.'

Hannah stood, holding Jack in her arms and staring down at the clothing. 'No. I never said that.' She squatted and ran a hand over Jack's head and continued studying the clothing. 'All I said, Mr Gibbens, was that your clothes were filthy and soaked in blood. And that I gave them to a man to be burned. Obviously, they weren't. Burned, that is.' She studied them a moment longer, then said, 'The truth is, I never took a close look at them. All I did was pull them off of you and looked for wounds on your body.' She paused. 'There was so much blood, I was afraid you had punctured an artery.'

She was staring straight into my face now with eyes that seemed to pierce through me. She didn't look or sound like a liar. 'After I got you cleaned up, I took everything out of your pockets then took the clothing downstairs and asked an old man to burn them because they were such a mess.' She continued looking at me. 'That's all I know.'

'But you can see now, can't you? You can see that I was shot and killed. Just like I said.'

She knelt, still holding Jack, and reached a hand down and touched the hole and the dried blood with her fingertips. Then she looked back up at me. 'The hole. Yes. I can certainly see that.' She paused. 'But I can also see that you are here with me. Alive, Mr Gibbens.'

'That's right,' I began again. 'But I don't have any wounds. And that's impossible. How do you explain that? Did God tell you about that, too?'

She looked up at me and shrugged her shoulders and raised her eyebrows, the gesture sincere and caring. 'God did not tell me anything about you. I'm sorry. I wish I could help you.'

'Yes,' I continued, my voice more forceful. 'Yes. You can help me. You know something.' I studied her features hard. She gave nothing away with her looks. 'What happened to me?'

'I can't help you.'

'Yes. You were there. You claimed that your voices sent you. What did they say? What did you see?'

'I can't explain something I don't understand myself, Mr Gibbens.'

'What did the voices say?' I pressed. 'Tell me that.'

She stared down at the ground for a time and then she looked up at me, 'The voices said, "The one you seek is in the alley."' Her eyes didn't look fully focused.

I was confused. 'Why were you looking for me?'

'I wasn't.'

'Then why did they say: "The one you seek?"'

'I don't know. I honestly don't know, Mr Gibbens. All I know is that God wanted you found.'

That was poppycock, but I didn't tell her that. I just took a deep breath and started in again. 'What did you see?'

'Blood,' she said quietly, her eyes focusing on an empty piece of air as she remembered back.

'So you saw a wound.'

'I heard a shot. And shouting. When I turned into the alley I saw that you had fallen back through a window. People were running and screaming. It was dark . . .' Her voice drifted off.

'What else?'

She seemed to pull herself back from whatever she was thinking about and looked at me in a surprised way . . . as if just realizing that I was there beside her for the first time.

'What else?'

She straightened the fabric of her dress. 'I knelt next to you and saw blood seeping out of your shirt.' She paused. 'I pressed my hand against it to try and stop you from bleeding to death, Mr Gibbens. And I prayed for you. That's all I know. I paid two men to carry you to my room. I kept my hand pressed against your chest while they went to find a doctor. While I waited, I stripped your clothes off. When I soaked up the blood, there was no wound. Nothing.'

She walked to the fire and stood looking down into it as if watching distant memories moving inside the flames. Jack was quiet in her arms. 'There are things that happen in this life that we can't always explain, Mr Gibbens. God touched you. That's all I know.'

'Humbug. I can explain things.'

She turned and faced me. 'No you can't, Mr Gibbens. I can't either.' Her voice had that edge to it again that made me squirm.

My voice was rising. 'I understand things. I'm not some damn fool who hears voices.' I was immediately sorry I'd said the words, but there was no taking them back.

She stared at me for a long time – definitely not a woman who scurried for cover when somebody stamped a foot. In fact, as I stood watching her, I had the uneasy sense she was fighting to control herself again. From doing what, I wasn't certain. She cleared her throat.

'Tell me about Nellie.'

I froze. 'What about her?'

'She was stillborn. A baby girl, dying the week before your wife.'

She turned back to the fire, plainly on the prod again, the way she'd been when I'd accused her of lying. Suddenly I didn't want this conversation. But I was learning fast that Hannah Morgan didn't like to be pushed around.

'Mr Gibbens.'

'Yes?'

'Nellie. Where did she come from?'

I shifted my feet.

'You know where children come from,' I snapped.

'Not the act of procreation, Mr Gibbens.'

'I don't understand.'

'Don't pretend to be an idiot, sir,' she said, returning in kind the insult I'd given her.

I could feel the blood rushing to my face.

'I know where babies come from,' she said in a frank way unusual for proper women. 'Tell me about the short life of Nellie Gibbens. Where it came from.' She watched me for a moment, then said, 'You can't. No more than I can tell you why those Indians believed I was a goddess. Or what causes a seed to sprout after it has lain a thousand years in a desert tomb.' She sat down with Jack still in her arms. 'You can't. And I can't tell you about that hole in your clothes and the fact that you bled but had no wound. There are things like that, Mr Gibbens.'

I was about to respond when Jack's ears perked and he growled out at the night. I turned and studied the surrounding darkness. It was empty except for the moon, the stars and the night shadows. But Jack wasn't one to sound false alarms. Something was there.

I reached and pulled the leather thong off my pistol. The little terrier hopped out of Hannah's arms and trotted a few yards out from where we stood, the hair rising in a thick ridge down the centre of his small back. Martha let go with a throaty half-bark to let whoever or whatever Jack had heard know she wasn't to be trifled with.

I hadn't seen anything by the time Hannah quietly said, 'Mr Gibbens, you best get a grip on your dogs.'

They had come in quiet like fog along the Pacific Coast and were standing in the shadows some sixty feet from the camp. Even looking straight at them, I didn't see them right away; then I caught the reflection of moonlight off white pigment and began to make the figures out in the dusky air. There were ten of them. They'd come up on foot. They were armed and most had the characteristic band of pigment running horizontally across their noses and cheeks, just under the fierce black eyes. Not a good sign since it was their version of war-paint.

I was no Indian expert but I knew Jicarilla Apaches when I saw them: more like plains Indians than Apaches with their braided hair and handsomely beaded buckskins. They were horse lovers. Maybe that's why they were here. The sorrel, the bay and the woman's black gelding were all nice animals. But no, this many bucks didn't come walking up on a camp like they were collecting money for the school library, not for three horses. They were here on other business. And I didn't like the smell of it. Not after seeing Dunnet's grave.

Mixed in with the Jicarilla were a few Mescaleros, mountain Apaches. As I watched, a bare-chested shaman dressed in a long deerskin skirt and wearing the hooded mask with the towering head-dress of the Gan, or Mountain Spirit, walked out a few yards ahead of the others, carrying a long knife in each hand. Slowly he began to chant and dance in place, the steady incantation floating into the night air like a warning to the soul.

Jack and Martha were getting ready to charge and I was deciding whether or not to reach for my pistol, when Hannah made the decision for me.

'Get hold of your dogs, Mr Gibbens. It would be unwise to attack these people.'

I agreed.

None of the Apaches moved when Hannah started toward them in the moonlight. The Gans dancer continued his slow, rhythmic movements. I could see no women or children among them. Not a good sign. Hannah was still moving slowly forward as I finished strapping the dogs' collars on.

'Don't push your luck, ma'am,' I called, picking up the shotgun and walking to the edge of the camp. The scattergun was nothing against this many, most armed with modern rifles.

'Mr Gibbens, put your gun down and stay where you are.'

I was surprised that standing with her back to me, she'd known I was carrying the gun and about to join her. She was nobody's fool.

'I wouldn't get cosy with this crowd.'

The woman and the Gans dancer had both stopped and were staring at one another, separated by a few yards of night air. The man looked tense, ready to run or fight. I wasn't sure which. Then he made a few symbolic stabbing gestures towards Hannah. Things weren't looking good. From what I could tell, they hadn't come to worship the woman . . . they'd come to exorcise a devil.

Watching her from the back, standing straight and tall and seemingly little worried by the wall of warriors staring sullenly at her, Hannah Morgan looked as strong as any woman I had ever seen. There was something oddly warrior-like about her, the way she stood, her head up proud, her thin shoulders squared against the line of braves, something that spoke of fortitude and conviction that would match any man's. She was a strange mix: vulnerable yet capable; winsome but strong. I felt a deep urge to stand beside her. But I did what she'd asked.

Jack, on the other hand, wasn't to be trifled with. He'd claimed the woman as his and he wouldn't have cared if there'd been a thousand warriors out there in the night. A fight was a fight. Especially when his own true love was involved. In one wiggling backward tug, the little terrier slipped his collar, then whirled and sprinted out across the sands like the cavalry to the rescue. Not a halfway dog, he hit the shaman's ankles hard, snarling as he snapped at the man. Caught by surprise, the warrior took to hopping around and swinging the daggers. Jack dodged and then darted in for another quick bite. The man swung and missed again. I knew that once started, Jack would not break off an attack. Both Hannah and I rushed forward.

Hannah reached him first, diving and grabbing the terrier, the shaman stepping back as if frightened and then hopping forward until he was standing over the woman where she lay sprawled on the sands clutching the struggling dog, his daggers raised menacingly over her.

I cocked the shotgun. 'Don't,' was all I said. I could hear the warriors cocking their weapons as well. It was over. I thought about my wife and daughter.

'Mr Gibbens. Put the gun down,' Hannah said firmly.

'When you get out, ma'am.'

'No. Now,' she said, her voice rising slightly.

I uncocked the shotgun and lowered the barrels until they were pointing at the sand. It didn't have any effect. The dancer was still standing over Hannah ready to plunge his knife. She was talking quietly to him but I couldn't make out the words.

I was trying desperately to figure how to break the stalemate when I heard rumbling above. I glanced up at the dark sky. 'Come on,' I urged. 'Do it!'

Then, as if in response to my plea, the clouds discharged a single bolt of lightning to the hot sands. The impact point on the desert floor was no more than a hundred yards away, causing an instantaneous flash of blinding white light across the land, illuminating Hannah and the little dog and the Apaches in its harsh glare. Then it was gone. Blackness falling hard again. The earth trembling. The sky roaring as if mountains were collapsing. I recoiled from the awesome power, bracing for another strike. But none came. Just that one bolt.

The effect of the lighting on the Apaches was immediate. This was the second time. In their collective, superstitious mind Hannah Morgan was truly one of the Thunder People. The Gans dancer began to back nervously away from her as if she might destroy him with a flick of her hand.

When I looked from the shaman to the place where the warriors had stood, they were gone. Gone so quickly and silently that I wondered for a moment whether they had ever really been there. But that was silly.

Hannah Morgan sat on the sand with Jack in her lap. The dog was whining and looking up at her face. I squatted next to her, continuing to stare out at the empty shadows of the desert to make certain no young buck would try and settle things differently. Satisfied that they were gone I turned back to the woman. 'I'll take him,' I said, softly.

Hannah Morgan didn't respond.

I turned and looked at the side of her face. She looked dazed, staring off into the night as if she had been stunned by some unseen blow. I wondered if the fright had thrown her into a trance of sorts.

'Ma'am?'

She didn't move or speak. Then, slowly, she opened her mouth, but nothing came out. I reached for Jack and the little dog whirled and snapped hard at my hand, and I fell back on my rump.

'Jack, what the hell?' The little dog had never growled at me before . . . not even the time I'd stitched his belly up after a horse had split it open.

At the sound of my voice, the terrier seemed to come to his senses. He shook hard once then whined pitifully and hopped out of the woman's lap and crawled wiggling over the sand on his belly. He was seemingly as surprised as I was.

'It's OK,' I said, laying a hand on his head, but not taking my eyes off the side of the woman's face. She was sitting stiff and erect. 'Just a mistake,' I continued. 'We all had a scare.' Jack whined as if in agreement.

I had seen people who'd been gunshot act the way the woman did. She was pale, her skin cold and clammy to the touch. Tiny beads of sweat clustered on her brow and her breathing was shallow, her pulse rate fast.

She hadn't moved when I picked her up and carried her back to the camp. I laid her down on a blanket then covered her with another. And now I was sitting nearby, studying her face, Jack and Martha quiet on either side of me. Jack came over and licked my hand as if to say he was sorry again.

'Forget it,' I said.

He seemed temporarily relieved and plopped down on the sand. When I looked back at the woman I could see her mouthing something. I bent, turning an ear to catch the sound. I heard what I thought were sentences but couldn't understand them.

The night was still and cold now, the way high desert turns after midnight. I put my hand gently to the woman's cheek.

Her skin felt icy. I pulled the blanket up under her chin and then went and grabbed my spare saddle blanket and spread this over her as well.

I knew people in her condition sometimes just up and died for no reason. So every so often, I rubbed her hands and feet to get the circulation flowing. Then suddenly, as if a lance had penetrated her, the woman's face contorted and she was racked by groans. Then she sat bolt upright and screamed a scream that seemed to penetrate deep into me. A scream that I thought maybe I'd heard before. Maybe I'd made it myself. I shuddered.

I tried holding her down, talking to her, shaking her to awaken her . . . but nothing worked. On and on she struggled in the grip of something invisible. Tossing and turning and calling out as if she were having a hundred nightmares in one. I held her in my arms, struggling to keep her still, and talked to her for a while and it seemed to help some but then she went back to her fretful turning and moaning and I laid her down and covered her with the blankets.

Then I heard a noise behind me and whirled, pulling my pistol out. Lucia and the two little Dunnet boys. The boys were holding hands and staring big-eyed at the muzzle of the gun. Lucia was watching Hannah Morgan. Every once in a while her dark eyes jumped to me as if I'd done this thing to the woman. She walked over and knelt beside her. Pretty for sure, but just a kid who looked frightened.

'Enfermo – sick,' I said.

Lucia continued to stare down at the woman with concern.

'She OK?' the older of the boys asked.

I nodded.

'You going to shoot us, Mister?' the smaller one mumbled.

'Sorry.' I lowered the pistol and slid it back into my holster. They'd both been crying. They were skinny, handsome kids.

Poorly dressed in pants and shirts that were worn out and too small. But nothing dulled their cuteness. They'd either slept through the lightning or been too frightened to move until now. Probably the latter.

'Aunt Hannah – is she OK?' the younger one asked again, his lower lip quivering.

'Just a nightmare. You ever have one?'

The boy nodded.

'She your real aunt?' I asked, wondering if she'd married into the Dunnet family.

'No,' the older boy mumbled. 'She just said we could call her that.'

I nodded. It was the right thing to tell two boys who had just lost their father. Even if I didn't understand much else about her, I knew Hannah Morgan had a good heart.

'What are your names?'

'Junior,' the older one said. 'James,' the little one followed quickly.

'Tucker Gibbens. My dogs: Jack and Martha.' The dogs were sprawled on the sand staring at them like they were from another planet. They hadn't spent much time around kids.

I checked the woman – no change – then walked back to the boys.

'You seen my pa?' James asked.

I was struggling with an answer when Junior said, 'Pa has gone to heaven.'

James came and stood in front of me.

'You hold me?' he asked.

'Sure.'

He settled into my lap and I could feel him trembling. We sat that way for a long time, just staring at the fire. Then I put them to bed and listened to their prayers.

When they were done I said, 'Where you from?'

'Places,' Junior said. 'Pa did horse-breaking for people.'

'Where you heading?'

'Don't know.'

'Any kin?'

He shook his head. James just stared up at me as if searching for something in my face.

'You boys get some sleep.'

I was turning back toward the fire when James said, 'Mister.' I stopped and looked down at him.

'You be here when we wake up?'

I nodded. He shut his eyes.

I went and stood by the girl and stared down at Hannah Morgan. She hadn't come to but she'd stopped struggling and was breathing normal. Again, I felt Lucia tense at my closeness.

'La senora vive – The lady will live.'

She ignored me. Lucia was wearing a cotton nightgown, probably what Hannah had found her in, and shivering hard in the cold night air. I put my jacket on her thin shoulders and she twisted away, letting the coat fall to the sand. Then she stood and walked quickly back to the blankets.

I sat down by the fire and thought about things. About death and kids and this woman.

CHAPTER SEVEN

Hannah Morgan and the children were gone when I awoke. I was checking my saddle blanket for burrs and complaining to the dogs. They were ignoring me, sitting side by side and looking out over the desert like they hadn't a care in the world and were stone deaf to criticism.

'You could have barked. You're damn good at barking when you shouldn't.' I put the blanket on the mare. 'That's what you're supposed to do when somebody comes or goes.' Jack just yawned and Martha laid down with a groan.

Finished saddling, I walked the mare to the edge of the camp and put a hand over my eyes and peered through the bright morning sunlight at a nice mix of prairie primrose and red mallow. I could hear meadowlarks.

'Hell,' I said, directing words over my shoulder at the dogs, 'I'm surprised you two didn't throw in with her.'

I stood thinking about the woman. About her talking to God and how none of it made sense. Then I swung up into the saddle determined to move on. Fifteen minutes later, I was just sitting there staring down at the ground. I forced myself to focus on the hoofprints of the woman's horse as they led out of camp.

It was almost as if she were following a compass – she was back riding in the original direction she'd taken out of El Paso. Wherever she was headed she wasn't about to be thrown off for long. After I caught myself still just sitting there on my horse like I was coldcocked, I decided I'd follow her a while. Not far. Just far enough to see what she was up to.

An hour later, after tracking her for miles across hard-caked alkali flats that were broken only by thin stands of greasewood, I reined the sorrel to a halt. What did I care about this woman's affairs? Nothing. Nothing other than what she knew about El Paso. And she wasn't telling me a whole lot. I watched a devil's tail twist its way across the dusty horizon.

It was still early morning and already the day was a blisterer. It would get hotter. Maybe up to 118. Dangerous heat out here on these dry flats with wind that felt like it was coming out of a horno – a Mexican oven.

I rode to the top of a small sandhill and stopped and panned the desert that sprawled in front of me with my binoculars. This country was filled with sage. It loved the place. I could see purple, silver, black and pigmy. And off in the distance, some Big Sage – as it was known in these parts – growing fifteen or more feet up and living, I'd been told, a hundred years or more. I spit. That was too long for anything to live. I kept moving the glasses over the landscape.

A rivulet of sweat ran into my eye and caused me to blink hard. These deserts were known as vengeful because they froze you at night . . . then burned you during the day. Whatever, the sagebrush liked it.

I couldn't see her. The hot air was floating over the land, dancing and distorting everything that was more than a couple hundred yards off and kicking up dust spirals that drifted haze over the horizon. The dogs waited for me in the shade of a stunted scrub oak, having lost interest in the woman.

I watched a coyote trot out of some brush and moments later bolt a jack rabbit from under the thin shade of a dead thistle.

The two of them were off on a hot run. Poor living, I thought. Speaking of livings, I had a prisoner sitting in a jail in El Paso. I panned the land with the glasses again. Nothing was moving. I had to get back.

'Let's go.'

I'd take Husker to Los Angeles, then ride out to the Pacific and finish it. That sounded good. The woman and El Paso were just some mixed-up dream. There had to be an explanation but I wasn't going to be around to worry it out. I forced myself to think about Jack and Martha and their future.

They were good dogs, and I was going to miss them. I'd give them to Sheriff Matson. The man liked them and had a big family. They'd have a nice life. The thought burned into my chest. I put heels to the sorrel and started down the trail, headed south. Then Jack barked.

When I looked back, both dogs were still sitting on the sandy knoll. Jack was looking off across the desert in the direction Hannah Morgan and the three kids had gone. Martha was just watching Jack, going along with him. She usually did. She was in love with him. It didn't matter. I turned back in my saddle and whistled hard. They didn't budge. Not liking their stubbornness, I rode the sorrel to the bottom of the trail, then turned out of sight behind some big rocks and waited. Ten minutes later, I clucked the mare out from behind the rock and looked back up the trail. They were still sitting there. Damn stubborn.

CHAPTER EIGHT

The trees appeared out of place and time in the bright sunlight of this Utah morning. I'd seen these same kind in California. They fit out there. But here in this high desert they seemed wrong somehow. There were close to a hundred of them edging the dusty road leading to a small town in the distance – a hundred date palms looking like shaggy umbrellas stuck in the parched earth. I shifted my focus to the riders: Hannah Morgan and the kids, some four hundred yards ahead of me.

I'd spotted them an hour earlier and been riding to catch up ever since; she was moving fast again, dragging these kids across the wastelands like they were being pursued by dangerous elements. But whenever I glassed her, she never looked rushed, never out of sorts. She was definitely strange – maybe she was missing something vital in her head.

I kicked the mare into a slow canter to save my backside. The woman was obsessed about things. Her voices, I guessed. Were they bringing her here? I studied the buildings at the far end of the road, fairly certain she hadn't stumbled across this crusty little place by accident.

All morning, I'd watched her making clear, sharp turns down arroyos, climbing over sand drifts, skirting cactus patches, but always returning unerringly to the same nick on the compass; slicing across these windblown spaces toward this solitary place

– moving as if drawn by some invisible pull in the ethers, moving in the same hurried way she'd moved toward Robert Dunnet, Sr and his boys.

As far as I could tell, the town looked well worth missing. But that was my opinion. And from the way she was moving, Hannah Morgan didn't share it. At two hundred yards, little James turned his head and saw me and waved, then he said something into Junior's ear. Junior yelled to Hannah Morgan, and they reined in their horses and sat waiting. All but Lucia – she didn't bother to stop or look – a tough cookie. Then Hannah called out to her and she reluctantly pulled in the stocky little bay she was riding and sat with her back to me.

Hannah Morgan smiled as I pulled alongside. 'Good morning, Mr Gibbens.'

She had a red scarf tied around her head that made her look gypsy-like. Jack was beside himself, barking at her from the rump of my horse, joyous as always to see her. I was trying to look stern.

'Morning,' I said, over the yapping. 'Why'd you run off?'

'Mr Gibbens?' she said, studying the desert in front of her horse.

'Why'd you run off?' I said again.

'We didn't,' she said, her expression suddenly serious, her eyes studying the desert in front of her as if searching for something. 'We simply got up, performed our morning necessities, said our prayers, packed our things, curried and saddled our horses and left.'

I squirmed a little and squinted towards the town, finding it hard to believe I'd slept through all that.

She made a small sighing sound and then turned and smiled at me again. 'In fact, sir, we made so much noise I was surprised we didn't wake you.' Hannah Morgan knew how to twist the knife. She looked innocent, but I figured she knew what she was doing.

94

'Whatever,' I said, trying to slip the subject. 'What town is that?' I asked, tipping my head back and pushing my chin out in the direction of the buildings in the distance.

'As I recall,' Hannah Morgan continued, ignoring the question, 'you said you were going back to El Paso today.' She tipped her own head back, closed her eyes, pursed her lips and seemed to send her contemplations heavenward for a moment. 'I think your exact words were: "Can't be wasting valuable time riding around out in the middle of nowhere with you and a bunch of kids." ' She'd done a pretty good imitation of my voice and she was pleased with herself and chuckled.

Despite my best efforts, I was grinning.

'Obviously you didn't have to go back – and you had at least some time to waste,' she continued, a small sound of glee in her voice. 'Or are you simply lost, Mr Gibbens?'

'No.'

'But you did ask what town that was,' she teased.

I didn't respond.

'Lost or not, we're glad you're here. Aren't we, children?'

'Yes,' the Dunnet boys said in rough unison, their faces squinched up in happy grins. Lucia didn't comment, but I caught her sneaking an unfriendly peek at me. Then she dropped her head and stared down at the ground beside her horse as if she were alone in the middle of this desert. Gone was the flannel nightgown of the night before, replaced by a freshly hemmed red dress that looked too big for her.

I looked back at Hannah, surprised to see that her mood had suddenly shifted again. She was sitting on her horse and gazing across the scraggy sagebrush-covered land towards the little town, seemingly oblivious to everything around her – her expression melancholy.

I cleared my throat. 'Everything OK, ma'am?'

It took her a moment to answer. 'Yes, fine, Mr Gibbens,' she murmured, her voice distant, her looks strained and strangely haunted. Then slowly she seemed to pull herself away from whatever was troubling her and turned back at me. 'It's so nice to see you,' she said, her face altering in a pleasant way.

The boys hadn't stopped grinning at me, as glad as Hannah Morgan that I'd magically reappeared out of these vast wastelands.

'Children, tell Mr Gibbens good morning,' Hannah said, in that cheery tone of hers. 'And then let's say a prayer of thanksgiving.' She could get excited over little things.

'Good morning, Mr Gibbens,' the boys responded in gleeful unison, hopping off their horse.

'Junior, James,' I muttered. Both of them looked tired and maybe they'd been crying – I knew how they felt. I glanced sideways at the girl. 'Lucia.'

She didn't look up or say anything, just started down off her animal.

'Lucia,' Hannah said softly.

'Hola,' the girl replied sullenly, her face still tilted down toward the ground as if searching for something she'd lost. Maybe her childhood.

Hannah nodded gravely at her awkward greeting as if she'd just uttered something wonderful. Then she, too, dismounted and the lot of them knelt in the sand by the side of the road. I continued to sit on my horse, until the woman turned and looked up at me.

'Mr Gibbens.'

I started to tell her to go on without me, but the pressure of her look was on me full and I waivered, then swung a leg down. I knelt and listened to her spiel about grace and forgiveness, how the children were one big happy family and the world a wonderful place. None of it very accurate, but it sounded nice. I was letting my thoughts drift, hoping she'd finish soon, when I heard her say, 'And we pray for Mr Gibbens's wife and his child. May their souls rest in Your holy arms, Father.'

I tipped my head back and looked hard at the sky.

Minutes later, we were back in the saddle and headed once again toward the little town. I studied the side of her face for a moment, then said, 'Thanks.'

'Mr Gibbens?'

'For what you said about my wife and child.'

She just continued to stare off into the distance in a contemplative way. She stared so long that I turned my head and tried to see what she was looking at, but there was nothing there. Nothing but sand and heat.

'We'll have breakfast in town, Mr Gibbens. Then move on.' She was suddenly studying the buildings again with that worried stare of hers.

'Where?'

'Mr Gibbens?'

'Where you headed?'

She waited a moment, then said, 'Just to a place I have to be.' I started to ask her if she was following her voices again, but her horse was prancing and whirling where it stood and she was trying to control it.

'You're pushing these animals pretty hard.'

'Yes,' she said, as though she had absolutely no choice in the matter, her eyes still fixed on the little town. 'We need to go,' she continued, and started off at a brisk trot, the children following.

The town wasn't much. Certainly not what a person would expect after seeing that grand line of exotic palms. The name at least fit: Oasis. But the dirt-coloured café that we pulled up in front of didn't look like my idea of any garden spot.

The whole place was grey and dusty, with rickety boardwalks and mesquite hitching posts. The buildings, a dozen maybe, were false-fronted clapboards that looked like they'd been sitting here defying the sun and sands for a thousand years.

Not a speck of paint on anything. Instead most of the buildings were covered with old posters for Saganaw Indian Oil, Dr Smith's Curatives and a variety of ancient theatrical billings. I stepped down out of the saddle and began loosening the cinch on my animal.

It was Wednesday. The train I'd booked seats on left El Paso in two days. I could make it but it would be a hard ride. I determined to breakfast with this woman, ask her a couple more questions about that alley, then clear out. The street had some folks on it. Across the way a few oldsters were reading papers on the hotel porch. Normal small town. I liked small towns.

Then I noticed Hannah Morgan. She was continuing to sit on her horse, turning in her saddle and looking around as if searching for somebody or something, her eyes carefully studying the faces of the people. Something was bothering her – just like earlier on the road.

'Problem?'

She shook her head. I wondered.

After Hannah and the children had washed their hands and faces at a nearby water pump, I pulled open the rusted screen to the café and then stopped and stared at the wooden door. There was a hand-painted sign square in the middle: 'No Indians, Mexicans, Chinamen or coloureds.'

I was starting to turn back when I heard Hannah Morgan behind me. 'It will be fine, Mr Gibbens.' She was looking at me with those dark eyes of her that looked like the eyes of a doe.

But it wouldn't be fine. And I didn't want to embarrass the

children. 'I'll buy some grub – we can cook outside town,' I offered.

'It will be nice for the children to eat inside.'

'They don't need this,' I whispered. I had turned and was watching her staring blankly past me at the door. She looked as if she wasn't focusing – as if lost in her thoughts. Then she turned sideways and gazed around the street again as though still searching for someone or something. The children were behind her. She looked back and nodded.

'This café is fine.'

'No use stirring things up,' I said, my tone stiffer, my head nodding confidentially toward the sign.

She smiled a smile at me that wasn't a smile at all and said, 'Mr Gibbens, please.'

I still didn't move.

Then she inclined her head toward me. 'Are we ready, sir?'

I don't know who had made her the boss, but I turned and opened the door and walked in. The café was better looking inside than out. There was a long black-walnut serving bar that had been polished to a high, reflective sheen and tables with clean red and white checked cloths on them.

There was a man in an apron behind the kitchen counter. He was big, bald and rough looking, but clean. Not a bad joint, I figured. From the smells wafting in the air, my guess was that the cooking was good. Every small town in the West had a place like this where you could get a good meal at a fair price.

The man smiled when he saw me and said, 'Name's Jake. Pull up a chair. I got honey-roasted ham. Fried chicken. Biscuits. I'll bring hot coffee.'

'Great,' I said, knowing the hospitality was for me and Hannah, that he hadn't noticed the children.

There were maybe six or seven other men in the place. They'd seen the kids. And one of them said, 'Jake.'

The man turned back. 'Yeah?'

'Better take a look.'

I was certain that Hannah Morgan had heard and knew what it meant, but she didn't hesitate. She just moved the boys and Lucia to a table near the front window and set them down like they were royalty and picked up a menu and began to study it in earnest. The boys were peering around the place with wide-eyed looks, obviously not used to restaurants, James peeking my way every so often. He'd been stealing sad, affectionate glances at me since we'd met. I knew he missed his pa badly.

I'd just taken a deep breath and started for the table when I heard the man, Jake, clear his throat behind me.

'Mister. May I talk to you?'

I looked at Hannah Morgan. She didn't bother to return my glance. She just looked ready to order breakfast. I was getting mad. There was no call for her to put these kids in this situation.

I turned back to the man. He towered over me, looking embarrassed. But no matter how apologetic he was acting, I knew it was going to be hard for me to hold my temper. He was bigger than I'd first thought and completely bald, not even eyebrows – his head and neck looking like a big pink thumb with a face on it.

'Those kids are coloured,' he said, his voice low, his looks those of a carnival strongman. 'The girl's Mexican.'

'Right,' I said, fighting the anger growing in my chest. 'We're passing through. The boys just lost their father. The girl has had a rough time.' I paused and looked hard into his face. 'You could make an exception.'

The man squirmed in front of me. 'I'd like to – but it wouldn't set right with folks around here. Some are Mormons, some

Southern. Neither cares much for Indians or coloureds. If it was just me. You understand.'

I was starting to lose it. 'No. I don't,' I said.

All my life I'd never been able to stomach certain things: people hurting or killing other people, bullies and such. I'd had a big brother who'd been born crippled with arms and legs that looked like dried sticks. He'd been teased and picked on bad by other kids. He was gone now, but I remember that I'd fought a lot of fights that he couldn't fight. I hadn't won all of them. But it was funny. I hadn't lost any either – just fighting them was winning. Maybe that was where this bad feeling in my gut had gotten started. I'm not certain. It didn't matter. It was just there.

I looked into Jake's small eyes and started to say something that was going to lead to the trouble I was trying to avoid. But I'd never been able to hold my temper once it started to boil and it was bubbling now. Then for a reason I can't explain, I just stopped and said, 'Tell the lady. She's in charge of the kids.'

I watched as the man walked over to Hannah, surprised I'd grabbed hold of my temper. As for Jake, my guess was he wasn't mean – just trying to make a living in this town. As I was working out what I'd tell the kids after I'd taken my best shot at Jake and we finally got tossed outside, Hannah Morgan looked up from the menu into the man's face. I could see her slowly scanning his features as if looking for something.

She wasn't smiling, but then I can't say she was frowning either. She just looked at him as if she might be asking him a tough question: 'Why are you here? Why would you think it was OK to come to this table and ask me such a thing?' But as far as I could tell she didn't say anything. She just sat looking at him with that steady gaze of hers. I'd been on the receiving end of that look. It could frost.

I'm not certain how long Jake stood there by the table, maybe half a minute. It seemed a long time. Everybody in the café was watching him, the room quiet as if something was going to happen. Junior and James were staring down into their plates as though they'd done something wrong. I felt badly for them. Lucia was looking out the window, tense as a snared bird, trying to ignore the whole thing – trying to ignore life and what it had done to her.

I looked back at Hannah Morgan. She still wasn't saying anything. Neither was Jake. They were both studying each other. Then I saw the man pull out his order pad and start writing and the place seemed to go back to normal again. Hannah Morgan was smiling and talking and the boys were laughing and shoving each other.

Nobody seemed to care much about me or Hannah Morgan or the kids any more, as if some silent understanding had been reached. Whatever it was, it was just there in the room and made things OK. Hannah was talking to Jake and looking like she had never doubted his goodwill.

When the man walked by me on his way back to the kitchen, he smiled and said, 'Nice woman. Nice kids.'

'What did you say to him?' I whispered, as I sat down at the table.

Junior and James were standing at the window watching people moving along the street, enjoying themselves, their minds momentarily off their dead father and what had nearly happened here. Lucia was standing behind them looking a little more relaxed.

Hannah Morgan had pulled her knitting out of her big canvas bag and was going at it like there was no tomorrow. She looked up at me over the tops of her little glasses.

'Pardon?'

'What did you tell that man to get him to change his mind?'

'Nothing. He just changed it.'

She glanced out the window, her eyes lingering on the scant traffic in the street longer than one takes with a casual glance. Once again, I had the feeling she was searching for someone. Was this the place she had been riding so hard to get to ever since El Paso? I didn't have a clue.

When she caught me staring at her, she said, 'I didn't say anything to him, Mr Gibbens. Really I didn't.'

I knew that was the truth. She hadn't said anything at all. But something had happened.

'Oh, I almost forgot,' she continued, 'I ordered you ham and eggs.' She went back to her knitting. 'Aren't the smells wonderful in here?'

'You what?'

'I ordered you ham and eggs.'

I liked ham and eggs fine but didn't like her taking it upon herself to just order for me like that. Like I was the same age as Junior and James. 'Why would you do that?'

'Don't you like them?'

'That's not the point.'

'If you don't, you better tell Jake.'

'That's not the point,' I repeated.

She stopped knitting and looked up at me.

'Do you or don't you like them? I think that really is the point.'

'I like them fine. But I also like to do my own ordering. It's not your place to go around ordering for me.'

'I see,' she said quietly. She had returned to her knitting and was looking as if her feelings were hurt.

I shifted in my chair. Convinced that I was right. Then I cleared my throat and said, 'I like eggs and ham.'

She didn't say anything.

'I like them a lot.'

She continued to knit.

James had returned from the window and was standing and holding on to her arm now. 'Aunt Hannah,' he said.

She looked up from her knitting and smiled at him. 'Yes, James?'

'This is a nice place.'

'It is lovely, isn't it? And Mr Jake is going to fix us a special breakfast.'

James grinned at the big man behind the counter. Jake smiled and nodded his head at the boy.

'I like eggs fine,' I tried again.

Hannah Morgan didn't answer me.

It was a grand breakfast. Jake even put a little bouquet of wild flowers – Sweet Everlasting and Goldenrod – in the centre of our table and made us a batch of free sandwiches for lunch. Clearly, he was smitten by Hannah Morgan, hanging around the table talking to her, keeping her coffee cup full while we waited for the food.

When the meal arrived, Hannah made us say our prayers again. I didn't like squirming in my chair in front of the people in the café – but when I looked I saw most of them mouthing what looked like prayers themselves. Jake was standing and watching in the same respectful way and I felt better. Even so, I was getting worn down on all this religion. Not that my opinion on the subject mattered much to Hannah Morgan. She seemed determined to pull these kids and me screaming and kicking toward some state of grace.

But when the prayer was over, she was all business – plowing through buttermilk pancakes, scrambled eggs and home fries, a stack of toast covered in jelly. Then she topped the whole thing off with a couple of pieces of butterscotch pie and a green apple. Seeing how much she enjoyed the apple, Jake brought a big burlap bag of them for her to take along.

As much as I knew she disliked the sign on his restaurant door, she'd quickly forgiven the man and the two of them carried on as if they were old friends.

The kids were enjoying themselves as well, laughing and eating. Hannah had shown them how to hold their forks and knives. Lucia hadn't seemed to be paying much attention, but when James couldn't get it right, the girl stood up from her chair and leaned over his back and worked with him until he was cutting and stabbing with the best of gentlemen.

'Thank you, Lucia,' Hannah said. 'James?'

'Thank you, Lucy.'

By the end of the meal, Hannah and Jake were calling back and forth across the room, gabbing and laughing about cooking, politics, schooling, the weather and day-to-day life in Oasis. I was learning fast that there was little Hannah Morgan wasn't interested in, or didn't have an opinion about. I just sat enjoying their good-natured talk – so did everyone else.

Every so often somebody would add something and as soon as they did Hannah pulled them into the middle of this meandering talk. The warm sound of it, its genuine good-heartedness, reminded me of conversations I'd heard my own mother and wife in. There was something distinctly female about it. It seemed to glue everyone in Jake's café together. For a moment, we all seemed to belong to one another. There was a magic in that – something men couldn't pull off.

Maybe that's why they loved women: because females made them feel part of something bigger and better than themselves. Whatever it was, it was seeping into my bones. And it felt good. The children were enjoying it as well. Even Lucia.

*

We'd just finished breakfast and were standing in the street out in front of the café, when a small, thin man somewhere in his sixties walked up. He had thick grey hair and was wearing a brown business suit wrinkled like a dry leaf. I suddenly sensed from the dazed way he stood looking at Hannah Morgan that he was the person she'd been searching for earlier.

Hannah was standing on the other side of my horse and I couldn't see her but I could hear her saying things to the man. I just couldn't make the words out. Then he was walking away. 'Nice day,' I called to him, trying to figure out what was going on.

He turned and smiled at me. He was wearing rimless glasses and had a genial face. 'Yes. It is that.'

'Name is Tucker Gibbens.'

He stuck his hand out. 'Michael Johnson.'

I nodded, shaking his hand. 'You a friend of Mrs Morgan?' I saw her struggling to get up into her saddle. I'd noticed before that she wasn't real good at mounting.

'Who?' the man asked.

I looked at Hannah Morgan. She was frowning at me now, her personality taking one of those quick turns it often did, becoming serious and a little bristly whenever she figured I was accusing her of something. I ignored her. 'Mrs Morgan. The woman you were just speaking to.'

'Oh. No. We just met.' He raised a hand meekly and made a little wave towards her. 'Ma'am.'

Hannah smiled at him. 'Doctor Johnson.'

Then he turned and started across the street. Hannah was back to frowning at me.

'Why do you always question the things I do, Mr Gibbens?'

'Because so much of it doesn't make sense.'

'To you perhaps.' She paused. 'To me it makes perfect sense.'

I just smiled.

'Regardless,' Hannah said, choosing to ignore me, 'I would appreciate it if you would not interfere in my business.' She turned her horse away from the hitching post. 'Children.' Lucia was glaring at me like I'd done something awful.

'Me interfere?' I called after her. 'Me? You bought me this pink shirt. Then you go around ordering my breakfast without so much as a howdy-do to me. You march around the desert like the Queen of Sheba without saying anything to anybody. Then . . .' I stopped before I said something I'd really regret. People on the sidewalk were staring at me. I didn't care. 'Fine. I won't interfere with you. You don't interfere with me.'

'Fine,' she said, over her shoulder.

I swung up into the saddle and watched as the woman and the children rode across the street and disappeared up an alley. I shook my head. Now what? I followed at a trot.

'This isn't the way out of town,' I said, pulling the sorrel alongside her horse.

'I know that, Mr Gibbens.'

'Where you going?'

'We agreed you weren't going to interfere in my business.'

'Curious.'

She looked at me as if she'd caught me in a lie or something. 'Your inquiries, Mr Gibbens, are rarely based on simple curiosity. You think I'm some sort of a criminal.'

'Lady, your business is your business. I've got things I need to be doing.'

Hannah chose to ignore me and stopped in front of a small clapboard building. Gold letters painted on the glass window read: Michael Johnson, MD, the name of the small man I'd just met. I was itching to ask what was going on, but knew she'd probably refuse to tell me – or worse, start one of her lectures again. I could do without that.

'Junior and James,' she said, 'stay with the horses please. Lucia, please come with me.' Then she turned and looked up at me. 'Mr Gibbens, I need you as well.'

'I thought I was to keep out of your business.'

'Act your age, Mr Gibbens,' she said, turning and opening the door of the building. 'I need your help.'

She said the words as if there was simply no question that I would give it. I started to protest but she was already through the doorway and inside the shadows of the room. When I glanced back at the children, Junior and James were grinning at me while Lucia was just giving me her dead-fish stare. I could feel blood rushing to my face. 'You behave yourselves,' I said gruffly.

The girl was nine or ten and lying in a bed in a darkened back room off the doctor's office. She had a pretty face and nice caramel-coloured hair that spilled over the pillow. The top of her head was wrapped in white gauze. I knew immediately why we were here. It was crazy, but Hannah Morgan had done it again: found somebody else in trouble. I wondered if she'd done it with her so-called messages from God.

I looked at the side of her face and cleared my throat quietly to get her attention, but she wouldn't look at me. The place was so dark and still that I felt like I was in a church or some sort of sanctuary and removed my hat.

'She asleep?' I whispered, stretching my neck so that I could see the child.

'Coma. Since we found her.'

The room was silent until Hannah Morgan moved by a cage with a canary in it and the little bird suddenly cut loose with a wild trilling of shrill notes that were jarring in the shadows of the room. She moved away and he quit. I wondered why. Wondered why a song bird was singing in a dark room. Then

I gave up wondering. There was too much to wonder about. Hannah stopped at the bedside and stood staring down. Johnson watched her.

This time – having seen her riding toward this little town, seen her searching the faces of the people in the street – I knew she'd definitely come here on purpose. The doctor claimed he didn't know her. Still, he'd seemed to seek her out on the street. He was the one that had done the approaching. Had he been lying about not knowing her? I'd watched him outside the café – there'd been a small look of recognition on his face as he walked up to her. Still, I didn't think he was lying. There was no sense that they knew one another.

Fact was: there wasn't much sense to any of it. I held my hat in both hands and followed the little man as he stepped closer to the bed. I was thinking about the silence of other sick rooms – about my wife and kid – and bit at my lower lip.

'Freight driver out of Denver found her on the desert south of here a month ago,' Johnson said. 'We've no idea where she came from. How she got here. Or how she's lasted this long.'

'What's wrong with her?' I asked.

Johnson bent forward and unsnapped a brass safety pin from the gauze bandage on her head and slowly began to unwrap it. I was standing a few feet behind them and I watched as Hannah touched the back of the girl's hand with the tips of her fingers. Then she slipped her index finger inside the child's hand. I jumped. The little fingers had wrapped around Hannah's, clutching at it.

'She moved,' I mumbled.

Johnson looked down at the child's hand.

'Yes. That's not unusual. She'll grip things. But she's not awake.' He had the gauze completely unwound now and I stepped closer to take a look at the top of her head. I wished I hadn't. There was a saucer-size hole – no skull bone, just a mucousy looking film over what appeared to be exposed brain.

Johnson was talking again. I forced myself to focus on his words. 'You can see why I didn't think she would last this long.'

'What happened to her?'

'My guess? She got cut on the top of her head somehow. Then wandered around in the sun without a hat, the wound exposed and festering. The sunlight just burned her skull away.'

I looked at Hannah. She hadn't moved to look at the wound, she just stood staring down at the child's pretty features. Then Lucia stepped up beside her and gently pulled Hannah's finger from the girl's hand and inserted her own in its place, her eyes fixed on the small still face on the pillow. Hannah studied both children for a moment, then she turned toward the doctor. 'I'll take her this afternoon.'

I couldn't believe it. I looked at the man. He was staring at Hannah like everything was normal. Like what she'd just said was normal. It wasn't. It was madness.

'That's fine,' he said.

'Are you crazy? That child doesn't have a top on her skull.' I looked from the doctor back to Hannah. 'Where would you take her?'

Hannah had turned and was walking toward the front door of the office. Johnson was rewrapping the gauze around the young girl's head. Lucia stood watching Hannah with a satisfied gaze, her finger still held by the sick child.

'You can't let her do this,' I said to Johnson. 'It'll kill the kid.'

The man didn't look up. 'There's nothing more I can do for her. She'll die here as well. This is for the best.'

'For the best? You don't even know this woman. Now you're going to let her take a dying child from your care?' I looked hard at the little man. 'Why?'

'I don't know. Just a good feeling about her.'

'Good feeling? You're loony as she is.'

Hannah Morgan was sitting on her horse next to the boys when I left the doctor's office, her head tipped back, her eyes shut, and basking in the bright sunlight like she might be relaxing at the seaside instead of getting ready to take over the care of a deathly ill child. Jack and Martha were sprawled lazily on the sidewalk.

'I don't know what your game is, lady, riding around collecting these kids. But you can't do this. She'll die.'

Hannah opened her eyes slowly and looked at me. 'Mr Gibbens, please.'

'Maybe that doctor is crazy,' I said, swinging up on to my horse. 'But I doubt the sheriff is going to stand by and let this happen.' I turned my horse back toward Main Street.

'Where are you going, Mr Gibbens?' She sounded like one of my old schoolteachers.

'To find the sheriff.' I kicked my horse into a trot.

'Mr Gibbens.'

I ignored her until she called my name a second time, then I reined in and looked back at her. Jack and Martha were still sitting next to her. Damn turncoats. 'What?'

'I need your help.'

'You don't think I'm going to help you do this?'

'I need your help,' she said again.

'No.'

The afternoon sun was burning into my back and I was thinking about it destroying that kid's skull. It was an ugly thought. I stood and pulled my shirt back on before it did the same to me and then I wiped sweat from my forehead with a rag. I'd been working on the contraption for the past three hours. I hadn't gone to the sheriff. I don't know why. Maybe because this woman was so convinced that I was going to help that I couldn't bring myself to disappoint her.

She'd just finished off one of Jake's apples and was sitting on a blanket in the shade of an old cottonwood tree, knitting on her pile of black-nothing like it was vitally important that she finish. But there was nothing to finish. It was crazy – all of it. Every once in a while she would look up at me and a faint smile would form on her face.

For a moment, I thought it was because she'd won: me helping instead of getting the sheriff after her. But that wasn't it. Even though I'd only known her a short time, I knew Hannah Morgan wasn't one to gloat over things. She just liked to smile. She smiled at everything. Bugs, a cold drink of water, the children's play burps, wind in the trees – anything could make her smile. It was a near affliction with her. I guess as afflictions go it wasn't such a bad one.

She had all kinds of different smiles: one that teased, one that questioned, one for little pleasures, one for big ones, another for appreciation, one for moments of confusion, and now, the one she was wearing, the shadowy, confidential smile that seemed meant specifically for my benefit, as if it was a secret between us, but always baffled me.

I could hear James squealing with joy somewhere off in the distance and, true to form, Mrs Morgan smiled her 'little pleasures' smile at the sound. The boys were playing dodge ball with a bunch of town kids down the road. Jack and Martha had trotted along to watch, and I was certain that Jack was trying to figure out how to steal the ball and get away with it. It did the boys good to get their minds off their pa.

Lucia hadn't come out of the doctor's office. When I asked

Mrs Morgan what the girl was doing, she'd just said, 'She wants to stay with the child.' I could understand that, remembering back to my crippled brother.

I stood now and stretched the soreness out of the small of my back and then glanced at her. She was knitting and smiling to herself as if she'd just heard something funny whispered into her ear. I wondered if her voices told her jokes. I cleared my throat.

'Ma'am. Why are you doing this?'

'Mr Gibbens?'

'Why collect these kids? What's the game?'

'Game?' she said slowly, as if the word were a bad taste in her mouth, her lovely smile disappearing. 'It's not a game, sir.'

'Fine.' I stopped talking for a second – then tried again. 'I still want to know why you're doing it.'

She sat and studied the dirt at her feet for a time, then said, 'You act as if I'm collecting baubles for a necklace.'

Her shiny metal knitting needles had been flying moments before, reflecting sunlight like minnows in a shallow stream. Now they were poised over the yarn, her eyes continuing to stare blindly into the dirt beyond her high-topped shoes.

'They need help,' she said almost to herself.

'Yes. But you won't send them to orphanages. You've got three in tow and about to pick up a fourth – but you don't want people who get paid to care for kids like these to do what they get paid for.'

She didn't respond right away. And for a second, I didn't think she was going to. Then she gave me a long look over the half-moon of the lenses. She didn't appear particularly angry, just impatient about something – as if I should definitely know better.

'There should be no pay for the care of a child, Mr Gibbens.'

There was a finality in her words that made me want to answer, 'Of course.' But as a lawman I was a selective listener and ignored the comment.

'Now, you're taking this little girl near death –' I stopped talking and stared directly at her face. 'Why?'

She pushed her glasses back up and began to knit slowly. 'I've already told you why. That's all. There's nothing more.'

'I don't figure it that way, ma'am.'

'And how do you figure it, sir?'

'I'm not certain – I just figure you're up to something.'

Neither of us spoke for a while after that. Hannah set her jaw and went back to her knitting while I worked on in the sunlight. When the silence got the best of me I said, 'That girl can't travel. She won't live two days. These negro boys need coloureds to look after them. The Mex girl –'

'Lucia,' she interrupted stiffly. 'Her name is Lucia. The boys' names are Junior and James.' She paused and I could tell she was gathering up her anger. 'It sounds so much nicer, Mr Gibbens, when you call them by their names.'

'Lucia,' I grumbled. 'She needs her own kind.'

Hannah Morgan stopped and looked up at me. 'It's their chance, Mr Gibbens.'

'What's that mean?'

'Their chance,' she said again, as if I would immediately understand. I didn't.

'For what, life? They won't die at an orphanage.'

'To know God loves them.'

'Why would they know that?'

'Because I've come for them, sir.'

Hannah Morgan was staring blindly into my face and I sensed that she was drifting off into one of her odd states again and I didn't want that. I definitely didn't want that, didn't want to be stuck with these kids running around town and her out cold, so I backed off. Moments later, she seemed to drift back to the present some and began to knit again. I shook my head and went on with the work.

'I'll figure it out, ma'am,' I muttered. 'It may take me some time, but you can bet I'll figure it out.'

Hannah Morgan looked disappointed with me again. 'I do so wish you would stop looking for conspiracies in everything I do, Mr Gibbens.'

I ignored her and went on working. I don't remember ever agreeing to help. I was just doing it. Probably because the woman was so pig-headed about things. Anyway, I'd measured the girl, then hunted up the undertaker's shop on Main Street and purchased a padded coffin that would give her plenty of room. I'd borrowed tools from the undertaker's carpenter and set to work in the alley behind his place.

That's where we were now. At least when the little girl died, there'd be a proper box to bury her in. That was something, though I didn't figure that Hannah Morgan had any such notion in her head. As far as I could tell, she truly believed that the child would survive being dragged around the desert. Where? – I didn't know. I kept telling myself that it wasn't my affair.

I'd taken the lid off the coffin and had the blacksmith make four heavy metal straps that I could bolt into the lid and the top of the coffin, raising the cover up a good five inches above the box. The back two straps were hinged at the top so that I could raise the lid just as when it was first built – the raised cover provided air circulation and served as a roof to keep the sun and rain out. I was handy with tools from my days on my folks' ranch.

When I'd finished with the coffin, I'd purchased a second-hand X-pack frame and was now working to secure the box inside the top of the X. Once that was done, the pack and coffin would be carried on the back of a quiet little ginny mule I'd also bought. I took a look at the animal grazing in the field behind the alley. She was old, calm and gentle, dead-white in colour – well broke and well used to packing far heavier loads than this one. She'd do just fine. I started whistling, things feeling OK for the first time in a long while.

Half an hour later, I was done.

'It's wonderful!' Hannah said, so excited she grabbed my hands and then in her enthusiasm leaned forward and kissed my cheek. 'Thank you, Mr Gibbens.'

I turned away so she wouldn't see me blushing. 'Just be careful you get the pack cinched up tight on the mule. That's your only worry, ma'am.'

I could feel her eyes on me.

'I've got to get back to El Paso,' I said. 'I have that prisoner.'

'Of course.'

'I'll show you how to put the child inside.'

'Yes.'

I still hadn't looked at her. But it wouldn't change things. I had to go – had to get matters squared away. Even as it was, I'd probably miss the train and have to wait a week for another. I was surprised I hadn't thought about shooting myself in a while. But when I did now, the painful wave of desolation swept over me, leaving me with the fixed sense of heavy brooding that had grown so familiar.

The child was lighter than I'd guessed, something tugging inside me as I held her. So pretty, so at peace, yet so close to death. I was in front of the doctor's office, standing alongside the mule on the little A-frame ladder I'd built for the purpose, lifting the child into the open coffin. Lucia was reaching up, as if I might carelessly drop her; Hannah was behind us, her arms crossed over her breast, watching with a satisfied look on her face.

I settled the girl down gently on to the satin padding, carefully adjusting her damaged head on a small green pillow that Hannah had purchased, then lowered the lid. Instantly, she was covered in deep shade. Lucia continued to look anxious.

'No preocupar – Don't worry,' I said. She paid me no mind.

Doctor Johnson was on the sidewalk watching the whole affair. He seemed as mixed up about everything as I was.

'Thank you,' Hannah said to me. I wasn't certain whether she meant the coffin or what I'd said to Lucia. It didn't matter. Either way, it embarrassed me whenever this woman thanked me for something. She was always so sincere and serious about the smallest of things – making them seem so much bigger and better than they were. But still, it brought a nice feeling.

'That's all there is to it,' I mumbled. Hannah was standing next to Lucia, looking up with a tight smile that was threatening to turn sad. I shifted awkwardly on my feet and pretended to check the mule's rigging. Jack and Martha were lying in the middle of the road as if they owned the town. I'd stationed the boys at the mule's head to make certain she didn't start walking; they were holding on to the halter with clinched fists, as if they thought the old mule might suddenly bolt for Siberia.

'Mr Gibbens,' Hannah Morgan began, then stopped as if suddenly she didn't want to say anything.

She shook the doctor's hand in a vigorous way and then he went back into his office and she turned and held out her arms, clamping her eyes shut, tears rolling down her cheeks. I was ready to run, knowing what was coming.

'Children, let's join hands. Mr Gibbens.'

I made busy with the mule's cinch.

'Mr Gibbens.'

She'd opened one eye and was looking at me like I was a lost soul, so I joined the circle. As soon as this had happened, she pressed her lips together hard like something miraculous had occurred. She seemed to think this every time she saw me in one of her prayer sessions – and I could see she was fighting tears now. This was wearing.

On and on she went about everything under the sun, blessing this and that, lizards and pond scum. Then just when I thought we were finally finished, she took a deep breath and launched another round of heavenly thanks. I listened but I wasn't so certain we had much to be thankful about. Still, I kept my mouth shut. At the end, she said, 'Pray for one another as sisters and brothers. Promise me.' But that wasn't the worst of it. The worst of it was when she stopped for a second, opened one eye at me again, shut the eye, and said, 'Children. Let us pray for Mr Gibbens.'

I wanted to protest but figured it was best if I kept my mouth shut. So I just squirmed as they all mumbled things under their breaths. At the end, she asked us to remember we were sisters and brothers.

I nodded – not because I was feeling these ragamuffin kids were my kin – but rather to get this over with before I died of old age or embarrassment. Finished, Hannah Morgan moved to her horse and struggled to mount. I started to give her a hand, but stopped short knowing she didn't like being assisted when she could do a thing herself. Stubborn and independent.

When she'd finally gotten aboard and was ready to ride, I reached over and handed her the mule's lead rope. 'She's well broke to trail so you shouldn't have any trouble.'

Hannah Morgan nodded and sat looking down at me with that peculiar gaze of hers and I got nervous she was going to launch into another damn prayer session. She continued to stare. I had the uncomfortable feeling that having brought me to what she thought was a reasonable state of grace, she didn't want to let me go. I took a deep breath. 'I'll ride a while with you, just to make certain everything works.'

'That would be nice,' she said, turning her horse and starting off at a brisk gait. I just stood and shook my head. Nothing was going to delay Hannah Morgan from her appointed rounds . . . whatever they might be.

The side street was empty but when we turned the corner on to Main, it was like we had ridden into the middle of a parade, the whole town lining the sidewalks. I felt for a fleeting moment the way I had in the café, as if something strange was happening – nobody saying anything until Jake came out into the street, beaming, and held a huge hand up to Hannah Morgan which she grasped in hers.

'Mrs Morgan,' he said.

'Jake. I am so glad we met.'

The man didn't respond for a moment, just walked the best he could sideways next to Hannah's horse, his large hand holding hers. Then he held something up to her with his free hand. It was wrapped in heavy butcher paper. She took it and smiled down at him, fighting her emotions.

Reluctantly, they let go of one another and Jake repeated, 'Mrs Morgan,' as if her name meant wonderful things he never wanted to forget. He was smiling as he stood in the street watching us riding away, but I think he wanted to cry. Hannah Morgan brought out funny feelings in people. I could see tears on her cheeks as well. It made the hair on the back of my neck tingle to see this woman crying, so I turned away to gaze at the crowd.

Folks were looking at us like we had done something important – the Dunnet boys thoroughly enjoying it. So was Jack, sitting on the rump of Hannah's horse barking like he was sunstruck.

I glanced at Hannah Morgan: she was just riding with a blank stare, scanning the faces of the people with a look that's tough to describe. She didn't appear surprised or sad, happy or grateful, and certainly not proud. By her way of thinking, God meant for her to collect this band of misfits and, therefore, she was going to do it or drop dead trying. It was that simple – and she that uncompromising.

I searched the faces of the people on the sidewalks, trying to understand what they were thinking but couldn't. I'd seen a lot of crazy things in my lifetime, but this one was bumping its way to the top of the list. Then a bunch of town kids started following close behind us and I was about to tell Martha to move them back before they spooked the mule, when Hannah said, 'It's fine, Mr Gibbens.'

I started to say we didn't know a damn thing about this mule and what she might do, but stopped and just reined my horse closer to the ginny and let the town kids follow along behind us. As it turned out, she'd been right.

The kids followed us a good mile down that road lined with palm trees without so much as a shout or handclap, just walked along nice as you please, a silent escort sending us off on our journey. And the mule hadn't minded. I wondered how this woman knew these things. She was just lucky, I figured.

About three miles northwest of town, as we rode down a gentle slope and out on to the desert once more, I looked over at her. She was bent forward slightly in her saddle, her eyes staring down at the sandy earth, her mouth moving and forming silent words as if she were communing with a ghost.

'What'd that man give you?' I asked, worried she might be slipping into one of her trances again, leaving me stuck with all these orphans when I was needing to turn off and head south. It seemed to take her a moment to pull herself back from whatever distant place she'd been in her mind.

'Jake?'

I nodded.

She looked at the slim package she still held, as if she'd just realized she was carrying it; then reined her horse closer to mine and handed it to me. It was hard and stiff, felt like a plate or something. I ripped the brown paper off and sat staring down at the object. It was the sign from the restaurant door.

Hannah glanced over at it, then looked off toward the far horizon in that dreamy way she had. It was a look I liked to see on her – it made me feel good. I'd seen the same one on my mother and wife. Seen it on kids gazing into camp-fires – even on my dogs when they were fed and contented and dozing in warm sunlight. A look that said: life is good enough. I guessed most animals could make that same look.

But then, a few moments later, I saw her shudder and draw herself up straighter; she was squinting now and turning her head back and forth slightly as she scanned the far horizon. She looked to be searching for some distant landmark to set her bearings by, suddenly tense and on edge. Each time I witnessed this quick shifting of her moods, it bothered me.

'Everything OK, ma'am?'

'Yes,' she said, her voice distant, her eyes still narrowed hard on something I couldn't see in the beyond. Something I felt I might not want to see.

'Ma'am?' I said, holding up the sign.

'Sir?'

'You want this?'

She turned and looked at me for a long time before she asked, 'Why?' The way she said it made it sound as if it were the most absurd question she'd ever heard.

'Memento?'

She didn't smile, didn't respond in any way.

'Right,' I mumbled and sailed it off into a thick pile of nearby brush. Once she was moving in the direction she wanted to go, she relaxed some and began to hum a quiet tune that sounded nice.

'What the hell am I doing here?' It was almost dark, with not enough light left to travel without risking the horses. So here I was sitting under a canvas cover a good 125 miles from El Paso, having just finished rigging the awning between some mesquite trees to keep the night dew off Hannah Morgan and the children.

I was feeling relieved. The coffin-pack had worked. The girl hadn't been hurt as the mule had made her way up and down hills, across streams, even sliding down a huge sand dune on her haunches. Nothing had happened to the child, she just rocked gently along inside the padded box.

That made me feel good – but it didn't explain what I was still doing here when I needed to be kicking for El Paso. I stood and tossed the water that remained in my cup on to the sand and watched it disappear into the parched soil. This dust could suck up water and lives of people.

The sun had gone down about thirty minutes before and evening shadows were deepening over the landscape, melding the far mountains, the sand and scraggy plants into the dense substance of night. I turned in a slow circle and looked around. We'd made camp in a decent little pocket of grassy land behind a sandy hillock some fifteen miles northwest of Oasis.

There was fresh water and graze for the horses and the hill

would block the prevailing winds. Hannah Morgan had made us a big meal of chicken, rice and red beans, then eaten so much that I was worried she'd burst, but it didn't seem to faze her. Minutes before she'd polished off one of Jake's apples. My eyes were on her now.

She'd just finished taking the children through the evening ritual of bathing, hair-brushing, cleaning out ears and fingernails, hunting ticks and washing clothes for the morning; then prayers – making each one say theirs separately – and pleasant talk about their families, their pasts and their futures. Watching from the safety of the horses, these things reminded me of evenings I'd spent with my own mother: a warm and wonderful sense to the sounds and movements that made me feel good inside.

Hannah was funny about things. She didn't shy away from the reality of the world, didn't sugar-coat the problems these children faced. She spoke to them about their fears with calm and courage. For myself, I winced when I heard her asking James about his father. But maybe it was best.

It seemed to clear things for these kids. They looked settled and relaxed: sad but satisfied there was a rhyme and reason to this world. And that was about all a person could hope for. I wished I could feel that myself.

I forced myself to stop worrying over things I couldn't fix and wondered again why I was still here. In some ways, I guessed, it made sense. This woman was wandering around in the desert with two small boys, a young gal who was mad at the sun, the moon and the stars, and a dying girl. They needed all the help they could get. That was OK – but I needed to get my things done as well. I sat and drew in a deep breath of night air and listened to a junco chirping in the nearby brush.

The boys, after protesting that they weren't tired, were sitting by the fire roasting tidbits of a desert bighorn that I'd shot that afternoon in a small canyon. When each piece of meat was done, they'd make the dogs do tricks for it. They were the world's biggest beggars anyway, so I didn't care. And both sides were enjoying the game.

I turned again and saw Hannah Morgan kneeling in the clean sand beside the coffin talking to the injured girl as if the child were hearing every word. She'd been doing this all day long, bringing her horse up alongside the mule and carrying on about everything under the sun: school clothes, the girl's hair and how it was going to grow back once her wound had healed and how they could fix it until it did, books and learning, boys, all kinds of things. I caught myself listening the way I had in Jake's café.

The junco had stopped chirping and I heard her say, 'You will grow to be a beautiful woman.' Something stuck in my throat. She wouldn't. She had no chance – I didn't care what Hannah Morgan said. I took a deep breath and shrugged off the melancholy that fell like a heavy blanket over me.

Milagros was the name that Lucia had given the child, since no one knew her real one. Milagros. It was good: Mexican for miracle. And that's what it was going to take for her to survive much longer. With all the harsh changes in temperature and the jostling on the back of the mule, I figured she'd be gone in a day or two.

Still, Hannah was right: it was better to die in open air, surrounded by other children and sunlight, than alone in the silence of a dark room. But watching the woman talking and fussing over the girl's injured body, it didn't look like she thought death was a possibility. Lucia was sitting at the head of the coffin, listening and looking down at the still face of the little girl in a longing way, as if they were real sisters and she'd forgotten to tell her something important before she'd fallen asleep.

The sounds of the desert night were coming alive – the scurrying of lizards, the winds, the distant calls of coyotes and hunting owls. Hannah Morgan rose up on her knees and leaned over and placed her hands on top of the child's bandaged head and didn't move – just stayed that way. It was eerie.

I didn't move either, shivering at the thought of the child's brain and remembering that Hannah had touched my chest in that alley in El Paso. And when I awoke, there was no wound. Was she a faith healer? I'd heard of such people. People who claimed a strange gift. There was no question she was different.

After I'd waited a time and Hannah Morgan hadn't moved, I walked over and stood beside her. Her face looked chilled except for tiny beads of sweat on her forehead, her features rigid in the same way as the night with the Apaches.

'Ma'am?' I asked quietly. She didn't move or say anything. I knelt beside her and touched my hand gently to her shoulder. There was still no reaction. Then suddenly Lucia yanked my hand away and stood glaring down at me as if I'd done something awful by touching her.

'No mal, dano,' I said. 'No harm.'

The girl just glared at me. 'No mal, dano,' I repeated, then looked back at Hannah and the child in the coffin. While I might have wished it different, the little girl was not stirring. Carefully, I removed Hannah's hands from the bandaged head, then carried the woman back to her blankets, covering her so she wouldn't chill. Lucia, torn by her concern for Hannah and the girl, followed until she was halfway between the two, dropping down on to her knees in the sand and watching both by swinging her head back and forth.

'No mal, dano,' I said again as I moved by her and spread

an extra blanket over the coffin. But my thoughts weren't on Lucia. They were on Milagros.

Looking down at her, I wondered. Hannah Morgan had touched her – then gone into one of her trances. Was it possible? I had to know. My heart was beating hard as I began to unwind the gauze. I pulled my breath in slow. No. The horrible gaping hole was still there. Hannah Morgan had not cured her. 'I'm sorry,' I said to the little face and remembered the time I'd looked at my dead brother's face. It made me hurt, thinking about the two of them trapped in bodies that wouldn't work right. I forced my thoughts back to the woman.

If Hannah Morgan couldn't cure this child, then it followed that she hadn't saved me. If not, then what had? I didn't care for the possibilities.

I was rewrapping Milagros' wound under Lucia's cold stare when Jack growled. The sound caused me to turn in a half-crouch, my hand dropping to my side. Too late. There were four of them: two Mexicans and two whites. One of the Mexicans was holding a pistol to the head of Junior. The muscles at the back of my neck bunched involuntarily. I could see the dogs about to launch an attack.

'Martha – Jack! Sit!'

'Smart,' said a big man with a Texas accent and an inoffensive face. He was leaning over the flat horn of a Mexican saddle holding a pair of binoculars, sandy brown hair falling down over his forehead from under a sweat-stained hat that he'd pushed up some.

Seeing those binoculars, I knew what they were after: Hannah Morgan. My guess was they were on the run – had spotted us earlier through the glasses, probably when I shot the sheep – had trailed us here, let it turn dark, then ridden in against the wind so the dogs couldn't scent or hear them.

Confirming my speculations, the one with the binoculars said, 'Where's that handsome little lady?'

'Dying of the white death,' I lied, motioning towards Hannah, hoping they'd be afraid. They hesitated and I took a good look.

There was no question they were outlaws – carrying enough heavy hardware to hold off the Argentine Army, bandoleers of spare ammunition hanging from saddlehorns, every man riding with a spare horse at his side. Nobody bothered with saddled spares unless they expected to be in a race they couldn't afford to lose. I'd chased men like these all my working life – knew them with just one look. These were filthy looking. My guess was they'd been on the run for a couple of months. Which meant they hadn't been in a town . . . and more than likely hadn't seen a woman in that time. So Hannah Morgan was driving them crazy.

'Bull,' the Texan said finally. 'Pull that blanket off her.'

That's when Lucia stepped from the shadows, the first smile I'd seen lighting up her face. Then this pale, thin girl – more child than woman – dressed in her black-flannel sleeping gown, said something in Mexican that sounded older than her years. The ones who understood it were grinning. Though my Mex-talk wasn't much good, I could figure what she'd said. She'd offered herself for Hannah Morgan.

'Silencio,' I snapped. She ignored me and continued walking toward the men, her hands on her small hips. I started for her but the Texan drew down on me. One of the Mexicans bent and swung her up behind him on the rump of a big white-socked chestnut.

The men were grinning now and I started to ease toward my holster when the Texan cocked his pistol and said, 'Pull that out and throw it aside.' I did it – but the familiar burning was in my throat. Still, there was no way all these kids would survive a head-on fight. The outcome wouldn't have mattered to me, but it wasn't right risking them.

'Walk to that rise and sit,' the Texan ordered. 'Or we kill the boy.'

I could hear James crying. Junior was trying to be brave but he was shaking badly and sucking in big gulps of air, the muzzle of the pistol jammed hard against his skull. I moved to the little knoll some ten yards away, and squatted. One of the Mexicans nodded at me, spitting out the word, 'Cobarde' – coward. I forced myself to look away so I wouldn't lose it. I didn't care for men saying things like that to me. Never had. Never would.

Martha and Jack were watching me closely, itching for some signal. I shook my head slowly – a sign they knew well. Jack growled, not liking things one bit.

Satisfied I wasn't going to do anything, the Texan swung down out of his saddle and started toward Hannah. Lucia yelled at him. She was no longer smiling. Then the Mexican in front of her turned and hit her hard with his open hand. She spit at him and he hit her again.

In the confusion, I undid two buttons on my shirt. The little belly gun was within reach now. Riding with Hannah and these kids, the men had no idea I was a lawman. And lawmen and outlaws were about the only people who carried hideaways any more. I noticed Lucia glaring at me, angry I wasn't doing anything. She didn't cut me much slack.

My mind was racing as one of the Mexicans swung down and joined the Texan approaching Hannah Morgan. It was clear they were planning to take her with them, conscious or not. I couldn't let that happen. If they got the horses, the woman and the girl, I'd never catch up. Even if I tried, Milagros and the boys would die out here. No – I stopped them now. Or they stopped me.

The belly gun had four shots. Unfortunately it was small calibre – meant to finish close-in fights. It wasn't looking good.

I turned slowly and faced the two who stood admiring Hannah. Them first. They'd left their horse reins trailing the ground. If I could kill them and grab a pistol, I might bolt the other two. They'd have the girl. But I'd have a horse and a gun. And I'd never lost that game. At least not yet.

The Texan squatted and yanked the blanket back off Hannah Morgan, expecting her to flinch. She didn't. I heard one of them whistle and say something about her looks. That's when it happened.

The Mexican standing next to the Texan suddenly straightened up and stared off into the night, pushing his hat back so it wouldn't interfere with his vision, and pulling his pistol. He said something in a voice that sounded nervous.

The Texan followed his line of sight into the night, both of them freezing for a moment, then they were backing hurriedly toward their horses, leaving Hannah Morgan behind. Unfortunately, the Mexican had grabbed up my pistol. I squinted off in the direction they'd been looking – couldn't see anything but a Spanish yucca on a small hill. Surely that hadn't spooked them.

But something had. They were on their horses and the four of them were kicking hard as if they'd just seen the US cavalry. Again I studied the darkness. Nothing. Absolutely nothing. No sound. No movement.

They'd dumped Junior. But Lucia was still on board, and they had all the horses. Things were better – but not great. I took off running at an angle away from them. My figuring was that they'd come out of the arroyo about a mile south and would head back for it and try to lose whoever it was that had stamp-eded them. As far as I was concerned, the only thing behind them was the wind, the moon and me. They'd scared themselves. That wasn't unusual for outlaws.

I was running for all I was worth, jumping cactus, skirting boulders and driving hard, hoping they'd make the turn I was counting on and I could cut one of them off or they'd lose a horse in their panic. I spotted them in the moonlight about a quarter of a mile out of camp, but I was shot, my lungs bursting, and they were moving at a smart clip under the stars. I wasn't going to catch them. I pulled up and tried to get my breath. Sonofabitch, I muttered. Then I saw the two shadows and hope surged. It was possible, though not likely. Martha was pulling hard behind the last rider, her large tan frame stretching out and eating up the distance. When she wanted to take something down, she could run. Jack was maybe two hundred yards behind her, his little legs digging to stay up.

'Gawddammit dogs! Run!'

I took off again, sucking wind and pumping hard. Martha was a good hundred yards behind the man, holding her own but not gaining; then the outlaw made the mistake of his life, deciding he'd peel off and screw his buddies by slipping away in the dark and letting them hang. But he hadn't reckoned on two dogs with enough heart to run him down. He'd never believe it. But then he didn't know Martha and Jack.

I could tell from the way he was riding that he had no idea they were behind him. He was still galloping, but he had slowed some and was picking his way quietly through the dog holes and brush. I kicked it for everything I was worth, sweat pouring down my body, my lungs ripping for air. But I couldn't quit. Martha and Jack were doing this for me and they deserved all the backup I could give.

I'd just made it to the top of a small sandhill when I saw the rider come trotting out a stand of mesquite brush a couple hundred yards below me. Martha was still a fair distance behind him, but closing fast now. I didn't know where Jack was until I saw the little dog suddenly dart out of the brush and lunge for the horse's nose.

The terrier had all the right instincts. Basically lazy, Jack had guessed where the man was headed and taken a short-cut to get there before him . . . and now he was hanging off the nose of the horse, his spindly little legs kicking in the air. I lost sight of them as the horse bucked its way back into the brush, Jack hanging on for all he was worth.

I was digging hard again when I heard a shot. I'd never make it in time. Never. He was going to kill my dog. 'You sonofabitch!' I yelled. Then I heard a scream and knew that Martha had finally caught up.

The man was dead by the time I got there. The dogs were sprawled in the sand beside the body, panting like they were both going to expire as well. Martha had caught the man with another of her throat clamps. It was becoming a real bad habit. I rolled the man over and pulled his pistol belt off and buckled it on my hips. It was one of the Texans. I brushed the sand off his face, straightened his legs out and crossed his arms over his chest so that he looked like he was taking a blessing from a priest.

'Good dogs,' I hollered as I swung up on the back of the man's second horse and started for the arroyo and the other three. The dogs trotted after me. 'No,' I hollered, 'go back to the camp!' I saw them both pull up and sit down. At least they weren't following. I figured when they caught their breath, knowing that I'd told them not to follow me, they'd probably head back to where they knew Hannah Morgan and the boys were. Water was there and food – and Hannah Morgan – and Jack loved the woman.

*

I was trying hard not to be seen, but figured I might be. Especially when following outlaws who knew if they relaxed they'd be shoved against a wall and shot. I crawled down off my horse and approached the wide strip of sandy trail that led some thirty feet down into the dusty little arroyo. I could hear water at the bottom and was working hard at being as quiet as possible. All I wanted to do was to check the tracks to make certain that all three had gone down into the gully.

Once I'd established that, I planned on riding a few yards back off the rim until I either found where they'd exited and made a run for it, or holed up. My guess was that with a moon as full as this one, they'd stop down below and let whoever they thought was pursuing pass in the dark. I wondered again what had spooked them. Men on the run were naturally jumpy – but it was still odd.

My plan of taking them from the top was sounding better the more I thought about it. They'd be expecting pursuit from down inside the gully . . . from somebody who'd tracked them into it.

I was thinking these things as I squatted in the soft sand of the trail reading the signs. They'd headed down, moving at a good clip. Now all I had to do was ferret them out. Hopefully they had some of their attention on Lucia. That bothered me. What she'd done had been foolish. If she'd let me handle things. But that wasn't fair. She'd done her best – risked herself to save the woman. I had to get to her.

I was just straightening up when I saw a shadowy shape a few yards below, then saw the flash and knew I'd be hit before I heard the explosion.

The bullet seared skin on the side of my neck, kicking me face-first into the sand. I was groggy, but not so I didn't hear the sound of a new round being chambered and then the crunch of boots. And I knew if I didn't do things right, the second round would be in my head.

'Clear your thoughts – clear your thoughts!' I kept repeating silently, as if talking to somebody else – kicking myself for getting caught like this.

I held my breath. If I moved now, he'd shoot me. Wait – just wait. I had one arm down by my side, the other out in front of me, loosely gripping the pistol. My eyes were clamped shut to keep the grit out of them. I was listening hard, not breathing. Timing was everything. Not too soon, not too late. From the jangle of his spurs, I figured he was Mexican. Not even Texans wore crap like that. If I was right – which I'd damn well better be – that would put his height at five-eight or so. I worked on the angles with my face stuck in the sand.

The man stopped. From the last sound of the metallic clinks, I figured it was three feet. Three feet, I told myself. Again, I worked the angles. My guess was he'd do two things.

First, he'd check to see if I was moving. If he saw anything, he'd shoot me or smash my skull with the rifle. If he didn't see anything, he'd assume I was dead or knocked cold and would let his eyes scan the horizon to see if anyone else was coming. When he was pretty sure I was alone, then he'd finish me. Probably with a knife. Either way, he wanted me dead.

'Not too soon – not too late,' I repeated. I had to wait until he was searching the night. It was my one chance. I tensed. It was almost time. 'One-thousand-one, one-thousand-two.'

All I moved was my wrist, raising the pistol up to where I figured he was and fired blind. The slug caught him low and blew him back. I shot him a second time, tearing a hole in his forehead. Then I wiped sand off my face and took his wide-brimmed hat and walked quickly down into the shadows of the arroyo. My neck was stinging and I tied a bandana around it, then searched until I found his horse. I untied it and started walking, trying to sound like I owned all of Utah and using the horse for a shield without looking too obvious.

I knew the shots had his partners' attention. They were calculating that either their friend was dead, or he'd done the killing. Either way, they weren't going to be caught playing canasta. The sombrero was too small, but it was all I had so I stuck it on my head and tried to walk like a Mexican.

Nothing was moving in the darkness in front of me. The small creek was talking over shallows and bordered with thick stands of marsh reeds and tamarisk bushes, making it perfect for hiding. There wasn't much I could do about that. I was in the middle of this damn thing and had to play it out – good, bad or whatever. My eye caught a faint shifting of shadows in the bushes to my right.

Like I said, I had the sombrero pulled low over my eyes, my hand resting on the grip of my pistol, standing close against the horse. Then the same blotch of shadow moved again and both outlaws were suddenly there in front of me, Lucia jammed between them. For a moment they thought I was their compadre: a bad mistake. By the time the Mexican's eyes were widening I was already firing. Lucia was smart enough to drop flat.

Both men were hit, but only one was down. The Texan was dead with a clean round hole in his throat, the bullet having entered his windpipe and exited his spine, breaking his neck, his head hanging down like a doll. The Mexican was still alive, wounded and stumbling away in the darkness, crashing through brush. I quickly reloaded behind the horse, then cut the rawhide on Lucia's wrists and pushed her up into the saddle. If she was at all glad I'd rescued her, I couldn't see it through the stony glare on her face.

'Wait for me at the top of the trail,' I said in my best broken

Mexican. 'Comprende?' I looked hard into her young face. She understood. I could see that. 'You wait for me. Comprende? Understand?' She didn't respond, just turned the horse and started off at a walk. She was a tough one. She'd just been in the middle of a gun fight, one man shot to death beside her, another spurting blood over everything, and she was acting like this was an everyday occurrence.

I watched her a moment longer – she was functioning OK – then I was off hunting the wounded Mexican. He was dripping blood over the ground and therefore easy enough to follow, even in the dark. The only surprise was when I flushed some spotted doves out of a scrub oak near a small water spill. Twenty-five yards further down the narrow gully, I found him. He was leaning back against the sandstone wall, trying hard to reload his pistol. He got a shot off but it was in the dirt near my feet.

'Drop the gawddamn thing!'

He didn't do it. Instead, he raised the pistol again. My shot took him chest-high, slamming him back hard into the wall. He slid down it until he was sitting and making a bad gasping sound. I came at him from the side because he was having trouble looking anywhere but straight forward, yanking the pistol away before he tried to pot me again, and squatted down. He was sucking wind through the hole in his chest; I knew he'd be done in a few minutes. From the faraway look in his eyes, he knew it too. I felt bad.

'Habla inglise?' I asked. 'Speak English?'

He nodded, blood trickling out the side of his mouth.

'Any whisky?'

He shook his head.

'Anybody you want me to tell anything? Wife, kids, mother?'

He tensed for a moment as if what I'd just said made dying

suddenly real and hard for him, then he relaxed as if he didn't care any more and shook his head slowly. I nodded and put my pistol away and took his hands and held them, so he could feel somebody with him at the last of it. He was young, maybe early twenties. Too young for this. He just looked at me – the pain and fear leaving, replaced by something empty. I didn't want to bother him, but I had to know.

'Back there with the woman – what scared you off?'

He didn't say anything for a while, then he mumbled, 'Too many.'

'Too many what?'

'Gringos,' he said, wheezing hard. 'Whites.'

'Just me.'

'Shit,' he said, spitting blood.

Then his eyes were glazing and he was gone. I stood and tried to shake off his death and wondered what he was talking about. 'Too many gringos?' Had there been riders moving past the camp in the night that I hadn't seen or heard? Nothing else made much sense. I picked him up in my arms and carried his body back to where I'd told Lucia to wait. She was gone. The girl was starting to irritate me.

I buried the three men in shallow graves and made a flat cross over the sand with river stones because I figured the Mexicans were probably Catholic and would want it, then I caught up the horses and started out of the arroyo. That's when I heard it. Faint at first, but growing louder.

There was no question what it was: a horse trotting through the night in my direction. I moved my animals into a shadowy stand of mesquite, pulled my pistol and waited. Was this one of the gringos that the Mexican had seen? Maybe.

The rider made the mistake of coming in too close to the bushes where I was standing and I stepped out and grabbed reins and jammed the barrel of my gun up into Hannah Morgan's face. She looked surprised but not frightened.

'Mr Gibbens,' she sighed. 'You're OK.'

I nodded.

She sat there for a moment staring down at me with a hand over her mouth as if she was holding something trapped inside. Then she took the hand away and smiled. 'I just had a bad dream. And when Lucia returned without you –'

'I'm fine,' I said, feeling awkward.

She turned her horse and started off at a trot. 'We best return to the children.'

I shook my head. It was a sacrifice for her to let these kids out of her sight for a minute. Nothing was going to come between this woman and these brats. Nothing. Not the devil or dust.

Back at camp, Hannah knelt in the sand and prayed over the children for a long time, mentioning my name in a couple of places and making me squirm. I made like I was busy checking saddles and bridles, until I caught her staring at me like she was worried about something and I took to wondering about that dream she said she'd had. Wondered if her voices had said something about me that I should know. But that was silly thinking.

Then she said good night and turned in herself. I field-hobbled the horses and picked up my rifle and walked out into the moonlight toward the little yucca on the sandy hillside. Martha and Jack followed. This was the place where the dead Mexican had been looking when he suddenly panicked, where he claimed to have seen 'Too many gringos.'

I searched for an hour but couldn't find a thing. Not one thing. Not a footprint, a hoof print, nothing. The man must have been high on mescal or needed glasses.

CHAPTER NINE

Everything is exaggerated in the desert. Heat and distances and mirages. I knew this well. So the next day, nine hours after I'd started back for El Paso, I wasn't surprised to see evening throwing down blue light over the land. I wasn't surprised or particularly interested.

Hannah Morgan had taken off with the kids before dawn – once again leaving me sleeping like a baby. She was like a match tossed into dry hay, the way she burned across this desert. Following her so-called voices, I guessed.

Like the last time, I'd slept through the commotion and the dogs had let her go. I chalked it up to the three of us being worn out by the events of the night before. It didn't matter. The woman obviously had something to do that didn't involve me. That was fine – I just wasn't going to hang around waiting to be whistled up next time. Nope, my curiosity was waning. I'd wasted too much time traipsing around this desert after her, trying to find out what had happened to me. She either didn't know or wasn't telling.

I was tired and rode out of the sagebrush flats down into a creek bottom. Since I wasn't going to make the train in El Paso anyway, I might as well take my time getting back. The land here had begun to turn sandy and sparse. It would get leaner until the Rio Grande. After that, it would get leaner still. I looked around: the place seemed as good as any to make camp.

Down by the water, purple sage and prairie astor were in bloom, and I could see butterflies – yellow Sulphers, Indian Skippers and sooty-brown Hairstreaks – bobbing and fluttering in the dry air over the flowers, enjoying themselves. The perfect spot to go collecting. And a year ago I would have leaped at the chance. But not now. There was no point to it now.

I reined the mare in and sat staring blindly at the ground, thinking about what my life had once been like. And never would be again. The noise of the water brought me back. Old cottonwoods edged a stream that ran out of some harsh looking shale hills, the trees broken and haggard like widows in mourning.

The creek ran fast in the shallows, then pooled in a deeper, slower moving place, reflecting the rose-coloured sunset off its glassy surface. I sat listening to the random squeaking of saddle leather, half-thinking this was a nice place, but not really caring. The dogs stood watching me and wondering what the heck I was doing. I sat up straighter and looked around. The banks of the waterway were spotted with blackberries and peachleaf willow and the dusky air was filled with the calls of magpies and kingfishers.

I don't know how long I sat there. All I know is that I was still in the saddle, staring blindly at my thoughts, when Jack barked. Five miles back I'd shot a mule deer that Martha had jumped up in a rocky canyon. I was carrying the best parts and Jack was dreaming about that meat. The little terrier sat on his skinny haunches and looked at me in his cheeky way, and barked again.

'I hear you, dammit.'

Twenty minutes later the sun had gone down and I was

squatted beside a small mesquite fire turning three chunks of venison over the flames and watching a muskrat swimming the creek a few snaps ahead of Martha's jaws. Jack was barking free advice from the shore. The big dog was gaining.

I whistled her off and she bit the water in frustration and came treading her way back across the creek. Jack trotted over and sat down in front of the fire, trembling and staring at the venison as if he might be able to command it to leap off the spit. When this bit of conjuration failed, he began to bark indignantly.

'This isn't a restaurant,' I snapped. Jack wasn't persuaded. He continued to whine and grumble, trying his damnedest to cast magic on the meat.

I ignored him and ran an oily rag over my pistol. Then I picked up the saddle carbine, opened the breech, stuck my thumb inside and put an eye to the mouth of the barrel, tipping the rifle until firelight reflected off my thumb-nail and up inside, illuminating the shining metal and spiralling rifle groove that gave the bullet its controlling spin. Burnt specks of gunpowder clung to the slick inner walls.

I forced a cleaning rod down it, then chambered a fresh round and set the butt on the ground and held the barrel in both my hands. The muzzle was pointed at my face. I began to tremble, the desire suddenly growing in me to push the trigger down. I would never see my wife again.

'Joan,' I moaned. Even as I called her name I saw her face in my thoughts, then just as suddenly she was disappearing. Then I felt something tug on my sleeve and I looked down at Jack.

The little beady eyes drilled hard into my face, then he barked and turned his head and looked at the meat. I got his point: 'There's plenty of time to blow your brains out after we've eaten.' Martha was behind him. She woofed once in agreement.

I straightened up and stared at the two of them. They stared back at me. Estancacion Mexicano – a Mexican stand-off. Then I laughed. 'Real pals,' I said. But they were right. I couldn't kill myself. Not now.

I would take Husker back to Los Angeles and turn him over. Clean out my paperwork. Get Jack and Martha settled. Then I'd finish it. That was the right way.

'Let's eat,' I said. The dogs jumped around like the postponement of my death so they could eat was great news.

After the meal, I built a cigarette and looked at the land around me: stark and dun-coloured with windswept mesas, deep sandstone canyons and long ridges, an empty land that kept tilting south until it ran into Mexico a few hundred miles away. I didn't know much else about it. The first landmark I knew was Old Dad Mountains a hundred miles southwest of here. Here, I knew nothing. Nothing but the fact that the graze wasn't good; and maybe how to find water and shade.

I took a long deep breath of air spiced with the sharp smell of purple sage. Two years ago, I'd have felt this spot was a slice of sweet pie. Now it was just a stopover on my way out. I drew hard on the cigarette and sat there while my mind began the endless replay of events in the alley in El Paso. I went slowly over each detail, refusing to move on until I was certain I had reconstructed every fragment of that night. For a reason I didn't understand I felt driven to answer what had happened. Some things in life are so momentous they cry out for a person to act on them. My wife's death was one. This was another.

It would have been easier if Lessing had just finished me with that shotgun. But he hadn't, and that fact – that I had been delivered from a certain death – was as unsettling as anything that had ever happened in my life. I didn't know why I'd been spared – didn't have a clue. It just raised questions I'd never considered before.

I stood and walked down to the edge of the creek, the cool evening air of the desert reminding me of Los Angeles, clear, bone dry and thin. The aromatic scent of the sage mixed now with the damp smells of the river and was not unpleasant. I'd grown up breathing these same smells and they brought back good memories: of being a kid, my mother and father, my brother, the old ranch, my courtship. Then these thoughts began to sour in my mind. My parents and brother were gone, the ranch, my wife and baby. I went back to thinking about El Paso.

I recalled with complete clarity John Husker's shaking hand as he took the drink, then the nervous jump of his eyes as he checked the door and the windows of the cantina. I also remembered with a clamminess the realization that I had been set up . . . that Lessing was now hunting me.

I took another long draw on the cigarette, holding the smoke and reliving in my mind the sickening sound of Lessing's footsteps, the turn, the awful flash from the gun barrels, the numbing concussion and the burning gas and pellets that drove me backwards. Stop! I told myself. Thinking about it does nothing. But I couldn't stop.

I wiped my damp forehead with a handkerchief, then refocused on what had happened next; trembling now as I let the cigarette smoke out of my lungs . . . lungs that shouldn't be there. I replayed my backward crash through the windows and the sound of screams. That was all. That was it. Finito. I was falling backwards and calling out. I tensed with that last thought as if a cold hand had grabbed the back of my neck.

I didn't move for a time. Just stood thinking over and over again those last moments in the alley. Yes. I was certain of it.

After I'd been shot, I'd called out. Called out in fear and desperation, thinking about nothing but death, afraid of it, wanting it only on my terms, not ready for it in that alley, at that dark moment in time.

Yes, I'd called out. I'd seen death exploding out of the barrels of that gun and I hadn't wanted to face it, and I had screamed. I ran my fingers through my hair, damp now with sweat. My hands were shaking. I almost thought I could hear the faint echoing sound of my frantic plea: 'Mother of God – help me!'

It took me some time before I could collect myself. Again and again I rethought the words until I was sure. I'd called out in reflex. The way Joan had taught me when she was trying to get me to join the church. I'd yelled to the Blessed Virgin for help. The ash on my smoke had grown long and fell now on to the front of my shirt. I brushed it off, then dropped the cigarette and crushed it into the ground and stood looking down at the sandy dirt, thinking. My heart was beating hard in my chest. My mind thinking it wasn't possible.

I had called out to the Mother of God . . . and when I awoke, Hannah Morgan was there . . . and I was still alive. Not even bruised. I shook my head. It couldn't be. Things like that didn't happen. Only religious freaks believed in things like that – not me. I walked down to where the dogs were lying on the creek shore and watched the water flowing in the little stream. Hannah Morgan had said that she had touched my wound. She had said that. I tried to ignore my speeding thoughts, but couldn't.

Jack came and stood up on his hind legs and danced like an old man around me, then put his paws on my leg. I squatted and picked the dog up and held him tight in my arms until he got uncomfortable and wiggled loose. My hands were shaking badly now. I needed another cigarette and reached for my shirt pocket and tobacco bag, forgetting that I'd left it on the blanket.

But I felt something else in the pocket and pulled it out . . . my heart flopping harder inside my chest. Robert Dunnet's letter.

With hands shaking so badly that I could barely control them, I unfolded the paper and read it – then again. Then just the last paragraph: 'I prayed to the Virgin but she has not come.' My eyes remained fixed on the words. 'But she has not come.' Over and over I repeated those five words, remembering the sudden turn in the woman's trek north . . . then her wild dash south into the reservation lands.

She had found the prospector, but too late. The thought was numbing. Robert Dunnet had prayed to the Virgin Mary and the woman had been reached by what she claimed were God's messengers. This God who hadn't bothered to answer my prayers for my wife and baby. Did he exist? I tipped my head back and stared up at the stars as if I might find some answer there – might hear celestial voices. But there was nothing. Nothing but the night winds penetrating the silence of the empty land.

Jack had decided to give me another chance at being normal and brought me a stick and dropped it at my feet. I ignored it and thought about Hannah Morgan and the things I'd seen. I thought about the man in the café unable to confront her; about the doctor giving the dying girl to her – a perfect stranger – and not knowing why he'd done it. I returned to the camp and began to pack. People, I figured, got one or two chances to make big decisions in their lives. Maybe this was mine.

CHAPTER TEN

Los Angeles. 3 March 1997

Father Richard Mulcahy put the manuscript down on the desk and stretched in his chair, feeling the familiar shortness of breath that came whenever he was tired or over-exerted. He'd known most of what he'd read so far from his talks with Father Cordova. Still, there was something interesting in the detail of it. Interesting, but not much more. He'd been hoping that he'd find something of what it was that had given such spiritual sustenance to Father Cordova over the years. He hadn't.

It was the same warmed-over cabbage: a visitation from the Virgin. The old priest rubbed his eyes, feeling tiredness falling down on him. The hallway outside his office was dark, the archdiocese quiet now, the hour 9.33. He wondered what had held his attention. It wasn't a bad story. Better than most. He was interested in this woman, Hannah Morgan. She was more to his liking than what the Church tried to pawn off.

He smiled at the joke they used to tell when he was a boy in choir: 'I don't care what the angel says, Mary – you're still in big trouble.' That summed it up for him. He believed that a woman named Mary had given birth to Jesus. He just didn't believe she was a goddess or the nativity virginal. The Church had let things get out of hand.

Besides mothering a royal son, what had she done to deserve worship? Nothing. She'd barely been mentioned in the Bible.

Respect, yes. But worship was silly. And all of these sightings around the world – it was an infectious madness that ate away at the body health of the Church.

Mulcahy felt his heart quickening and forced himself to slow down. He didn't need to die over this manuscript. His thoughts leaped to Father Cordova and he mumbled a quiet prayer for his soul, praying that the talk of suicide was just talk.

He sat turning a pencil over and over and thought what he knew of the Mother of Christ. The Roman Church had ignored her for hundreds of years after the death of the Saviour, viewing her mainly as an intercessor with her Son. But as the centuries passed, Rome had come to realize she was one of their greatest assets. So they'd canonized her and held her up to the masses for devotion. And like a rock star who never grew old, she packed the believers in by the millions, century after century.

Hannah Morgan, the old priest thought, certainly had the dignity, the sense of self, the beauty to be the Mother of God. Best of all, she hadn't drifted down out of the clouds as some sort of omnipotent, ethereal being, spouting little sound-bites for the late-night news. No. So far, she seemed much more as he believed the real Mary might have been – and would remain today: aware of the mystery, part of it, without being all knowing, all powerful. She was, after all, only human. Weak as the rest of us. Beseiged by her frailties and fears. Good and compassionate, but no Joan of Arc riding to battle.

He yawned. Yes. This was the way to portray the Virgin. Whoever Tucker Gibbens was, Mulcahy agreed with his fiction.

He sat staring blindly at the shadows of the hallway beyond his open office door, wishing he could believe again. 'Let me,' he whispered. Had he secretly been hoping these yellowed pages would resurrect his faith as they had Father Cordova's? He didn't know. All he knew for certain was that he was desperate to lose the cold, glass-like hardness inside him that was so foreign a feeling. He forced himself to calm down again.

He stood and stretched his back and wondered: was it pure fabrication? Or had something happened to Tucker Gibbbens? Father Mulcahy returned to his desk chair and sat looking at the manuscript.

The thought suddenly crossed his mind that he should treat Father Cordova's memory and Tucker Gibbens's manuscript with greater care. Either Gibbens was a liar or he believed what he'd written. Cordova believed it was the latter. Therefore, he told himself that, at the very least, he should check the story's facts.

He yawned again and ran his hand through his grey hair, determining that he would begin in the morning to document the details of Gibbens's story. The events had taken place over a hundred years ago, but proper record-keeping in this country was deeply entrenched by the 1700s. There was little one couldn't find if they put their mind to it.

Mulcahy picked up a pen and thumbed back through the pages, writing down notes – names, events, dates and places. He was soon feeling better, but didn't know why.

CHAPTER ELEVEN

Utah Territory. 21 July 1887

Four Walls was halfway prosperous looking as mining towns go. There was a sign on the wagon trail leading to it that read: Population 1,000. I doubted it, but didn't care. The collection of weather-beaten buildings was squatting in the foothills of the purple mountains that rose from the flatlands where Hannah Morgan had left me the day before. I could see lights burning in a number of places and, given the lateness of the hour, I took notice. I stopped and checked my weapons. It was habit.

Finished, I gave the sorrel a nudge from my heels and started thinking about Hannah Morgan and her God. Then later, when I realized I was sitting on my horse in the middle of a dark street and didn't know how long I'd been there, I forced myself to think about where I was and what I was doing.

I had no idea why anyone would give a town a dumb name like Four Walls, unless they were drunk or didn't give a damn. I surely didn't. All I wanted – now that I knew the truth – was to find the woman and get to the bottom of things in my life: like whether she knew my wife and baby . . . and how they were getting along. Where they were. And how I could find them.

My breath caught with the next of it: whether I had a chance of getting in where they were headed. I doubted it. But I was still going to try. But I was worried that I had postponed going after them too long. I might never catch up. Anyhow, after I'd found out these things, I'd return Husker to Los Angeles, then do what I had to.

I leaned out of my saddle some and followed the hoof prints of the three horses down the main street of town. I'd been following them so long that I could do it easy enough in the moonlight, the little triangle nick in the metal of the black gelding's shoe clear and distinct. I trailed the prints until they disappeared in the jumble of other animal, human and wagon tracks that criss-crossed the dirt here. Then I straightened up in the saddle and reined the mare around a sign that said: WALK YOUR HORSE.

I'd pushed my animals hard all day and the lot of them looked filthy and beat. I guessed I looked the same. I tied the sorrel and the bay to a rail in front of a café that was still open. The place was run down, but the whole town looked like a good sneeze might finish it.

Turning in a slow circle, I scanned the street looking for the woman's and the kids' horses. They weren't here. Either they were stabled somewhere for the night or perhaps they'd just passed on through. Something in my gut told me they were still here.

It was 11 p.m. as I stepped up on the wooden sidewalk and headed for the café door. Jack started to follow. 'No. Stay. Both of you stay and watch the horses.' I reached and slapped the pack on the bay's back, then pointed a finger at the ground, so they understood. Jack walked over and relieved himself on the hitching post, I figured to show his displeasure. Martha just sat. She never minded her work.

I slid on to a hard wooden seat at the bar and ordered a beer. The place was filled with family types, which seemed unusual for the hour. A few men were drinking and some were playing cards, but most were talking in tight knots around the tables. Nobody paid me much mind, which was equally unusual in a town this size and this far out in the barrens. From the buzz of voices in the room, I knew something had happened. Did they already know about her? I listened but couldn't catch enough words.

A skinny, freckle-faced girl of maybe seventeen approached me from my side of the bar. She had thin red hair and smiled a greeting with a mouth full of bad teeth. 'My name's Ruth.' The accent was Irish. 'Whataya drinkin'?'

'Beer would be nice,' I said, nodding toward the keg on the bar.

'Would ya buy a girl something?'

On closer inspection she couldn't have been much over sixteen. Pushing drinks and other things to survive. And from the looks of her cheap dress and broken-down high heels, survive was the right word. I felt sorry for her and thought about Lucia. I nodded at her. 'Sure.' I scanned the room for Hannah Morgan. She wasn't there.

Ruth ordered the most expensive whisky in the place. I'd known she would and I watched her sloshing the small puddle of golden liquid around in the bottom of her glass as I laid five dollars down for the man behind the counter to pick up. Ruth leaned into the bar, propped up by thin girlish arms.

'I'm looking for a woman,' I said quietly.

Her eyes brightened, but behind them I could tell she was fighting off some sort of sadness and was in no mood for romance. But for money she'd do it. I wasn't interested. I'd never bought a woman in my life and didn't plan on starting this night – especially a kid. The Virgin around or not, the idea had never set well with me. I stared at Ruth's freckled face and wondered what it was that was making her sad. But it wasn't my cat to skin. I had my own worries.

'Ya've come to the right place,' she said, trying her best to make the voice and the smile seductive. It wasn't working.

I smiled back at her in an appreciative way. 'Thanks. But I don't have the time.' I didn't want to hurt her feelings. I'd always felt something for women who lived out their time in places like this – risking so much of themselves just to keep kicking.

'I'm looking for a specific woman. One who rode into town with a bunch of kids, two of them coloured.'

The change in Ruth's expression was immediate. She frowned and blurted, 'Ya know her?'

Most of the people in the room were staring at me now – not all that friendly looking. 'Depends who you're talking about.'

'Long dark hair. Early thirties.'

I could see her stifling a cry. 'Sounds like her,' I said.

'You a friend?'

'Yes.'

Ruth stared at me for a moment, then slapped me hard across the face and turned and walked away, slowly climbing the stairs that led to the rooms upstairs. My cheek was stinging like hell but I didn't touch it. I felt like an idiot standing there, blood rushing to my face, my cheek on fire, everybody staring.

What had the woman done to this girl? Humiliated her in some way? I'd have guessed Hannah Morgan – of all people – would have befriended her. Surely she understood her. Taken pity on her. It made no sense.

I watched her disappear into an upstairs room, then felt someone move uncomfortably close against me. I turned and looked into a dark bearded face. The wild black hair, the pale skin and the intense blue eyes were features that fit a preacher. But I was guessing, from the cold professional way I was being crowded, the man was law. I didn't care. I just wanted room. I took a backwards step, my expression telling him not to press.

'What do you want with that woman?'

'I usually get a better greeting,' I said, my cheek still stinging, my hackles rising.

'I asked you a question.'

I studied the hairy face, my thoughts whirling. Perhaps Hannah Morgan had performed some miracle gone bad. Maybe they were just stunned by who she was. I didn't blame them.

'Just want to talk to her,' I said, trying to shake my temper.

'About?'

The population of the café was crowding around. No time to get tough. I reached slowly into my coat. In response the bearded man put a hand on the butt of a pistol. I pulled my wallet and showed my brass deputy-sheriff shield. It worked. Big-city badges did in small towns. The man turned toward the bar and called for half a beer.

'Harold Adams,' he said, offering his hairy hand. 'Sheriff here.'

'Tucker Gibbens.'

Adams leaned into the bar and watched me pull my coat off. 'Get that shirt in Los Angeles?'

'El Paso. Gift.'

Adams nodded and then leaned over and said something to a man standing beside him and the man immediately left the café. I doubted he'd gone to El Paso for the sister shirt, figuring instead he was going to telegraph Los Angeles to confirm that the badge and Tucker Gibbens were real. I'd have done the same. Adams sloshed the beer around in his glass, peering down into the amber-coloured fluid like he was looking for something – maybe some answers – then took a drink. 'I don't know what California wants her for, but she's not leaving here.' He paused. 'You don't have any of those extra-something papers –'

'Extradition,' I offered, trying not to sound like a smartass. I took a drink of warm beer. 'Nope. Just want to ask her some questions. Small-time stuff. Illegal trespass on reservation lands. Nothing big. Just things like that.' My brain was scrambling as I tried to figure what the hell had happened.

Adams nodded, staring down again into his beer. 'Fine. Not a problem. She's in my jail across the street. Any time you want to see her, you let me know.' He paused. 'Just understand. She's not going anywhere.'

I nodded, stunned the woman had been arrested. 'What's she locked up for?'

'Murder.'

At first I thought it was a joke. When I figured it wasn't, I took a deep breath I didn't need and said, 'That can't be true.'

Adams was staring hard now at me. 'Why?'

'Just can't be.'

'What do you know about this?' he said, putting his beer down on the bar.

'Just that she didn't murder anybody.' I was struggling to keep from rushing my words.

'Opinion? Or you know?' Adams asked, watching my face.

'Opinion.'

'Mine is she killed three men in a boarding room.' The sheriff turned back to the bar and took another pull on his beer. 'Three,' he repeated, as if talking to himself. He tipped his head up toward the door where the skinny red-headed girl had disappeared. 'One was Ruth's brother.'

I started to shake my head, then thought better of it and forced myself to finish my beer.

The room was in deep shadow, illuminated only by the low burning flame from a kerosine lamp. The bodies were lying under blankets on tables that had been pushed against the far wall. There were large blocks of ice stacked under each table and a chill on the place. I could hear water dripping into tin pans, the sound unsettling in a strange way. I thought about my wife's and my baby's bodies . . . not on ice, but decaying in the earth. I thought about my own coming death, imagined my face rotting into an ugly goo. Then other bodies that I'd seen, some I'd killed myself: green and bloated and smelly. I forced myself to stop thinking these things.

Not believing Hannah Morgan had anything to do with the murders, I had asked to see the corpses first. I was standing beside the sheriff while the town barber, who was also the town undertaker and veterinarian according to a sign outside, pulled the room's blinds to keep the crowd on the other side of the windows from gawking at the remains. Professional courtesy, I figured. That, or it made the slender man in the neat linen suit and bow tie look more important. Probably some of both.

Though I'd seen my share of dead people over the years, I'd never gotten comfortable looking at them and I braced myself for these three, trying to decide what the strange but vaguely familiar smell was floating in the room.

'You've never seen a thing like it,' Adams said. 'Not in Los Angeles. Not in Paris, France.'

As the sheriff was finishing, I placed the smell. It was the odour that came into the low atmosphere after a lightning strike that was too close for comfort. Something burned. As I was thinking this, the little barber pulled the first blanket off like he was unveiling a work of art. The air reversed in my throat and I just stood staring in disbelief at the body. The sheriff was right – not in Paris, France.

'Isn't that the damnedest,' Adams offered. The big man was squinting at the corpse.

I stepped closer to the table, my eyes narrowing. 'Turn that lamp up?'

The increased illumination only made the scene more grotesque. I wasn't viewing a body . . . I was looking at parts of a body that had been pieced together like a jigsaw puzzle on the tabletop. I took a deep breath and held it, then bent forward and took a close look at the cut that had severed the man's upper arm, slicing through the heavy humerus bone, ligaments, muscles, veins and arteries. It was sliced clean as warm butter. But the strangest thing was the fact that the cuts were seared the way a piece of meat sears in the frying pan, the ends of the bone scorched brown.

'Crazy,' the sheriff continued. The barber nodded in sombre agreement.

The small man looked up at me wanting to be helpful. 'I handle bodies for a living, sir. Explosions. Things like,' he said. I noticed his voice was high. 'But never like this. Took a day to put them together. Pieces everywhere. But no blood. Drop here and there.' He waved a slender hand at the bodies, waved it the way a female would. 'You should have been able to swim in it.' The man stopped talking and pulled at the hair on one side of his head.

'Best we can figure,' Adams said, 'whatever made the cuts fried the flesh. Cauterized it.' He looked at me. 'You ever seen anything like that?'

'No.'

After I'd looked at the other two bodies, diced in the same gruesome manner, I turned toward Adams. 'What happened?'

He shrugged. 'Passer-by heard a scream from a boarding room. Came and got me. When she didn't open the door, we kicked it in.' He wiped his mouth with his hand. 'This is what we found.'

'And the woman?'

'When we got inside?'

I nodded.

'Half-naked on the bed. Dress down to her waist. Looked dazed. Made me think of my old man's stroke.'

'Assaulted.'

'Or playing black widow.'

'No.'

'You're looking at what we found.'

'Where were the kids?'

'She'd rented rooms with the Johnson family just outside town. After dinner she told them she had something to do. The kids were there when it happened.'

I looked back at the bodies, a fly landing on one of the faces. I brushed it away and then I turned to the barber and said, 'I want to talk to the sheriff alone.'

As soon as the man was out the door, I turned on Adams. 'She didn't do this. I don't know who did . . . but it wasn't Hannah Morgan –'

'Gibbens.'

I didn't like the way he'd said my name.

'She confessed to it.'

'Confessed? You have a confession from this woman that she butchered these men?'

'As much.'

'Like what?'

' "I'm so sorry this happened." She kept repeating that.'

'That's it? That's her confession?' I frowned at the man as if he was a babbling fool.

He stepped out of the shadows, his face looking a little uncomfortable.

'That's not a confession! Hell, I'll tell you the same thing: I'm sorry this happened.' My eyes were narrowed and I could feel the veins on my neck standing out, and I knew I was getting close to kicking the can over.

'Not the best.'

'The best? It's nothing. Jesuspriest, man, that's not a confession. She was numb from what she'd seen. Sonofabitch, I am too.' I couldn't stop looking at the bodies. 'Adams, listen. Did she say she'd done it? Did she say: "I killed these men"?'

The sheriff pursed his lips beneath his heavy moustache and then shook his head. 'No. But she was the only one in the room.'

'How the hell do you know?' I was getting mad again. 'You have a witness?'

Adams looked off across the room and let the silence accumulate. He rolled his head on his neck trying to rid himself of tension. It was obvious he didn't care for the few facts he had, but he wasn't ready to fold to me. He cleared his throat. 'Listen,' he said, looking directly into my face. 'When I asked her what happened – hoping she'd give me something – she had nothing to say. Claimed she blanked out. That's a little ripe.'

'No it's not. She has that problem.'

'You a doctor too?'

'No. I just know she didn't do this.' I looked back at the carnage on the table and felt the urge to tell Adams who Hannah Morgan was. But I knew I wouldn't be believed. So instead, I said, 'She didn't do this. She couldn't have.' The words implying more than Adams could possibly understand.

The sheriff squinted at me. 'What's with you, Gibbens?' He paused. 'She your girlfriend? Or you just poking her?'

I forced myself to listen to the ice dripping into the pans for a while. I'd been fighting not to lose it. But now I was close. I turned slowly and faced Adams. 'She's not some common whore. Don't say she is.'

I took a careful, measured step backwards and Adams knew instinctively what the move meant. He just wasn't certain why

I was doing it. What he was certain of, I sensed, was that he didn't want any part of this. He wasn't a coward, he just didn't want to kick the lid off the can for no reason.

'Just wondering,' he said.

'She's innocent.'

'Your opinion. Just remember: you work in Los Angeles.'

I ignored the remark, still facing Adams. 'What'd she kill these men with?' It was another challenge, just not as angry.

'We don't know. Maybe a hot sword.' Adams sucked at the inside of his cheek. 'But that supposes she could hold it without burning her hands off, and swing it hard enough.'

'That's crap. You haven't found anything.'

'Right.' Adams focused his eyes on me, and said, 'Maybe she had an accomplice. How'd you cut your head?'

'Arrest in El Paso.'

'You work all the towns?' It was a little jab.

I studied the man for a moment, then said, 'She didn't do it, Adams.'

'Maybe.'

'Maybe, hell. No weapon, no confession, no witness. You don't have anything. You couldn't convict –'

'Gibbens.'

'What?'

'It's too late. She was found guilty this morning.'

I stared at the sheriff for a long time before I said, 'Are you people crazy?'

The man was rocking back and forth on his large feet like he was getting ready to start out the door. 'I told the judge I didn't think she'd done it. He partly agreed. Didn't do any good. Jury found her guilty.' He hesitated. 'Voted death.'

It was like somebody had plunged a hand into my chest, grabbed my heart and squeezed hard. I was stunned. I stood staring at the sheriff's face until I was able to speak. 'That isn't going to happen.'

'What?'

'Her being put to death.'

Adams was watching me carefully now. When he spoke his voice was low. 'She'll be shot in the morning. What you and I think doesn't put any cheese on the cracker. We just do what we're told.' He paused. 'Comprende? You got evidence, fine. Otherwise, stay out of it.'

I could feel sweat breaking over my back. 'You don't know who she is.'

Adams was studying me closely again, as if beginning to seriously wonder who I was. 'Who is she, Gibbens?'

A nerve exploding somewhere deep in my mind kept me from blurting out what I knew. I didn't need to get thrown into jail for being a dangerous lunatic, so I turned and started for the door. 'I'll want to see her in a little while.'

'No,' Adams said.

I stopped and turned back to the man. 'What?'

'Not with that attitude.'

'I've got to have a certain attitude to see her?'

'Yeah. One that says: No trouble. No shit.'

'Fine.'

The sheriff watched me for a moment, then said, 'Your weapons. Now.' He continued to study my face until I began to unstrap. 'I don't like this either,' he added.

I didn't comment.

CHAPTER TWELVE

The alley was dark and smelled of rotting garbage, a narrow space between run-down buildings that were abandoned or used for cheap night rentals. I was moving carefully, following Hannah Morgan's footprints in the dirt and wondering what had happened here.

Like all high country after sundown, the air was chilly, but even so I was sweating. Since El Paso I'd had strange moments of happiness followed by jolts of confusion. I was feeling that way now, sweat pouring into my eyes.

I pulled my hat off and ran a hand through my damp hair and continued to slowly unravel her movements in the dust, seeing clearly where she'd made her way along in the darkness, stopping every so often, turning in tight circles, as if searching for something.

I thought about her doing this same thing in the town of Oasis. Thought about the child and the doctor. I reset my hat and started moving again. It was darker here under the eaves of a two-storey building, so I bent closer to the ground and continued moving slowly along, the story of what had happened written clearly in the dirt.

She'd been walking fast when they grabbed her, the three men coming at her from different directions in the cramped passage. She hadn't resisted, but that didn't surprise me.

In my mind, I could almost see the look on her face as the men held her, a look so self-assured that it sometimes seemed haughty. That look alone should have stopped them. But it hadn't. They'd been fools.

Then an errant thought passed through my mind: these men may not have had a choice. Maybe Hannah Morgan drew people to her in a marked way – good and bad alike forced to some predetermined place and time of chance and destiny . . . none able to resist these ordained moments.

The Apaches, the outlaws, the doctor, Jake – had they been drawn to her? I stopped moving and took a breath I didn't need. Had I? Was that what happened in life? Were we pulled face to face with our gods – our fates determined by these final confrontations? I didn't know. All I knew for certain was that I was here. As confused as when I first met her, but still here.

I kept moving down the narrow course between the buildings, trailing what was now a jumble of footprints to a staircase at the back of a boarding house a few yards down the alley. They'd been rough with her, shoving her along in front of them, knocking her down once, and when she hadn't moved fast enough, they'd dragged her forcibly. She hadn't cried out or begged the men to release her. She wouldn't yield to fear or force. She would yield, I was certain, to no one but her God.

I shook my head at her mulishness. Still, for all her un-compromising stubbornness about things she thought were right, there was yield and compassion in her. I'd seen it before. Even as she opposed her enemies, she was bawling over them. It was hard as hell to figure.

As I studied her movements in the dust, I was drifting again in my thoughts until it seemed as if I were sensing the foreboding silence of her as she was forced along this way . . . sensing it like a scent of danger that lingered in this dark place, a remembrance of her. And I wondered again how the men could have been such absolute fools.

Then I recalled the first time I'd met her. Certainly I'd recognized her great beauty – but nothing more. I had asked if she were a prostitute. No, the men would not have known. They'd been left to their own fate. They'd seen the beauty of the woman, but not inside her heart. They'd never suspected.

My thoughts began to drift again.

I stopped and stood staring blindly into the darkness, feeling once more what had happened to her here, sensing her physical presence somehow still drifting in this passageway, sweat moistening my skin. I don't know how long I stood there wrapped in these disturbing thoughts before I shook my head and forced my mind to clear. I had no sense of time – all I knew was that I had none to waste.

The stairs led to the second-floor room where the men had met their deaths. I knew the place without knowing how I knew. I studied the darkened doorway for a few minutes, trying to understand what had happened inside, feeling a strange foreboding stealing over me as I peered up at it; then I turned back, my thoughts drawn again – almost against my will – to the alley, and I stood searching the shadows for some detail, some clue as to why she'd come here. The question seemed to gnaw at me. I didn't know why. All I knew was that I couldn't leave this alley until I had an answer.

I kept asking myself: what had she been hunting? What had caused her to leave the boarding house and children late at night in a strange town and to come alone to this filthy place? Was she looking for whoever it was that ultimately killed the men? The same person or persons that the dead Mexican and Texan had seen on the little sandy knoll?

A chill ran over my backside: I'd found no tracks out there

in the sands. No riders – no men on foot. Nothing. What had they seen in that desert night? Or thought they'd seen?

I didn't believe in ghosts – but I'd been a lawman long enough to believe in evil. I just didn't know its source. But I wasn't about to laugh it off because I didn't know what hole it crawled out of. The muscles tensed across my shoulders. Something was bothering me about the upstairs room, my eyes drawn once more to the darkened windows.

I started for the stairs, then stopped. Whatever it contained had to wait. The answer I needed – the answer that had placed the woman in harm's way – was down here in the alley. The same answer she'd been seeking. And for a reason I couldn't quite grasp in my mind, I felt compelled again to know what it was.

I turned in a slow circle and scanned the place. Had the three men laid a trap for her, luring her here on the pretence that someone was hurt and needed help – perhaps calling out from the alley's shadows? I rolled my shoulders, trying to release the building tension that was beginning to ache.

No. Hannah Morgan hadn't been tricked into coming down here. She wasn't somebody to be tricked, she was filled with uncanny practicality, and she'd come here, I was sure, of her own free will. The men had more than likely seen her turn into this dark passageway, followed her, then forced her into the room. Their mistake. Their moment with destiny.

I retraced my steps to the last place she'd been standing before they'd taken her, turning and facing in the direction she'd been facing. I could tell from the small spurts of dust on the backside of her footprints that she'd been moving fast just before she encountered the men, moving in that determined way she had when she'd made up her mind about something. But what had she decided? I saw it lying in the dirt next to the building where I stood: a little well-chewed apple core. I smiled.

Convinced that whatever she'd been searching for she'd already spotted by the time she'd reached this location, I placed my boots over her footprints and squinted against the darkness and tried to see what she had seen. There was nothing in front of me. Nothing but a broken water barrel and a pile of old lumber stacked helter-skelter against an open lean-to shed . . . that was all, that and the looming darkness.

I let my eyes drift up and over the roof lines of the buildings, along the darkened doorways, into blotches of shadows. Nothing. I moved forward a few feet and then stopped and waited for the moon to break from behind clouds, waiting so that I could take a closer look around me. Then I heard it: a small sound that on any other night I'd have dismissed as nothing more than a rat in the woodpile.

But on this night, with my senses sharply focused, I knew it was no rodent. Something had carelessly shifted one of the boards. I stood turning my head back and forth trying to pick up more sounds in air. Nothing. I could hear a woman laughing in a nearby room, but nothing else.

The longer I stood there staring at that pile of wood, the more the jumbled pieces began to make some kind of sense. My heart was thumping hard against my chest. There was a large flat plank lying roof-like on top. And I thought I could make out a small dark tunnel of a hole in one end. My skin crawled. What was hiding down in there?

I reached slowly for the plank and then stopped. Was the person or thing that had killed these men crouched underneath? Perhaps waiting for me? I unbuttoned my shirt and pulled the belly gun, then gripped the board and yanked it fast.

I guess I should have known all along what I'd find. Hannah

Morgan was a woman full of surprises in some ways . . . and predictable as tomorrow in others. This was one of those predictable others.

The little girl was curled up asleep, a bottle of water and a loaf of bread beside her and a filthy looking blanket under her. She was maybe eight and, from the look of her, she'd been beaten up some. Her nose was crusty with blood, her eye blacked, a lip puffed and liver-coloured. She was sleeping the sleep of a kid too scared to sleep until she'd finally collapsed in exhaustion. Now the clap of damnation wasn't going to faze her.

I pushed my hat back and shook my head. Hannah Morgan could surely ferret out these lost brats. I put a hand on the child's shoulder.

'Hey. Time to get up.'

I thought that maybe the kid would let out a scream or try and run for it. She didn't. She just opened her eyes and looked at me and then smiled, until her badly puffed lip caused her to grimace. Then she raised her arms as if she'd been waiting for me all along. I picked her up. She was thin and shivering and dirty.

'What's your name?'

'Olive,' she said in a small, unsteady voice.

'Mine's Tucker Gibbens. Where do you live, Olive?'

She shook her head hard. 'I don't want to go there –' She stopped suddenly as if frightened. She was clutching hard at my neck.

'OK. You don't have to.'

I was starting to say something else when the little girl tensed in my arms and whispered, 'Mister. There's somebody in the shadows there.'

I turned and lowered her to the ground and pulled the belly

gun. Olive was right, there was a shadowy shape standing a few yards down the darkened alley, watching us. I nudged the little girl toward the building, then cocked the pistol. Seconds later, Lucia stepped out of the darkness. She didn't look particularly angry this time, more like she was impatient with me. As if I'd failed to do something that was important.

'What are you doing here?' I said, trying to recover from my start. Then I realized I'd used English and was starting to translate when she spoke.

'Looking for you.'

'For me?'

'Yes. Miss Hannah told me to find you.'

'The woman told you to find me?'

'We go with you,' she said, matter-of-factly.

I slipped the little gun into the holster inside my shirt and held up both my hands, palms out, chest-level. 'No you don't. You're to go back to the house where you are staying.'

'She's in jail.'

'I know.'

'You are to get her out.' Lucia said matter-of-factly, again as if I were dilatory in my behaviour.

She stepped forward and picked Olive up, throwing out her hip and expertly setting the child on it, then started checking the little girl in a thorough and caring way. Her movements told me she was used to taking care of kids, liked them.

'Nothing hurt?' she asked, poking a finger into the little girl's belly, a rare smile on her face.

Olive grinned and shook her head and in that one second of time, I could see that she was for ever Lucia's. She couldn't stop looking at the older girl who held her so nonchalantly on her hip, like a mother or a sister. Probably like one she'd never had.

'Good.' Lucia turned back to me, her expression once again solemn and distrustful. 'You are to get her out,' she repeated, as if I'd been sitting around drinking tea and eating cake all night.

'I'm working on it. Now you take Olive back to the others.'

'No. We go with you,' she repeated firmly.

As I was getting ready to tell her that she was flat wrong about that notion, Junior and James came leading the mule and Milagros out of the darkness. Jack was trotting along, happy to be a part of this late-night excursion.

'Howdy, Mr Gibbens,' Junior said. James looked dizzy from fatigue, his eyelids drooping sleepily; but he managed a small grin when he saw me.

'Boys,' I said. Then I glowered at Jack. He'd left Martha to watch over the horses while he went off and played. That was typical Jack. 'You get your fanny back to the horses.' He lowered his head as if he was sorry . . . but not sorry enough to obey. 'Jack!' He turned and started down the alley on the trot. I walked over and looked in the coffin.

The children had wrapped Milagros in a warm blanket and she was breathing fine, moonlight spilling over her face and making her look like a picture. It was amazing she'd lasted this long – maybe it was all the excitement of these kids dragging her around as if she were up and about like them, caring and fussing over her, talking and laughing, maybe that was what kept her going.

Lucia, Olive riding her hip, checked Milagros as well, as if I couldn't be trusted to do a job right or maybe might mess up the blanket. Satisfied, she turned to face me again, looking more determined and dissatisfied than ever.

'We go with you,' she started in again. 'Miss Hannah say so.'

'You don't go with me. I don't care what Miss Hannah says. You go back to the home you were staying at, you go to bed, you get up in the morning, you wait. But you don't go with me. Understand?' None of them said anything. 'Milagros needs to be out of the chill – before she catches pneumonia.' I could see that this bothered Lucia and figured it was time to act.

Calculating the best way to get them to obey was to show them I wasn't kidding. I marched off without them. It worked. The next time I looked back, they were walking in the opposite direction. I buttoned my belly gun away under my shirt and started for the jail.

Then I heard Olive's little voice in the darkness and turned back. She was looking at me over Lucia's shoulder. 'Mister Tucker. I can't go home.'

'Don't worry,' I said, not certain what I meant.

She smiled through the darkness at me.

I arrived as Hannah was completing a big meal, empty plates spread around the jail cell. I was holding a small clutch of little yellow flowers behind my back. I'd only given flowers to one other woman in my life, but I'd seen these at the side of the jail and thought they might cheer her.

It was close to midnight and she was sitting on her cot with a last tray of dishes balanced across her lap, finishing off the food. I couldn't help but laugh inside, the mysterious happiness overtaking me again. Nothing, but nothing, seemed able to cut this woman's enormous appetite.

When she saw me, recognition warmed her eyes and she touched the corners of her mouth with a napkin and then smiled up at me. She looked as if she might be sitting on a country porch somewhere at evening time rather than in a jailhouse waiting out the hours until her execution. I let my eyes move slowly over her face, a feeling of awe spreading through me. The Holy Mother.

'Mr Gibbens,' she said quietly, her features softening into a broader smile. 'How are the children?'

I took a deep breath and held it: even on the eve of her death, she was fussing about these kids. 'They're fine,' I said.

'Milagros?'

'Fine.'

She just sat there on the cot gazing up at me as if I'd done something grand. I knew the sheriff was behind me, watching all this and it made me uncomfortable. I cleared my throat. 'You OK, ma'am?'

She nodded. 'I'm sorry I left you out there on the desert again, but when I woke up you were still asleep – and you looked like you needed it.'

I thought I could detect the same old teasing beneath the surface. But I wasn't certain.

'And there was someplace I had to be,' she went on.

Her eyes lost focus for a moment as her thoughts seemed to drift away from me, off somewhere distant, off to a place that I sensed I'd never ever know. There was something final sounding to the words that had bothered me. 'Where was that, ma'am?'

My voice brought her back and she glanced at me, either forgetting or refusing to talk about this thing she'd been so determined to do.

'I'm sorry I left you,' was all she said, vaguely.

'That's OK,' I mumbled. I couldn't take my eyes off her – this woman that my wife had prayed to until her death. I didn't understand how she had gotten to this desolate place or why she'd come . . . all I knew was that she was here . . . and she was the Blessed Virgin. I was as certain of that fact as anything in my life.

The sheriff and his deputy had both searched me and missed my belly gun. I wondered if that had been divine intervention. I turned to them. 'I want to talk with her alone.'

Adams looked at my face for a moment and then crooked a finger at me. When I was close to him, he whispered, 'Deputy sheriff of Los Angeles or not, you try anything slick . . . I'll have you shot.'

Hannah Morgan was humming softly.

I nodded.

The sheriff tipped his head respectfully at Hannah. 'Mrs Morgan.'

'Mr Adams.'

Hannah had set the tray down on the floor and was sitting with her long tapering hands folded in her lap, staring out through the bars with those eyes that seemed to reach inside me somehow, a pleasant half-smile on her full lips, as handsome as ever. Nothing seemed able to dull her radiant features, not even the portent of a violent end just hours away.

Then slowly her features began to change and I could see concern for the first time on her face. 'Mr Gibbens,' she said softly, but with that touch of urgency I often felt in her voice. 'There's something you must do.' She examined my face. 'In that alley –'

'I already did, ma'am,' I interrupted.

'Sir?'

'I found her.'

'Who?'

'The child – Olive.'

She stopped and pressed her lips together as if stopping up something inside before it could spill out of her. 'Is that her name?'

'You didn't know?'

170

'No.' She paused, then looked at me with a quizzical expression. 'How did you know where she was?'

I grinned. 'I'm getting on to your game.' I was feeling good. 'I told you I would, sooner or later.'

Hannah Morgan sat and looked at me for a long time and I thought she might laugh or cry, but she didn't do either, she just bit at her lower lip.

'Olive?'

'Yes.'

'What a beautiful sound,' she said, staring quietly at the floor of her cell as if trying to see the child's face on it.

I wondered if she were listening to the voices again. 'She doesn't want to go home,' I said.

Hannah looked up. 'Do not take her home,' the words sounding like an order, their chill taking a moment to work on me.

I hesitated, not certain what to say to this woman, then cleared my throat. 'Ma'am, with all due respect, it's one thing to pick up kids who don't have anybody, but you can't just walk off with somebody else's child. There are laws against that.'

'Laws?'

It didn't sound like a question, so I didn't say anything, just waited. When she didn't continue, I said, 'Maybe you don't like them. But they exist.'

Hannah squinted at me as if trying to bring my face into focus. 'Olive will not go back,' she said. A hollow sound in her voice caused the hairs to rise in slow waves over the back of my neck. 'Promise that,' she continued.

'Me? Promise?' I was scrambling in my head for a way out of this. 'Ma'am, I'm a lawman, not a judge. Judges decide.'

Hannah just stared at me as if she thought that was the silliest thing she'd ever heard. After I'd squirmed for a while, I said, 'No, ma'am. I can't promise. I'm sorry.'

She still didn't say anything, just continued to look at my face. She didn't appear angry or upset, she just looked at me until I suddenly felt I had to do something to get her to stop. 'Let me think about it,' I said. 'I'm not promising anything.'

She didn't respond.

'I'll just see what can be done. If that's not good enough, then you'll have to figure something else.'

Hannah Morgan picked up her knitting from the cot. The large black blob of knitted yarn had grown significantly larger since I'd last seen it.

'Ma'am, did you hear?' I wanted to make absolutely certain that we had an understanding – that she knew I wasn't assuming responsibility for Olive or any other member of her merry little band. All I'd agreed to was to check into the child's situation. 'Understand, ma'am?'

'Yes, Mr Gibbens. If you say it will be done, I believe you.'

I didn't like the sound of that – not at all. 'Ma'am. I only said I'd check.'

'That's fine.'

I still didn't care for the way she said that – so matter-of-fact and confident sounding – but I was more worried about her immediate situation than arguing whether or not a kid went home. I rubbed two days' worth of stubble on my chin and wondered why she'd come back to earth. Just to die? Could people in a nothing town like this really kill her? Then I remembered her Son and knew. Perhaps there was some great reason for her death. But if there was it escaped me completely. Or perhaps there wasn't any reason – perhaps that's why I'd been brought to this place. To stop it. I shivered at the possibility.

Suddenly the door to the office opened a few inches and Jack came scooting through on a dead run, dodging Adams and the deputy, hopping through the bars and up on to her lap, licking her madly. Again, her mood took one of its swings. She had her eyes and lips pressed tight and was making a laughing noise as she had three nights before when Jack had licked her.

The door opened wider. 'We tried to stop him,' Adams apologized.

'He's an old friend, Sheriff,' Hannah said, running her hand over Jack's back. After Jack settled down some, she wiped her face with her napkin.

'We're working on those apples,' Adams said, keeping his eyes on Hannah Morgan for a moment as if he wanted to say something more to her. But he didn't.

'Thank you,' she said, looking past me at the man like he was an old friend rather than her executioner. The door closed. She returned to looking at me. 'You were going back to El Paso, Mr Gibbens.'

'Yes.'

'Why didn't you?'

I cleared my throat. 'Because of you.'

She nodded as if she had expected that response. 'I'm sorry but I can't tell you anything more than I have about what happened to you there. I honestly can't.'

'That's not why I came.'

'Then why?'

'To be with you.' I felt funny saying those words. Yet in some way, I felt strangely intimate with her, as if we were old friends.

'That's wonderfully kind of you, Mr Gibbens.' She waited a moment and then said quietly, 'It is comforting to have you here.' She leaned down and kissed the top of Jack's head. 'Both of you.' The little dog squirmed with pleasure.

'Are you injured?'

'Sir?'

'Those men,' I said, averting my eyes. I'd dealt with rape

and assaults against women my entire working life. But with this woman it was different and made me uncomfortable.

'No. I'm fine.' She paused. 'They – ' She stopped as if she didn't want to say anything more . . . couldn't bring herself to. She looked down at her hands as if they belonged to someone else, then raised her face to me. 'The sheriff and the others – '

'No,' I said, my voice low, my eyes fixed on hers.

She seemed to press back into the shadows of the cell.

'You didn't kill anyone,' I repeated, trying to see more of her face in the murky light.

She didn't say anything.

'But somebody did. What happened?'

'I'm not certain.' She sat staring down at her hands again. 'No more than I know what happened to you in El Paso.' She looked into my face as if I might be able to help her plug the empty holes in her memory.

'Nothing?' I could see where she had pinned the top of her dress closed. 'Do you remember them grabbing you in the alley?'

'No.' She looked down at the floor. 'I sometimes lose consciousness, Mr Gibbens. I don't know why.'

It was my turn to study the floor between my feet, recalling the lightning storm, the Indians – the night she'd put her hands on the sick girl's head. She'd fallen into trances each time. It was no act. Perhaps when she got worked up enough over something her brain just shut down.

Opossums dropped over if they were badly worked up. People said that they were just pretending. I didn't believe it. My guess was they went into some sort of a stupor when they got excited enough – a protective sort of thing that nature had provided them. Maybe it was something like that for Hannah Morgan – something perhaps that had been provided for her. Maybe.

174

I nodded. 'I've seen you do that.' I continued looking into the soft eyes that were watching my face as if she were worried about me. 'Are you escorted by someone – someone who might have done this to protect you?'

'Escorted?'

'Yes.'

'No.'

'Those men at the camp – one of them told me they ran because they'd seen men near our camp.' I studied her face closely. If she knew anything, she didn't let on. 'But there weren't any men there. Weren't any footprints. Nothing.' I watched her face for some sign that she knew. I didn't see it. 'You don't know anything about that?'

'No, sir.'

I believed her. Of one thing I was certain: she was no liar. 'Have you ever been accused of something like this before?'

'I've been accused of many things, Mr Gibbens, but never anything like this.'

Suddenly I realized that I was still clutching the flowers behind my back and I awkwardly pushed them in through the bars to her. She didn't move for a moment, then slowly she raised a hand and put it over her mouth, smothering a smile that looked like it hurt, and blinking her eyes hard a couple of times.

'They're so beautiful, Mr Gibbens,' she said, taking them and brushing them softly against her skin, as if nuzzling a child. 'Do you know what they're called?'

'St Johnswort.'

She nodded. 'Yes, because they bloom on John's festival day.'

'I didn't know that,' I mumbled.

She nodded again, pressing her lips together hard. Then she closed her eyes and took a deep smell of the flowers as if they were an elixir for all her troubles. When she finally opened them again, she seemed her old self once more, smiling happily, as if the scent of the blossoms had truly helped.

'These tiny dots on the leaves.'

I took a closer look.

'They're scars, Mr Gibbens. Scars from when the devil pricked this little plant with a needle almost two thousand years ago. He tried to frighten it into submission because it had been named after the great saint.'

I nodded, only half-listening, not interested in the plant, watching her lovely face. I could see her drifting off, her mind bent on some distant thought, her eyes slightly unfocused. Was she remembering the evangelist dressed in animal skins, the ranting redeemer raging to save men's souls, the son of her cousin, Elizabeth, baptizer of her own son? Was she seeing him again in her thoughts wandering in the desert wilderness, wading the waters of the Jordan? It seemed not impossible to believe. Then she shut her eyes for a moment. When she reopened them, she was fully back with me.

'Yes, Mr Gibbens. The devil tried to frighten this beautiful little plant into forsaking its holy name. But it resisted, unwilling to yield, falling on the protection of its creator. In the end, the devil could not shake its faith. And for ever after he has feared the courageous will of this tiny plant.' She studied my face. 'The legend, Mr Gibbens, says that little St Johnswort protects man against Satan's cruelty.' She paused, squinting at my face as if trying to read something in it. 'Do you believe in legends, sir?'

I hesitated. Did she know that I knew? 'Some,' I said.

'Yes. So do I.' Her words seemed to drift slowly away, drift across the cell and out through the small window into the starry night, drift as if they would never stop drifting until they reached her God.

My hands were gripping the bars, and I was unconsciously

squeezing them until my knuckles turned milk-white. Jack was staring across the cell as if listening to something nobody else could hear. Hannah reached out and laid a hand on mine, my head swimming with emotions.

'Everything will be fine, Mr Gibbens.'

'Everything won't be fine.' I paused, not wanting to say the words but this wasn't the time to hesitate. If destiny had brought me here, brought me here to save this woman – then I would play my part boldly, no matter what.

'They plan to execute you in the morning.'

'Your shirt looks nice,' she smiled, as if she hadn't heard me. Then, as if the shirt had reminded her, she said, 'Mr Gibbens. I have some money. The sheriff is keeping it.' She stopped talking for a time, then took a deep breath and continued, 'Please use it to buy a new dress for Lucia. Milagros has an extra one. But Lucia has none. And the boys need shirts and pants. Make sure they are warm – wool or heavy flannel. All the children must be warm. You'll have to see about Olive's clothes.' She suddenly stopped talking and stared hard into my face.

I waited for her to say something. When she didn't, I said, 'Ma'am? Did you hear me?'

She continued to ignore the question. As if it really didn't matter, wasn't important. The children were something else.

'What does she look like?'

'Who?'

'Olive.'

I pushed my hat back on my head and pursed my lips and tried to conjure up the child's face in my mind. 'She's got curly hair, blue eyes, and she stands about this high,' I said, holding my hand hip-high. I was smiling despite my worries over what was going to happen here. 'She and Lucia act like sisters.'

Hannah was crying silently now, crying with a kind of joy, tears streaming freely down her cheeks. I was amazed how much she laughed and cried, the two emotions seemingly inextricably woven in her. She didn't bother to wipe the tears away. 'They are sisters,' she said, sniffing softly, saying the words as if there was no question about it, her eyes gazing off across the shadows of the cell.

I didn't venture a comment. If she said these two kids were sisters, they were sisters. It didn't matter. What mattered was what was going to happen to her. And what I had to do about it.

Then, suddenly, Hannah Morgan was back to business again. She might believe in things of the spirit, but she was as hard-headed practical as any person I'd ever met. 'They will all need jackets. Remember to get good heavy ones – with collars that can be raised and buttoned up.'

I wondered why she was so worried about getting jackets that were so warm when we were riding around in a desert. There was no question that the nights got chilly, but she seemed eager to outfit these kids for a trip to the North Pole. I pushed the thoughts away and repeated, 'They're going to execute you.'

'Yes,' she finally said.

'You've got to do something.'

'Mr Gibbens?'

'You know.'

She looked at me with a puzzled expression for a moment, then said, 'No. I'm afraid I don't.'

'There are things you can do at a time like this.'

'Sir?'

'Pray for help,' I suggested, as if leading a child to the right answer.

Recognition altered her expression. 'Oh I have, sir,' she said, taking a second deep smell of the little bouquet. She placed the flowers on the cot beside her, then adjusted her little glasses and pulled her knitting over her lap and began to work her needles rapidly.

'And?'

'Sir?'

'Will help be sent to you?'

She looked uncertain how to answer. 'Yes,' she ventured. 'I prayed and God will certainly send me all the help I need.' She spread the black mass of knitted material out over the floor. It was large as a blanket.

I relaxed and let my breath slowly out, watching her knitting away, relieved that her God was going to save her.

'How will He do it?'

'Mr Gibbens?'

'How's He going to save you? Take you out of the cell – knock the wall down? Or what?'

She studied my face for a time with one of her disappointed looks, as if all her prayers over me had been wasted.

'He will give me the strength to see this through, Mr Gibbens.'

'And somebody to save you,' I added quickly.

'Sir?'

'You prayed to be rescued?'

'No. I prayed for God's love.'

'Your voices – you told them you needed help?'

'It doesn't work that way.'

'How does it work?'

'The voices tell me things. When God wishes something done.'

'Yes. But they'll send somebody to save you – now that you need help? That's only fair.'

I didn't like the way she was looking at me, as if I might be beyond salvation. That was enough for me. If she was going to stubbornly refuse to do this her way, then I'd do it my way. I looked worriedly over the heavily barred windows and the rest of the room: no back door, no side door, only one way in and out . . . and Adams and his deputy were guarding that. As my eyes moved around the cell, I wondered again about this God who would use this woman to save others but who would abandon her in her time of trouble. I thought again of my own prayers for my wife and baby – prayers that went unheeded. It made no sense and seemed so unfair. I fought the anger welling in my chest and looked again at the cell.

The walls were adobe, some three feet thick, and I was willing to wager the mud had been plastered over heavy logs bolted together with straps of iron. It would take a week to dig through. The bars were an inch and a half thick, the window sills sunk down into the walls. This was a tight little cage. I put a hand up and absently touched the belly gun through my shirt.

'No, Mr Gibbens.'

'Ma'am?'

'You are not going to use whatever that is under your shirt.'

I studied her face closely for a long time before I spoke again. 'Ma'am, let me make this clear. If you aren't going to be rescued – ' I waited a few moments, then continued, 'then something else has to be done.'

'No, Mr Gibbens. Nothing has to be done. God will provide.'

'That's all I'm talking about: Him providing for you.'

'I have already told you. It doesn't work that way, Mr Gibbens.'

'How's it work then? He sends you out to rescue everybody under the damn sun – but when you need help, He doesn't send it? They're going to kill you tomorrow.' The words scratched out of my throat. 'Kill you for something you didn't do. I won't – '

'You won't get involved, Mr Gibbens,' she interrupted. 'That's what you won't do.' She smiled a smile that almost wasn't a smile: her mouth didn't open to show her teeth, her eyes didn't squint, but still she had smiled and was peering over her glasses into my face, and it made me feel wonderful.

'I have to.'

'No. You do not. Will not.'

I didn't respond.

'Mr Gibbens? Did you hear me?'

I wanted to go on sitting there with her hand on mine for the rest of my life. I hadn't felt that way since that last night when I had held my wife's hand and watched her slip away into the dark mystery. 'I can't let them –'

'Yes, you can. And, yes, you will,' she said more forcefully this time. 'You will do nothing to stop this. Do you understand?' She waited a moment, then continued. 'I am not your concern.'

I shook my head slowly, studying her eyes, noticing again how tired they seemed, almost as if she were sick with fatigue. Those eyes bothered me more than ever now. I sensed in them a resignation that I could understand but didn't like to think about where this woman was concerned.

When I finally was able to talk, I didn't want to. I just wanted to go on sitting with her hand on mine, staring into that gentle face, not saying anything. Life seemed bearable that way. But I had to say it. When I finally spoke, my voice was low. 'You don't have to pretend with me.'

'Mr Gibbens?'

'I know who you are.' I watched her, waiting for some acknowledgement that she understood what I was talking about, but didn't see it. She simply raised her eyebrows in a questioning way.

'Who am I, Mr Gibbens?'

I took a deep breath. 'The Holy Mother.'

Frown lines formed between her eyebrows and I could tell she was waiting for me to go on. When I didn't, she said, 'Mr Gibbens?'

'You know who,' I mumbled as if I were being toyed with.

'No. I'm afraid you have me at a disadvantage.'

I looked down between my boots and then raised my head again and looked into her eyes. I was sweating hard. 'Mary.'

'Mary?' she asked, seemingly more puzzled than before.

'Yes. Joseph's wife.' I continued to study her face. Still there was nothing in her expression that said she understood. 'You're making a mess of this,' I told myself.

'The Virgin,' I began again.

Hannah cocked her head to one side as if confused and then smiled a funny smile at me. 'You think I am the Virgin Mary?' she asked, as if finally understanding.

I nodded.

Hannah Morgan didn't speak for a time, she just sat smiling that same funny non-smile at me, as if expecting me to admit that I was only teasing. Then she quit smiling, but her face retained its quizzical expression. Finally, she patted my hand. 'That's wonderfully kind of you, Mr Gibbens.' Then she frowned and laughed and asked, 'Do I look that old?'

I ignored her. 'The Mother of Jesus Christ.'

'Mr Gibbens. I'm afraid you think that I saved you in El Paso. I didn't. Nor did I cause lightning to flash in the sky that night when the Indians came to our camp.' She smiled again, the familiar teasing look forming on her face. 'I'm not too great a disappointment to you, I hope.'

I was shaking my head slowly back and forth. 'I know who you are,' I repeated. 'I don't know much religion, ma'am, but I know the Virgin was just a woman,' I said, not willing to drop this, my eyes searching her face, hunting for something that would give me the answer I already believed . . . and wanted acknowledged. I didn't see it.

'You brought me here, didn't you?'

'Mr Gibbens,' she said, as if such talk was silly.

'You did. You brought me here.'

'You have a wonderful imagination, sir.'

I didn't say anything, just looked down at the floor.

'Mr Gibbens.'

I looked up at her, searching her features again for the answer.

'Don't.'

'Don't what?'

'Seek your dreams through me,' she said.

'El Paso was a miracle.'

'We are surrounded by miracles.'

I ignored the remark. 'You're the Mother of all who live and all who die.'

Hannah Morgan looked increasingly weary. 'All mothers are that, Mr Gibbens. It's our blessing and our curse, sir.' She stared at me through the bars for a while, then she patted my hand.

'You must do something to save yourself,' the sound of desperation underscoring each word.

'Do you think this is another Jericho, Mr Gibbens? Do you have a trumpet? Will you cause the walls of this cell to crumble?' Through the sadness there was a touch of mirth at the edges of her eyes.

When I didn't answer, she asked again, 'What would you have me do?'

'Rescue yourself. Call on God to rescue you.'

'Though it may surprise you, Mr Gibbens, I can't.' She looked stern. 'Even if I could, I wouldn't. Nor will you, sir.'

I was shaking my head back and forth now in defiance. The

woman watched me for a moment as if deciding something, then looked down at her hands.

'Let me tell you a story, Mr Gibbens.' She paused. 'May I?'

I didn't respond.

'There once was a young woman, Roman by birth, Christian by belief, the mother of three children. The year was 203 after the death of our Saviour.'

My eyes darted to her face. But she gave nothing away with her expression. She was concentrating on her story, seeming to reach back in her thoughts for it.

'This woman had just given birth to her third child, a baby girl – her life and the life of her family stretching before her like a lovely stream. But it was not to be. Her name was found by Roman officials on the rolls of a secret Christian sect in Southern Italy.

'There was a trial of sorts and she was condemned to die as a Christian martyr because, when asked, she would not give a pagan sacrifice to the long life of the emperor . . . though she was begged by her husband and father to save herself, to make the simple sacrifice.' Hannah looked into my eyes. 'Nor would she call on her Lord to save her.'

'On the day of her execution, the Roman crowds took pity on her and begged her to call her god or to forsake him, holding her husband and children up on the wall of the arena so that she could see them and come to her senses. Human compassion was there, Mr Gibbens, even in that mad crowd.' Hannah stopped talking and lowered her head and took two sharp hard breaths.'

'Ma'am?'

She looked up at me, but I wasn't certain she saw me, tears flowing down her cheeks.

'Are you OK?'

She didn't answer, just continued to sob silently for this young woman who'd lived so long ago. 'What happened?'

'You already know, Mr Gibbens.'

'No I don't,' I snapped, not certain why I was angry.

Hannah Morgan looked up into my eyes and I thought for a moment that she might call me a liar. But she didn't. She just looked back down at the floor of her cell and sat thinking for a while. Finally, she said, 'She did not forsake her god or beg him to save her – didn't give the sacrifice, Mr Gibbens . . . and she was condemned by the Roman procurator and thrown into the arena with wild beasts that had been starved for days.'

Hannah was trembling now and my anger was gone. I wanted to reach out and hold her, but couldn't because of the bars. She moaned slightly and I knew she was drifting away from me again, drifting back in time to witness that woman's suffering, her body shuddering as I imagined her hearing the woman's children and husband crying out to her.

'Ma'am?'

'The animals tore at her for over an hour,' she said quietly, her voice hollow and distant. 'Dragging her around the arena. But they did not kill her. And the people marvelled. Nor did she cry out in pain or fear. A crazed bull was put into the ring with her and she was trampled and gored, but still she clung to life and would not call on the Lord to save her.' Hannah took a deep breath that seemed to hurt, as if her own lungs had been punctured, her eyes gazing at the shadows across the cell. 'In the end, a gladiator was brought in and she guided the blade of his knife to her throat, as if she realized that nothing could kill her unless she willed it.'

'What did it gain her?' I mumbled. 'What?'

'God's love, Mr Gibbens.'

'But cost her life.'

I could barely hear her when she next spoke. 'Gave her life.'

She was staring down blindly at the floor as if seeing the young woman's horrible end in her thoughts . . . her own end in sight as well. I waited, then asked, 'Did you know her?'

Hannah looked quickly up at me as if she didn't know where she was or who I might be. And for a fleeting moment, I was certain in my heart that Hannah Morgan had been in that arena that day with that woman. Perhaps she had even been that woman. Could that possibly be? I had no answers. Not for any of it.

'Did you know her?' I asked again.

'Who?' she said, still sounding as if she were dreaming.

'The Roman woman.'

She seemed to come back to me and sat up straighter on the cot.

I waited for her answer. She didn't give it.

She picked up the flowers and rose from the cot, held Jack in her arms and walked over and stood beneath the small barred window of the cell, leaning against the wall and tipping her head back to look up at the stars. 'It is a beautiful night. Is there a moon? I so love moonlight –' She caught herself as if she were afraid to let her emotions begin to control her.

'I know who you are,' I repeated once more.

'Mr Gibbens?'

'I know who you are.'

She was fully back with me now, her eyes sharply focused on the present. 'Most of the time we aren't even certain who we are ourselves, or where we're going in this life . . . let alone knowing who others might be.' She turned and looked at me with compassion. 'You had a frightening experience in El Paso. I understand your confusion. But I was being honest, I don't know what happened to you. You must believe me. It is true

186

that the voices sent me to find you, but you must not attribute great and miraculous things to me. I am not a goddess – I am simply a woman who does what God asks. Attribute wondrous things to the Lord – not to me. Do you understand?' She was looking out the window again.

'You're not just a woman,' I said shaking my head. 'The world is at your feet.'

'The world is not at my feet, Mr Gibbens. You can plainly see that. I am to be put to death.'

I was shaking my head hard. 'My wife prayed to you.' I tried to recall the words. 'Hail Mary full of grace,' I mumbled, 'the Lord is with thee. Blessed art thou among women.' I continued staring at the back of her head. 'Surely you understand? The Lord is with you. Call to Him. Call to your voices.'

She turned toward me and for a moment, in a flicker of light that seemed to escape her eyes, I saw it, saw the recognition . . . then it was gone and I wasn't certain.

'I'm tired, Mr Gibbens. I want to prepare myself.' I noticed the weary sound in her voice as if she were carrying some awful burden that she desperately wanted to lay down. But I couldn't let go of it.

'When I was shot, I cried out for the Mother of God to save me. I should have been dead. But instead I woke up in a room alive . . . with you.'

'If you were saved, Mr Gibbens, it was done by God . . . not by me.' She sounded impatient. 'I will not, on the night before my death, take credit for the Lord's work.'

This fresh mention of her pending death spurred me on. I grabbed at the prospector's letter in my shirt pocket and read it to her . . . repeating the words: 'I prayed to the Virgin but she has not come.' I stopped and looked up anxiously at her. 'But you did come – didn't you? You were riding north, and then suddenly you took a turn to the south and began a race to this man. You saved his children.'

'I have already spoken about that, Mr Gibbens. I had been told about them by my voices.' She seemed to withdraw somewhere inside herself, then her lips were moving and she said softly, 'The children.' She paused. 'Sometimes I see them in my thoughts. I don't know why. I just do. But that doesn't make me a goddess.' She looked at me. 'I found the man and buried him. Nothing more, Mr Gibbens.' She waited a few moments. 'According to you, I should have saved him – raised him from the dead.'

I didn't say anything, just sat watching her face.

She put Jack down and went and sat on the bed again and stared down at her hands as if recalling all the things that they had held over her lifetime. Jack was sitting at her feet looking up at her in a rapturous way.

'Mr Gibbens, tomorrow I will leave this earth. I need time to prepare myself. You may stay if you wish, but I would rather not talk any more. I hope you understand,' she said, reaching and touching my hand once again.

The sensation was as wonderful as before. I felt suddenly ashamed. 'I'm sorry. I'll leave you alone.' I stood and looked down at her lovely features in the dim light of the hall lantern. 'I just wanted you to know that I knew. That tomorrow I will be there . . . and I will know. I don't care what you say, or what name you call yourself, I know who you are.' I stood without saying anything for a long time, then I cleared my throat and said, 'Ma'am, I'm going to free you.'

'No. You will not. You will leave here and go on with your life.' She waited for me to respond. When I didn't she said, 'Mr Gibbens. Did you hear me?'

'Yes. But I can't let you die. Knowing who you are.'

She let out a deep sigh as if she was tired of arguing the point with me, her shoulders seeming to sag. 'You know nothing, sir. That's all we both know: that we know nothing. Maybe that's all we're supposed to know.' She paused. 'Good night.'

I forced myself to walk away from the cell, stopping and looking back at her from the doorway. She had gone to the window again and was staring up into the night sky, a black velvet sprayed with specks of gold. Jack stood beside her.

Watching her there in the shadows of the cell, her hair uncombed, sweat dampening her dress even though the room was cool, her features straining under the tension of what she faced, I realized that nothing – nothing at all – could marr her austere beauty. I took a deep breath and let it out. She turned and stared at me across the room.

'Pray for me, Mr Gibbens.'

'I'll pray to you,' I said.

'No,' she said firmly. 'Do not, sir. Pray to God. And pray for me.' She turned back to the window.

When I didn't say anything, she continued, 'Do you understand?'

I didn't answer her. Instead, I mumbled, 'Thank you.'

'I did nothing for you, Mr Gibbens.' Her voice was tired sounding.

'Not for me.'

'Who then?'

'My wife. She died slowly. Over time.' I stopped and looked off into the shadows and swallowed hard. 'In pain. But because of you, she died in peace.'

She stared at me for a while and I thought for a fleeting moment that she was about to acknowledge who she was, her true self . . . but then she looked away to the window once more. 'Leave me, please, Mr Gibbens.'

'Where are they?'

'Who?'

'My wife and baby?'

Hannah Morgan turned and looked at me and an expression of compassion formed on her face. 'Mr Gibbens. I'm sorry. I wish I could tell you all that you want to know. But I can't. I honestly don't know the answers.'

I watched her for a moment longer, then said, 'Jack.' The little dog didn't budge. 'Jack,' I snapped in frustration. Still, the little terrier stood his ground, unwilling to leave the woman's side.

Hannah reached down and patted his head. 'Go on, Jack,' she said. The dog whined in protest. 'No. You go on with Mr Gibbens.' As if he understood, Jack turned and trotted out of the cell. At the door leading out of the room, I stopped and looked back at her one more time. She was staring out the window at the night sky again.

I started to say something but before I could speak, she said, 'Good night, Mr Gibbens.'

I felt as heartsick and lost as I had the night my wife died. The sheriff and the deputy didn't say anything as I walked past, they just kept looking at the door to the cells as if they thought Hannah Morgan might appear any moment. They were as bothered by this thing as I was. Finally Adams called my name and sat down in his swivel chair and picked up a piece of paper from his desk, then leaned back with a creaking sound.

'Got a telegram from your sheriff. It says: "Get home. Blue Marlin jumping. Bonita running."' Adams studied my face. 'Sounds like a decent proposition.' His deputy nodded in agreement.

'Yeah,' I said, continuing for the door.

'Gibbens,' Adams continued. 'I'm sorry about her.'

I stopped and looked back at him.

'Why don't you? Go home and go fishing.'

'She didn't do it,' I said.

'I don't know that. But there's nothing I can do about it.'

I turned and started for the door. Adams and his deputy were good men, just doing their jobs. I'd been in their position too many times to think any differently. In fact, I didn't want to think at all. On this night I didn't want to think about anything. I just wanted to forget. Forget the woman in the cell, forget what was going to happen to her at dawn, forget that I was walking away and not doing anything. I shoved the door open and stepped outside into a dark street splashed with pools of flickering yellow lamplight, then stopped and stared.

I couldn't believe it. They were just sitting there on their horses, dressed and ready to go, like we were a team or something: all five of the children. Olive looked fresh and clean like she'd been given a quick bath, her hair brushed. I looked hard at Lucia's face to let her know I wasn't happy about this. It was the second time in two days that she'd ignored what I'd told her to do. I frowned harder.

If I thought that extra intensity of my frown would cause her to feel guilty and shuffle her feet, I'd thought wrong. She might be young, but she had a strong sense of herself and a stronger backbone. She returned my frown with a pretty good one of her own. Olive was sitting behind her saddle, watching me. It was obvious the little girl had thrown in with Lucia. Junior and James were up on their grey pony – looking a little worried about my mood. I figured these two at least were used to obeying their father. Lucia and Olive had been on their own too long.

'Well?' Lucia asked, as if I'd been on some sort of a personal errand for her.

'Well what?'

'Where is Miss Hannah?'

'You know where.'

'You were going to get her out,' she continued, her tone accusing. 'You said that.'

'No I didn't say that, young lady. I said I was looking into things. And anyway, I told you to go back to the Johnsons' and stay put – so get.'

She shook her head. 'We stay with you.'

'No you don't.' I walked over and checked Milagros in the coffin. Satisfied she was fine, I turned on my heel and walked back into the sheriff's office. Adams raised his eyebrows at me.

'Gibbens?'

'There are five orphans out front in the street. You need to do something with them.'

Adams looked confused and pulled at the hair on his cheek. 'Mrs Morgan said you'd take care of them.'

'Me? Why the hell would I be taking care of five kids that aren't mine?' I told myself again that I had made it perfectly clear to Hannah that I wasn't mothering this pack of brats.

Adams shrugged as if I might have a decent point. I walked across the office and pulled the door open and looked into the cell at Hannah Morgan. She was still standing and holding the flowers, staring out the little window at the night. She turned towards me.

'Mr Gibbens? Are the children all right?'

Damn, she couldn't go five seconds without worrying about them. Hell, she ought to be worried about herself and me, we were the ones who were going to die soon. I watched her face for a moment, struggling with these thoughts, then cleared my throat and said, 'Yeah. They're fine. Just wanted to see if you wanted anything.'

'No, Mr Gibbens. And thank you.'

I started to asked her what she was thanking me for – then I suddenly didn't want to know. She was good at obligating me to things I didn't want to do. 'Good night, ma'am.'

I shut the door and started for the open one behind me. Before I got there, Adams spoke.

'You taking them, Gibbens?'

'Nope. You got an orphanage in this town?'

'Too small.'

'Then I'm wiring the authorities in Salt Lake. They can figure things out.' I turned and looked at the man. 'I'll pay for their room and board for a month. That should give everybody enough time to decide what to do. You figure?'

'Yeah,' he nodded. 'Probably about right,' he said, leaning forward and handing me my gun belt across the desk.

'I'll tell those orphanage people to come see you,' I said.

'That's fine.'

I didn't look at Lucia and the others when I walked back outside the jailhouse – I just started down the darkened street, walking and whistling, even though I didn't feel much like whistling. My guess was that, tired as they all were, they'd head back to the Johnsons' and hit the hay. They had to learn to mind. It was a matter of character. I turned down a side street, still whistling like I was enjoying myself. I wasn't. My mind was rushing over Hannah Morgan's bleak situation. There had to be something I could do. I just didn't know what it was at the moment.

'Goodbye, Mr Tucker,' James called in a sad voice.

The sound tugged at me but I forced myself to ignore the feeling. 'James. All of you – go to bed.'

I walked on down the empty road feeling rotten about having

left the kids, but knowing it was best for them; then I remembered and stopped and stared up at the canopy of night sky: thick velvet blasted through with a million stars. Hannah Morgan had asked if there was a moon. There was: bright and full and beautiful as any I'd ever seen.

'Yes,' I whispered, as if she could hear me.

I glanced behind me. The little street was empty. The kids had finally gotten the message. I tipped my head back again and watched the moon for a while, thinking about the woman. I knew so little about her, had known her for such a short time, and yet once again the sensation that I had known her my entire life flowed over me. A dog howled somewhere in the night, the sound cutting through me. It wasn't one of mine but it brought me back to the present and I turned and started walking.

I stood studying the second-storey room where the murders had taken place, staring up from the shadows of the alley near where I'd found Olive, feeling as if the room's dark windows were eyes staring down on me. And it wasn't a friendly stare.

The hour had grown late, the town silent: a restless silence. People were sleeping but I figured they weren't sleeping very well considering what they knew was coming with the dawn.

Like the sheriff, these weren't bad folks. Somebody had just come into their town and killed three men they knew . . . and they were going to avenge those deaths. Their only mistake was that they had the wrong person, had no idea who the beautiful stranger was. Nor were they willing to admit that the men were not innocent, that they had tried to rape the woman. Why didn't she just tell them who she was? Give them some sign so they could believe?

I froze as soon as I placed a foot on the bottom step of the stairs that led to the room, standing motionless, listening hard.

The sensation had come quickly, firmly, like a hand on my shoulder. I tried to shake it off but couldn't shake the sense that someone was watching me. I turned in a slow circle and let my eyes probe the shadows. Still nothing. No one. No sound. No movements. I ignored the nerve that was still firing a warning deep in my brain and started cautiously up the stairs.

There was a sawhorse in front of the weathered door with a sign tacked to it that read: 'Keep Out. Sheriff Adams.' I put a leg over the horse and tried the brass knob. It was open. I pulled my pistol and shoved the door in and stood listening for movement inside, then I stepped in, the gun still in my hand, and shut the door behind me, pressing my back against the wall and waiting. I was breathing hard and tried to calm down. The room was empty except for its scant furnishings.

I stood in the darkness letting my eyes adjust and smelling the faint sickening-sweet smell of death that still lingered in the stagnant air. Finally when I could see well enough to make out the objects in the room, I moved to a small table that held a kerosine lamp and struck a match. The flame in the glass globe cast a dull yellow glow over things. The place didn't look much different from the room in El Paso. It contained a bed, a chest of drawers, water basin, and plenty of dust. Adams said that it had been rented on a weekly basis by one of the dead men.

I could see dried blood splattered on the walls and a few dark stains on the wooden floor, but the barber had been right, there was hardly any. Certainly not what you'd have expected after three grown men had been hacked to pieces in this room. I'd spilled more blood killing a hen for dinner. It didn't make sense. It was as crazy as El Paso. Still, I believed her: she didn't know anything about it, hadn't played a role in it. But who had?

I made a thorough search of the room, finding nothing except three buttons on the floor. I figured they'd been yanked from

Hannah Morgan's dress as the men wrestled with her. They'd had one intention: to rape her. They'd caused their own deaths. I reached down and picked the buttons up and held them in the palm of my hand.

The change came over the room very slowly. At first I hardly noticed it, but the longer I stood there holding the buttons the stronger the sensation became. I wasn't certain what it was – just a change of sorts. The room looked the same in the dull light, but it wasn't. It seemed as if there was suddenly something in it that I should be able to see or smell but couldn't. I slipped the buttons into my pants pocket and pulled my pistol and felt foolish standing there with a drawn gun hunting for ghosts in an empty room.

I don't know how long I remained there until I realized I was afraid to move, even to breath. Whatever it was, I was listening for it, dreading it. I wanted to start for the door but couldn't.

Move, I told myself. Don't be a damn fool – move! But I couldn't. Then as if the thought had just suddenly popped into my mind, I was thinking of the buttons. Quickly I pulled them out and tossed them on to the bed – tossed them away as if they were burning hot. Slowly, I began to feel better, the panic dissipating like fog in sunlight. I moved toward the door, leaving the buttons behind, shivering and then wiping a sleeve across my forehead. Something wanted those buttons left here. Something I wasn't going to challenge. I felt stupid but I still wasn't going to try and get out of the room with them.

I was standing with my hand clamped on the cold brass of the doorknob taking one last look around and trying to figure out what had happened here – to the three men, and, moments before, to me – when I saw it. It was a thin sliver of reflected light coming from beneath the bed.

Cautiously I returned, nervously eyeing the buttons that I

was convinced had triggered the unsettling feelings moments before. Swallowing my fear, I pulled the bed frame away from the wall and knelt and studied a small silver cross that had fallen into a crack in the floor-boards. My eye had chanced upon it, catching a slight reflection of the room's light along the edge of the metal. Or had it been chance? Had I been meant to find this cross? Was it part of the answer that I was seeking?

The sheriff and the others had missed it, even though they'd combed the room. Maybe because they'd been looking for bigger things . . . burning swords and such. But maybe not. I reached for it and then stopped, my thoughts returning to the buttons and the strange sensation. No, I told myself, this was somehow different. The buttons had been violently torn from her – this was her possession, something she loved, it represented what she believed in . . . what her Son had died for. Something deep inside told me it would be all right to pick it up. Still, my hands were shaking as I touched the metal.

I held the small cross up in the lamplight. I was certain it belonged to the woman. It looked ancient. Further proof, I told myself, that she was who I believed. The metal had been worn thin in places as if the small cross had seen constant use through millenniums of pain and suffering.

From the rough cut of it, I figured that, even new, it had been a primitive job of foundry work. Now it just looked very old – polished smooth with time and tears. I remembered my wife in her deathbed fingering her own crucifix and understood the gentle rubbing of human fingers that had burnished this cold metal wafer-thin. I turned it over and squinted in the weak light and tried to make out some faint letters that had been etched into the back. They didn't look English. Then I tensed.

Blood was rising to the roots of my hair and a tingling sensation moved across the back of my neck. Though I hadn't heard a sound, I got the same prickly feeling of unease that I'd had before. Someone was in the room with me, standing behind me, watching me as I examined the small cross under the lamp's light. Whoever it was, they were good at this game. My senses had been honed to a sharp edge over the years and it was rare for someone to be able to sneak up behind me. Maybe it was the sheriff. No, something in my brain told me it wasn't him. It was the person or thing who had killed the three men. I felt my body dampening with sweat.

Though gunfighter was the last word I would have used to describe myself, I wasn't slow at getting my revolver out of its holster when I had to, and I whirled now and pulled the weapon . . . poking the barrel out into the murky light, poking it at nothing. The room was as empty as before. I checked the door and the stairs leading to the back alley. Nothing. No one. But there had been someone. I was certain of it. I shook off a hard shudder, stuffed the little cross into my shirt pocket and hurried out, moving as if I were trespassing. It had nothing to do with the sheriff's sign to keep out. It was something else. Something that made my stomach churn as I moved back into the night. There was a narrow opening between two buildings. I took it on the trot. A dark passageway turned left. I followed. Then there was an arched opening. I went through it, still moving fast.

When I hit the main street of town, I stopped and turned back and stood catching my breath and listening, my eyes studying the shadows behind me. No one was following. At least nobody that I could see. I shivered and pulled the cross out and examined it again in the moonlight. It cast a large shadow on the ground.

I didn't care who she admitted to being. I knew the truth and would always be haunted by it. By what I'd not done. How could I know this and allow her to be killed? I felt numb and put the cross away and started to turn back to the jail. I couldn't let her die.

But she'd told me to leave. Warned me not to try and help her. Told me I had things in my life I must do. I kept telling myself that there was a chance all this was meant to be: her death intended. But why? What earthly good could possibly be gained by it? These people knew nothing about her. She wasn't dying for any cause. There'd be no victory. Nothing. Nothing but death. Senseless and meaningless.

As I trudged through the darkness, I wondered if she had truly walked the earth for two thousand years? No wonder those eyes looked so tired. The thought of her gentle face caused me to stop and turn back again. But no. She had told me to go. And I would do as she wanted. I turned away once more, trying to ignore the pain. Then I stopped still.

Again, I had the unnerving sense that someone was behind me in the darkness, watching me. All was still and silent. The moon was casting deep shadows into doorways, under eaves of buildings and close in by the walls. Waiting and listening, I heard nothing. But I was convinced someone was here.

Starting to turn away, I yanked my body to a halt. Had that been a sound? I strained to hear the slightest movement. Putting my thumb on the hammer of my pistol, I pulled it back slowly until I heard the metal click and felt the trigger go rigid. The bright moonlight made the blotches of shadow seem darker as I peered into them, probing, waiting.

There was a faint sound of gravel stirring. I whirled and started away at a quick walk. If they were going to take me, then they'd do it on my terms, where I chose to fight. I made a sharp right turn and went quickly down another alley, then halfway down in the thickest part of the darkness, I ducked into an open gate that led into a small yard. I waited. They were coming. I could hear the footfalls moving quickly down the alley. There was more than one of them. The Mexican must have been right. Thinking about the three dead men and the way they'd been horribly dismembered, I felt sweat begin to break over my back. They might get me, I told myself, but not before I got at least one of them.

I listened, timing the footsteps of the first pursuer, waiting until I saw the blotch of shadow crossing in front of the gate, then I drove forward, tackling the dark shape, using my strength to carry the surprisingly light body across the alley and slamming it hard into a fence on the other side. I straightened up and took a deep breath and tried hard to control my rising anger.

Lucia was sprawled on the ground – opening and shutting her mouth, as if she were drowning in the air. I watched to see that she wasn't seriously hurt then I said,

'Are you trying to get yourself and these kids killed?'

Lucia's only reply was an awful gasping sound. Olive was standing behind her, her own small hands on the girl's shoulders.

'Mr Tucker, she can't breathe,' she said, sounding scared.

'She's lucky that's all she can't do,' I snapped, then I leaned down close to the Mexican girl's face. 'Go back to the boarding house and leave me alone. Understand?'

Lucia just glared at me, still hurting for breath. Then she wheezed, 'You promised to get her out.'

'You keep saying that. But it's wrong. I said I was going to see what I could do. And I'm doing that . . . when you aren't wasting my time.'

I bent over and picked her up in my arms and carried her struggling and kicking down the alley, Olive trotting along beside us. Junior and James were out on the street holding the horses and watching over Milagros when we emerged from the dark passage. I went muttering by them as James said, 'Hi, Mr Gibbens.' I ignored him and plunked the girl on to her horse. She glared at me, still struggling to fill her lungs with air.

'Now go back to the boarding house.'

I took a quick look at Milagros, then tipped my hat and said, 'Boys,' and started down the road, determined these kids weren't going to get the best of me. 'You head on back to the Johnsons'. Hear?'

As I moved, I focused on the hopelessness of the woman's situation. Dead at dawn, if I didn't do something. I had to do something. But what? Then I heard the horses behind me and turned back. Damn – I didn't need these kids at a time like this. As usual, Lucia was leading the pack, Olive sitting behind her, then the Dunnet boys, the white mule and Milagros.

The little Mexican gal looked like she'd finally gotten her breath back, but it hadn't improved her attitude any. Not at all. She was still looking at me like I was doing something awful. I shook my head and kept walking; turned left down a street, right down another. These kids could do whatever they wanted, I told myself. It wasn't my concern – no matter what the woman had told them. I'd told Hannah Morgan plainly enough that all I was going to do was check on Olive's situation. That was all. Zero, nada . . . nothing more. I had my own problems.

My dogs and horses were where I'd left them. Jack whined as I approached. The children were following at a safe distance and I was walking with a stiff jaw, continuing to ignore them.

I sat down on the edge of the sidewalk and put my head in my hands and felt miserable. Then the children pulled up in front of me and Lucia sat eyeing me like I'd finally lost it, like I was a mean, worthless sonofabitch . . . so I straightened up a little and tried to look more respectable, more in control . . . as if it were normal for me to take a seat on a sidewalk at two in the morning and clutch at my head like I was keeping it from exploding.

Martha and Jack sat down in front of me as well and stared at me just as closely. They'd seen me looking like this a lot since my wife's death, but they still didn't like it. I moaned inside and Jack whined as if he'd somehow heard it and Martha cocked her head trying to understand the why of things. I could have told her there was no why in this life.

Lucia cleared her throat.

I ignored her.

'You cannot,' she snapped.

'Cannot what?'

'You cannot just sit here. You promised.'

'Will you quit saying that? I didn't promise anything. I just said I'd think about her situation. And that's what I'm doing. So go stare at somebody else – I'm thinking.'

'Asno,' she muttered.

I knew what 'asno' translated meant. Roughly: burro . . . or if she wanted to twist it slightly – which I believe she did – it became the thing I was sitting on.

I continued to ignore her, letting my thoughts drift back to that first fateful day when I'd met Hannah Morgan. It wasn't even a week now, but it seemed like for ever. I pursed my lips and shook my head. It was a confusing mess.

'Good dogs,' I said, feeling miserable, confused, cowardly. This woman – if the legends were to be believed – had the courage when she was still a young girl to change man's destiny by agreeing to give birth to the son of God. This woman – prayed to for almost two thousand years – had bothered to come when I had cried out to her. And she had saved me, whether or not she admitted it. And now I was leaving her to die at the hands of people who had no idea what they were doing.

I forced myself to my feet and cinched the sorrel up and mounted, then headed west out of town towards a small stream where I could think. Think until the coming of the dawn. The children trailed along behind, looking more dejected now. It made me feel bad, but there wasn't a thing I could do about it. So I rode.

CHAPTER THIRTEEN

I was on the edge of town, riding slumped forward, deep in thought. It was that hour of night when darkness and silence meld into emptiness. I was staring at my hands clutching the saddlehorn, idle hands that had always been effective in the past at stopping wrongdoings, hands that didn't seem like they were mine any longer. What was happening to me that I would allow this? I reined in the sorrel and sat looking at the building . . . the children stopping a few yards behind me.

It was covered in moonlight and looked small and oddly comforting. The sign said 'Methodist'. But it didn't matter. If she was the Holy Mother, then one church was as good as any other. And she'd asked me to pray for her. I could do that, even if I didn't believe in her God. I swung down and left the horses standing in the street and walked rapidly toward the building. Lucia started to climb down.

'No,' I said. 'I'm going in alone.'

She frowned at me for a moment, then stayed put. The dogs started to follow me, then stopped as well, instinctively knowing I'd want them to guard the horses and these infernal kids.

Jack barked at me to see if I would clarify the situation but I ignored him. I glanced back from the darkened doorway of the church. The little terrier continued to sit, trembling and worried, and took to whining and watching where I'd disappeared in the shadows. Martha just plopped down in front of the two horses with her familiar weight-of-the-world groan, as if to ensure that the sorrel and the bay didn't take it in their minds to wander off down the street to look for food or water.

Lucia resettled herself in her saddle, crossing her arms over her breast and staring stoically at the shadowy doorway where I stood, while Olive wrapped her small arms around the girl's waist. The Dunnet boys and Milagros pulled into line next to them. Damn, they were a stubborn lot.

It was 2.30 a.m. and the little church was pitch dark inside. I searched the altar area for a statue of the Blessed Virgin. There was nothing but a large wooden cross and some candles and a collection plate. I lit the candles on either side of the cross, remembering that it was the Catholics who had statues to the saints, not the Protestants.

I felt funny standing in the wavering candle light in this little church and walked over and sat down on one of the pews exhausted from the hour, the long ride and the strain of what was happening. Thoughts of my dead wife crowded into my mind.

She had been strong, compassionate and fiercely loyal to family and strangers alike. Decent down to her soul. Every so often over the years I'd caught myself giving a young criminal an extra break or feeling a tug at my heart when I witnessed some tragedy, knowing it was her magically pulling the strings of my conscience. It was a funny thing the influence she had over me. Women men loved were amazing things, I guessed.

The thought caused me to tense, thinking of Hannah Morgan again. I knew Jesus had to feel the same about her as I did about my own mother and wife. That had to be true. God had to feel the same things man did. Otherwise we had nothing in common. It made perfect sense. Anyhow, I hoped it did.

I was shaking hard now in the still coolness of the small

sanctuary, the faint blue-white light of the moon shining through the row of tall windows, mixing with the yellow glow of the candles and illuminating the cross on the altar. The cross cast a tall shadow against the wall behind it, reminding me of the shadow cast by the smaller cross and I fished it now out of my pocket and held it tight. I wished my wife were here. She'd know what to do. What to say. The Virgin had asked me to pray for her.

I guessed I had always believed in something bigger than myself. But I'd never tried to reach that 'something' except when my wife and child died. And my pleas hadn't been answered. Maybe it was because of the life I'd led. Shooting people, hitting them over the head, throwing them in jail. I sat straighter in the pew. That didn't matter now. The Virgin had asked me to pray for her. And I was going to do it the best I could, willing to make a pact with the devil, if that would save her.

I cleared my throat, and clasped my large hands together feeling clumsy. 'Jesus –' I said, then stopped and thought some more. 'Your mother –' I stopped for a while. 'She asked me to pray for her. So I am. She's too good to need prayers. But You know that.' I stopped and sat looking down at my hands. 'I don't know what to say. You love her. Don't let her die.'

I sat and tried to cry in the dark, but couldn't, moaning instead, remembering my own mother and wife; the moans releasing things, good and bad. I thought about what else to pray. 'Please help her. Or tell me to do it. All I want is for You to tell me what to do.'

I listened, hoping that I would receive some sign. But I received nothing. I guessed I hadn't expected to. It was just like my prayers for my wife and child. All for nothing – wasted words. Nearly exhausted, I tried to talk to my wife but the words wouldn't come, just the old anger at a God who had let her die so senselessly.

If I shot my way into that jailhouse, innocent people would die. If I succeeded in freeing the woman, I would have to kill people who didn't deserve it. Even though she was the Holy Mother, that wouldn't be right. Hadn't she already told me not to? Could I do that? I didn't know. The woman had read my thoughts and warned me away. I felt the moans coming up again and tipped my head back and stared at the ceiling. But could I deny her? Could I allow them to shoot her like a common criminal and not try to stop them? I shuddered. 'Tell me what I should do,' I whispered. 'Please.' But I heard nothing.

My mind churned with the awful dilemma.

'Joan,' I moaned. I paused, waiting to see if she would speak to me or make her presence known in some way. I clutched hard at the little crucifix. 'Please talk to me. I need your help.'

The room remained silent for a long while, then I heard a stirring in the back and I whirled and studied the dark shadows. My eyes locked on a large darker blotch of murkiness. Then I watched as it pulled away from the other shadows. Someone or something was moving in the back of the church. I fought the disbelief and trembling in my body. Was it Joan? Or the person or thing who had killed the men? Had it followed me here, tracked my scent like some feral beast?

'Joan?' I called again, slowly slipping the pistol out of its holster. 'Joan?' Only silence. Then anger surged through me as I thought it was Lucia. But no, the shadowy shape was too large for the girl.

Then I heard footsteps and raised the weapon, holding it steady in both hands, until a heavy-set man in his sixties, half-dressed and half-asleep, walked a few hesitant steps down the centre aisle of the church toward me. He stopped and stared at me and the muzzle of the gun. My first thought was that he looked like a over-sized cherub. I slowly tipped the pistol up toward the ceiling, so badly disappointed that it wasn't my wife that I had to force myself to breathe.

'Son,' the man said, 'may I help you?'

When I had recovered enough to speak, I asked, 'Who are you?'

'The minister of this church. My wife and I live off the back and we heard you talking.' He took another careful step forward. 'Are you in trouble?'

'Ben?' a woman called from the shadows.

'Just a visitor, Mother.' He smiled at me. 'My wife.'

'Would they like a cup of coffee or something to eat?'

The old minister looked at me and raised his eyebrows in a silent question. I shook my head no.

'No, Mother. But thank you. You go back to sleep now.'

I stood up and started to walk out of the church, then stopped. A crazy thought had suddenly come to me. Perhaps my wife had indeed answered me. It would be just like her to do something practical like wake the minister up in the next room and get him on the job. Who better to help me prevent the death of the Virgin Mary?

I stood looking at the heavy-set old man for a long time until he finally said, 'Son?'

'Come here,' I said. 'Sit down, please.' While the minister was doing this, I took out my wallet and the prospector's letter, showing him my badge. 'I'm a deputy sheriff in Los Angeles. I'm telling you that so you don't think I'm crazy. Some bum off the desert. Understand?'

The minister had a pleasantly round, fleshy face and he smiled at me and said, 'I think we're all a little crazy. Don't you?' There was a nice twinkle in his eyes.

I liked him immediately. 'Yeah, maybe. But this story I'm about to tell you may make you think I'm running ahead of the pack on the subject . . . but you've got to listen to it.' I checked my watch: 2.45 a.m. 'We don't have much time.'

The old minister reached out and patted my shoulder with his fat hand. 'We're on the Lord's time, son. Therefore we have all we'll ever need.'

I stared at the man, finally nodding. 'I hope so.' I extended my hand. 'Tucker Gibbens.'

'Benjamin Fellows,' the old man responded, smiling and grasping my hand in both of his.

Fifteen minutes later, I had finished telling him the entire story as accurately as I could, from the moment I was shot in El Paso, to the room, the clothes with the hole in them, Dunnet, the Indians and the storm. Benjamin Fellows sat with his eyes narrowed, watching my face and nodding at places. He had prayed over the three corpses in the barber shop the evening before and therefore was aware of the strange and frightening butchery that had taken place in that little room off the back alley.

Relieved that the episodes of this fantastic tale were out in the open, I took a deep breath and then let it rush through my clenched teeth, feeling better that I'd told everything I knew to another human being, to someone who would feel about the woman the same as I did, to a man of God. Benjamin Fellows just sat watching me. I found it hard to read his face. His expression wasn't disbelief or scepticism as much as non-committal, his thoughts seemingly far away.

'Reverend?'

He visibly jumped at the sound of my voice. 'I'm sorry. I was just thinking back to my college days.'

'What are we going to do?' I asked.

Fellows leaned back in the pew and took a scrutinizing look

at me. 'In divinity school, Mr Gibbens,' he began slowly, then stopped and seemed to be remembering back in time. 'In divinity school we were taught to avoid religious zealots who would see Christ sitting across from them in a poker game or taking the waters at the local hot springs. We were also told to avoid those with overly active imaginations who would constantly receive visitations from the saints or the Virgin Mary, or the devil.' He paused. 'We Methodists are a funny lot. We leave exorcisms and stigmata to our Catholic brethren. They're so much better at it.'

I didn't say anything for a moment. Then I stood. 'You don't believe me.'

The old minister continued to sit and think. 'Didn't say that, son. I just said that we Methodists are not big on religious demonstrations. We're much more literal minded, if you get my drift.'

'Get my drift, Reverend. The Mother of your Christ is in the jail down the street and less than three hours from now she is going to be murdered . . . murdered in the same mindless way her Son was.' My voice was sharp and condemning. 'Are you telling me that as a man of God you're going to just let that happen?'

If I had meant to frighten or shame the old minister into action, it wasn't working. Benjamin Fellows continued to sit in the pew looking like he was daydreaming. When he finally stirred, he glanced up at me and let out a little mirthless laugh.

'At seminary there was a wonderful inscription over the door that led to chapel.' He pulled absent-mindedly at one of his many chins. 'I can't recall whose quote it was – some French philosopher from the eleventh century, I believe. It doesn't matter. What it said was, "Satan's cleverest wile is to convince us he doesn't exist."

I just watched him. Suddenly, Fellows slapped the tops of his fat thighs and hopped up, surprisingly nimble for his weight and age. 'Maybe that's what he's done here,' he said brightly.

'Meaning?'

'That perhaps the devil feels if he convinces us that he doesn't exist, then we won't believe that God or the Blessed Virgin exists either. Come along, Mr Gibbens,' Reverend Fellows said, marching down the aisle toward the church door. 'Let's go talk to Hannah Morgan.'

I looked up into the darkness of the high-peaked ceiling and said, 'Thank you.' Then out of the darkness at the back of the church, I heard the sound of shuffling feet and watched as Lucia – Milagros in her arms – Olive and the Dunnet boys walked slowly down the centre aisle of the church. The minister just stood with his mouth open as the children moved silently past. Then he turned and looked at me.

'Yours?'

'No,' I said quickly. 'The woman's been collecting them here and there around the countryside.' I was squinting hard at Lucia, trying to make her feel uncomfortable that she'd disobeyed me once again. She ignored me, placing Milagros down carefully on a blanket that the Dunnet boys had spread on the floor. Then Lucia knelt in front of the altar, followed by the other three. They looked like little angels. I shook my head.

'What lovely children,' Fellows said.

'I wouldn't make snap judgements,' I mumbled. 'Come on.'

'But the children?'

'Leave them. I've been trying to get rid of them all night.'

'Sir,' Fellows said a little stiffly, 'we can't just abandon them.'

'They've got a place to stay – the Johnsons' house. Only they won't stay there. So leave them.'

Fellows looked from me back to the children for a moment, then he cleared his throat. 'One moment, please.'

With the minister gone, I could focus on the kids. 'You don't mind at all, do you? You just walk around doing whatever you please. Just because this old man thinks that you're sweetness and light . . . you don't fool me.'

They didn't say anything for a moment, then I heard Lucia – her head bowed, her hands clasped in front of her – saying the woman's name, God's name in Mexican, Milagros and the names of the other children.

'No. You don't fool me one bit.'

'Shhhhhhh, Mr Gibbens,' Olive said in a formal little voice.

I started to say something else, then felt bad about it and turned and walked out the front door. I could hear Fellows and his wife talking somewhere behind me in the church.

The Reverend Benjamin Fellows had been inside the jail for the past hour, while I paced back and forth in the cold shadows of the street. The old man had wanted to be alone while he questioned Hannah Morgan, not wishing to put her on public display in this her darkest hour, and I had no interest in talking to the lawmen waiting in the front office.

All the minister had told the sheriff was that he wanted to talk and pray with the prisoner. Not an untruth. He had carried his Bible inside. I wondered if this was to test her knowledge of the Word. But somehow I thought not – Fellows didn't seem like the testing type. The old man would simply ask her the big question, I figured, and believe. I was sure of it. Fellows was, after all, a man of God. He would naturally sense the woman's divinity.

Jack paced at my heels, shivering and grousing. Martha sat off to the side watching the two of us, as if wondering why we were out here in the middle of the street when we should be holed up someplace warm. It was cold – but at least the kids weren't here. Mrs Fellows – a good double for Mrs Santa Claus – had gathered them around her in the sanctuary. I figured they were either still there in the church or back at the Johnson place. Didn't matter which to me. Just so long as they weren't crawling up my backside.

I looked up at the spray of stars floating over the little town and thought of my wife's death. It had taken painful months of agony for her strong body and stronger will to waste away. Through it all, she had prayed to the woman who sat talking to Benjamin Fellows.

Thank goodness, I thought, that I had found him. As if the minister had been summoned by this very thought, the front door to the jail opened, spilling light into the night, and the old man stepped out. He leaned back in and said goodbye to the sheriff and turned toward me.

His head was down, his chin resting on his chest as he walked, obviously deep in thought. I stepped quickly to his side. Fellows was headed back down the street toward the church, walking slowly.

'You saw her for yourself,' I said.

Fellows nodded, continuing his contemplations. I watched him, frustrated that he wasn't speaking.

'Now you believe.'

Fellows stopped in the middle of the street and looked at me. 'I believe she is an extraordinary woman.'

I didn't like the sound of that. 'She is more than extraordinary – she is the Saviour's Mother.'

'She makes no claim to being anything but a mortal woman.'

'I told you that,' I snapped. 'But Mary was nothing but a mortal woman.'

'True enough,' Fellows said, turning and starting off again at a slow walk toward the church. I marched at his side.

'You've seen her. You've spoken to her. Therefore you know!'

Fellows stopped again and looked at my face with eyes that understood my anguish. 'Yes, I've seen her. And, yes, she is an extraordinary woman . . . in her beauty, her calm dignity in the face of her fate, in every human way.' He paused. 'And I've seen you, Mr Gibbens.'

'What's that got to do with anything?'

'A great deal.'

'Exactly what?'

'Simply that when I look at you, Mr Gibbens, I see a man in love with a condemned woman. A man who cannot bear to face that. A man who would do anything – believe anything – if it would save her.'

'That's absurd! She isn't normal flesh and blood. She's from God. And my guess is one of His angels killed those three men – killed them for daring to lay a hand on her.' I stopped and caught my breath. 'Isn't that what the Bible says: "He'll give his angels charge over thee"?'

Fellows nodded. 'Yes.'

'Well you can damn well bet they're watching over this woman.'

'I pray so,' the old man said softly.

I stood peering into the preacher's face in disbelief. 'What kind of a minister are you that you can sit down and talk directly to the Virgin Mary and not know it?'

'I guess an old, tired-out one, sir. One who has seen too much of man's hate and too little of God's grace. But that's not the point. I asked her for some sign of her divinity, Mr Gibbens, and she just laughed.'

'So did her son.'

For the first time, Fellows looked slightly shaken by what I'd said. It was one thing to be an honest sceptic and quite another to turn your back on the Virgin. No man who cared for his soul would dare do that. He stood in the centre of the street as if not certain what he should do, then he turned and marched off resolutely toward his church.

I trotted after him and grabbed one of his shoulders and spun his heavy body around. 'Here, look at this. I found it in that room where the murders took place. Look at it,' I snapped, pushing the little cross out to the man. Fellows took it in his chubby fingers, put his glasses on, and examined it under the moonlight.

'It's old, isn't it?' I challenged.

Fellows nodded. 'Very old.' He had turned the cross over and was trying to make out the faint etching of letters in the thin metal. 'I'd say those are Greek letters.' He paused. 'I don't know how old it is,' he continued, handing it back to me, 'but I'd be willing to guess it's ancient Greek unless it's a forgery.'

'It's no forgery. It belongs to her.'

Fellows took his glasses off and stared at me for a long time before he said, 'Son, that still doesn't make her the Mother of God.' The old man turned again and began walking steadily toward the small white church. I didn't move. I just watched him go.

'May you rot in hell,' I barked at him. Martha took a couple of quick steps after the minister as if to follow up my harsh words with a few well-placed bites. Then I snapped my fingers and she relaxed and sat down and watched the old man put a foot on the lowest step of the church. He looked tired and confused.

Benjamin Fellows said nothing, just continued climbing in a slow gait up the steps of the pretty little church that sat looking so safe and secure with darkened windows in the moonlight. 'Damn phony,' I muttered.

I watched him and fought the urge to chase after him, to grab him and slap some sense into him. I felt a physical tug and looked down to see Jack pulling on my pants.

'Let go.'

The little dog released me, backed up and barked hard, as if urging me to do something to save the woman.

'Be quiet.'

The children's horses were gone from in front of the church.

The sky had lightened. It was almost imperceptible but I sensed the dark heavens fading toward dawn. I was sitting on the sorrel at the edge of town, staring back at the jailhouse. I couldn't do it. I couldn't wait for the sun to rise and to watch them take her to the place of her execution, to see her eyes, to watch them blindfold those eyes. I felt like screaming.

'I know who you are,' I said to the shadows. 'I know! I know you can hear me. You heard me before.' I choked back the feelings rising in my throat. 'You understand that I can't stay to see this. I can't. If you want me to let them kill you – then I have to leave. Or I'll try and stop them.'

I turned the sorrel's head and put my heels to her and started across the field at a walk; the moon was sinking fast toward the horizon, casting the land in deep, pre-dawn darkness. The coming day was one the world would regret, I figured, like it had regretted only one other.

I pulled my hat off and ran my hand through my hair. 'Why didn't you tell that old man?' I said, talking to my horse's neck. 'What's so grand about dying for a crime you didn't commit?' I pulled a handkerchief and wiped the beads of sweat from my face. 'It makes no sense.'

I rode with my head down, Jack sitting silently on the horse's rump, while Martha and the bay trudged along behind. I was heading south out of town back toward the flatlands and beyond them down through New Mexico to the Texas spur and El Paso. I was lost in my thoughts. Then Jack growled and I heard men talking and reined the sorrel in and listened.

The sound was coming from a small sandhill a hundred yards off. Something about the men's voices, subdued and tense, told me what I didn't want to know. These were the men who would have to carry out the execution. I walked the sorrel over to where they stood. There were six of them. Just normal looking men . . . none of them wanting to be here . . . all of them sick and scared to do this thing. I studied their faces for a few moments, then looked out across the dusky air at the tall post sticking out of the ground, and beyond it the small hill that would catch the bullets that tore through her.

'Mister,' one of the men said. 'You aren't supposed to be here. There's going to be an execution. Nobody is to be allowed to –' The man stopped and studied me hard. 'You next of kin?'

I didn't answer him, just continued to stare at the dark post, imagining the woman tied to it, the sound of the rifles cocking, the explosion of sound, her body jumping as the rounds collided with it.

'You kin, mister?' the man asked again.

I still didn't answer. I just sat staring down at the ground next to the horse.

'You wait. She'll be here in about an hour. We got some coffee over there.' The man looked up into my face. 'I'm sorry.'

I nodded, then turned the horse and put my heels into her flanks. I couldn't do it. I couldn't. No matter what happened. If

I got her out, I'd pray for forgiveness. My wife would understand. Would feel that I'd done the right thing. Then I'd kill myself and try to follow.

I kicked the mare harder, the young animal leaping forward into a run. I had to get back before the crowd began to form in front of the jail. I didn't want to hurt anybody I didn't have to. From the look of the man, the sheriff wasn't going to let me waltz in and out of his jail with a condemned prisoner. He would do whatever it took to try to stop me. I wouldn't have expected any less from him.

He was a straight-talker, a hardworking lawman who hated what he had to do this morning . . . but would do it. With compassion, but still do it. It would be hard to shoot a man like him . . . but I would. That's why the woman had told me to leave. She had sensed that. Had seen into my soul.

There was a thin strip of pink on the eastern horizon now. I rode slowly down the main street of Four Walls, my eyes and ears taking in the sounds and movement around me. The town was still sleeping. Either that, or they had no stomach for this morning's doings. I didn't blame them.

I rode by the little church, the windows were dark. The old man hadn't even seen fit to stay up and pray for her. Hadn't even lit a candle for her. I shook my head in disgust. While I understood the sheriff and the rest of the town not realizing who she was, I didn't feel that way about the old man. I'd expected more from a so-called man of God.

I yanked a saddle off the back of what I figured was a deputy's horse and put it on the bay, adjusting the stirrups to the woman's height. We'd be riding hard. Next I tied the things from the pack on to the backs of both saddles, stuffing what I could into the saddlebags. Finished, I pulled the shotgun, checked my pistol and ordered the dogs to wait. Then I crossed the street.

There was a man coming toward me slowly on a horse. It didn't matter. I couldn't pick and choose the time. That was lost. What I had to do, I had to. I turned the knob of the door and stepped in and threw down on the men in the room. There were two of them. Neither moved. 'Give me the keys.'

'Put it away, Gibbens,' Adams said quietly, 'before you get into shit.'

'The keys.' I cocked one of the shotgun's barrels.

'You don't need them. Take a look.'

The other man in the room was the old minister, Benjamin Fellows. He was gazing at me with a smug expression that I had an urge to wipe off with a hard rap of the shotgun butt.

'Weapons on the floor,' I said.

'Not wearing any,' Adams said, picking up his coffee cup and swirling it until steam rose into the air. 'Go take a damn look, will you please.'

I backed to the door and kicked it open behind me, banging it hard against a wall. I stood expecting either the sheriff to make his play, or the cell room to be filled with deputies. Neither happened. My eyes jumped to where they'd been holding her. She was gone.

'You sonofabitch. You've already done it.'

Adams was watching me over the rim of his coffee cup, steam rising around his hairy face. The reverend was sitting and looking contented with himself and the world, his chubby hands in his lap, his thumbs twittling in a steady motion. I cocked the other barrel of the shotgun for emphasis.

Adams shook his head slowly like a monster in the mist. 'Listen,' his voice was careful and steady . . . realizing that I'd crossed the Rubicon. 'We haven't done anything.'

I just watched him.

'She's riding north out of town.' He looked at Fellows.

The old man's eyes were filled with happiness. He stopped twittling and slapped the tops of his thighs. 'That's correct, Sheriff. Hannah Morgan rode north at a nice brisk trot, followed by those wonderful children.' He paused. 'My goodness, she travels fast.'

My eyes jumped back and forth between the men's faces. The only sound in the room was the hiss of the kerosine lantern burning overhead. 'What are you talking about?' The shotgun still levelled head-high.

Adams leaned back in his chair and took another drink of coffee and continued looking pleased. 'Reverend.'

The old minister beamed. 'We agree with you. She wasn't guilty.'

Adams put his cup down and clasped his hands behind his bushy head and leaned back. 'The reverend and I sent a note to Judge Williams's house last night, telling him that we didn't think she was,' Adams continued. 'The judge had my deputies wake the jury up – most of them weren't sleeping anyway, worrying about having condemned this woman – and had them vote again. It was unanimous.'

'Acquittal, Mr Gibbens,' Fellows said, his eyes filled with a happiness that seemed to leap out in invisible waves at me. 'If I was you, I'd ride after her.'

I lowered the shotgun and just stared at the two men in disbelief. 'You let her go?'

'No. The judge and jury did.'

I was starting to grin now myself. I walked over and laid the shotgun down on the desk and then tossed my arms around the fat reverend and hugged the man off his feet, waltzing him around the room. 'Damn, I owe you a big apology!' I let the embarrassed man down and turned to the sheriff, who quickly held up his hands to fend off a similar show of affection. I extended my hand. 'Adams, I'm proud to know you.'

'Thanks. Take the reverend's advice.' The men were having a good time, tickled with themselves, relieved that they wouldn't have to participate in the death of the woman.

I couldn't stop grinning at them.

'Git,' Adams barked.

I started for the door.

'Oh, Mr Gibbens,' Fellows said.

I looked back. 'Yes?'

The old minister had stopped smiling. 'She's a fascinating woman. Mysterious in many ways. But, Mr Gibbens, she's flesh and blood. Don't waste time thinking she's anything more.' Then the old man smiled. 'She's lovely enough. Don't you think?'

I just grinned. I couldn't stop grinning.

'Git! Before you try kissing us or start making up verses.'

I walked outside and stopped and stood and continued to grin like a grown fool, my eyes on the eastern horizon that was quickly turning a bright, glorious pink. I watched it for a while, feeling all kinds of good things, then walked quickly over and uncinched the saddle that I'd been about to steal and put it back on the horse where it belonged. Finished, I swung up on to the mare and rode out of town, whistling and meaning it this time. I hadn't done that in a while.

I reined the sorrel in when I came to the front of the little church and sat staring at the coloured windows, the steeple and the cross. I didn't know what to do or say. Finally, I just took my hat off and said, 'Thanks.' I still wasn't certain who I was thanking. It didn't matter, I figured. Something just told me that saying thanks – and meaning it – was enough.

CHAPTER FOURTEEN

Los Angeles. 5 March 1997

Father Mulcahy stood at the edge of his desk only half-listening to the morning noises of the archdiocese spilling down the hallway outside his office, anticipating the rumbling sound of the grand organ two floors below, but not caring, just wondering at the sudden hollow aching inside him that the phone call had caused.

He was staring at the half-read manuscript sitting on the corner of his desk. He couldn't believe it. He was numb. Then he realized that he was still holding the telephone in his hand and put it down. The call had been brief, but so very unsettling. Why? Had he wanted it to be different? He wasn't certain.

For two days now, he had been collecting information about Tucker Gibbens and Hannah Morgan. Bits and pieces gleaned from dusty books and files, delivered by fax or telephone; talking to the state historical folks in Utah, Texas and New Mexico; asking for help from court clerks and checking death certificates and the like; searching the big genealogy computers run by the Church of the Latter Day Saints, which were, without question, the best at tracking down people.

Slowly it had been coming together. Tucker Gibbens was no liar. He had killed two outlaws in El Paso just like he'd said. There was a Sheriff Eli Matson. Junior and James Dunnet had indeed lived. And there had been a town called Four Walls, now known as Simmons, and a Sheriff Harold Adams.

The old priest felt his pulse quickening and he moved around the desk to his chair. He coughed. He didn't know why, but he was feeling funny, his mind somehow momentarily separate from his body. He glanced back at the manuscript, at the places where he'd scribbled in the margins, his eyes stopping on the name: Hannah Morgan. He coughed again, wincing with a pain so deep inside he sensed rather than felt it.

She had existed.

He almost couldn't believe it. He had been certain that she was going to be the one great fabrication in Gibbens's tale. But she wasn't. That was what the last phone call had been about. A clerk at the county court house in Simmons had been kind enough to go to the library – where the town's archival records were being kept – to look up Hannah Morgan in the old court records. Father Mulcahy took a long, deep breath and held it.

Hannah Morgan had been arrested on 20 July 1887 for the murder of three men. She had been sentenced to die. Then acquitted of the same crime on a revote of the jury the next day. All of it just like Gibbens had written it.

Hannah Morgan was real.

There was a sound building in the priest's head. A faint shrieking that seemed to come down through the ages to him and made him want to clamp his hands over his ears. He was sweating hard now, hearing the beating of his pulse replacing the shrill sound, wondering what it all meant. He trembled, dimly remembering other times, other hopes, other dreams. He wiped his forehead, unsure what the horrible sound had been. Then not caring. He sat up straighter in the chair. Because a woman named Hannah Morgan had once lived did not mean that he would find salvation through her. Nor that she was the Virgin. That was silly. The familiar cold feeling returned to its place in his gut. She would not soften this hardness that was constantly with him, had become like some artificial organ inside him.

He picked up the unread part of the manuscript and sat staring at it, drawn to it, but now afraid of it. He began to read again – not because he wanted to but because he felt compelled to finish the pages.

CHAPTER FIFTEEN

Utah Territory . . . 1887

The air was alive with heat. I should have known Hannah Morgan would find a place like this. Ten miles northwest of Four Walls, sitting on the side of a road that cut across a wide stretch of alkali flats, the building looked like a former Sabbath house, complete with spire. It was a road station now where coaches between Denver and Salt Lake could change teams and their passengers take care of private matters and get a drink or a hot meal. That last thing was most certainly why Hannah Morgan was here.

There was a large wooden sign in front of the place with an enormous fat man painted on it that read: 'I eat here.' I shook my head and grinned. That had to have attracted her. After all, it'd been a whole four hours since she'd had a decent meal – so she was wasting away to near nothing. I laughed out loud, the mysterious happiness engulfing me again.

The only thing I was wondering about were the tracks of five horses that had followed Hannah Morgan and the kids out of Four Walls. She'd been trotting hard-pressed as usual and they'd followed just as fast – making every turn she'd made, so I knew they were trailing her. I wondered if these were the 'gringos' who'd run the outlaws off; then slaughtered the three men.

Inside the barn, I checked Hannah's horses and the white mule and unsaddled my animals and pitched them fresh hay, leaving the dogs to watch over things. Curious, I took a look at the five horses. Normal enough, nothing mysterious. The saddles were worn and repaired, just like mine, just like most of the saddles in these parts. They were carrying ropes and canteens and three had saddle carbines – but no sword. Still, that didn't mean anything. They could have stashed it somewhere. I turned and went inside.

It was a smoke-darkened tavern, hot, but clean enough. The front room had a long bar and a few gaming tables. An old man was tending drinks and there were two tables of card players. Nobody paid me much mind.

'Woman and kids?' I asked. The old man nodded toward an open door. I went through it and down a tight, claustrophobic passage, stopping a few feet back at the far end.

Hannah Morgan didn't look like a woman who'd just escaped death: she was sitting at a table smiling and talking, her head tipped down over her knitting as if it were critically important that she get each and every weave of the black yarn perfect. I chuckled at the thought of her knitting her way rapidly along in order to make absolutely nothing out of the black mass.

Milagros' coffin was resting on two chairs that had been pulled close and Lucia was bent over fussing with the child. The Mexican girl looked tense. I wondered if Milagros was worsening. But no, Hannah Morgan would have been worried if one of her brats was in trouble. It was something else. I moved my eyes slowly over the other children. They too looked nervous.

Nobody had noticed me, so I continued to stand back in the hallway looking at things. Hannah was still knitting, still talking up a storm. But she'd be doing that in the middle of a tornado.

There was a grey-haired serving woman washing glasses in a tub – and closer by, a group of men at a table. Five men. The ones who'd trailed her, I figured. Suddenly, I was remembering the fleeting thought I'd gotten in the alley the night before: that perhaps encounters with this sainted woman were not by chance. Slowly, the hairs began to rise on my neck. Was this one?

I took a good hard look at the men: too seedy to be heavenly. Late thirties and forties, dressed in dirty clothes, needing baths and haircuts. I could use those things myself but it looked permanent with this bunch. Maybe they worked for the mines or some local spread. That I couldn't tell. But what I could tell was that they were mad about something.

I'd made my living too long walking into rooms just like this one and taking a fast read of the inhabitants. Read right and walk out. Read wrong and you never knew. I'd become a damn good reader. And these men looked too ready for trouble. I didn't know why. I just knew I was right.

I slipped the little leather thong off the hammer of my pistol, pulled my hat down hard on my head so that my hands were free, then started walking and looking friendly.

'Mrs Morgan.'

She glanced up over her little glasses, her face flushed from the heat, and broke into a wonderfully wide smile that made me feel like taking a step back. 'Mr Gibbens! What a wonderful surprise.'

But looking at her, I had the unsettling sense that I saw something deep in those eyes that wasn't surprised at all . . . that she in fact had been expecting me. And that bothered me – as if I had no free will. All my life I'd done things the way I wanted to do them. I didn't like the possibility that that had changed.

I shrugged the feeling off, noticing that the little clutch of flowers I'd given her the night before was sitting in a glass of water by her plate. It made me feel good. Maybe the legend was right: maybe the tiny plant had protected her from satan. I stiffened. Perhaps I hadn't picked them by chance. Again, I didn't like the thought. Regardless, I was glad she was alive and here on earth. I took a quick look at the kids.

Everyone but Lucia seemed glad to see me. Nothing new there.

'Hello, Mr Gibbens,' Olive and the Dunnet boys said. Lucia also said something that passed muster as a greeting with Hannah. She was brushing Olive's hair now. I looked at the child's face, into her eyes: she looked about to faint and suddenly I put it all together. Or thought I had.

'Join you?'

'Please,' Hannah beamed, turning to the waitress. 'Ethel. A good friend has arrived. I'm sure he's starved.'

The waitress's features warmed. 'Let me get a menu.'

'Aren't you famished?' Hannah said.

'Sure,' I lied, my mind on the men. I pulled a chair next to Lucia and took Olive on to my knee, testing what was wrong. She was shaking like a snared bird.

'Everything's fine,' I whispered.

Lucia's eyes darted to the men and then back to my face in a silent warning.

I nodded. 'Anything starts, get the kids down on the floor. And keep them there.'

She didn't say anything, but I knew she'd heard and would do it. She might be stubborn, but she knew how to survive. Olive wouldn't look at me but I felt her steady trembling. Lucia was humming a soft little tune now that sounded nice and I knew was intended for the frightened child. She was good with kids. Hannah was pressing her lips together and watching all of us as if she were proud or something. I couldn't believe she didn't know what was going on here or wouldn't acknowledge it.

228

The Dunnet boys were snatching uneasy glances at the men.

'How are you, James? Junior?'

'Fine, Mr Tucker,' they said in close unison, forcing worried smiles, then glancing back at the men, fiddling nervously with their napkins and chairs.

If Hannah even knew the men were nearby, she didn't show it. She just continued knitting and talking, looking at all of us between the movement of her needles with loving glances . . . like we were sitting at heaven's door. But we weren't.

Olive was starting to suck in sharp hard breaths.

'Everything's OK,' I repeated quietly, but it wasn't. Some unfortunate play was about to start. We both sensed it.

Then I heard a chair scraping hard over the floor-boards, and knew my theory was correct and also knew what was coming. Olive's body stiffened.

'Steady, sister,' I whispered.

The man wasn't tall, just wide, a well-used barrel of a body stuck on two average-sized legs. He was wearing a brown range hat that was too small for his big head. There was no mistaking the power in the neck, the arms and hands. He would be a formidable enemy. I took a deep breath to make certain I had enough air if I needed it and said, 'Mister.'

From fights won and lost, I knew that a man who hit after lulling you with a simple smile hit with twice the impact. And looking at this thick, stubby body standing in front of me, I knew I was going to need all the impact I could get. My guess was that he had me by fifty hard pounds. So I smiled.

Lucia reached and took Olive without making a commotion. The Mexican girl knew trouble. And what to do about it. I liked that about her. Olive was taking sharp hard breaths again, more audible now in the quiet that had fallen over the room.

229

'What are you doing putting your filthy hands on my little girl?' the man asked, pulling his pistol and holding it pointed at the floor. 'You like little girls?'

'Olive's a good kid,' I said, ignoring the unseemly accusation and the gun. 'I wouldn't hurt her.' I paused just long enough to get his attention. 'Nor let anybody else.' Once again, I was surprised by my new-found sense of composure. Normally a comment like the man's and a drawn weapon would have brought me up and kicking my chair back. I was turning into a regular diplomat, smiling until my cheeks were hurting.

I continued to ignore the gun, knowing from experience that if I focused on it I'd get the urge to shove it up one of his nostrils and out the top of his skull.

'I asked you something,' he snapped.

'What?'

'If you like little girls?'

I bit hard at the inside of my lower lip, feeling myself losing control, my hand sliding slowly down toward my hip. Lucia had moved Olive out from between me and the man. Smart kid. Even if I did everything right, this was going to be close. I wished the children weren't here to see it, especially Olive. But it wasn't my play. My hand was continuing to slip lower, the movement almost imperceptible, but if the man knew about such things, he knew where it was . . . and where it was headed.

Then, as if she were oblivious to everything that had just happened, knitting needles still flying, Hannah said, 'I can smell our food, Mr Gibbens. Can't you?'

I looked over at her. At times, she was certifiably loony. And this was certainly one of them. She was knitting away and smiling, acting like we were at a picnic, oblivious to the real world around her. I shook my head. It seemed odd, her being the Virgin Mary and still sometimes seemingly so featherheaded. But it was undeniable. As I was thinking this, I saw her suddenly stop knitting, make a half-turn in her chair, and look up at Olive's father as if she'd just realized he was standing there. She squared her shoulders to the man in that defiant way she had. If she saw the gun, it didn't faze her. I could see her expression changing.

I got myself ready for something decidedly unpleasant on her part, wishing she would just stay out of this. She was tough in her way, a woman to be reckoned with, but the problem was, she didn't have any finesse when it came to dealing with trouble. She just jumped it head-on, no bull, no dodge. And that's what she did now.

'She's not your child,' she said quietly.

'What?'

'She's not your child,' she repeated, her voice steady and soft, but as firm as any voice I'd ever heard in my life.

'The hell!' the man bellowed.

Hannah's eyes seemed to collide with his. 'Listen carefully,' she went on, her words nearly a whisper. 'Olive is no longer your child. She is going with me. You need to understand that. You must agree with it.' The words were cold, hard and sharp like a jagged piece of ice that cut into a person. 'You have no choice. In God's name, you must do this.'

The man stood staring down at Hannah for a moment, then he turned back to me. 'Hand her over,' he said, pointing the pistol at my face and reaching a hand for Olive.

'No,' Hannah said quietly, but I could tell she was starting to lose her temper.

'Maybe we should talk this over without the pistol,' I suggested.

'Shut up,' the man snapped.

'The child is going with me,' Hannah repeated, returning to her knitting, seemingly not too concerned with my predicament.

But I was.

Things weren't looking good at the moment. I could hear the children beginning to whimper and Lucia was murmuring a prayer in Mexican that I doubted was for me.

Great. Here I am, sitting with a gun in my face, surrounded by bawling kids, while this woman just goes on knitting and trying her best to piss off the gunman. I didn't move a muscle, figuring I was up against it good, my mind racing over the choices left me. There weren't many.

'Now!' the man yelled.

'Listen,' I said, trying to sound friendly. 'You've got to do like she says.' I paused, scrambling hard for something impressive to say. 'You've got no idea who she is . . . you really don't,' I continued, trying to sound as mysterious as possible. 'You really don't.'

The man squinted hard at me. 'Yeah? So tell me: who the hell is she? Cleopatra?'

The men behind him laughed and shoved each other, as if he'd made some grand joke. Hannah was frowning, which made me even more nervous. She was about as trustworthy in these situations as Jack.

'Better,' I offered. 'She can do wondrous things. She does magic.'

'Mr Gibbens, please,' she said, her voice sounding thoroughly exasperated. I didn't care.

She gave me one of her 'Don't act like a child' looks over her glasses. 'This man will do what I have said because it is right,' she continued with that matter-of-fact tone of hers. 'He has no choice.' She paused. 'I have made my demand in the name of God.'

Wonderful, I thought. I was dealing with a killer and a woman who was a god but also crazy.

Finished with her declaration, Hannah went right back at her knitting as if there was no man threatening to blow my skull to smithereens. I couldn't believe it: she was knitting-and-purling like this was any old day. The children were crying pretty good now and Lucia had stepped up the volume of her praying. At least somebody realized the seriousness of things. Fat lot of good that would do.

'What'd you say she did?' the man asked, cocking the hammer on the pistol with a loud metallic sound.

'Magic. She does magic.'

'I do not do magic,' she said firmly.

Since it was my head he was aiming at, I ignored her. 'Yes she does. She's just being modest.'

The man stood thinking for a second, before showing a lot of bad teeth. 'Then have her float me and my friends out to our horses. We want to go riding.' He turned his head back to his pals, snorting like a pig at his originality.

I would have gone for my gun but I knew he'd get off at least one shot in reflex and might hit a kid. So I waited.

'Want to go riding, boys?' he chortled. They were nodding like a bunch of defectives. The man turned back. 'Yeah. Float us out to our horses so we can take a ride.' The men behind him were chirping and grunting and slapping their legs. 'Horses are in the barn in case you're wondering where to deliver us. Mine's the big black-and-white pinto with the blue eyes,' he grinned.

Then we waited.

'Mine's a Roman-nosed palomino,' one of the men chimed in a few moments later.

Then we waited again.

And waited.

'OK,' I said, looking over at the woman. She didn't look like

233

she was getting down to doing anything that would save me. She just looked angry, knitting faster than before. 'OK . . .' I repeated, nodding at her. 'Any time.'

'Come on,' the man groaned, sounding like a spoiled child. 'You said she could do magic.'

Hannah Morgan didn't stop knitting or looking upset with me. I could feel the sweat breaking over my body. What was she waiting for? Then I recalled the talk I'd had with her in the jail – when I'd asked her if she'd prayed to save herself. The recollection caused a sinking feeling in my gut. She wasn't going to do anything. Maybe she couldn't do anything. That's what she claimed. It made no sense. But I could definitely see that nothing that even resembled a miracle was happening.

'Ma'am?'

'Mr Gibbens, this is ridiculous,' she said, not bothering to look up. 'This man is going to do what I've said. Because it is right – because God has ordered it.'

'I don't think so.'

'Yes –'

'You lying bitch!' the man screamed. 'You said you could do magic!'

I'd seen it happen before: Hannah Morgan stiffening and seeming to physically change shape and content somehow before me, growing somehow larger and more imposing, the light in her eyes fading some, as if all her energy were being sucked inward, concentrated on some mighty purpose. She was doing it now. Normally she was calm and collected, but call her a liar or treat her or the children with disrespect . . . and watch out. She'd stopped knitting with the man's insult and was staring down intently now at the table, as if focusing hard on something in the wood's grain. I watched her. The men watched her. The children did as well.

For just a moment, I half expected the five men to begin to float out of the room, wafted through the still air by the mystical powers of this strange woman. But it didn't happen. Nothing happened. We all just stood there watching her and waiting, the room dead silent. Then she shuddered hard as if suddenly chilled and slowly returned to her normal self. Studying her face, I thought she looked slightly disappointed. I knew I was.

Finally, I said, 'Mrs Morgan?'

'What?' she responded, sounding stiff and irritable.

'Are you?'

'Am I what?'

'You know . . .'

'No I don't know, Mr Gibbens.'

'Are you going to float these men out to their horses?'

'I am no magician, Mr Gibbens. And I don't want to discuss it any more.'

'I'm afraid it's not that simple,' I countered.

'It most certainly is.'

As I was getting ready to yank my pistol as a last desperate move, a sudden barrage of hollering and banging broke loose in the other room – the explosion of noise sounding like somebody was tearing the place down board by board with sledgehammers, men shouting, glass breaking, tables tipping.

I'm not certain what I expected when Olive's father yanked open the door to the narrow hallway. What I didn't expect to see was a riderless black-and-white pinto horse with blue eyes stuck halfway down the little passageway, with another horse – a Roman-nosed palomino – just as stuck right behind it, both animals struggling wild-eyed, kicking and stomping to get down the little hallway and into the dining room, like they had some urgent appointment to keep.

'That's my gawddamm –' The man stopped suddenly, as if

235

the words had been torn off at his teeth and lowered his pistol, then turned slowly and stared hard at Hannah Morgan's face. His expression was frightened, his mouth open like his jaw had been broken.

I was looking at her as well, convinced more than ever that God had come amongst us. I didn't care what she said, I was a believer in her as a divine spirit in human form. But she wasn't admitting to anything. She sat now ignoring us both, knitting again, her head bent down close to her work. Though I can't say for sure, I thought I saw a flicker of satisfaction on her face.

Then the anger that I'd corked up inside me broke and I was out of my chair and going hard after Olive's old man. I was doing it for myself . . . for the way he'd spoken to Hannah Morgan . . . and what I suspected he'd done to Olive over the years.

I'd gotten him spun around and hit hard a couple of times and was following him down to the ground to finish him off and to get ready for his pals, when I heard Hannah Morgan say, 'Mr Gibbens, please.' She said the words in a flat tone, again sounding very tired of my behaviour.

I stood up and stared down over the man, blood trickling from his nose. I was crowding him hard, ready to hit him again.

'Mr Gibbens,' Hannah said more firmly.

'Fine,' I muttered, stepping back but my eyes still on the man. 'You get your horses unstuck and out of here. Fast. Olive is going with Mrs Morgan. Understand?'

The man nodded.

'You agree?'

He nodded again, faster. His friends had lost their enthusiasm for any trouble related to this woman as well. They'd have gone for me. But not with Hannah Morgan sitting there knitting. They just stood shuffling their feet and staring at her as if she were a dangerous, demonic woman – as if she might turn them into toads if they didn't behave. Two of them had pulled their hats off as if this simple gesture might save them.

She smiled in a warm way, her eyes filling with water. I couldn't believe it: Hannah Morgan could fight with the best of them, but as soon as the fighting was over she was crying and moaning over the plight of her enemies. It was daffy. I shook my head and watched the work starting on the two horses jammed in the hallway.

Somebody was yelling for grease and they were pulling and shoving to get the animals unstuck and out of the tiny hallway. When it was over, the men led their horses toward the back door. Hannah was watching them now.

'Sir?' she called.

Olive's father turned back with a nervous glance at her.

'Thank you for doing what is right. I will make certain that Olive is loved and cared for during her life.' She paused. Then she raised her arms up, palms towards the heavens and said, 'May God forgive your sins.'

Afterwards, I watched as she dabbed at her eyes with a handkerchief, snuffing over a snake who'd have gladly blown my head into small fragments. She was truly the Mother of Mercy, though I was having a hard time agreeing with her about this big tub of guts who was still standing and staring at her like he was daft.

He watched her for a moment longer, a muscle over his right eye causing the lid to jerk nervously, then he nodded and went stumbling out the door like he was late for something important. I was sucking on my teeth when I felt something brush against me and looked down to see Olive. She took my hand and stood for a while. It was a sort of thanks and made me feel good. The two of us watched Junior and James putting on a mock fist-fight, mimicking the one they'd just witnessed. Hannah Morgan didn't look any too pleased.

'Boys,' she said sternly.

The kids were looking relaxed again. All except Lucia, who seemed to feel that she'd wasted a perfectly good prayer on my behalf and didn't like it. Olive went and joined her.

Later, after the children had taken two heaping plates of food out to Martha and Jack, and the room had fallen quiet with their absence, I turned and looked at her. In response, she pursed her lips and looked over her little half glasses with an unhappy expression and said, 'Yes, Mr Gibbens?'

'Nothing,' I mumbled, suddenly not sure what to say.

'You're thinking your wild thoughts again.'

I didn't respond.

She was buttering a piece of toast. 'It's best not to think exaggerated thoughts, Mr Gibbens – it throws everything in your head out of kilter.' She took a bite, savoured it for a moment, then seemed to remember something important and frowned at me.

'And by the way, sir,' she lectured, 'that man would have done what God wanted done. There was no call for you to say I work magic. I don't believe in magic or sorcery or tricks. And please don't tell people I do. It's not honest.'

'Those horses?'

'Things happen, Mr Gibbens.' She cleared her throat. 'I've told you that before,' she said, her tone sounding as if I was a dilatory child.

I shook my head. She wasn't going to give in and admit who she was. No matter what. She was determined to have me believe her nothing more than an ordinary woman. But I knew – knew she could help me find my wife and child. I was sure of it. Still, there was no use coming at it head-on. She wasn't going to fall for that. I'd wait. She was bound to make a holy mistake.

I walked over and looked down inside the coffin at the face of Milagros: peaceful and pretty. But seeing her lying so still while hearing the laughter of the other kids through an open window touched something deep inside my gut. She hadn't done anything to deserve this living death. It was just the way life was: cruel and arbitrary. Hannah had tied a sprig of the little St Johnswort into the child's hair.

It wasn't fair, this little girl stretched out here more dead than alive. I was thinking about my wife and child and suddenly feeling that Milagros – like I – ought to just give up and let go of life. Then Hannah Morgan was beside me.

'She's fine, Mr Gibbens.'

'She's not fine. She's almost dead.'

Hannah Morgan just stood there a moment, as if trying to control herself. When she finally spoke, her voice was low and carefully controlled. 'Don't ever say that.'

Emotions whirled inside me. 'She may as well be.'

'No,' Hannah snapped. 'You will not empower death. You will not.'

I was stunned by the harshness of the words, then surprised at the firmness of her grasp as she took my hand and brought it down to the coffin, slipping my index finger inside Milagros'. The child's reaction was instant, her little fingers wrapping around mine and squeezing gently, as if silently welcoming me to her dark world. The sensation of the pressure of her soft grip seemed to surge through my body and I felt odd emotions – again my thoughts were drawn to my wife and child . . . as if this child were somehow connected to them, could convey my thoughts and feelings across the sea of black ether that separated us.

'Never wish her dead,' Hannah said, her voice still strong

though no longer harsh. 'Never surrender life. God gave you that.'

I wondered if she knew what I was planning. Maybe. It didn't matter. It was my business. I studied the still features of the child. 'Why don't you save her?'

The woman didn't respond. She was talking to Milagros now, as if I were no longer there. Then she suddenly stopped and looked out a window that faced the mountains, as if she'd heard her name called. She appeared to be listening to something and I wondered if she was hearing her voices. I cocked my head and tried to pick up any sound in the quiet room. There was nothing. Nothing but the ticking of an old clock on the wall. She just stood there staring for a while – then turned to me and said, 'I must be going, Mr Gibbens.'

Six hours later, I was sitting on my mare and watching the woman riding through a foggy river canyon two hundred yards below, her gaggle of small fry strung out on the trail behind her. Her horse looked jumpy. But this whole thing was an act. It had to be. She almost certainly knew I was here. She liked to tease, I knew that. Nothing else made sense.

I'd left her and the children at the stage depot and headed south for a few miles, as if riding for El Paso, then doubled back and taken up her trail. If she wasn't going to admit who she was, I was going to prove it, at least to myself. And after I'd proven it, then I was going to find out how to get to my wife and child.

The air was turning chilly and I was whistling a quiet tune, my binoculars focused on her. She was moving parallel to a small stream, leading the white mule carrying Milagros, the mule followed close behind by the Dunnet brothers who were in turn being followed by Olive with Lucia up behind her. I spit. Quite a parade. Hannah Morgan and the Mexican girl were like two book-ends when it came to protecting these kids.

The stream waters had the black horse nervous. The animal was afraid of its own tail, dancing and spooking at rocks and grass clumps. I brought the binoculars down and sat calculating what I knew.

Hannah had headed north as soon as she'd left the depot, doggedly resuming her old trek, determined as ever. I'd had no problem catching up even though she'd been pushing herself and the kids hard again. I wondered where the heck she had to get to that was driving her so . . . had driven her since El Paso. No clue. I just knew it had to do with her voices.

After I'd caught up, it'd been easy enough to keep watch on her while staying out of sight. I'd been doing it for hours, and seen nothing . . . nada . . . goose egg. Still, I was convinced that any moment I was going to spot something extraordinary. Something divine.

Any moment . . . but so far the only thing I'd seen was a proud and determined woman riding a half-broke horse in the middle of lonely mountains, leading a band of scruffy kids. Nothing miraculous in that. The miracle was that she'd risked her neck out here – poorly dressed and riding this lunatic animal. I understood now why she'd bought the kids warm clothes in Four Walls. She'd definitely known where she was headed. Nothing as simple as chance . . . not with this woman.

I rubbed my eyes and felt the tiredness rolling over me, remembering that I hadn't slept for a night and a day. The sorrel stomped an impatient hoof and then began to spin the smooth Mexican roller in the metal bit with her tongue, plainly bored. Jack was just as cranky, trotting around wetting every-thing in the small clearing, as if there might be a thousand love-crazed females within spitting distance.

Martha, bless her soul, looked contented, sprawled on her side in a patch of fading sunlight. The bay was nibbling on the white flowers of a yarrow plant, the aromatic smell tickling my nose, my back hurting from having been in the saddle too long. Nobody was having any fun.

I put the glasses back on the woman and wondered the same old questions. Would she suddenly be whisked away on a white cloud? Who'd killed the men, an avenging angel? That sounded as far-fetched as believing that Hannah Morgan was the Mother of God.

I moved the circles of glass over the rugged moss-covered rock soaring up both sides of the canyon. No one was in sight. I'd checked her back-trail three times that day but hadn't spotted anyone.

Once more I watched her kick the horse into a jolting trot. Where was she going in such a hurry? It was almost dark and she needed to make camp while she could still see. Or could she see in the dark? I guessed maybe – guessed she could do any sweet thing she wanted.

Since I'd been watching her, she'd never hesitated about which way to go. Hour after hour, she'd climbed into these mountains as if she were dead reckoning her trail. But where? I doubted there was anything but hoar frost and mountain goats up these lonely passes.

I put the binoculars back to my eyes. She was urging the black across the creek now but the horse had convinced himself he was going to drown in six inches of water. I spit. He was as worthless as armadillo crap in these wilds, backing up now against the woman's futile pleading. I sat cogitating. This had to be an act.

Surely the Mother of God could exert a little divine power over a jolt-headed nag. A small bolt of lightning up its rump would about do the trick. As I was thinking this, the black suddenly crow-hopped across the water rolling Hannah Morgan off its rear in a less-than-graceful somersault. She landed on her own rump in the sand, her feet out in front of her, her long dress up and over her head. When she finally stood, she conducted a careful examination of her posterior. I swallowed a laugh as she straightened her clothing, talking rapidly to the horse. I couldn't hear the words but I could guess. Then I watched as she felt her backside once more. This was her third fall in four hours and I imagined she was getting pretty sore. But she was game, I'd give her that.

Earlier, she and the horse had come tripping down the mountain in a not-very-dangerous gravel slide, ending with her pitching over the animal's head. Not long after that, I'd watched the gelding buck her off when she accidentally backed him into the sharp spines of a yucca plant. It was a good show. Maybe she was doing it for the children's benefit. At the very least I'd have expected a few bars of celestial music in these steep rocky gorges. But there was nothing. Nothing but the howl of cold canyon winds against rock.

I watched now as she tried to jump the stream on foot. She didn't make it, not even close. Her long blue dress was wet up to her thighs and night was almost on them, the temperature dropping. Jack whined.

I ignored the little dog and watched Hannah trying to wring the water from her clothes. Her horse was grazing in a stand of meadow grass and she was talking rapidly to it again. I decided I wouldn't give that nag much of a shot at horse heaven.

From what I could see, she wasn't carrying a change of clothing and, unlike the kids, she hadn't bought herself a jacket. I bit at my lip. She needed a fire. As I was thinking this, she looked around as if thinking the same thought. My interest rose.

243

From the damp look of the rocks and trees below, a fire wasn't going to be easy.

She unstrapped her saddlebags, fishing through them until she found what she was looking for. Matches, I guessed. Again, my interest rose. Matches weren't going to start wet wood . . . not without some sort of help. This thought made my heart pump a bit harder: the moment I'd been waiting to witness was perhaps close at hand.

But it wasn't to be.

I watched as she sent up one little black puff of smoke after another in a futile attempt to get the wood burning. Now she stood and marched off into the surrounding brush, returning moments later with an armful of grass. From her stiff movements, I could tell the cold was getting to her. Grass wasn't a bad idea – only it wouldn't work either – wouldn't burn long enough or hot enough.

She was kneeling again and I was watching the flame sprouting fast but, as I'd guessed, not igniting the kindling. I shook my head – she didn't have a clue how to start a fire in wet country. Then suddenly the wind picked up in the trees and I felt a hard chill in the evening air and untied the mackinaw behind my saddle and pulled it on. I'd been in the woman's place before and didn't envy her, but she wasn't in any real physical danger, so I decided to watch a while longer.

Surely, I told myself, I was about to witness what I'd been tracking her all day to see: divine intervention. I felt bad knowing she was cold, then caught myself. If she was the Holy Mother she wasn't cold at all. God wouldn't let that happen. He might not answer my prayers but he surely looked after the Virgin. I waited: the canyon light fading fast, the fire remaining unlit.

The woman was sitting on the sand beside the wood, when suddenly she stood and crossed her arms and rubbed herself hard up and down to fight the cold. The children were standing around her, looking warm enough in their new garb, but worried. Hannah Morgan, goddess or not, was wet and without a jacket and looked badly chilled. Still, I could hear her talking cheerfully to the children like she was warm as toast. She was a piece of something.

Like water, cold air tumbles downhill into places like the canyon where the woman stood shivering. My guess was that it was ten or fifteen degrees chillier down there than where I stood . . . and when you mixed in the moisture off the stream, it was damp and cold. She should have known that . . . but she didn't appear to. That surprised me.

As I watched her hugging and rubbing herself, trying to get some warmth into her body, I saw something that I'd have never believed possible. It wasn't an angel, or the clouds parting to show a strange beam of heavenly light, or the wood magically bursting into flame. It was none of these. What I saw was Hannah Morgan step behind a large boulder, out of sight from the children, and kick a stone on the beach – kick in frustration, and then stamp off around the rock back to Milagros and the other children, walking as if nothing was wrong.

Something in the act – kicking at the stone, then checking on this child even though she was chilled to the bone – stirred my sympathy, even as it brought a new wave of confusion to my mind. What she'd done had looked so human. There was nothing Madonna-like about it. She was simply cold. As I continued to watch, Hannah leaned into her horse's shoulder, hugging it, trying to get warm, still keeping up her happy chatter with the children. I felt crummy.

My thoughts flew back to the words of the old minister in Four Walls: 'She's a fascinating woman. Mysterious in many ways. But, Mr Gibbens, she's flesh and blood. Don't waste time thinking she's anything more.'

Could I have created all of this craziness in my head? She had accused me of that very thing. But if that was so, then – I stopped myself from replaying everything all over again. There was no gain to it.

Maybe there were other natural explanations that had nothing to do with Hannah Morgan. Maybe she wasn't the Virgin – maybe she was just an inspired being who could see things, hear mysterious voices. Maybe she was telling the truth: that they just came to her and told her what to do. I didn't know the answer. I'd been so certain. Now I was questioning it again. Then I stopped myself. No. She was the Virgin. Crazy as it sounded, it was the only thing that made any sense, that explained any of what had happened to me. And she was my hope to find my wife and child. She had to be the Blessed Mother.

Fog was rising off the river by the time I reached the place where Hannah had tried to build the fire. I knew I was in the right spot because I could see the little pile of kindling and the burnt matches, but the woman and the kids and their horses were gone.

'Hello?' I called, peering hard into the water vapours drifting across the sandy beach like dreams.

I held my mouth open so that my breathing wouldn't interfere with my hearing, and listened for Hannah Morgan and the kids. There was nothing but the sound of the rushing waters and wind talking its way down off the mountains.

'Hannah Morgan?' I hollered, then listened as my voice bounced back and forth across the canyon walls, slowly climbing higher and higher, echoing to a soft faint sound as if I were whispering her name to heaven. Still no reply. I reached up and picked Jack off the sorrel's rump and set him on the ground. The little dog began to shiver harder and to step carefully around the damp spots in the sand, looking miserable as he moved.

'You damn sissy.'

I scooped him up and put him down where the woman had been squatting beside the wood, so he couldn't miss picking up her scent. The dog put his head down and began sniffing hard. He had her trail. 'Go find her.'

Jack didn't need any urging. He had taken to Hannah Morgan in a big way and seemed ecstatic that she was nearby. 'Hell, you should be so happy when you smell me,' I said. 'I'm the one who feeds you. And keeps the coyotes from eating your skinny body.'

The little dog didn't wait to debate the matter, he just darted off into the darkness, me trotting in pursuit. 'Martha,' I called back over my shoulder, 'stay!' The last thing I wanted was to lose my horses in these mountains. The big dog would make certain that didn't happen.

I couldn't see Jack in the misty night but I could hear him scurrying and whining his way up the rocky trail. Then I stopped and held my breath and listened. As I had back in the alley in Four Walls, I now felt a sudden and unsettling sensation that something or someone dangerous was close in the darkness. I pulled my pistol and tried to scent the air. Nothing. Then as quickly as it had come, the feeling passed and I trotted after my dog.

Jack found Hannah and the kids in a blind gulch a few hundred feet from the stream. I could barely make them out in the swirling mists. They were gathered in a group at the top of the trail, the children clustered near the horses, Lucia standing in front of Olive and the boys, Hannah Morgan standing a few yards in front of her. She looked every inch the she-wolf ready to defend her cubs. Having ridden through damp trees and brush, she was even wetter than before, pale and cold and shaking hard. The eyes of her horse were rolling white with fear. The kids looked scared as well, even Lucia. But not Hannah Morgan.

She stood peering down into the mists toward me, as if searching through the smoke of war for an ancient enemy, ready to do battle to protect her charges. To protect them from what, I had no idea. All I knew was that something in the way she looked – the way her shoulders were squared, her head held high, her hands clasped in front of her as if in prayer, gave her a bearing oddly not of surrender but of absolute defiance.

It was a posture and look that made me stop climbing and study her as if seeking permission to approach any closer. I'd never felt that way before in my life. When she finally recognized me in the clouds of vapor, her face broke into a wide smile and she lowered her hands as if she no longer had need of their prayerful protection. It was strange – this sense of power in her gesture of supplication.

'Mr Gibbens. It's so nice to see you,' she said, her breath blowing white in front of her face. She bent and picked up a bouncing Jack. 'Children, it's Mr Gibbens,' she called, her teeth chattering with the cold. 'I think he's lost again.' The smaller kids laughed, then said their obligatory hellos with genuine enthusiasm. Even Lucia seemed somewhat relieved to see me.

'Yep. Lost again,' I grinned, tipping my hat at the lot of them. 'That horse is badly spooked.'

'There's something down the trail.' She looked off toward a dark clump of brush below us on the trail.

I studied the spot but saw nothing.

'Probably coyotes.' The black was still dancing, so I walked up to it and reached to rub its neck and the animal shied hard and I yanked it down before it did damage to itself or somebody else. Looking at the soap-like sweat on its neck and the wildness in its eyes, I knew it wasn't coyotes that had spooked it.

'You OK?'

'Yes,' Hannah said, cheerfully. 'We've had an exciting day. And now you're here.'

The children didn't look quite as happy about things. But then, it was hard for anyone to have as much enthusiasm about things as this woman.

I studied the trail below us again: narrow, bordered on both sides by thick brush, the river close enough to be heard but not seen. I looked back at the woman. 'Ready?'

'There's something you should know, Mr Gibbens.'

'Yes?'

'I smelled it.'

'Smelled it?'

'Whatever is down there.'

'What'd it smell like?'

'Putrid.'

'Putrid?'

'Yes.'

There was something controlled and calculated-sounding in her voice. The flat, emotionless words of a field commander sizing up the enemy position just before a charge. And in the sound was the sense that I would know – somehow understand as she did – what had caused the smell. But she was wrong. I had no idea.

She returned her gaze to the shadows of the trail. No sign of worry on her face, simply alert and ready for something that she fully expected was waiting for her in those bushes. What? I wondered. It made me uncomfortable. I pulled my binoculars and glassed the dense thicket. There was nothing to see in the dark shadows. 'It's gone.'

It didn't appear as if she believed that. But whether she did or didn't, Jack was looking contented and that was enough for me. I watched her turn and stride back up the hill, looking strong and sure of herself; she checked Milagros, tucking the child's blankets in tight against the cold. Lucia was still giving me her drop-dead stare, not one to give up a fight – though I didn't have a clue about what we were fighting over.

So I ignored her and settled my hat low over my eyes and tried again to figure what had caused the smell. Skunks could be winded and not seen – but skunks didn't scare horses like this.

And if it had the power to harm the Mother of God – that bothered me. I had no interest in running into anything that had that much power.

I turned the horse around and then took Hannah Morgan's upper arm and helped her on to the animal. It was a natural thing that men in these parts did for women who were trying to mount a horse, especially one who had as much trouble getting up on an animal as Hannah Morgan did. Still, it made me uncomfortable to grasp her arm – she felt wonderful to the touch, lean and strong, her body moving with grace and assurance.

I checked to see that the mule's pack was tight and that Milagros was strapped in OK. She looked chilled and that bothered me, so I slipped my hand under the blanket and slid my finger into her hand. She clutched it and I felt the same wonderful, silent greeting and knew she was OK. When I turned back, I saw Hannah Morgan watching me and looking like she wanted to cry. I didn't want that so I turned away.

Stepping quickly to the black's head, I spoke a few harsh words to it to let it know I wasn't putting up with any crap. It snorted as if shocked by my insinuations, then blew its nostrils clear of white vapour and sucked in air to check the breeze for scent. A cold wind was kicking up and I could see the woman shivering hard. I figured she'd freeze to ice before she'd complain. 'We need a fire,' I said, handing my mackinaw up to her.

'No. You keep it.'

'I'm OK. This shirt gives off a lot of heat,' I grinned.

'It looks very nice on you, Mr Gibbens,' she said. 'And you must remember, it was on sale.'

I let out a little laugh and pushed the jacket up closer to her. She hesitated, then took it. 'Thank you. I am a little cold.'

I watched her pull it on, looking up at her lovely face, drawn to it, then feeling uncomfortable, beginning to notice that I'd stopped thinking and hurting about my wife whenever I was with Hannah Morgan. That wasn't right. I forced my thoughts to her. I don't know how long I stood there daydreaming before Hannah leaned down from the saddle and touched my shoulder.

'Mr Gibbens?'

'Yes?'

'The children could use that fire.'

'Sure.'

If she noticed my discomfort, she didn't let on. She just pulled in the lead-line of the white mule until it was alongside her animal, Lucia urging her horse close on the other side of the coffin, wedging the mule and Milagros between them, then Hannah Morgan took hold of her saddlehorn and made herself ready. When she was set, she looked back at the children and smiled. 'Children, Mr Gibbens is going to take us out of here.'

'Everybody stay close. Understand?'

Hannah, the boys and Olive all nodded. Lucia just made like she was fussying over Milagros. She wasn't going to budge.

I slipped the leather thong off the hammer of my pistol, took a fresh grip on the black's reins, and started down the trail toward the river. Jack trotted a few feet in front, looking like he didn't have a care. That made me feel better. Better until the little dog suddenly froze, his hair rising in a stiff ridge down the middle of his tiny back.

'What is it, boy?' I asked, pulling my pistol and trying to follow his gaze into the dark blotches among the trees. I couldn't see a thing. Then I heard the woman say something and looked up at her.

'What?'

'The smell, Mr Gibbens.'

The heavy wave of fetid air rolled over me just as she said the words . . . as rotten as any carrion I'd ever scented. Jack growled and started for the bushes a few yards down the trail.

'No!' I snapped. 'Jack. You get down to the beach.' The black was dancing again, forcing Hannah to tighten her grip on the saddlehorn and the mule's lead-line, while I concentrated on the brush and trees.

We were hemmed in on both sides, our vision cut by the floating droplets of moisture. Instinctively, I wanted out of here. I couldn't manoeuvre if things got desperate – couldn't see worth a damn. I started forward, my eyes locked on the wall of plants to my left.

'Jack, get going!' The dog obeyed, growling fiercely as he went. 'Knock it off.' He didn't, but he lowered the volume some.

Then, off to my left a few yards, I heard a limb snap – the sound bringing me to a hard stop. But search as I might, I couldn't make out any shape I recognized as being alive. Still something was slipping through the mists toward us, I was certain of it. I brought the hammer back to full-cock on the pistol. Then I started the horse and mule slowly down the trail. The last thing I wanted was to take a charge in this dark cramped place. Again, I heard a stirring in the brush. Whatever it was, it was moving with us. Stalking us.

I checked the woman. She was watching the shadows as if there was something she didn't like in them. That bothered me. She didn't look scared. She just looked ready for something . . . as if it was an old adversary out there in the darkness waiting for her. Something or someone she'd faced before. Ancient scores to even.

A breeze brought another wave of stench lapping over us – a smell that I thought I knew. I'd smelled it the night my wife died, then again with Lessing and Ramon, and in the barber shop in Four Walls: the effluvium of death. There was no mistaking it. As I was thinking this, I heard a sound that made blood rise to my scalp: a low rumbling roar that shattered the stillness of this isolated canyon, dying in a couple of menacing throaty coughs. Then the night fell ominously silent again.

I'd never thought of evil as a living thing that existed, not until I'd met this woman and seen the bodies of the men in Four Walls, not until I'd heard this unearthly sound. It was like nothing I'd ever heard before.

I started the gelding and mule down the trail at a fast trot, the children following. Jack gave us rear protection, bravely holding the trail for a few moments to make certain nothing was following, then he shot after us, glad to be leaving behind whatever smelled and roared like this. He was courageous, but no fool.

When we broke free of the brush, Martha's familiar shape standing in front of the two horses was a reassuring sight. She was poised at the edge of the river sand, barking her low-volume challenge, and though I felt like it, I didn't stop to hug her. Instead, I made certain Hannah and the children had their animals under control and then swung up into the sorrel's saddle and started down the shoreline in the direction I'd come. We rode at a steady trot – Jack, his ears laid back flat against his head, leading the way now, Martha lumbering along behind.

A mile down river, we passed the spot where Hannah had tried to start her fire. I kept going, putting another mile between us and the narrow trail before I reined in, concerned that in the dark we were going to hurt one of the horses on the river rocks. I turned in the saddle and took a look around. The beach here had begun to widen, was covered with deep clean sand, and with a fire, it would make a decent camp . . . open enough that I could defend it. But from what?

CHAPTER SIXTEEN

Hannah Morgan had the children sitting in a row on the sand. She was moving along behind them, checking their heads for ticks and lice, making sure they'd scrubbed behind their ears and done a decent job of washing their faces. She was humming and making periodic comments, glancing at me every so often as I squatted next to Milagros' coffin. I'd been studying the child's sweet face for a while, thinking about my wife and child, when I reached in and let her grasp my finger. The same wonderful surge of emotion flowed through me and I just sat there and let her hold me and thought about things. I wanted to cry.

A few minutes later, I tucked the blankets in around her and moved off to the pile of wet kindling I'd gathered. Hannah Morgan joined me, watching as I began to build a teepee with the sticks.

'What was back there?' I asked, my voice low so the kids wouldn't hear.

'Sir?'

'On the trail.'

'I don't know.'

'You don't?'

'No, Mr Gibbens.'

'You looked like you did.'

She didn't say anything for a few moments. Then she shook her head. 'I thought I did. But I'm not certain now.'

I messed with the sticks for a while, then asked, 'What did you think it was?'

She didn't hesitate. 'The devil, Mr Gibbens.'

I didn't say anything, just sat watching her face, waiting for her to grin or laugh. She didn't. She looked back with a levelling stare.

'You're kidding?'

'No, sir.'

'You think the devil was up that trail?'

'The smell – it seemed the same.'

I straightened up some and made a face at her. 'You've smelled the devil before?'

'Twice.'

'Twice?'

'Yes.'

'That's crazy. The devil doesn't come after people.'

Hannah squinted at me for a moment as if I'd missed some essential lesson in life, then said, 'Of course he does, Mr Gibbens. Every day. Remember the pricks on the St Johnswort.'

'That's just an old tale.'

She was staring hard at me again and when she finally spoke she sounded hurt, as if I'd been somehow unfaithful. 'You told me you believed in legends.'

'Some,' I said quickly, peering at her through the night air, trying to figure if she was just pulling my leg again. It didn't look like it. 'Let's say maybe I believe in the devil – which I don't – why would he be after you? What have you done?'

'God's work, sir.' She stopped and seemed to be weighing whether or not to continue. Finally, she said, 'The same as you.'

I jumped. 'The same as me?'

256

'Yes. Helping to care for these children.'

I didn't like the sound of any of this. She was either the Mother of God or certifiable. Right now I didn't know which. All I knew for sure was that I didn't want to get sucked into her affairs. I had my own problems. So I put the last stick on the teepee and stood. 'Let's get this burning.'

Hannah stared at the pile of wood, her thoughts somewhere else. I stood looking at the side of her face in the shadows, drawn to it once more, not knowing how long I'd been watching her when she finally cleared her throat.

'I'm not, Mr Gibbens,' she said softly.

I jumped. 'Pardon?'

'You're thinking I'm some goddess.' She paused. 'I'm not.'

'I'm not thinking anything.'

'Yes,' she persisted.

'You just looked concerned.'

She smiled at me with that look of hers that could stun and took one of her great turns of direction. These quick emotional movements always left me lagging far behind her. And this one was no exception.

'If I seem concerned, Mr Gibbens,' she grinned, 'it's just that I don't think you'll get a fire going with that wet wood. I tried earlier.'

I had the urge to ask her more about the devil but stopped. I didn't want her telling me how I was a part of everything with her and these kids. I wasn't a part of anything. That was my problem. I was somehow cut off and separate from things. From people and life. And I didn't want to talk about it. Especially with this woman. Especially with her. So I switched subjects. I was getting as good at that as she was.

'I cheat,' I said, turning and studying a stand of pines a hundred yards off. 'I'm going over there to get the stuff I cheat with.'

'May I join you?'

I don't know why I thought it, but something in the way she said the words made me feel as if she wanted to be there to protect me. That made me feel odd – being protected by a woman. I shrugged. 'If you want.'

She stood and dusted off her dress and hands and said, 'Ready.' She turned and looked at the kids. 'Children, we'll be right back. Mr Gibbens is going to try and start a fire. Isn't that right, Mr Gibbens?'

She was making one of her jokes, so I ignored her and headed for the trees.

'Yes. That's what he is trying to do,' I heard her teasing. She followed, walking fast to catch up with me. 'Please pray for him.'

I could hear the children giggling.

'May I give you some advice?'

I nodded.

'The wood is too wet. The air too damp,' she lectured as we approached the dark band of conifers. 'You may be expert at starting fires . . . but I'm an expert at not starting them,' she chattered happily. 'So you should listen to me.'

'You want to bet?' I asked, making idle conversation, watching the shadows around us. It was as if I'd suggested something wonderful to her. She clapped her hands together in front of her and bounced on the balls of her feet a couple of times like a schoolgirl.

'Yes. I love bets.'

I laughed to myself. She could surely shift directions. If she thought the devil was still after her, she didn't look too concerned about it.

'OK, it's a bet.' I wasn't paying much attention to her now, my eyes searching the dark tangles of brush along the tree line for movement. It was still and silent, but that wasn't a whole lot of reassurance. I started to step into the trees when Hannah grabbed my arm. I jumped. 'What?'

'What are we betting?'

'What do you mean?'

'We can't have a bet without betting something.'

I let my heart slow, then thought for a moment. 'OK. If I lose, I'll cook dinners as long as we're in these mountains.' I was still fighting the shaking in my body, 'But next time – don't grab me like that.'

She nodded. Then she pursed her lips and squinted her eyes some and nodded again, appreciatively this time. 'That's good.' She hesitated. 'Now what should I bet?'

She was crazy. 'How should I know?'

'OK. OK. I have it. If I lose, I'll knit something for you.' She looked at me for a reaction. 'Good, right?'

'Yeah. Fine.' I wasn't hearing her. Rather, I was trying to listen to the night and the silence in the trees just ahead and wishing she'd stop talking. She was as bad as Jack at times.

'This is a good bet,' she said quietly.

'Shhhhh.' I frowned. Hannah smiled back at me and silently mouthed the words: 'Good bet.' I shook my head and took a step into the trees and all hell broke loose in a wild explosion in the branches overhead. Shoving the woman behind me, I went down into a fast crouch, pulling my pistol and looking for a target. Nothing. The silence returned, broken only by Hannah's hard breathing. I'd shoved her backwards and she'd fallen hard on to her seat.

'Fool's hens,' I said sheepishly. 'They nest in the low branches.'

She was sitting and gasping for the air that had been knocked out of her.

'Ma'am?'

'Yes?' she gulped.

'You OK?'

'Yes,' she wheezed.

'Sorry about the shove.'

She was opening and shutting her mouth without sound.

'Good thing I'm not jumpy,' I said, trying to make a joke, embarrassed that I'd knocked her down. I helped her up. She was still sucking hard for air, making little gasping sounds in the night and putting a hand on her breast and closing her eyes.

'Yes. Very calm,' she said, forcing a painful little smile, her eyes still shut.

The absurdity of her words caused me to laugh. She was a sport. It took a while for her to recover her breath. When she was breathing a little better she said, 'I like to hear you laugh,' her voice sounding hoarse.

I didn't say anything – just wondered if she could see me turning red in the shadows.

'You don't do it often.'

When she was breathing normally, I started moving through the pines again, examining trees. Hannah followed close behind once more, intent on carrying on a conversation as if we were strolling through a city park somewhere.

'You should laugh more. You have a lovely laugh.'

Again, I acted like I hadn't heard. If she cared, it didn't show. She just continued carrying on her conversation.

'I used all my matches trying to light a fire,' she continued, suddenly grinning. 'I don't believe in being pessimistic, Mr Gibbens, but you won't be able to.' She paused, then chuckled. 'Can you cook without a fire?'

'You a good loser, ma'am?' I asked, running my hand over the trunk of a large pine in the darkness, examining the bark until I found what I was looking for.

'Yes. I happen to be a very good loser. Excellent. But I'm afraid you won't find out,' she said with a little laugh. Then she did a strange thing. She stopped and wrapped her arms around herself and shivered and looked off into the shadows. 'Perhaps we should just find someplace – a cave or something – Mr Gibbens, where we can get out of the wind and the cold.' For a moment, she looked concerned.

'You see something?'

She didn't respond.

'Ma'am. What's wrong?'

'Nothing.'

It was my turn not to respond. The gesture and words just seemed so unlike her – so unsure. Then, seconds later, she was back to her happy energetic self, moving close to watch over my shoulder, forever curious about every little thing.

The yellow balls had hardened into clear glass-like clumps, adhering with the tenacity of glue to the bark of the tree. I knocked off three large pieces the size of plums. Hannah continued to stand close behind me – bumping into my back every once in a while as I worked. All my life, I'd hated to be crowded. And with anyone else, I would have asked them to step back some. But not with this woman. Though I didn't like to admit it, it felt good having her close. It had been that way with my wife, too.

'What's that for?' she asked, reaching an arm around me and touching the hardened clumps.

'For cheating.'

'Mr Gibbens.' She paused. 'I don't know why you won't listen.' Her eyes were filled with laughter.

Back at the camp, I slid the yellow globs inside the teepee of twigs then struck a match catching a glance at Hannah's face as it flared. I could see she honestly didn't think I had a chance

261

to get this pile lit. I smiled. The children were standing in a half-circle around us, cold and shivering.

I held the match just outside the teepee. 'Still time to back out.'

She shook her head. 'No sir.'

I touched it to the balls. Instantly they began to burn, flames licking up through the teepee of wet kindling with an intensity that left no doubt that the wood itself – damp or not – would soon catch fire.

Hannah's expression changed slowly.

'Mouth's open,' I said.

She looked genuinely torn between the relief of getting a fire burning and disappointment that she'd lost the bet.

'Better get to knitting.'

'I don't believe it.'

'Whether you do or not . . . you still lose.'

'But you cheated.'

'I told you I was going to.'

'Where'd you learn that?'

'We had pine on our ranch,' I said, feeling good. This woman made me feel good – something I hadn't felt since after I'd found out about my wife's sickness.

'Mr Gibbens, there's something I must tell you.' Her voice sounded concerned.

I sat up straighter and stared across the shadows at her. She looked serious, the wavering light of the small fire deepening the lines on her face. Here it comes, I told myself. She's going to confess. She's going to admit to being the Mother of God. I sucked in a breath and said, 'Yes?'

She hesitated for a few moments, then said, 'I've never knitted anything in my life.'

'What?'

262

'Honestly. I never have.' She paused. 'I should cook the dinners.'

I looked at her to see if she was joking. She wasn't. This was serious with her. Just like the time when I'd accused her of lying. She took these kind of things very seriously. She'd entered into a bet, given her word, and she was worried about living up to her end of it. She was strange that way.

'Sure,' I said, disappointed she hadn't confessed. 'Whatever.'

She looked at me, mistaking the sound in my voice to mean that I was sorry she wasn't going to knit me something. She sat up straighter. 'No. That's not right. A bet is a bet. I'll knit you something.'

I couldn't believe her. Worried about a simple thing like this. 'We were only playing.'

'Yes. But we gave each other our words. So I'll knit something.' She forced a brave smile on to her face.

'Suit yourself,' I said.

'Fine.'

I stared at the yellow flames licking back the shadows of the night. They were growing brighter and brighter, the children crowding closer. Hannah had pulled out her knitting and was making some sort of calculations in her head, then on the sand, then the palm of her hand, scribbling invisible things hard and talking to herself and, every once in a while, looking over to stare at me with an appraising squint.

I ignored her. My thoughts drifted back to the day my wife had come home to Santa Monica by train from the specialist in Tuscon. She hadn't said anything through dinner or while we sat on our porch and watched the winter surf pounding the sand, but I knew the lump she'd found in her breast wasn't good. I just hadn't expected she wasn't going to make it.

That she wasn't going to live to see our child grow. That we weren't going to buy the ranch we'd dreamed and saved for. Weren't going to grow old together and take our grand-kids camping on the beach, hunting for sea shells and pirate treasure.

We weren't going to do anything together. Nothing but watch her die. I closed my eyes and forced myself to think about other things. I cleared my throat and looked at Jack crawling into Hannah's lap. It made me feel better.

I found my thoughts drifting away again, until a few minutes later I was feeling as if I knew how ancient man had felt when he first found fire, sitting around these magical flames with the woman he loved.

For a fleeting moment I felt as if I were actually there, thousands of years ago, could see the shadowy shapes of others – kinsmen – around me in the stifling darkness of a towering cave. I had never felt anything like it before in my life. It was as if I were awake but dreaming. I shuddered and shook the sensation off. I continued to stare at the fire – then at Hannah. Suddenly I knew fire wasn't only warmth and protection. It was hearth. One of the Creator's great gifts to man – a succouring focus for everything human in the cold night of the world.

I stared at her face and listened to the sounds of the children and wondered about this fleeting sensation of having travelled back in time, this ghostly revelation of where family and home began. This odd sense that I had actually been sitting in a cave somewhere with this woman and others – others who were related to me – thousands of years ago. Then Martha groaned peacefully and I was fully back in the here and now, with Hannah Morgan next to me, the children close gathered around us, at the edge of a river in these high mountains.

I took a couple of deep breaths and then said, 'Resin is the reason pine forests go up fast in fires.' She nodded in a daydreaming way, staring into the flames as if she too were watching something in the past that I couldn't see. Then she went back to her knitting. She was so incredibly beautiful, I thought. I forced myself to stop looking and began to feed the flames in earnest.

The sap had burned long and hard enough to ignite the teepee and the larger sticks I'd added. I waited until these took off before adding more. Hannah seemed to suddenly realize that I was there beside her and she looked at me and smiled and set her knitting aside and began to help feed the flame. She did a good job of it, careful not to destroy the fire's natural draw. I wondered where she'd learned. I liked the feeling of working with her.

'Hungry?'

The children were nodding hard.

'Starved,' Hannah added.

'What were you planning on eating?' I asked, amazed once more at her almost total lack of preparation. She'd left Four Walls at a trot with little or no food for her and the children.

'I don't know.'

'No?'

She laughed. 'I had some things.'

'I can see that. Lots of yarn.'

'And other things. I thought I'd find a ranch before now where I could buy more.' She had suddenly returned to staring into the flames as if thinking her dark thoughts again. She wasn't being rude, just seemed deeply distracted. It was an odd mannerism. One I was getting used to.

I started to ask her a question, then my stomach growled and I stood and walked to my pack. 'I've got some makings.'

She swam out of her deep contemplations.

I took my pack and began pulling things out. That afternoon in a grassy mountain meadow, I'd shot a couple of rabbits and three squirrels with a little meat rifle I carried. These had been gutted and cooling all day under the canvas pack. I brought them out, along with my cooking pot.

Earlier I'd also found a stand of wild carrot and burdock. Both were good in stews and I'd pulled them and dropped them into a burlap sack. I dumped these things on to a flat rock near the fire now. Slim pickin's considering there were five kids, two hungry adults and two dogs.

Hannah took the pot down to the river, carrying it easy on her hip like she'd done it a thousand times before, and scrubbed it clean with wet sand and water. When she returned she stood watching me dressing the game with my pocket knife.

'Not much,' I said. 'I've got flour and salt and pepper. Some bacon.'

'With a little help, it'll be more than enough,' she said, turning and looking off up the sandy beach. 'There's a pond up there, Mr Gibbens.'

I didn't say anything. I certainly wasn't going fishing at this hour.

'I saw cat-tails.'

'Yes?'

She'd turned and was walking away in the moonlight toward the green spikes with their familiar soft brown heads. I watched her. She was a tall, athletic looking woman who stood and walked straight – without any interest in having anyone look at her. She belonged only to herself, gave away nothing to others. Therefore whatever she was seemed so much more valuable. I got up and brushed the sand from my knees and followed.

'Cat-tails?' I called after her. I knew red-winged blackbirds liked to nest in them but I didn't figure they were worth anything as food.

'Quite good,' she said.

Fifteen minutes later, we'd harvested an armful of different plants. Plants I'd never before done anything with but look at. Hannah had taken off her shoes and tied her damp skirt up above her knees and was wading around in the icy waters of the pond now, laughing and wiggling her toes down into the frigid mud to locate the heavy egg-like tubers of the arrowhead plants that hugged the shoreline. She'd kept up her happy conversation about everything under the stars, fighting the chattering of her teeth and the cold. Finished with the arrowhead plant, she'd gone digging in the same way for the cat-tails.

I liked the way she went right at things, happy and industrious. There was nothing prim or fancy about her. She might have the looks of a sophisticated beauty, but she could and did get down and work at practical things. And she enjoyed it, laughing and talking as she dug in the mud. Jack and Martha and the kids watched from the shore. Me, too. Everybody but Lucia seemed to be having a good time.

Hannah Morgan was as alive as any woman I'd ever known. I watched her now tugging hard at a cat-tail. I was feeling tired from the day, but not her. She seemed to have enormous reserves of everything stuffed into her slim body.

Standing with my arms full of dripping plants, I watched her wade ashore one final time, playfully hitting me over the head, club-like, with one of the soft cat-tails, the children running on ahead. She laughed that deep laugh of hers and I got embarrassed. I'd never been much for games, especially with women. I wasn't without humour, I just had a hard time joking with females. I'd spent too much of my life separate from them – herding cattle or hunting men – to be much good around them.

As we were heading back to camp, she spied some milkweed and purple-flowered thistle and happily ordered me to harvest them as well. She was cold and shivering in the misty air, but thoroughly enjoying herself. I dutifully carried out the order, though I couldn't imagine eating prickly thistle.

Beside the fire, which I'd built into a nice blaze, I watched as she cleaned and tossed things into the boiling water, the contents rising to just below the pot brim. The stew was steaming with mounds of Solomon's seal, milkweed, burdock, wild carrots, diced cat-tail and arrowhead tubers. She moved quickly and surely around the fire, as if used to it, cutting with decisive movements, stirring, seasoning, poking at the embers beneath the pot. Then she browned the squirrel and rabbit meat in a skillet with a little flour and grease and dropped these into the water, adding salt and pepper . . . and soon the wafting aroma of the brewing meal had the kids and dogs and me salivating.

Next she took some flour and mixed it with the coloured pollen from the cat-tail heads, using part of it to thicken the stew. The rest she mixed with water and baking soda and rolled the resulting dough out into long strands that she wound around green sticks and baked over the coals of the fire to make some stick bread.

Hannah Morgan knew how to rustle grub.

With the bright stars in the dark canyon sky seeming to float just over the tops of the mountain, the warm flames jumping into the brisk night air, Hannah suddenly rose to her feet and held her hands up high toward the sky and readied herself to speak over the food. I'd never seen anybody pray like that – like they were calling down all the power of heaven on the world. Always a little awed by this uninhibited gesture of hers, each and every one of us lowered our heads, listening as the low sound of her voice kicked in, the supplications flowing easy and nice. She could spin gold with her voice. Once, I heard my name and shifted uncomfortably. Then she was done and smiling and dishing out the food. We ate hardy.

Afterwards, she produced a bag of wild raspberries she'd collected that day along the river's banks. And we feasted on those and hot coffee. A truly wonderful meal. At the end, I could only sit – stuffed and thoroughly satisfied – the dogs sprawled in the hot sand near the fire, sipping my coffee and studying this amazing woman who so confused me.

The kids collected a big stack of wood and carried hot coals from the main fire to start one of their own back near their blankets. They were sitting around it, poking it with sticks and talking and laughing while Lucia combed out their hair. The dogs were with them. Kids and dogs: good company. I watched them for a while, then looked back at the woman.

She was still wearing the mackinaw jacket and staring down at the flames again. Whenever she did this the lines on her face seemed to deepen and she looked tired and even lonely. It was as if her face bore the marks of other people. Their pain, their sorrows. I continued to stare at her until she looked up and smiled.

'Yes, Mr Gibbens?'

I glanced away, uncomfortable that she'd caught me gazing at her again like some schoolboy in knee pants. 'Nothing.'

'Yes, something. You are still thinking your crazy thoughts.'

I didn't answer.

'Isn't that correct?' She continued to watch me, her half-smile slowly changing until the lines of her face were serious. 'Mr Gibbens, I don't know how to convince you.' She paused. 'I hear the voices of God's messengers. That's all.'

She turned back to the fire without saying anything more – the two of us watching the flames and listening to the mountain's great solitude. Every once in a while I noticed her squinting off into the sheets of darkness beyond the firelight, as if searching for something on the fringe of the night. I wondered if she were who I thought – wondered what happens to a deity who lives for ever? Alone without family, no friends. Sadness crept over me.

She looked back at the fire and pressed her lips together, poking at the coals with a stick, a trail of bright sparks soaring into the night sky like angry words. Whenever she was tired and contemplative, I would think I could see the ages, like the wear of countless hands on marble, burnished subtly into her features, the cut of a million life sentences.

'Where you headed, ma'am?'

She continued to watch the fire. 'I don't know.'

'No?'

She held the damp folds of her dress out to dry. 'This pass.'

'Where's it lead?'

She shook her head.

'You're climbing these mountains to get to a place you don't know?' My tone suddenly sceptical. 'I thought your voices told you these kind of things.'

She was gazing down at the ground. Slowly, she brought her head up until she was staring level into my eyes. 'I'm supposed to be here,' she said. 'I know that much.' She paused. 'But I don't know where it leads. There's a house with three chimneys. I've seen it. But that's all I know.'

There she was again, making certain everything was perfectly accurate. No exaggerations. No mistaking what she'd said. And she could turn cold as a toad's belly in response to my questioning. But I'd been a lawman too long to stop asking questions because somebody didn't like it. Even this woman.

'You're trying to find a place you're supposed to be – but you don't know where it is. Right?'

'Yes.'

I could see her cheeks changing colour and her body stiffening. I ignored it, driven to know the truth about her. 'How will you know?'

'Sir?'

'If you don't know where you're heading – how will you know when you get there?'

She ignored the question and stared down into the steam rising from her coffee cup. Understanding her somewhat better now, I decided she wasn't going to answer me anyway, so I sat building a cigarette. She waited a while and then went back at her knitting. She could madden a soul. Talking just enough when pressed.

She was a piece of work. Out here in the middle of nowhere, unarmed, poorly dressed, dragging a bunch of kids up a towering mountain, riding a half-broke horse. Trying to find her way through mountains to a place she'd never been . . . all because she heard voices. I spit. She'd better be the Mother of God . . . and hope the voices were right. She might be immortal, but I had the unsettling sense that the world was going to make her pay a bitter price for holiness.

She was lucky I'd been looking out for her. I froze. Or was she? Had I been brought along to do just that? I didn't like the possibility. I'd always done what I wanted, when I wanted. And nothing – not even this woman – had changed that.

I was nudging a small stone around with the toe of my boot when she asked, 'Why are you here?' She hadn't looked up from her fast moving needles. She was still upset. I jumped, wondering if she'd read my mind.

I stalled for time. 'Pardon?'

'Why are you here?'

'Just thought I'd check to see you were OK.' My voice trailed away and I got embarrassed the way I did around her.

'I'm fine,' she said coolly.

I was suddenly mad myself. I'd been running around this desert trying to take care of her. Following her all over the damn dusty place. And here she was acting like I owed her. She was still knitting. I'd be damned if I'd let her keep me from finding out things. I'd been ready to kill men over her. That, I figured, gave me rights. I looked at her.

'Those three men –' I stopped, suddenly not wanting to continue.

'Yes, Mr Gibbens?'

'Nothing.'

'What do you want to know?' Her voice was firm.

'You don't remember anything?'

She looked up from her knitting and stared long enough for me to squirm a little. 'I find you strange, sir.'

The words took me aback. 'How's that?' I mumbled.

'One moment you grovel before me . . . telling me I'm the Mother of Christ. The next, you act as if I'm a liar.'

I didn't move.

There was something inexpressibly cold and hard-edged – something condemning – in the words and her expression that made me want to stand very still and say nothing. Which I did.

Hannah knitted hard for almost an hour by the fire, while I repaired saddle leather. Then she took the dinner dishes downstream to a place where the waters slowed, the kids and dogs chasing around her like banshees. I leaned over and tried to see what it was she was knitting so hard on, but couldn't tell. It just looked like a mess. I shrugged and started getting the camp ready for sleep.

Hannah was singing one of her soft songs down the beach,

Jack sitting close beside her as she squatted washing the dishes. I closed my eyes and listened for a while and thought about all the good things that had been my life. Then I stopped and just sat listening to the woman's voice: nice in the soaring majesty of these mountains. The words seemed to float on the air, drifting as if they would drift higher and higher up these steep granite slopes, drift on for ever.

I stirred from my thoughts and spent the next few minutes rigging a canvas over Milagros to block the breezes and keep the mists out. Finished, I knelt next to the child and slipped my finger inside her little hand and felt the warm squeeze. 'Don't quit,' I muttered.

The night sky was clear. We'd get a dew but there were blankets enough. As long as it stayed above twenty degrees, Hannah and the kids would be comfortable. I looked back down at Milagros.

'Don't quit.'

Milagros gripped harder when I tried to pull away. It had never happened before and it made me hurt in my chest, this clinging to me as if she were lonely. I sat down next to the coffin and let her hold my finger for a while and thought about things. Martha was on her side in the sand nearby. I smiled. I hadn't felt this at peace in a long time.

I didn't look up right away when Hannah stopped singing, not until I heard Jack growl. There was a mist in the air. Not much but enough that I missed seeing it in my first glance down the darkened beach. I moved my gaze back over the dark terrain, following the direction Hannah and Jack were looking. That's when I saw it.

She'd been right: the devil. The dark shape was standing some ninety yards down river from Hannah, melding with the shadows, towering like a feral monster in the shallow water.

The kids were cowering on a little sand bar between it and Hannah.

I started for them – but it was too late. She was already moving forward, wading out into the stream toward the children who stood frozen looking at the creature. I would have expected nothing less from her – expected that she would go after anything that threatened these kids. She'd reached them now, turning each child around and saying things to them that I couldn't hear, moving them gently but firmly off toward the shore. Finished, she turned back and faced it, stepping off the sandy strip and back into the frigid waters, seemingly drawing herself up to her full height, as if readying herself for some final struggle – unarmed but defiant in a way that was almost frightening to behold.

Jack was growling and kicking sand on the shore. 'Stay out of this,' I hollered at him. Then Hannah waded a few feet closer toward the beast, again, as if readying herself for single combat with this frightening creature. It wasn't what I wanted her to do. The waters of the stream whirling around her calves, her arms held down at her sides as if by force, her fingers spread wide and tense as if ready to fire bolts of energy from their tips.

'You should not be here,' she said to it, her voice sounding as if it were laying down the right and wrong of things for all centuries.

'Just start backing up,' I called, trying to keep my voice even and moving slowly down the beach toward her, pulling the hammer back on the rifle. But she didn't back up. Didn't move. I hoped she wasn't sliding into one of her trances. The kids moved by me, whimpering and looking back at the woman, but driven along by the firm hand of Lucia.

'Get them up into trees,' I snapped.

I turned back to the river.

274

'Ma'am. Take a slow step back. Now.' Still, she didn't move.

The shadowy shape in the darkness was massive. I squinted through the river mists and tried to make out the details of it, but couldn't. Maybe it was seven or eight feet tall – 1,000 pounds. It was turning its huge head in the shadows, trying to catch Hannah's scent in the air. Then it started.

Hannah had taken another step toward it – seeming to challenge the creature's right to threaten her and the children. That was enough. The beast let go with a rumbling roar, dropping to all fours and going for her. It was running in a deadly headlong charge, water spraying out on all sides, its teeth clicking.

Though I'd never seen a grizzly bear before I'd heard about them, knew the legends of their speed, power and meanness. And this one was proof those horrible tales were true. Its head down close above the water, it was bunching into a hard run through the shallows. No more than eighty yards separated it from the woman now. I expected her to turn and bolt for shore. But then I should have known Hannah Morgan better. She wasn't one to cut and run. Crazy as it seemed to me she took another combative step toward it.

I threw the rifle to my shoulder and immediately saw the back of her head in my sights. 'Down! Get down!'

But she didn't move, forcing me to run upshore a few yards. I knelt and pulled off the first shot. Even as I heard the explosion I knew I'd yanked at the trigger, pulling the barrel right. But I also knew from the bear's sudden bawling that I'd hit it. Even so, it hadn't slowed the charge.

I levered in a new shell and fired again. Again. Again. Everything happening in seconds. Still the bear was making its mad rush at Hannah. I fought the horrible thought ripping through his mind: I wasn't going to stop it. I fired twice more in quick succession. Still it came.

I chambered the final round and ran forward into the cold water for a better shot. Hannah hadn't moved. Hadn't turned like a normal person and run. She just stood there facing this mad charge. Then I saw Jack bounding through the water to meet the wild beast head-on. No matter that he was small, he wasn't about to let Hannah Morgan be attacked without going down first. Under any other circumstance I'd have tried to order the dog off, but not now. There was no time. Then I caught sight of Martha sprinting in long stretching strides down the shore to back up her tiny friend. Something pulled at me deep inside seeing Martha and Jack, knowing they were both willing to die for this woman and each other.

Without much hope left, I pulled the rifle into my shoulder, sighted on the lumbering mass of brown hair, held my breath, then squeezed. I felt the hard kick, saw the flash, heard the boom echo with authority off the steep canyon wall across the river, the splat of lead. Then I watched in surprise as the bear dipped its giant head into the water, shovelling sprays of sand and foam in front of its snout as it went down in a sliding heap, its head and heavy upper body ploughing into Hannah with a tremendous wallop. Flying backwards, the impact of the beast's collision with her was great enough to drive her body a couple of yards over the water's surface. Then Martha was on the animal, tearing at it with vicious growls.

I was fumbling for another shell – then stopped.

Just by looking, I knew it was dead. I waded closer. A small red hole in the centre of its forehead was trickling blood down on to the heavy snout. But just to make certain, I stuck the muzzle of my pistol against the side of its skull and fired. Twice. I saw Hannah wince from the concussion and close her eyes. I knew that her combativeness was gone now, that she was suddenly feeling bad for the animal. Then the smell hit me, a gut-souring stench that almost caused me to lose my meal. Someone – hunter or Indian – had wounded the bear in the shoulder and its flesh was rotting with gangrene.

Certain the fight was over, I moved through the water to where Hannah, her clothing soaked, was struggling to get up, spitting out sand and water.

'That poor beast,' she mumbled, then turned her head and seemed to be searching for something. 'Jack?'

'Jack!' I hollered. I was running in the river, the water numbingly cold. Searching desperately like a blind man under the surface. He wasn't anywhere. I ran upstream, then back, frantic now, Martha continuing to tear at the bear as if evening the score for harming her friend.

I stopped and stared. I couldn't believe it. Hannah Morgan hadn't moved. Jack was under these dark waters dying and she hadn't stirred a muscle to help find him. I'd never have believed that possible.

'He's dying,' I yelled. 'Where is he?' She looked frozen in place, her lips moving slowly, her eyes clamped tight. I wondered if she was trying to pray him to the surface or crying over his lost soul. Neither one would do much for Jack.

'Where?' I yelled again. Still she didn't move – whispering nonsense into the night. As I was thinking this, Hannah suddenly opened her eyes and looked across the dark shadows of the river at me.

'Underneath,' she said.

'Underneath?'

She didn't answer, just knelt down in the icy river, the waters rising to her waist, and began to search around the bear with her hands. Then the children were rushing back into the stream as well, and together, shoving with all our combined strength, we tried to roll the animal. Impossible. Jack had been down for at least two minutes. I sprinted for the horses while Hannah and the kids continued to hunt for him.

'Jack,' she said quietly, over and over, as if she were calling him to supper or to his grave. An odd, winsome sound. It wasn't so much that it sounded like resignation – it was something else. Maybe more like calling someone home. It scared me to hear it.

Still not convinced he was under the bear, but not having a better guess, I forced the sorrel close, the horse crow-hopping and snorting, wanting nothing to do with this dead beast. I didn't give a damn what it did or didn't want, tossing Lucia a rope and yanking the animal up hard to keep it from bolting.

'Loop that forepaw,' I yelled to the girl, wrapping the other end of the rope around the saddlehorn. When she was ready, I kicked the mare across the stream. The rope went taut, spraying water and stretching so hard I thought it would break, the sorrel straining, until slowly the carcass rolled. Hannah was standing up now, dripping wet, her eyes narrowed and searching over the surface of the dark river, searching for some clue that wasn't to be seen.

There was nothing. Nothing but shadows and the night-dark liquid, thick with mud from the river bottom. If Jack was down there, we'd never see him. I was swinging off the mare to begin the frigid search again when I saw Hannah take two quick, purposeful steps to her right, looking as if she were learning to dance. She stood still, her head cocked rigidly to the side like Martha did sometimes when she was trying to figure something out. I stepped beside her, hope surging in me, moving my eyes slowly over the waters. Nothing. There was nothing to be seen. No stirring. No bubbles. Nothing but the pitch-black liquid, dark as the mouth of a wolf.

Then she bent quickly, reaching down deep into the chill

river, submerged to her shoulders, and plucked Jack out of the swirling sand and murkiness without hesitation, as if there was no question she could see him. It was as if her voices had spoken, guiding her to this spot in the river. I looked at her face. Her mouth was half-open and she was nodding slowly. It made perfect sense. At least if you believed she was the God-bearer. Which I did.

Jack looked broken. He was still breathing, but barely. I swallowed down a cry in my throat as Hannah carried him to the fire, talking softly as she moved. I focused on her words, hoping they had some power.

I didn't notice anything at first. Then slowly – still listening to her voice – I was seeing flashes of other women. Women of different ages and races holding the sick and dying: strangers wed only by sorrow breaking into view before my eyes as if suddenly appearing out of some primal mist, then disappearing. Shoved from the stage by others. I leaned into the mare as if I might faint and rubbed my face hard, the images gone as quickly as they'd come. I needed sleep.

Minutes later, I was squatting in front of the woman and looking at the terrier. He was wrapped in a towel, still as death in her arms, his breathing fading even as I watched. Something twisted hard inside me.

It seemed so wrong. Small though he was, he had too large a heart to die so easily. He couldn't, I kept telling myself. So game, so willing to give himself for me, for this woman. I took a deep breath and felt miserable. Felt I'd been too hard on him, scolding him, telling him to shut up all the time. For his part, he'd been good-hearted and eager to please. I felt another moan building in me. 'I'm sorry. For everything. All the yelling. Everything.' I wanted to say more, something meaningful. But I didn't know what.

Hannah was staring down at him as if she were watching a sleeping child, not looking sad or scared. The kids crowded around and sobbed quietly. I was feeling rotten, when suddenly Jack shuddered as if he'd been touched with those electric wires I'd once seen in a carnival and sat up and began barking madly as though eager for round two. Martha joined him, her deep woofs echoing through the canyon night. The noisy racket of the two of them had never sounded so good.

Tears were flowing down Hannah's cheeks as she kissed Jack's sandy head, the kids whooping and jumping around. The little begger loved the attention, barking faster and faster, as if he thought it was his yapping everyone was thrilled over.

I sat down hard on the sand before my legs went out from under me and looked up at the night sky and blinked a couple of times, then chanced a look back at the dogs, the kids and the woman, all of them celebrating on the sandy shore. Hannah was talking and laughing as if this was the happiest day of her life. Maybe it was – but then every day was pretty happy as far as she was concerned.

She was marching the children, all of them soaked and shivering, back to the fire, talking loudly as she went, the dogs leaping around her like demons. She stopped only long enough to pull her shoes off and to pour the water they contained out on to the sand, laughing as if this was an enormous joke. Then after settling the children by the fire, she turned and hurried off into the darkness. She still hadn't dried herself and I could tell from the stiff way she was moving and the tight look on her face that she was cold. But she wouldn't stop and take the time to get dry. When she was focused on something, there was no stopping her.

I wondered if she'd gone to thank her voices. Maybe. She returned minutes later hugging an armful of soft green pine boughs, that half-grin of hers stuck on her face, and she plopped down in the sand and quickly wove these twigs into small head-wreaths for the children and the dogs.

She made one for Milagros as well – never willing to exclude her from anything – she and the children taking the little green halo to the coffin and placing it gently on Milagros' breast. They stayed by the girl for a while, Lucia rubbing the injured child's arms to help her blood flow, Hannah chattering away to the sleeping child.

Then she stopped talking and stared down into the coffin, her expression seeming to transform from happiness to a deep contemplation, different somehow from the moods I'd seen before, her eyes unfocused in that way she had, gazing inward, as if she could see something of the child's future inside herself. Then Hannah nodded as though she was saying yes to something unspoken, and smiled. It made no sense the way she talked to this sick child. But then very little about Hannah Morgan made sense to me. The kids just continued to talk and play around the coffin, Lucia rubbing on the little girl's legs now. I turned back to the fire.

Surprisingly, both dogs had let her stick the silly green things on their heads without pawing them off and then they were sitting in front of the flames like they were wearing crowns of gold. I laughed. The whole lot of them – the kids and these two animals – looked like pictures I'd seen of fairy nymphs.

As I was thinking this, Hannah leaned forward on her knees and put her hands on Milagros' head and went stiff and still again like I'd seen her do before. She was determined as ever to heal this child. The kids stopped talking and watched, silently drawn, as I was, to this strange demonstration of faith, shivering from the night chill and maybe something else. Moments later, Hannah stood and stared solemnly down at the still figure, wrapping her arms around herself as if she'd suddenly realized she was cold, then turned and walked back to the fire, the children following, just as solemn.

But solemnity was not something Hannah tolerated long and I could see her tossing it off now like a too-heavy garment, talking rapidly to the children and suddenly grabbing hands and hurriedly forming a circle. They danced and marched around the fire, hand-in-hand, as if it was some sort of maypole. Round and round they moved. This flowing circle of the woman and these lost children seemed strange to me for a moment, seemed to blend together somehow, their movements harkening to other times, other places. Times and places lost for ever in the lamentable silence of dead memories.

I just stood and watched. Watched until they all dropped down on to the sand, too exhausted to continue their lunacy.

After she'd tucked the children in and said their prayers with them, she moved off to sit by Milagros again. She seemed reluctant to leave the child this night – just sat staring at her, giving nothing away with her expression. Not sadness, not happiness. I half expected the young girl to suddenly sit up in the coffin, miraculously cured. A light breeze bent the flames of the fire and made me shiver. I got up and walked over to her.

'You best get dry.'

She turned and gazed at me in the moonlight until I got uncomfortable, looking at me as if she needed my help.

'Ma'am?'

She took a deep breath, glancing down at Jack now, picking him up and rocking him gently in her arms. She started to say something, then she stopped and turned, orienting slowly to the familiar northerly direction, peering up into the deep gouge between the mountains, her gaze fixed on something invisible that I knew drew her like an insect to a lantern's light. 'I must be going,' she mumbled.

'Not tonight.'

'No. Not tonight,' she agreed. She let Jack down and leaned forward and tucked the blankets around the child. 'Not tonight.'

Watching the intense expression – her face gently lit by the faint dance of moonlight off moving waters, her arms cradling the little dog – I could well imagine her on some ancient desert plain succouring the Christ Child. The Madonna: so strong and yet so tragically weak to the world's suffering.

CHAPTER SEVENTEEN

Milagros was gone when I got up the next morning. I guess I'd suspected it the night before but hadn't wanted to face it. I had to now. Hannah sat holding her cradled in her arms. Something tightened in my chest. I didn't want to see the child. Didn't want to look into that small face, so cold, the eyes closed against life, the features slowly changing back to nothing. No, I didn't want to. But I had to.

I stood behind Hannah without speaking.

'Go,' I heard her say, gently, as if trying to shoo the dead child away. I moved in front of her. Her clothing was still damp from the night before, her beautiful eyes sunken into her head. I knew she hadn't slept. She'd stayed with Milagros to the end. Would stay, I knew, with the world until the end.

I put a blanket around her shoulders and then took the body from her, rigid in death. Memories of my wife and child, my parents and brother – all dead and cold like this – rushed over me. Hannah sat with her eyes focused on the sand in front of her.

'Go on now,' I heard her whisper and knew she wasn't talking to me. I wondered if it was possible. Yes. Everything was possible with this woman. I knew that.

'You need sleep,' I said.

She didn't respond.

I laid Milagros in the coffin, fixing the blankets neatly over her, then led Hannah to the fire. After I'd made coffee, I returned, drawn the way we are to death. I studied the small face that had never looked at me and knew that, nevertheless, she had seen me. 'Goodbye,' I said. Emotion clawed at my throat, then I slipped my finger inside her hand. There was no warmth, no squeezing welcome. Nothing but the chill reminder of what once was and would never be again.

I don't know how long I sat there before the children came. They came slowly and quietly, as if afraid they might awaken her. I didn't even hear them. They were just suddenly there beside me. James crawled into my lap while Olive and Junior stood on either side of me, their hands on my shoulders, gazing at the dead child. James was trembling and I put my arms around him. Then Lucia came and began to brush out the child's hair, humming that small tune she liked. None of us said anything. And, yet, in some strange way, we said everything. I knew that.

Always practical, always focused on the living of life, unwilling to mourn for long, Hannah had tossed off her melancholy and was cooking. In a little while, she came and collected the kids. Then she returned.

'Mr Gibbens.'

I looked up at her. She stood smiling down at the dead child as if proud of something Milagros had accomplished.

'Why didn't you save her?' I asked.

'She was.'

'She's dead.'

'More alive than either of us, sir.'

'You could have,' I mumbled.

Hannah turned as if unwilling to participate in this talk, and walked back to the fire. I just sat and stared at the child again and wondered the why of things. Nothing about this life or woman made good sense. Nothing.

The sun jumped the rim-rock of the mountain some two hours later, and Hannah came again. When she spoke, I heard a sound that caused me to glance up. She was staring up the canyon, twisting a towel in her hands until I thought it might rip.

'What?'

'I don't know.'

I didn't want to leave the child, but the sound in the woman's voice had triggered something in me. I walked down to the river, climbing up on a fallen log near the water's edge and just stood for a while. Hannah was right. Something was wrong.

Since first light the sky had held constant: a lovely thin blue colour, high up. No breeze. And it had warmed considerably during the past hour. Everything was pleasant feeling. Still, I was sensing what she'd sensed.

Then I saw three mallard ducks speed past me, careening wildly through the air and disappearing down the river. They were moving fast, as if chased by a falcon, shooting desperately low over the water . . . too low. I waited and watched but saw nothing pursuing them. That small fact caused me to stop and look up and study the surrounding hills and forests. Nothing seemed all that unusual. But still I couldn't rid myself of the sensation that something was happening. Something I didn't want any part of.

I watched now as a group of goldfinches landed on the branch of a nearby aspen and huddled together in the bright morning sunlight. Moments later, I hopped down off the log and walked past where Hannah was digging Milagros' grave in the soft sand with an old coffee can – digging hard and fast. I could hear her making sounds as she worked. The two dogs were watching her and whining, not used to seeing her like this. I wasn't either.

Hannah looked up at me and squinted against the bright morning sunlight, then shaded her eyes with a hand.

I didn't say anything to her, just kept walking until I'd entered a small meadow behind the sandy shore, filled with wildflowers. I stood listening and watching, turning slowly in a circle. Nothing. I couldn't hear them, couldn't see them. On a perfect looking late summer day, in a meadow filled with thousands of flowers, I couldn't see a single bee. This place should have been filled with them. My heart began to speed. Then I turned and looked back at the camp where Hannah was now standing and watching me.

'What is it?' she called.

I didn't answer, my eyes on the fire. The smoke was having a hard time rising into the air, was hanging in a grey cloud just over Hannah's head.

There'd been no frost that morning. None whatsoever, even though I was certain that it had dipped below freezing during the night. Hurriedly, I searched the flowers until I found a spider spinning a new web, Hannah coming up behind me.

'Mr Gibbens?'

'We may have a problem,' I said, watching the spider. The web was small and tight, not large and loose like they normally spun. And when it was complete, the creature went and crouched near the centre. That was all it took to convince me.

'We've got one,' I said, turning and taking her by the arm and starting off at a brisk walk back to the camp.

Hannah looked from me to the spider web and back again. 'What kind of problem?'

I wasn't listening to her. Instead, I was studying the sky. It was still a thin blue but now I could see high, wispy clouds with long trailing strands that looked like they had been painted with a brush.

'Mare's tails.'

'Pardon?'

'Mare's tails.' I'd broken into a trot and was hurrying her along the sand to the camp.

'Mr Gibbens,' she said, pulling back, 'will you please tell me what you are talking about? What is the problem?'

'We've got to get down the mountain.'

'Why?'

'Blizzard.'

I wasn't paying any attention to her now – just surprised that the Mother of God didn't know the why and wherefore of natural things. She had this amazing insight into life, into people's problems, but seemed so woefully ignorant about other matters. I was hurriedly bundling our belongings in the heavy canvas tarp.

'Hurry,' I said.

'No.'

I stopped and looked at her. She was standing with the tin can she'd been using held in both hands. 'I must bury Milagros.'

The sky was still a lovely soft blue colour.

'No time.'

'I will make time.'

Something in the way she said the words told me that she could indeed make time. But that was silly.

'No.' I said the word slowly.

'I will not leave her. Nor will I go with you.'

I frowned at her. She was holding the coffee can in both hands tight against her belly. My expression had no effect. When I finally spoke my voice was low. 'What do you see?'

She turned slowly, looking at the fields, the trees, the mountains, the river. 'Nothing, Mr Gibbens.'

'What do your voices tell you?'

She looked suddenly uncomfortable. She took a deep breath. 'Nothing.'

'Nothing?'

'They have not spoken to me this morning.'

A chill ran across my shoulders like some feral creature.

'Haven't? Or won't?'

She stiffened again.

'They are not a telegraph service, Mr Gibbens.'

I returned to my hurried packing. 'Smoke isn't rising from the fire, bees are staying in their hives, birds are huddled together in the trees, ducks are heading downstream, skimming the water as they go.' I turned and looked up at her. 'They've got the same feeling in their guts that you and I do.'

She was staring at me as if I were a little boy who'd tried to play a trick on her that had failed to work.

'Smell,' I said.

She frowned.

'Smell,' I insisted.

She took a deep breath through her nose and held it.

'What do you smell?'

'Just things,' she said, confused.

'Too much: the grass, the river, the trees . . . everything too rich.'

I went back to trotting around the camp quickly stuffing gear into saddle-bags and the canvas pack, the kids watching closely now.

'Mr Gibbens, are you trying to tell me that you can smell blizzards coming?'

The words brought me up fast. I couldn't believe it – not

289

from a woman who told me she had smelled the Devil himself. But I didn't say anything, didn't need a fight, not at this time.

'Smell them. Hear them,' was all I said.

She looked up at the mountains around us, listening as if she thought I'd lost something vital in my head. 'Exactly what do you hear, sir?'

'Woodpecker for one.'

She listened a moment, then squinted her eyes at me, looking more worried about my sanity than the weather. 'It's just a woodpecker, Mr Gibbens.'

'Too loud. Too crisp and clear.' I looked up and studied the sky again and didn't like what I saw and hurried off toward the horses hobbled on a stand of grass behind the sandy shore. Jack had begun to bark.

'You're scaring him,' Hannah said, walking quickly along behind me as if she didn't want to leave me alone.

'It's not me.' She looked up at the sky.

I could tell she was surprised at the dove-grey clouds edging over the towering mountains to the east. Something in them looked ominous. For the first time, she seemed to understand that I was right.

'I must bury her,' she said, rushing back to the grave. 'But even then, I cannot go with you.'

She paused, studying my face as if searching for something in it that would tell her that I understood. I didn't. Nor did I want to. I began to squirm.

'You know that, sir.'

'All I know is that we've got to get down this mountain.'

Hannah Morgan started digging. 'Take the children.'

'You're going.'

'No.'

'You're going.'

'No, Mr Gibbens. I am burying this child. Then I will ride north.' She paused. 'I must ride north.' She was gasping hard in the thin mountain air as she dug. 'You know that I must do that.'

I was suddenly angry that she kept including me in her crazy conclusions like I knew things I didn't – had made pledges I hadn't. 'I don't know any such thing,' I snapped. 'All I know is you're going down this mountain.' It was an order.

'I am not.'

She was digging furiously at the sand again, the children helping her now with their bare hands. They looked scared.

I was cinching the saddle on the sorrel. 'Ever been in a blizzard?'

'I've been in snowstorms, Mr Gibbens,' she said firmly.

'Blizzard?'

She hesitated a few moments, then said, 'Probably never a blizzard, sir.'

'Probably?'

'Never.'

'Never seen anybody caught unprepared in one?'

'No, sir, I have not.'

I tossed Lucia's saddle on to the bay and began to cinch the animal up, driving a knee hard into the horse's paunch to force it to let the air out that it had swallowed. 'Never seen a person so cold they killed their horse,' I huffed, 'split its belly and crawled up inside to get warm, only to freeze into a block of ice when the animal's carcass froze around them?'

She didn't answer. The children were still digging but they were also watching me, their eyes growing wider.

I stared at her. 'Make you a deal. Admit – right here and now – who you are and I'll sit down, have coffee with you. Then we can ride north. Take our sweet time about it. Do anything you please.' I paused. 'Otherwise, you're coming.' I dropped my voice low. 'I'll make you.' I saw her body go taut. I didn't care.

She returned my stare for a moment, her pleasant features shifting into an immutable look of hardened resolve. I'd seen it all before. But this time the hardness made me want to step backwards.

'You will not,' was all she said.

The words almost sounded like a threat – the way a dog gives a low warning growl. My mind leaped to the dead men in Four Walls. But that was crazy. She hadn't murdered those men any more than I had. But somebody had. Somebody who surely wouldn't like me grabbing her, forcing her places. I didn't care. I wasn't leaving her.

I glanced back up at the slowly moving wall of clouds. 'Snow comes first. Then the temperature drops. Then the wind.' I waited a moment before I said, 'It's the wind that kills you.'

Hannah stood her ground. 'I won't go, sir.' She returned to digging hard. 'Children. Gather your things, quickly. You are leaving with Mr Gibbens.'

Lucia hurried them off to pick up their belongings.

'Together.'

'Mr Gibbens – you know I've made a promise.'

There she was again, talking like I knew certain things. But I didn't. 'What promise?'

She just stared at me like I was losing my mind.

'Who'd you promise?'

'Our God.'

I shook my head. 'Yours.' She stopped and tensed again. It didn't matter. I was tired of games. 'I don't care about your God, your word or anything else.' My voice was rising. 'You're going.'

'No,' she said, scooping sand faster with the coffee can.

'You'll go, ma'am. Whether you want to or not.' I paused. 'Don't make me force you.'

She looked up at me, her eyes flashing again and I thought for an uncertain moment that she was going to tell me to go ahead and try . . . if I dared. And I wondered if I could. There was something about her – something I sensed but couldn't see – that seemed unsettlingly superior. Physically, mentally, every way. It was the strangest feeling I'd ever had.

'I'll do it,' I said, not as certain as I sounded.

Hannah Morgan stared at the sand for a long time as if deciding my fate, before she said, 'If you'll help me bury Milagros – I will go with you.'

I let the breath I'd been holding go, sensing again the iron will behind that beautiful visage and glad I wouldn't have to challenge it.

CHAPTER EIGHTEEN

We'd been riding hard for maybe an hour when the snow came. It was heavy and wet, collecting fast over the trees and trail. Then the temperature was falling. Close to sixty when we'd started – now no more than thirty.

I didn't know how far it would drop, but guessed ten below wouldn't break records. And dressed skimpy the way we were, we'd have an ugly time at fifteen above.

Hannah Morgan was shivering in her saddle, staring down like a blind woman at her hands, lost in melancholy beyond Milagros. She was quick to cry over the living, hated death in ways I didn't understand . . . but she did not long mourn the dead. They had gone to her god. And she would never mourn that. I continued watching her, wondering exactly where her voices were driving her. Then the wind hit. It rushed down the canyon bending trees until they snapped, blasting snow and ice fragments into us like sand.

Hannah shuddered visibly. I pulled my horse close beside hers and plucked a miserable looking Jack off the rump of the sorrel. The children had one another's body warmth to help them survive. She had nothing.

'Open your jacket,' I hollered over the wind. Hannah unbuttoned the mackinaw and I stuck Jack inside. 'He'll get warm. Do the same for you.'

She smiled slowly at me and I could see she was badly chilled.

Martha was covered with snow. Still, as long as the dog kept moving and the temperature stayed above fifteen, she'd be OK. But if we didn't made it down soon, we were going to have to hole up. It was something I didn't want to do. Not with a bunch of kids and a woman who was already half froze. Too dangerous. We were still about 6,000 feet up. Safety was around three. We'd be there in an hour. Maybe.

I'd cut a hole for my head in a spare horse blanket, and was wearing it now sarape-style, the sides closed with leather strapping. It wasn't the best, but better than nothing. I'd tied towels and rags around Hannah's and the children's heads, knotting them under chins as if they had toothaches. Then done the same around my own.

'Getting colder,' she yelled over the wind's roar. 'The children?'

'OK for now,' I hollered at the top of my voice.

'The horses and Martha?'

'OK. Just keep riding.'

Thirty minutes later the wind kicked up another notch, driving the snow horizontally, burning exposed flesh and making it damn difficult to see. Worse, it cut our speed. The temperature was still dropping. I figured we had to stay in the saddle another hour. I glanced at Hannah Morgan and wondered if she could.

She was cradling Jack through the Mackinaw and leaning into the wind. I knew with her thin dress and light shoes she had to be suffering badly. She hadn't complained. She wouldn't.

I kept my eyes focused on the trail, wondering why this God of hers would let her suffer like this. What was the point? Hadn't she given enough? What more would he ask? Or was this her

choice? I didn't know. Had no answers . . . not about her life
. . . not about my own. All I knew was that she wasn't a woman
to let herself be enshrined. Not by her God . . . not by me.

I was thinking these thoughts when disaster struck. The trail
ran close to the river's edge and Hannah's horse stumbled over
a rock hidden by the snow drifts, the frantic animal sliding into
the river, dumping her into the frigid waters. It was the worst
thing that could have happened.

I leaped to the ground and quickly fished her out. Once she
was on shore, I shoved her down, rolling her over and over in
the soft snow, the snow sopping up most of the water before it
had a chance to penetrate her clothes. Most of the water . . .
not all. And at this temperature, water in clothes and against
skin was deadly. Fear for Hannah Morgan's life was pumping
through my body like poison – the same way it had in Four
Walls. We could go no further. We had to face things here, at
this elevation, in this place, now. We had no choice. Hannah
needed to get out of the wind and into a shelter with fire – and
she needed to do this in minutes . . . or she was going to die.

I looked at her and tried to smile. She smiled back, her face
pale, her lips blue. She was wet from her neck down, the water
beginning to harden in frozen sheets over her long dress.

'I'm sorry, Mr Gibbens,' she said, fighting the chattering of
her teeth. 'Keep going.' I could almost feel her drifting away
from me, into another place and time.

'No. We can't. We've got to dry you off,' I said, grabbing her
arm and leading her stumbling through the snow drifts toward
a large pine tree. The lower boughs were covered with heavy
snow and drooping down close to the ground. Carefully so that
I wouldn't knock the snow off, I poked a hole in through a
drift at the edge of the tree, a hole large enough to crawl
through.

I went in as if entering a teepee, tramping and packing the snow down around the tree's trunk. Then I climbed back out and ran to the horses and took the pack off the bay and carried it back to the shelter. Lucia had the kids off their animals and was building a second snow-cave like the one she'd seen me make. She was OK, that one. I tossed her extra spare blankets.

'Get them inside with the dogs. I'll be right back.'

She didn't say anything, just ushered the little ones in through the hole. Jack shot in, followed by Martha.

I turned back to Hannah. She'd slumped to the ground. I yanked her up and made her walk while I spread the tarp over the ground inside. Then I helped her in through the hole. She wasn't moving right: stiff and awkward.

'Get those clothes off and wrap yourself in these blankets.'

I tied the horses to one another behind a dense windbreak of pines, then climbed inside with the kids and hurriedly dug a small hole the size of my fist some six inches down in the dirt with my pocket knife. Finished, I opened a leather bag I carried and pulled out a handful of dry bark: white oak, tamping it down into the hole, shaving slivers of pine sap in on top, then lit it.

No flame and almost no smoke. But the bark had ignited and was burning slowly, the heat streams rising in the air. The oak shavings, starved for air, would burn coal-like for some sixteen hours, raising the temperature a good twenty-five degrees in the small shelter. Combined with the body heat from the kids and dogs, and protected from the wind, they'd be warm enough under their blankets.

'Mr Gibbens,' James said, his teeth chattering hard, 'are we going to die?'

'Nope.'

'Miss Hannah?'

297

'She's fine. Promise.' It was a promise I wasn't sure I could keep.

James smiled at me. I smiled back and then looked at Lucia. She was busy spreading blankets and making the shelter ready.

'Whatever you do, don't let this fire hole get covered up . . . and don't go outside.'

I thought I saw her nod. So I nodded, then went out, rushing back to the second shelter. I dug another hole and lit another handful of oak – then looked at the woman. Damn. She hadn't gotten her clothes off. Wasn't doing anything to save herself.

She was sitting and staring at the rising trail of heat as if she could see something inside it. I didn't like the rigid, withdrawn look on her face. She was freezing down, fast reaching the end of it. Her breath, whenever she breathed out, was no longer forming the same dense white clouds mine was. She'd lost too much body heat. She didn't have long to live unless I did something.

'Hannah,' I said, turning her face to mine with a hand.

She looked at me but her eyes didn't focus and she said nothing.

'Hannah. Stay with me! Understand? Stay with me!'

The oak shavings were raising the temperature in the little enclosure but it was still cold as the devil's scales. Warm enough to survive in, if the shelter kept the wind off us, and we stayed bunched together under blankets. And if Hannah was dry.

I looked at her and realized she was sliding into the final stupor of frozen death. 'Your dress. Get it off,' I said. She nodded slowly and I started to turn away, then realized that she was trying to unbutton her garment, but couldn't. 'Fingers,' she whispered.

Like heat stroke, once a person got too cold there was no saving them. And Hannah Morgan looked as if she were slipping over that invisible line. A minute later, I had stripped the wet, ice-covered garments from her body, then wrapped her in blankets and pulled my extra wool socks on to her feet, blown on her hair until the ice in it melted, rubbing it hard with a towel to dry it. Finished, I was rubbing her hands, arms and legs hard to get circulation flowing. Slowly she started to come back. She looked young and, in spite of her strong figure, still girlish.

'Mr Gibbens,' she said, fighting the trembling of her body and sitting up, the blanket falling to her waist.

'Yes?' I averted my eyes, uncomfortably aware of her close-ness, her nakedness.

'Children?' Her voice trailed off. I could tell from the pale blue look of her skin that she wasn't out of danger yet – but here she was worried about the kids.

'They're fine. Out of the wind – they'll keep each other warm. They've got the dogs. I've got oak burning for them as well. Lie on your side,' I said softly. When she had done this, I pulled the horse blanket I was wearing off and spread it over the other blankets, then I yanked off my clothes and slid underneath the pile and up behind her. I pulled Hannah Morgan's bare body tight against me. She felt like ice. I shivered violently. But even shockingly cold, her skin against mine was one of the most wonderful sensations of my life. I forced myself not to think about what I'd seen when I'd stripped her garments away, nor the soft feel of her now. She was still shaking uncontrollably and beginning to talk about travelling north, mumbling things I couldn't understand. I held her tight, sensing vaguely that her vulnerability was somehow also her great strength.

Once again, my arms around this woman, I was a man torn by a nagging sense of wrongdoing . . . it was a feeling very much alive in me now. And I didn't like it. I called myself more than a fool. All my life I had tried to do things honourably. My father had taught me that. And that was all I'd ever aspired to . . . never figuring that I was going to be able to do much more. No saint was I. But now, with her body pressed against me, I was struggling hard to deal with even these very basics of morality. Passion rising in me. Then a strange thing happened. I began to fall asleep.

With Hannah's skin warming against my own, I just stopped thinking about her, began to feel at great peace, then suddenly drowsy. And the passion I'd been experiencing was dissipating, seemingly lost in the howling night wind . . . swept out of the shelter with any carnal thoughts I'd held about this woman. We'd been surviving for too long, on too little sleep, I figured.

Outside the storm raged. Its fury would go through the day and far into the night. It didn't matter. Inside this shelter, with the bark fire glowing and holding this woman tight against me, it was wonderfully warm. So wonderfully warm. Hannah's breathing grew deep and rythmic now. I struggled to stay awake and listened to her.

'Hannah,' I whispered, fighting the fatigue that seemed to grab at me.

'Yes,' she said drowsily.

I jumped, thinking she'd been asleep. Then I couldn't remember what I wanted to say. 'Nothing.'

She murmured something.

I breathed in deeply of her, then slept, the night stitching threads of dark mystery through my mind.

'Tasukete!' 'Helfen!' 'Aiutare!' 'Socorro!' The cries came at me in a hundred languages from the lips of thousands, a cacophony of tragedy and terror that swirled like a whirlwind of death rattles in my ears. I could speak nothing but English, still I knew these were cries for help.

I'd been drifting off into deeper sleep, my arm around Hannah Morgan's shoulder, her bare body pulled close to mine, when the cries began. Then came the visions, a kaleidoscope of human suffering that burned into my sleeping brain until I was drenched in sweat and shuddering uncontrollably. In my mind's eye I lay helpless, as if paralysed, watching a storm of ruinous human catastrophe that seemed to blow down through the centuries.

Children died of disease before my eyes, some were crushed to death under the spinning wheels of wagons, sailors drowned in unknown seas, cities were sacked and burned, there were hangings of men, women and the young, and the pitiful beheading of an old Oriental man on a desolate plain; death and suffering in numbers too great, too overwhelming to be fully comprehended. The worst of it, I thought, was that every one of the victims seemed to turn in their agony and stare into my eyes as if I and only I could save them. If only I would try. I began to sob, shudders racking my body.

'I can't! I can't!' I moaned. 'There's nothing I can do!'

Still the terrifying calamities would not stop, the horrible, agonizing sounds of the pleading voices pounding against my skull like hammers against stone . . . the awful visions flowing over me like lava destroying everything in its path . . . as if humanity itself could not long survive this hellish onslaught of pain and destruction. Then the worst of it struck . . . as visions of my wife and dead child floated before my eyes, pleading as the others had for me to help them.

Unable to bear it any longer, I clutched my head as if to keep it from bursting and screamed a scream that felt as if it had been trapped somewhere deep inside me all my life, the sound every bit as frightened and hopeless as those yells that moments before had been flooding my head. Then I was awake and

301

Hannah Morgan was holding me in her strong arms. I moved away from her. Neither of us said anything.

I struggled to my knees inside the shelter and tried to shake off the nightmarish panorama of death and suffering that had been marching relentlessly through my mind, trying to see again the anguished face of my wife. I couldn't. She was gone. Gone inside the empty blackness. I wanted to cry out to her, to tell her I couldn't help. But I couldn't. The words lodged in my throat.

After I had sat staring at the tree-trunk for a long time, shivering in the cold and reliving the terror of the dream, I slowly collected myself, then turned and saw Hannah sitting up and watching me. The blankets were down around her waist. She was naked – as if we were together and creation was brand new. I felt blood rushing to my face and turned away.

Hannah Morgan did not seem embarrassed by the fact that we were both undressed. Yet she was not bold – nothing suggestive or wanton. It just seemed that she was not ashamed of our nakedness. Nothing carnal or wrong. Still, it made me uncomfortable and I quickly began to dress.

I was listening. The awful cries had stopped. But I wasn't searching for them. It was the wind I was listening for. It was gone. The blizzard was over. I could see the morning sun shining through the eastern snow wall of the shelter.

Hard as it was to believe, we'd been asleep for some fifteen hours. Maybe that was true, I thought, but I'm exhausted. I felt as weak and wobbly as ever in my life. I told myself that it was from lack of food but I knew that wasn't it. I'd gone for longer stretches without eating and hadn't felt like this. It was the terrible dream. It had drained me of strength and bled off my emotions until I felt limp and wasted. All I wanted to do was go back to sleep, but I forced myself to widen the hole out through the snow. I had the kids and Hannah Morgan to think about.

'It's over,' I said, without looking at her. 'I'll check the horses and then get a fire going to dry your clothes and get something to eat.'

'The children?'

I crawled out into the brilliant glare of morning over fresh snow and broke a hole in the children's shelter. They looked like baby mice bundled up snugly together. Nobody stirred except Jack, who raised his head and looked at me, then went back to sleep.

'They're fine,' I said, standing with my back to the open crawl hole and her.

She didn't say anything. But I sensed she was watching me.

An hour later, I handed her dried clothes in to her, then passed her a plate of hot red beans and bacon. The children were still sleeping. I went back to the fire, listening to her eating. She surely loved a good meal. Then I heard her knitting needles start clicking away inside the shelter and laughed. She was dogged about things.

The canyon was covered with some three feet of snow and looked pure and beautiful. The temperature was somewhere in the high twenties. No wind. Chilly but a decent day to ride down the mountain to the sagebrush flats.

Jack and Martha were out exploring among the nearby pine trees now. I took a sip of coffee and then a pull on a cigarette, holding the smoke inside for a time, then let it go with a rush. I was still trying to piece together the horrible fragments of the nightmare, when I heard her behind me.

She was bending down and peering in at the sleeping children. She'd finished the meal and dressed, wearing the mackinaw

303

and looking as wonderfully beautiful as that first day in El Paso. That seemed ages ago. I watched her muttering one of her countless prayers.

'Morning,' I said, turning back to the fire. 'Coffee?'

'Please,' she said, joining me. 'The horses?'

'Fine. Bunched together behind a windbreak of trees.'

She smiled.

I knew she meant it. She liked everything that was alive. I handed her a cup full of steaming black coffee. Neither of us spoke for a while after that. We just stood staring out at the snowy world that surrounded us.

Standing here in this desolate river canyon, a good seventy miles from anyone, I felt alone in the universe with this woman. It was a good feeling. Then I sensed that she'd turned and was looking at me. I was still uncomfortable about the fact that I'd seen her naked and I wondered if she was about to mention it. I shifted awkwardly on my feet. She wasn't.

'They came to you.'

'Ma'am?'

'The people.' She continued staring at the side of my face.

I didn't say anything.

'You saw them.'

I turned and looked at her, seeing again the fatigue and strain in her eyes and knowing now its tragic source. I didn't understand a thing about it . . . but I knew that I'd glimpsed the awful things she saw at night – the things that made her cry out as if in pain, that ground the dark circles deep under her eyes, underlining her great and good spirit with a constant melancholy.

'Yes.'

Hannah turned back and stared down into the flames of the fire.

'Who are they?'

'Always different.'

'Every night?'

She continued to gaze down into the fire, as if searching for the answer to my question in the burning embers. 'Most.'

I looked at her. 'Why did they come to me?'

She didn't respond, just stared blindly at the coals as if she could see the people writhing in them.

'Ma'am?'

Hannah turned her face up to mine. 'I'm sorry.'

'Why did I see them?'

'I don't know.' She stopped talking and gazed across the river at the sheer granite walls of the mountains soaring majestically toward the sky.

'You can escape –'

As if she had anticipated what I was about to say, Hannah quickly interrupted, 'I must be going, Mr Gibbens.'

'Because you gave your word?' I noticed that she didn't care for the way I'd said it, but she let it drop, straightening the pleats of her long dress.

I looked up the canyon toward the towering snow-covered mountains that were faintly etched against the morning sky and shook my head, 'Not that way.'

'It's the only way I know.'

'Too much snow. Your horse won't make it.' My voice was firm. I felt I had to be to get her to listen to reason about things.

She bridled for a moment, again not liking the fact that I was telling her she couldn't do something. I wondered yet again about her stubborn streak. It cut a broad swath up her backside – sent her charging headlong into trouble.

She put her plate down. 'Then I'll find another.'

I didn't doubt it.

CHAPTER NINETEEN

We rode down out of the mountains and on to the sagebrush flats around noontime. The kids looked sad over the loss of Milagros. I was as well. But not Hannah. She was just going about life, like always. She'd been knitting since we started out that morning and I'd been trying to figure out what it was that she was making me. I couldn't. It didn't look like anything I'd ever seen. At least nothing useful.

'What is that?'

She looked up from her work. 'This?'

'Yes.'

'This?'

I could tell she was avoiding the question.

'Yes. That. What is it?'

She seemed to lean down over her work a little closer. 'I'm not exactly sure,' she said quietly.

'Not exactly sure? It's more than halfway done.' I was smirking good. 'How can you not know what it is?'

She looked slightly annoyed. Or maybe defensive. 'If I'm not certain what it is – how can you know it's more than halfway done?' She paused. 'Anyhow, I didn't say I didn't know. I said I wasn't sure.'

'What's the difference?' I asked, turning back to scan the horizon over the mare's head.

She was getting huffy now. 'There's a big difference, sir. A very big difference.'

'What?'

She didn't answer me.

'None.'

'Pardon?'

'I just figured it out. There's none.'

She rolled her eyes as if I were incapable of understanding the simplest things and went back to knitting.

I shrugged. At least the yarn was black.

The air felt wonderfully alive, filled with the bitter-sweet smells of Spanish yucca, the broken stems of sage, and the sounds of honey bees and birds. The horses had begun to dance in eager anticipation of a good graze. Then Jack took to barking from his perch on the rump of Hannah's horse – barking for the pure joy of it – until I told him to shut up. He stared spitefully at the me, slowly realizing that his honeymoon of being able to do whatever he wanted after the bear attack was over. So he shut up.

I glanced at the woman. She was deep in thought. Knitting as fast as ever, but deep in thought. Hadn't even heard me yell. I shook my head. She could surely focus on things – burn holes in them – when she took a mind to. Nothing distracted her. Especially not once she'd given her crazy word and was carrying it out. We hadn't talked much during the ride down, Hannah seemingly caught in these unspoken concerns of hers, knitting up a storm as she worried.

This back-tracking, I knew, ate at her. She was tense as if she was late to something important. I studied her rocking in her saddle, needles flashing in the sunlight, staring down with unfocused eyes as if she could see a parade of things I couldn't. I thought momentarily of the horrible nightmare. And figured

I didn't want to see what she saw. I felt bad for her. She was strange in her way, pensive and moody, bearing great burdens, without being unfriendly or self-possessed. She was what most women wanted to be: mysterious without trying.

I continued watching her, as always finding it hard not to, sensing the ferocious energy contained within her – controlled like that of a caged panther. A raw, compelling womanhood.

She was riding bent forward over the mass of knitted material, her needles still now, staring blindly at the sandy earth, tangled in new and seemingly darker thoughts. Her lips were moving slowly as if she were talking to someone. But through it all, the fatigue, the depressing visions, the dirt, her moments of lunacy . . . her beauty radiated. And with the desert sunlight on her, I thought she looked the goddess she was. No matter what she admitted.

I forced myself to gaze off across the land. It was nice country: a mix of high desert and red sandstone hills that grew into the blue mountains. There were good stands of junipers in the hills and scrub oak and chokeberry down on the lower elevations. On the flats there was tumbleweed and yucca and sage. Yes, nice country. I'd grown up in similar surroundings and understood it. I felt good. Good that I'd saved this woman and the kids. Still, I couldn't throw off the sense of guilt that I was forgetting my wife . . . riding away from her, abandoning one who had loved me.

We rode into a sea of white flowered yarrow. The aromatic plants burned my nose as the horses broke a trail through it. Jack and Martha were having a good time chasing wood rats and ground squirrels as if they were pups again.

We continued on until I saw a good stand of buffalo grass near a small desert spring and reined the mare in. Hannah's horse stopped on its own and started to graze. The act seemed to bring her out of her deep thoughts and she turned and looked at me as if I were a newly arrived stranger.

'We need to let these animals feed,' I said.

She didn't answer, just looked like a woman awakened from a deep sleep, collecting herself before she spoke.

'Yes,' she said finally, still sitting on her horse. 'But I need to be going.'

I pushed my hat back on my head and swung down and loosened the cinch on the sorrel. Then I walked over and offered my hand. She climbed down.

'An hour or so. They need that. They've been going hard.'

'Of course,' she said, remaining beside the black gelding as if ready to crawl back into the saddle. 'Then I need to go.'

'Is there a certain day?' I asked.

She didn't answer.

'Ma'am?'

Hannah turned and looked at me again as if I were a total stranger. I could see beads of sweat on her upper lip.

'Ma'am, are you OK?'

Her eyes seemed to consider me again. 'Yes. I'm fine.'

'Do you have to be there by a certain day?' I repeated.

'Where?'

'This place you're going.'

'I don't know.' She sounded frightened.

'You don't know?'

'No.'

Hannah stiffened at the persistent questions. 'Is that acceptable?'

I watched her for a moment, then said, 'Your business.'

'Thank you,' she said, turning and walking toward the small spring.

I followed.

'Where are we headed?' I asked.

She had taken a tin cup and knelt and scooped up some water from a clean looking pool. She held it out toward me.

'After you,' I said.

She took a sip and then said, 'I have no idea. Just north. That's all I know.'

'You gave your word again?'

She ignored me.

I pulled my hat off and ran my handkerchief around the inside of the brim, then reset it on my head. 'Why are we going?' The familiar sound of the law creeping into my voice again.

When she finally spoke, her tone was cool. 'I didn't know you were. You seem always so ready to leave.' Her hackles rising.

I worked a rock loose with the toe of my boot, not wanting to get her ruffled. 'Figured I'd make sure you got there OK.'

'I can manage.'

I pulled my hat down lower over my eyes. 'Yeah, I can see that.'

She stared at me for a few moments, then took another drink, and slowly smiled at me over the edge of the cup. 'I've done alright, sir.'

'Yes, ma'am.'

'I do fine on my own, thank you,' she laughed.

'Absolutely.' I was grinning now.

She tossed the water that remained in her cup and scooped me another. She was standing close to me and the smell of her was in my nostrils. It was funny, how she could smell so naturally good.

'Thanks for the water,' I said.

She was staring off toward the north, her face turning serious again, the cold chill of this burden falling over her like a shadow of some feral beast.

'Mr Gibbens, you've been very kind to me and the children. But I don't want to delay you any more.'

'That's OK,' I said. 'Never been in these parts.' I was suddenly embarrassed. 'I'll get a fire going.'

Minutes later, when I chanced a quick glance at her, Hannah was sitting on the ground, her knitting in her lap, needles darting like minnows in a stream. I shook my head. It was the last time I'd ever bet her anything. She took things like her word and obligations too seriously. Then I saw her hesitate, examine the row of yarn she was working on, and then start talking fast. Upset. Dropped a stitch, I figured. I laughed.

CHAPTER TWENTY

The moon wasn't up yet and I couldn't see the face of my pocket watch very well in the darkness. Either eleven or twelve. And I was tired. We were all tired. But Hannah Morgan wasn't in a stopping mood. She was riding a few yards ahead of me, Jack lying on the rump of her horse. Martha was walking with her tongue out beside the sorrel. The kids were a few yards behind me, almost asleep in their saddles. From the look of Hannah's posture, straight and stiff, she appeared ready to dust another seventy-five miles.

'Can't go all night,' I called. 'These animals are shot.'

She turned her head and looked back over her shoulder at me across the wash of shadows. 'Yes. Just a bit further.'

'Where?' I snapped, looking off into the darkness ahead and feeling exasperated. 'You're not sure where you're going. You said that. One place looks as good as another to me.'

'Just a bit further, then we'll stop,' she said, her voice carrying that vague, distant sound in it that was nevertheless oddly intense and focused. Focused on what I had no idea. All I knew was that I was growing accustomed to it, even if I didn't understand it.

When she turned away to look over the ears of her horse again, I shook my head. She was going to drive us all into the ground at this pace. What was eating at her, I wondered? On and on, mile after mile, we'd ridden, talking only when I said something. Then lapsing back into silence.

Suddenly she urged her exhausted horse into a trot and was lengthening the distance between us.

'I'm warning you. These animals can't take much more of this,' I shouted into the darkness at her. She kept going. I shook my head. She was a strange one. I knew she loved and felt sorry for these animals, was always fussing over them and worrying about saddle sores and whether they were thirsty or hungry. But then when this thing, whatever it was that drove her, these voices I guess, took control, she seemed willing to sacrifice herself and everything else. Obsessed was the right word. The thought bothered me. I nudged the sorrel into a slow trot, the mare doing it, but I could feel the exhaustion in her. The Dunnet boys groaned, then they all followed.

A minute later, Hannah reined in at the top of a small sandy knoll. My first reaction was that I'd finally gotten through to her. But then I could tell from the way she was sitting in her saddle, still and alert, her head cocked down the line of the slope in front of her, that she was looking at something. Jack was up balancing on his feet on the rump of her horse, trying to get a look himself.

I reined the sorrel in beside her horse. Martha sat down next to us with an exhausted groan. There were lanterns burning in the ranch house that stood a hundred yards off down the hillside. It looked like a thousand other ranch houses that I'd seen during my lifetime in these lonely lands. The low cabin had been built of peeled logs and smoke was trailing out of the stone chimney.

I looked at the yellow lanternlight spilling out the windows. That was strange, I thought. Here it was close to midnight and these folks were up and doing. Something was wrong. Was this what had driven Hannah Morgan so? Was this the end of the mad rush that she'd been making since I met her? Did she even know why she had come here?

I struggled with my thoughts, looking alternately from the woman to the small house. What could have brought the Mother of God to this forsaken-looking place? Nothing she ever did seemed connected to large events or things. Just ordinary people. The people in her dreams. I took a deep breath and held it. That made sense.

I turned in the saddle toward Hannah and started to ask her what was wrong down in the little cabin, but before I could she had put her heels to the black and was starting down the slope toward the house. I wondered again whether she'd been told by the voices to come here . . . or whether this was a chance encounter. Wondered what problem awaited us at the bottom of this hill. Was there danger?

'Let's stop here,' she said over her shoulder.

'Did you know this place was here?'

She didn't answer me. And I knew from experience she wouldn't. I decided to take another tack. 'I'm not sure that's a good idea.'

'Why?'

'Maybe we shouldn't bother them.'

Hannah was already dismounting in front of the house. 'Perhaps they could use our help, Mr Gibbens.'

I didn't care for the way she said that and shook my head and swung down. 'Don't feel you have to take my advice all the time,' I said sarcastically.

Again, Hannah ignored me and ran her hands through her hair and then stepped up on to the porch and knocked at the door. I could hear movement inside and instinctively I dropped a hand down to the butt of my pistol. Then I heard a child's voice.

'Who's there?' She sounded scared.

'Friends,' Hannah said.

She had a nice-sounding voice and way about her, I thought. The way my wife had. Maybe the way good women did. Lord knew I was no expert. I just knew I liked the way she spoke and handled herself. Then I heard a man's voice telling the girl to open the door and light suddenly splashed out on to the porch and Hannah.

The little girl had been crying, her large eyes red and swollen. She looked thin and exhausted, wearing a worn dress that was too small for her and had once been a pretty blue colour.

'What's wrong, child?' Hannah asked, bending down over the girl and putting a hand on her thin shoulder.

The little girl shook her head and then burst out crying. Hannah knelt and put her arms around her and the child seemed to melt into her.

'Sarah?'

'Strangers, Pa.'

I stepped up behind Hannah and the crying child. 'Name's Tucker Gibbens, deputy sheriff from Los Angeles,' I called, trying to figure what was wrong here. I still had my hand on the butt of my pistol. 'Passing by and saw your light and thought you might have a problem.'

'It's my ma,' the girl moaned. Hannah stood and took her by the hand.

'What's wrong with her?' Hannah asked, stepping into the house without being invited. As if she wasn't going to be deterred from what she'd come to do. I shook my head. The children were slowly making their way to the ground.

I saw a tall balding man of about thirty-five step out of a

room off the back of the cabin. From the looks of him, he hadn't shaved or slept much during the past few days, looking as worn and haggard as the girl. I nodded at him, peering around the room to make sure this situation was everything it appeared on the surface. It looked that way. I nodded at the man again.

He was carrying a tray with dishes on it and looked barely able to stand. Looking at the man, I knew that Hannah Morgan was here because of her voices, not chance. She'd done it again: walked right into trouble. I glanced at the side of her face. She was pointedly ignoring me. A human divining-rod for problems.

Regardless, from the look of the man and his little girl, I was sensing that this was the last place I wanted to be. It wasn't that I didn't believe in helping folks. I did. It's just that I was getting a bad feeling about this situation. Like I'd been here before. The smell of the sickness, the worn, desperate looks on these two faces. The heavy, hopeless silence of the house. Yes, I'd been here and didn't want to be again. I thought of my wife and child.

'Name's Clive Hall,' the man said. 'Daughter, Sarah.'

'Hannah Morgan,' she said, stepping forward and taking the tray from him. 'Let me help you with that.'

The man let Hannah have the tray, as if relieved that this weight had been taken from him. 'My wife.' The man looked down sadly at the little girl. 'Sarah, get me that old blanket in the other room.' The child darted away. When the little girl was out of the room, he continued, 'Ethel's my wife. She's slipping away.'

I froze with the words, fighting the urge to turn and bolt from the house. It was too soon after Joan. Too soon to face this. I'd have fled if Hannah Morgan hadn't suddenly looked at me as if sensing this unease, something in her look telling me I couldn't run. That I had to stand and struggle with this thing. I didn't like that about her, the way she got me mixed up in dark things.

Things I didn't want or need to get mixed up in, but couldn't avoid because of her.

Again as if she sensed me waivering, she said, 'Mr Gibbens, would you please bring me my saddle-bags?' She stared at my face until I nodded and then she said, 'Thank you.' It made me feel somewhat better staring at her and hearing her voice. Not great, but better. Like I could at least do what she had asked without falling apart. Lucia had bedded the children down on the floor in the main room. She didn't let much grass grow under her, I'd give her that.

'Thanks,' I said to her as I moved to the front door. As was typical, she didn't say anything. She hadn't done it for me. That was OK.

When I was alone again out by the horses, I began to shake like I had malaria or the remains of a bad drunk. The moon had poked a hole in the night sky and I stood staring at it for a while, then turned and buried my face in the warm neck of the black gelding, my breath blowing soft into the animal's fur. I stood by the side of the horse for a time, trying to get a grip on myself, sweat forming over my back.

I had to do it. Hannah had asked for whatever was in her bags. She was waiting for me. The Virgin Mary was waiting for me inside that house and I was standing out here whimpering like a child. I forced myself to stand up straight.

She hadn't come here by chance. She did nothing by chance. My mind grappled with these thoughts, ordering and reordering the facts. She was the Virgin. She might deny it, but I was convinced she'd ridden directly to this lonely ranch house because of the woman who lay dying inside. She'd ridden here the same as she'd ridden to the Dunnets in that lonely canyon. I stopped. The same as she'd come to me in that alley. It couldn't have been chance.

Now, with this little girl's mother slowly turning her face to the wall in this lonely homestead, I was certain I would finally get some answers. Hannah Morgan was here. The God-bearer. She was standing in that house – had come, I was certain, to save the woman. Ethel Hall was suffering, but still alive. Her husband and daughter were crying and begging for her life. Hannah Morgan – Mary, Mother of Christ – would save this woman, this wife, this mother. I fought to keep my hands from trembling at the wonder of it, and untied the bags from the back of her saddle.

Jack was whining and looking miserable. I knew the animals were hungry and thirsty. I'd get them fed and watered in a little while. I took a deep breath and turned and headed inside. I would do what I had to do. If Hannah Morgan wanted me to face it – to witness it – I would.

The little girl was standing in the doorway of the room taking short, hard breaths and watching Hannah Morgan talking to her mother. The man was at the foot of the bed listening intently, looking lost and bewildered. I touched a hand to the little girl's head as I moved past carrying Hannah's bag. Sarah looked up at me and wiped tears from her cheeks and tried to smile through her sadness. I smiled back at her, then walked to Hannah.

I had warned myself not to look at the dying woman. But I couldn't do that. It wasn't curiosity that drove me. It was a basic human instinct to reach out to the sick, the hurt, the dying. If only to make eye contact for a moment in all eternity. Even so, I was sorry I'd done it when my eyes fell on her pale, feverish face, covered with heavy beaded sweat that looked like oil. Like her husband, she was thirty-something, not much older than my wife. But they didn't look anything alike. It didn't matter. Seeing the wasted face on the pillow, too weak to speak in anything but a harsh whisper, brought the dark memories flooding over me until I felt as if I were drowning in this room.

Hannah looked up and sensed this. 'Mr Gibbens,' she said quietly.

I didn't move or respond in any visible way, my eyes locked on Ethel Hall's face.

'Mr Gibbens?' she repeated more firmly.

I jumped and looked at her. 'Yes?'

'Could you and Sarah boil some water, please? I need it.'

I nodded and started to turn away. I knew Hannah was getting the little girl out of the room so she could talk frankly with the woman and her husband. Talk about God.

'Mr Gibbens.'

I turned back toward her.

'You might introduce Sarah to Lucia. And to Jack and Martha. They could use some special care from a girl like her. Sarah, would you help Mr Gibbens's dogs?'

The little girl snuffed and then said, 'Yes.'

'Yes, that would be nice.'

Hannah was right. It was the best thing for her: to put her in charge of the care of wild Jack and big Martha, and under the protective wing of Lucia. The two dogs were especially good with kids, though I had concerns about letting crazy Jack inside the house at such a solemn moment. Still, it would give the girl something to do while her mother slipped away from her, left her standing here in this house, never to hold her or talk to her again. I felt myself tensing. No. That would not happen. Hannah Morgan would save her. She had reached Robert Dunnet too late. Milagros had no one to live for. But this woman had a husband and daughter who desperately needed her. She would save her. I forced my thoughts back to Sarah, reaching down and taking her small hand. She was staring hard at her mother's gaunt face and shuddering as if she were cold. 'You have a dog?'

'No,' she said, her lower lip trembling.

'Well, I have two and they need attention. They've been working hard and are beat up and tuckered out. And there are some other children out here. But they've been riding hard and are probably asleep now. But my dogs, they've got to be checked for burrs and fed, brushed good and watered. You think you can help me do that?'

Sarah snuffed hard and then nodded, her eyes still on her mother as if she were afraid that if she looked away the woman would disappear. She was right. Soon enough. No, I told myself again. It would not happen.

'Good, Sarah,' I said softly, moving her toward the door. 'First let's start some water boiling.' She was watching her mother over her shoulder as I walked her out.

Then she pulled away and ran back, kneeling by the bedside. Sarah threw her arms around her, sobbing, 'I love you. Don't die. Don't.' I saw Hannah wince as if from a physical blow with the words, more certain than ever now that she would save this woman.

She gently took Sarah away from her mother, their eyes – mother and daughter – locking for a moment, and walked her toward the door. 'Your mother loves you.'

'Don't let her die,' Sarah repeated. She turned back and stared across the shadows at her mother. The woman was crying silently in the bed. 'Don't go,' Sarah said, then she turned and ran crying out of the room.

Later, I sat on a hard wooden chair and watched Sarah kneeling on the floor and carefully brushing Jack's fur with a curry comb.

Lucia was sitting beside her, talking quietly to her. The other kids were fast asleep. The two dogs had just finished gorging themselves on a meal of beef that the man had supplied and were warming themselves in front of the flames of the fireplace. The wood was mesquite and gave a nice smell to the room. I studied Sarah. She was skinny and cute and had been petting and fussing over the two dogs for the past hour. Thankfully, Jack seemed to understand the serious drift of things and was behaving himself. He could do that. There was definitely a sensitive, caring side to him. But not always.

Hannah had been right. Looking after the dogs was the best thing for Sarah, allowing her to escape for a moment from the dreadful mystery happening in the room a few feet away. Clive Hall had fallen into exhausted sleep on a bed on the other side of the room, snoring lightly. I felt for him, knew what he was going through – his pain made worse knowing Sarah was losing her mother and he couldn't shield her from it. 'Children make cowards of us all,' my mother used to say. I'd never understood what she'd meant. I did now.

I stood. Hannah had to save this woman. She had to. I moved quietly to the bedroom door, looking over my shoulder toward Sarah. The little girl was talking to Jack, her back to me. Lucia's eyes met mine for a moment, then the girl looked away. I opened the door and stepped quietly inside, shutting it softly behind me. I was shaking again.

Hannah Morgan was kneeling beside the woman's bed seemingly deep in prayer, her lips moving silently, her body rigid, perspiration dampening the back of her dress. I didn't know what to do, whether to say something or to watch until she finished. Would it be alright, I wondered, for me to witness? While I was thinking this, I heard her talking low, then another layer of sound, the awful rasping of the woman's heavy breathing; and in this dimly lit room I knew that Ethel Hall's lungs were gone. She couldn't live. Couldn't get air. Then something caught in my throat. My lungs had been destroyed as well. But I'd been saved. Saved by Hannah Morgan. She could save this woman. She was speaking again. I stepped forward slowly, reluctantly.

'So very hard,' Hannah was whispering. 'But it is very beautiful –'

'My baby?' the woman said, the words seeming to hiss out of her lungs. Then she was gasping for breath again. 'What will become of her?'

'She will be fine.'

'I can't breathe. I can't,' she said, a rattling sound in her throat.

It made me desperate to see this woman dying, asking for air. Dying the way my wife had. The words I'd heard bothered me. Then they began again.

'Will she remember me?' the woman moaned. 'What will happen in her life? Will someone love her? Who?' she rasped. 'Who will she marry? Who will care for her if I'm not here?' She was struggling in the bed now and Hannah was holding her down, whispering into her ear as if she were answering these questions.

When the woman quieted again, Hannah said, 'God will, Ethel.'

For a moment the woman was fighting to rise, Hannah holding her once more. Then Hannah said, 'Go now,' in a firm voice and the woman suddenly relaxed and I knew she was gone. Gone as if Hannah had ordered it. But no, it couldn't be. I moved quickly to the bed and looked down. Yes, she was dead. I turned on Hannah.

'You ordered her to die!'

'Don't be silly, Mr Gibbens.' She paused as if she were very weary. 'I helped her to let go of this world. That's all. I'm afraid that I don't possess the powers you want me to.'

'Bring her back!' My desperation had been quenched by a wild resolve.

Hannah didn't look up at me. 'I realize, Mr Gibbens,' she said, her voice sounding very distant and strained, 'that if I'm not some goddess then in your eyes I've lost the biggest opportunity of my life. I'm sorry to disappoint you, sir. But I can't do anything for this woman. She's gone.'

'You've got to,' I said, my voice growing louder as I remembered those first awful moments when I had suddenly realized that my wife had died – that she was not just sleeping. That she was gone. Gone for ever. 'That child needs this woman! God isn't going to do a thing for her.' I stopped and stood staring down at the top of Hannah's head. 'Where is this God of yours?' I demanded. 'Have Him set the damn terms – just save her.'

Slowly, Hannah turned to look up at me. She was crying, sobs beginning to rack her body as she crouched animal-like beside the dead woman's bed. Wild agonies flashed in her eyes. Even during her most tormented moments, I had never seen this expression on her face and it stunned me now. I reached and touched her shoulder and she flung my arm off with surprising strength.

'You're like those people!' she sobbed. 'All those people . . . crying, begging . . . pleading for things that I can't do! I can't, can't, can't! Don't you understand?' Hannah was up on her feet now and backing away from me as if I carried some deadly virus. I stood absolutely still, not knowing what to say or do. Whatever tensions and fears that I'd sensed bottled up inside her were now releasing in a wild emotional torrent as she stumbled away to a shadowy corner of the room like a mad woman. I followed and she whirled on me.

'Leave me alone!' she snapped. 'Don't ask me to do anything . . . for her . . . for them. Don't! I can't . . . I can't . . . I can't! Do you understand?' Her words sounded tortured.

'Yes. I understand.'

'Don't lie to me! Don't you dare lie to me! Not me! You understand nothing! Absolutely nothing. You think I'm some god . . . that I can magically make this woman rise from this bed . . . wave a hand and cure her of the rotting sickness and death.' She narrowed her eyes and stood glaring at me. 'I'm a woman. Nothing more! I am not the salvation of this world that you want me to be. I can do nothing for it except weep.'

And weep she did. Standing and looking lost and forlorn in the shadows of the corner, standing unsteady, as if she might collapse at any moment; Hannah Morgan cried for a long time. I let her. Was she crying for Ethel Hall? The faces in her nightmares? For the world? I didn't know. All I knew was that I was afraid to approach her and uncertain why.

'I understand,' I offered quietly, not even knowing what I meant. Only knowing now that she was not a celestial spirit. Not the Virgin Mary. Just flesh and blood of this earth, tragically possessed by these visions.

She pulled deeper into the darkened corner at the sound of my voice, leaning weakly against the logs, sobbing softly as if she would go on doing it until the end of time. I started to move to her, but didn't. Didn't know what to say or how to console her.

When she finally spoke again I could barely hear the words. She was staring at the dead woman. 'What could I have done? How could I have helped her? I prayed. That's all I can do. It's all I can ever do,' her voice trailing off into the shadows.

I didn't say anything.

'Why? Why must I see their faces? Hear their cries? Why must they come to me, Mr Gibbens? Why?' She was heaving without sound now. Then she looked up at me and said, 'They want so much. But I can't give them anything. I pray for the Lord to help them,' she said, running her words together now. 'That's all I ever do. All I ever do.' She looked across the room at the dead woman. 'But it's never enough. There are always more of them – needing so much more than I can give. I can't –' She was sobbing again, drenched in sweat and moaning. Then she clasped her head in her hands and squatted there in the corner. I knelt and held her tight.

'Can't you help them?' she cried. For a second, I wasn't certain she was talking to me. Then she shuddered hard and I heard her taking a deep breath and she seemed, a moment later, more aware of where she was and the fact that I was holding her. She forced herself to stand. 'Why do they come to me, Mr Gibbens?'

I couldn't see her face in the shadows. 'I don't know,' I mumbled. 'I don't know.' And that was the truth. All I knew was that I'd been wrong about Hannah Morgan. The old minister in Four Walls had been right.

'I don't know,' I repeated.

She didn't respond.

CHAPTER TWENTY-ONE

I figured it was the awful repetition of things – like water dripping against stone until it wore it away – that had finally brought me to it. Watching Joan and Nellie die and, now, so soon after, this woman. It had brought the foul dark waters crashing over me, triggering the floundering depression again. But it didn't really matter any more. What mattered was that I was finally ready. Secretly, I had prayed that Hannah Morgan was the Mother of God so that she would save me from this. Would help me find my wife and child. But she wasn't. And wouldn't. And whatever bright possibilities she promised, they were gone now, replaced by the dreadful melancholy that scoured my soul raw through the long days and nights until I wanted to scream.

I was squatting on a boulder at the bottom of an arroyo, half a mile from the ranch. The right time and place. The dogs could go with Hannah or stay with Sarah and her father. Their choice. Hannah, I figured, was right: she could get along without me. And she had her collection of children.

When I didn't return to El Paso, Sheriff Solomon would wire my boss and Matson would send someone to pick up the prisoner. That was it. Life would go on. With or without me. There was nothing else to worry about. I had no kin. Hall could make good use of my horses and weapons.

I was sitting and looking down at the pistol in my hand, my

thoughts on my wife and baby, when I heard a sound and looked up to see Hannah Morgan standing on the edge of the gully, holding something and staring at me like I was a schoolboy caught playing hooky. She appeared fully recovered from the woman's death. That was an amazing thing, I thought. How she could bounce back so quickly.

She smiled at me. 'Hello, Mr Gibbens.'

I nodded. I didn't want her here.

She came slipping and sliding down the steep trail like it was covered with wet eels until she was standing at the foot of the rock where I squatted. Hannah made a show of dusting her hands off, as if just getting to the bottom of the gully had been an incredible feat of daring. Then she leaned back against the stone, looking up at the night sky. She was carrying her knitting. Damn, she didn't quit once she got launched on a thing. She was humming a bright-sounding little tune.

The air was cool and still. Somewhere out on the desert, coyotes were yipping and I could see little cave bats flitting through the air. I shifted on my feet, wanting her gone. But also glad she was here. She was an odd mixture of pieces, I thought. One moment she was ministering to the dying, the next screaming and crying, then she was enjoying the living. Through it all, she cared. I knew the visions and the deaths tore at her soul. Perhaps that was it: perhaps she couldn't go on struggling with them, night in and night out, unless she found some joy and laughter in things. Even then, her moments of levity were fleeting. They were certainly there. And funny. But fleeting. Even as I was thinking this, I could see her facial expression turning serious again.

'I'm sorry,' she said.

'For?'

'That childishness.'

327

'Don't blame you.'

'I shouldn't have.'

'Forget it.'

We stood a while under the moonlight, not talking, just listening to the desert and smelling the sage and cooling dampness of the night.

'How'd you find me?'

'Jack.' She looked up and smiled. 'He loves you.' At the sound of his name, the little dog energetically leaped up a series of rocks until he was on the boulder with me, licking the side of my face.

'Quit it,' I said, slipping the pistol back into my holster. She'd leave soon enough.

'I've gotten Ethel ready.'

I didn't say anything, just looked down at the top of Hannah's head for a long time, thinking about things in my life, until my eyes blurred some.

'I thought you were the Virgin.'

She didn't say anything, just stared off into the night's darkness.

'Thought you'd come to save this woman. That you'd help me find my wife and child. But you can't. I understand that now.'

'No, I can't.'

I waited a moment, then said, 'You should go back to the house. Sarah needs you, Hannah.'

'So beautiful.'

'What?'

'My name from you. Like a gift.'

I was beyond blushing any more, but not beyond my feelings for this woman. I wanted to avoid them if I could. 'Sarah needs you,' I said again.

'When you are ready.'

'I'll join you in a little while.'

'Don't lie to me, Mr Gibbens. Please don't do that. Not at a time like this. It hurts too much.'

I bit at the inside of my lip and didn't respond.

'I had a husband. I loved him.' She turned and looked up into my face. 'I know, Mr Gibbens. I honestly know.' She reached up and held her hand out until I slowly reached down and touched it. 'Please don't.'

'What happ–'

'It doesn't matter,' she interrupted. 'Just don't.'

I pressed my lips together as if I were fighting to hold back words that were trying to escape.

She let go of my hand and turned and watched the night around us. 'You were created for some reason.'

'What reason?'

'I don't know. Maybe your butterflies. I don't know. All I know is that we're all created for something.'

'And you?'

'I assume I was meant to be leaning here against this very hard rock talking to you at this moment,' she smiled.

I laughed. She had a soothing way about her, I'd give her that. She could get me smiling even when I was ready to kill myself. 'You drew a bad assignment.'

She looked back up at me with a serious expression. 'No. No, I did not.' She continued staring and moments later she said, 'It's finished.'

'Ma'am?'

'The thing I knitted for you. To pay off the bet.'

I didn't care any more, but asked to be polite. 'You figured out what it was?'

'Of course. How else would I have known it was done?'

'Sounds logical.'

'I want you to try it on.'

'Later.'

'Mr Gibbens. After all the work I put into this, you will come down here right now and try it on.' She sounded very proud.

It was a sweater. The neck hole was a little tight – hurting my ears when I pulled it on – and the shoulders were a couple of inches too narrow . . . but I figured those minor shortcomings would eventually correct themselves when the material stretched.

Hannah was standing in a contemplative way with a hand against her cheek, supporting her elbow with her other hand, her eyes squinting hard as she gave her handiwork a critical appraisal. She looked concerned that I like it. 'What do you think?'

I was trying to contort my body into some sort of position that would fit the general shape of the sweater, rolling my back to give a little more slack to the shoulders, pushing my upper body down into my waist to make it look longer.

'It's fine. Great. Thanks.'

She was still squinting. 'Do you think the sleeves are off?'

'No, not at all,' I said, stretching my left arm down as far as I could without actually doing physical harm to myself to take up the excess length on that sleeve; and then trying to pull my right arm back up to get the sleeve down further than mid-forearm on that side.

'Hmmmmm, you're sure?'

'Positive. It's very nice. Thank you.'

She had stepped closer and was feeling a glob of excess knitting that sort of hung down from the chest area of the sweater.

'What's that?' I asked, curious.

'I think it's an extra shoulder.'

I just stood there looking at the glob of material and trying to figure how to respond to that. Finally, I cleared my throat and said, 'You can never have too many shoulders in a sweater.'

This finally struck her and she began to giggle, then laugh, then roar . . . until she was staggering around bent over. I helped her sit down beside me on the sand and waited for her to stop laughing.

'You really like it?'

'Yes! It's magnificent.'

'Good. Then I'll make you another.'

'No! No! You've paid off the bet!'

She was rolling with laughter. 'Just one more. Let me try one more.'

I gulped down a new wave of feelings and cleared my throat. And told myself my wife would agree. I cleared my throat again.

'Come away with me, Hannah Morgan,' I said.

Hannah didn't move or respond in any way and for a moment I wasn't sure she'd heard me. 'Hannah. Come with me.'

I watched her turn her face down and tried to read her thoughts. Afraid of them.

'I can't.'

'Yes, you can.'

'I must go.'

'You don't have to.'

She looked up, frowning playfully. 'You are a bad student. Remember? We are created for reasons.'

'So you say.'

'We are. I have this thing I must do.'

'Then afterwards,' I persisted.

'Afterwards what? So you can live with the visions? The screams.'

'Yes,' I said, and meant it.

Hannah turned and walked off up the gully. Soon I had lost her in the darkness. Was that her answer? To just walk away and say nothing? It didn't seem like her. But she was gone. Then a few minutes later I heard her coming back. She stumbled over something and let out a little yell. And I laughed. When she finally reappeared from the shadows she was holding her hands clasped together at her waist in a childish gesture. She grinned. Jack was half asleep on the rock and he looked up at her now, then returned to his nap. There was no question that he didn't like me cutting in on his woman, but sleep was definitely more important. And he returned to it.

Then Hannah Morgan nodded.

'Is that a yes?'

'Yes,' she said, still watching me with amusement. She didn't laugh but stared with a comic expression on her face. I liked that about her: the wonderful mixture of natural reserve and good, great humour.

'You'll come with me?'

'I will come with you.'

I had to force myself to breathe. 'I don't have much. A house, a job, my butterflies, these dogs and some things of my wife's.'

'I wouldn't want you to have much,' she said, her voice throaty sounding with emotion. 'Wouldn't want you to be grand with money and power. No. I like the fact that you are just you.'

I didn't say anything. It felt great to be alive.

'Let's go back to the house,' she said. She had turned and was starting to probe her way through the darkness again, stopping when she sensed that I wasn't following. She turned back.

'I want to stay for a while.'

She studied my face across the wash of dark air that separated us, then she smiled and said, 'Of course.'

Jack had followed Hannah back to the ranch house and the night was still and silent. I sat down beside a small fire that I'd made of tamarack wood and listened to its popping and crackling, watching its pungent smoke curling in the air. I tipped my head back and looked at the night sky.

'Joan,' I whispered. 'I'll always love you.'

I tossed some fresh wood on the little fire and watched it catch. Then I took my wedding ring off and put it in my pocket. 'I'll always love you.' I wiped my eyes on the back of a sleeve and headed for the house.

I'd slept in a rough adobe bunkhouse that stood a couple of hundred yards from the main house. I was stretched out in one of the beds now luxuriating in the warmth of early morning sunlight shining in through the dirty glass of one of the windows. Hannah had stayed with Sarah, sleeping in the little girl's bedroom to give her comfort.

Mrs Hall's body had rested in a rough wooden coffin that I'd hastily built that night from cedar planks in the barn. When it was completed, Mr Hall and I had placed the woman inside wrapped in a nice red blanket. Hannah had done her hair up pretty. And before we'd closed the lid for the night, Hannah and Sarah had brought some sage flowers to put inside with her.

Then the little girl had put a tin-type of herself inside with her mother, saying she didn't want her to forget what she looked like. I knew what she meant. Then Hannah and Sarah stayed in the barn talking to Mrs Hall, and talking about things. Hannah was good with children. Good with everybody.

I slept again.

When I awoke the sunlight was on the rough plank floor and it was time to get up. I stretched long and hard. Clive Hall and Sarah, I knew, had planned to leave before sunrise and to drive their wagon and the coffin to Denver, so that Mrs Hall could be buried in the family cemetery. They had relatives there – aunts, uncles, cousins – and probably wouldn't return to the ranch, Hall had told me. Smart. It would be lonely out here for the girl.

I hopped out of bed and took a look out the window. The wagon was gone. I could see white smoke snaking from the chimney of the log house and wondered if Hannah was still sleeping. Probably. She'd been pushing herself hard and we'd been up late last night. I felt wonderful just thinking about her. I looked around the small room: a fairly new steel hip-bath was sitting next to an old iron box-stove.

I took a good sniff of myself and figured I hadn't been picking grapes in the vineyard of the Lord. So I started a fire in the stove and put a couple of buckets of water on top to boil, then I dug my razor out and stropped a new edge on it on the saddle cinch. I'd washed the pink shirt out the night before and it was hanging over the stove on a cotton rope. It was clean and dry but, unfortunately, pink as ever. I shook my head and laughed out loud. I'd get even for that. I looked forward to laughing about it over the years.

An hour later, I strolled up the rise to the main house, knocking politely on the front door. I was surprised that neither Jack nor Martha let out a peep. And when Hannah didn't answer my second knock, I pushed the door open and found the house empty. She was gone again. The dogs were as well. The children were still sleeping. Still exhausted from their ordeal in the mountains.

The note was hanging from the fireplace. The little clutch of

St Johnswort that I'd given her that night in the jail at Four Walls – dried and stiff now – was tied in a little purple ribbon and hanging with the note. I sat down hard on a chair. I knew what it said before I unfolded it. What I didn't know the answer to was Hannah Morgan's true feelings. Had she only been toying with me? Had she said what she did – that she would come with me – just to keep me from killing myself? The awful possibility knifed through me. I looked down at the paper, my hands shaking.

Dearest Tucker

You know I have to do this. I ask that you not follow. Please. I have a bad feeling in my heart. You asked once what I was created for: it was simply this.

Take the children to El Paso. I promise – I will be with you. The flowers are for you to carry. To keep you safe from Satan.

Love, Hannah

Jack and Martha are in the barn.

CHAPTER TWENTY-TWO

I really didn't have much of a choice. Jack wasn't going to go to El Paso any more than the scrawny beast was going to volunteer to join the Mexican Army. Nope, the little terrier wasn't going back without Hannah Morgan, not unless I shot him and slung him over the saddle. And Martha pretty much did what Jack wanted to do . . . and they were my dogs.

As soon as I'd opened the tack-room door, Jack had sprinted outside, frantically checked the house for Hannah, then taken to sniffing out her trail like he'd gone crazy. When he found it, he was off, scrambling fast over the sagebrush flats with Martha bringing up the rear in her substantial way. So I'd shrugged and figured I really didn't have much of a choice. It was the humane thing: to take care of your dogs. Even if Hannah was going to be mad. But she had bought me that pink shirt. I grinned at the thought.

I woke Lucia and told her to take care of the kids until I got back. The girl hadn't answered me. But she'd do it. I was beginning to trust her.

I was reviewing these things as I leaned into the dark shadows under the eave of a small building that I guessed – from the soft sounds of clucking drifting through the wall – held roosting chickens. I studied the shapes and blotches of things ahead of me. Martha and Jack were sprawled on either side of me. It had taken us some nine hours to get here and Jack was completely shot through since he'd chosen to cover most of the distance on his own four spindly legs.

I cleared my throat softly and shifted my weight on my feet. I'd been waiting here in the shadows for almost two hours. Trying to figure things out. But I hadn't yet. Nobody had gone in or out of the big house. A chill ran over my back like some feral animal. The house had three chimneys – the house in Hannah's dreams. With a sour feeling, I was certain that this was the place that Hannah had been hunting all along. From the very day I'd met her. I didn't know why. It just had that feel about it. Still and dark and final.

I'd checked the bunk room and while it was obvious people were living in it, there was no one in it now. They were probably riding fence or in town. Wherever that was.

The hour was late: maybe two in the morning. I had no idea where Hannah was. All I knew was that her black gelding was tied in front of the big barn. I didn't like that fact. Nobody left a horse that had been travelling hard like this one bridled and saddled – especially Hannah Morgan. The animal stood with its head down, and I knew she'd pushed it getting here. I scanned the other buildings wondering what was so damn important about this place. I looked at the large two-storey clapboard house again. Nothing was moving.

I pushed away from the building and walked the dozen yards to the side of the barn, glancing back at the darkened silhouette of the large house. No light in any window. No movement. Still, something was bothering me. I didn't figure that Hannah had fought this hard to get here just to pick daisies. She'd come because of one of her damn visions. And I knew first-hand those weren't pretty. They were tragedies – tragedies of all kinds.

The muscles across my shoulders tightened with this last thought and I reflexively checked my weapons. I was fully loaded, head to toe, and toting the shotgun. I rarely made an arrest without it these days. It was one of those weapons that just talked horse sense to the opposition. Settled them down nice. Suddenly the moon broke from the clouds and spilled soft light over the barnyard. I pulled in tight against the wall to avoid being seen.

That was when I heard it. The sound caused me to freeze and my scalp to crawl. I'd heard it before. Most recently was in the Spanish quarter off the old Mexican Plaza in the centre of Los Angeles. I'd been standing at the foot of some adobe stairs that led to a cheap second-floor room, the door at the top of the stairs was open a foot or so and I'd heard the sound coming out the space. It had been three in the morning and I'd been on patrol when someone reported screams coming from this room.

I'd sent Martha up first. There'd been no commotion and so I'd followed. The woman had been huddled in a corner, her nose cut off at the end, and her arms slashed repeatedly from shoulders to wrists. Deep gashes. From the look of her broad face and the coal-black hair, and the cut-off nose, I knew she was one of the Apaches who worked on the sheep ranches around LA. I also knew she'd been unfaithful to her husband. That was the way they did things. Then she'd moaned. The same awful sound that I'd just heard from inside the barn: a woman's moan of deep, impossible pain. My mouth went dry and I brought the hammers back on the shotgun with one thumb.

I kicked a side-door open and went through fast with my dogs, the scattergun levelled at the ebony blackness. Nothing moved inside the cavernous room. I held my breath and listened.

A rope seemed to be straining against wood somewhere in the darkness nearby.

'Martha? Jack?'

I felt the mastiff's nose bump against my leg and Jack whined from a few feet away. I relaxed some. The room was clear of danger. I pulled a sulphur match out of my shirt pocket and flicked it into flame with my thumbnail . . . and wanted to scream. She was hanging by her wrists from a rope tossed over the barn's rafters, twisting slowly in the still cool air. She was naked and a strange pink colour.

'Hannah,' I said, as the match began to burn my flesh. I blew it out, struck another and hurriedly lit a lantern that hung on a post. Then I turned back to her and realized two things. One, she'd been flayed alive, probably with a whip in the hands of someone who knew how to use it. And two, she wasn't Hannah Morgan.

I spread a horse blanket over the ground and then cut her down and laid her on it as gently as I could. But still she moaned again as her raw flesh touched the wool. There was almost no skin left.

'I'm sorry. I didn't mean to hurt you. You're safe now.' I hated to bother this woman, but I had to. 'Where's the woman, Hannah Morgan? Did you see her? That's her horse outside.'

The woman looked up at me and tried to mouth something but I heard only air. I leaned closer. 'In the house,' she whispered, then was gone. I put a hand on her head and held it there for a moment, before I spread another saddle-blanket over her and turned for the door. The thing was rising in my throat. I fought to control it.

I'd come in through the back porch and was standing in the kitchen, still holding the cocked shotgun at the level – my only concern was not discharging it in reflex if Hannah came running at me from out of one of the darkened doorways. While I wasn't any good at it, I did it anyway, mumbling a prayer that she was still alive. Then I stood still and tried to get a feeling for what was wrong in this place. Something was. I could sense it. But what?

My mind asked a thousand questions but the house gave up no answers. It was just dark and silent, almost sullen feeling. I continued standing and listening for the floor-boards somewhere in the house to creak. They didn't. I flicked a match and lit the lantern again. I'd doused it before leaving the barn so I wouldn't give anybody watching a pretty shot when I crossed the yard.

The kitchen looked normal enough. There was a big batch of yellow noodles drying on a wash towel on the table and I could smell shredded cabbage fermenting into sauerkraut somewhere nearby. I heard a noise and whirled. It was only a bag of cheese dripping whey into a pan. There was a big iron cookstove and jars of canned fruit lining the walls. It looked normal as hell. But the woman in the barn meant it was a different kind of hell.

I moved slowly through the downstairs, checking the parlour, the dining room and a smoking room. The place was nicely furnished with what I guessed were store goods from Denver or mail-order stuff from further east. Again, it looked too nice and normal for what I knew to be the awful truth.

There was a big wide staircase in the entry hall made from walnut that had been shined slick by busy hands. I wondered if they'd been the hands of the woman in the barn. Probably. I fought the bad urge rising in my throat again, swallowing it down hard. My guess: I had a wife-killer on my hands. But where was Hannah? I stopped myself from moving fast through the house to find her. Hannah needed me alive.

The second-floor hallway was long and wide, maybe sixty feet long, with half a dozen doors on each side. The doors bothered me. But at least they were closed, so I'd have a chance to hear someone opening one. I'd left Martha and Jack downstairs to warn me if anybody was stalking behind me. It was a mean choice. I'd have sorely liked to have the dogs with me: Martha for backup and Jack for sense . . . but I also wanted to know that I didn't have to keep looking over my shoulder every few seconds.

'Get going,' I told myself. I was pushing the limits of luck standing out here in the middle of this darkened hallway second-guessing myself. I had to stop thinking and act. Men who thought too much in my profession got themselves blown into smaller versions of themselves. And I didn't want that to happen now. Not now. I kept telling myself this was like any other job I'd ever handled as a lawman. But the roaring of the blood in my ears said it wasn't like any other. I was looking for Hannah Morgan. The woman I loved.

There was nothing in the first three rooms I opened. They were furnished as bedrooms. Women's rooms. Nicely fixed with fancy curtains, lace, Belgium rugs and dark furniture. The whole place was smartly turned out. Whoever owned it had some money. As I was moving down the hallway toward the next door, I heard a sound in the ceiling above me and froze. Somebody was moving over the floor-boards. Not walking but shifting their weight.

I hadn't noticed the narrow staircase hidden in the shadows midway down the hall. It led to a third floor. I turned the lantern wick down into the kerosine until it was barely giving off light, then I took the stairs, climbing quickly but carefully, easing my weight up on to each step to keep squeaks down. It smelled musty to me. I sniffed again. There was something else. Maybe the smell of fear. I didn't like it. The entry to the room above was an attic-like trapdoor where the stairs stopped, and in the weak light I could see a padlock dangling from it. Fortunately, the lock was open.

I didn't relish lifting this door, but I had no choice. I climbed higher up the steps until I was bent over, my back and shoulders wedged up against the door, my hands still clutching the shotgun. I took a deep breath and held it, doused the lantern flame in the kerosine, and then began to raise slowly up, the door lifting smoothly and with very little sound.

I stopped as soon as I got a crack open that I could see through and squinted. The room above was dark but I sensed not empty. I just couldn't see anything. If somebody was there and awake, they already knew I was here. Sweat broke on my forehead. This wasn't unusual. I hated tight spots in the dark. I didn't mind a fight. I just hated tight places. They made me sweat. Still, whoever was up here hadn't fired at me yet.

Slowly, I pushed the door up a few inches more and glanced around. Somebody was here. I could almost feel them in the darkness. And they were watching me. I just couldn't tell who it was. But still nobody had shot at me. So, believing that you kept doing those things that were working for you, I continued easing up until I was finally standing straight.

I leaned the door back against the wall behind, then stopped, still standing with most of my body down on the stairs, and turned slowly studying the room, shotgun at the ready. Nothing. Somebody was up here but nobody was moving or firing. Maybe they just thought I was one of them. That was fine with me. Quiet as I could, I climbed up inside, crouching to provide as small a target as possible. I felt exposed. But even so, I felt better now that I was out of the cramped stairwell. I waited. Where is she? I kept asking myself.

Slowly my eyes adjusted and I counted four shadowy blotches that I guessed could be people. The shapes were down along the floor on the opposite side of the room. That made no sense. I slipped a shell out of my belt and tossed it to a corner of the room. Nothing. No movement. No gun cocking. Nothing. For a second, I had the awful thought that they – like the woman in the barn – were dead. Then I heard a chain pulling slowly through a metal loop and knew these people were alive and being held as prisoners. What the hell kind of place was this?

I flattened out on the floor, pulled the shotgun tight against my shoulder and pointed at the four blotches, and whispered, 'Hannah?'

There was a stirring. Chains being pulled and people sitting up. I still couldn't see anything. Shadows against shadows. 'Hannah?' I said again.

Then I heard her.

'Why? Why did you come?'

'Shhhhhh.'

'No,' she moaned.

In the light of a match, I saw Hannah, two women and a young girl chained to the floor of the small attic. All four of them looked like they'd been hit and slapped a great deal, their eyes puffing and blackened, their lips swollen and split.

Hannah was looking at me through eyes that were almost swollen shut, and shaking her head as if I were the last person she ever wanted to see.

I lit the lantern and squatted beside her and took her in my arms. She didn't seem able to stop saying, 'No.' She'd been shackled down hard by her wrists and ankles into a position that I didn't like the look of. She was sobbing and shaking her head back and forth hard, her hair flying over her shoulders. I put my hands on her head and tried to hold it still. There was an ugly rope burn on her neck.

'No,' she sobbed again.

I put my finger to my lips. 'Shhhh.'

'You've got to go. Now! Leave!'

I ignored her and began to try the keys on the ring until I found the one that fit. As I worked, she continued to cry softly and to moan 'Nooooo.' I moved on and unchained the other women and the child, watching Hannah collapsing in a sprawl over the floor as I worked. She looked wretched and I wondered if I was just witnessing one of the mercurial changes in her personality that I'd seen before over the past few days. She looked as if nothing could possibly console her.

Then she pushed herself up by her arms and looked at me. 'You don't understand!'

'Yes. I know.'

'No, you don't know!'

'Yes. Yes, I do.'

'You couldn't.'

'I figured it out. I know.' It was the lawman in me, I guessed. I had a good instinct for things. And I had done it this time. Knew I had even before she said it. That was why she hadn't wanted me to follow.

She stopped crying and supported herself on her arms and looked at me. 'What? What do you know?'

'You saw me in your dreams.'

Hannah just stared at me for a long time before she nodded. 'Yes,' she said softly. 'You were one of them.' Her voice sounded far away now. 'Don't you understand? I can't do anything for you. I can only watch. Go!'

I held her in my arms and stroked her hair. 'No. I won't go. Not without you.'

She was whimpering now. 'They're never wrong.'

'I don't care.'

'Go!'

'Hannah – stop!' I lifted her to her feet, waiting to see that she would remain standing. She didn't, crouching back down again like a wounded animal. She was sobbing without sound now. We had to get out of here.

I turned to the woman closest to me. She was maybe my age, pudgy. 'What's your name?'

'Marbeth,' she mumbled through badly swollen lips. She was wearing a nightgown and looked badly frightened. There was dried blood smeared over her face and down her front.

'Marbeth. How many are in the house? And where are they?'

'I don't know. I just know there is a man. He brought me here. Held me and –'

Before the woman could continue, Hannah had scurried over and was crouched beside me, holding my hands and talking rapidly. 'You aren't listening!'

I shook her shoulders. 'Hannah. Quit. I know you saw me. Know you think I'm going to be killed. But I'm not. I promise you that. I promise.' I tipped my forehead against hers and held her. 'I promise.'

She was shaking her head hard again. 'No, no, no! They're never wrong. Never! Please go!'

'They're wrong this time.'

She shuddered and seemed beyond reasoning with. For an instant my thoughts were on phantoms, tragedies and dark things that were just out of sight but not out of mind. Then I shook myself hard to get rid of them and quickly stood. 'I don't care what you saw. I'm here and I'm alive. And you and I are going. So hush.'

Hannah started to protest and I reached and put my fingers to her lips. 'Hush,' I said again. 'Everything is fine. I promise. You were created to do these things. I was created to be with you.'

Hannah got a funny look on her face. As if she thought I knew something, and had suddenly realized I didn't. 'No,' she said, quietly.

'No what?'

'You were not created to be with me.'

'Yes.'

'No.'

I didn't like the way she was squinting at me to see if I comprehended.

'For what, then?'

'For the children.'

I couldn't breathe for a second. When I finally could, I said, 'That's crazy.'

Hannah wiped the tears from her cheeks with the tips of her fingers. She seemed more in control. 'I thought you had realized that by now – realized that you cannot turn your back on them – that you are needed.' She paused. 'That you were chosen.'

Thoughts of El Paso, that night in the alley, the blast that hadn't killed me, of Hannah Morgan sitting dazed and moaning in the tiny boarding room, mumbling the words, 'He is the one,' moved through my mind.

As if she read my mind, she said, 'You are the one.'

I shook my head no and stood and pulled her to her feet and started moving her and the other women toward the small trapdoor.

We were moving through the darkness of the kitchen when I heard something behind me and turned. I'd been a lawman too long, I guessed, and found it hard to pull a trigger fast enough – that split second that gave one the advantage. I just couldn't do it, not without knowing who was on the receiving end. In this case, I probably wouldn't have pulled the trigger first even if I'd had the chance. The crabbed old man standing in the shadows of the doorway was pale looking, and from the surprised and fearful expression on his face, I took him for another victim. Took him for that until I saw the pistol, watched flame flash out of the muzzle.

Hannah was to my right, not far, but far enough that I was surprised she'd made it in time. Then we were both on the floor and I squeezed off a barrel of the shotgun that blew the old man back through the doorway. That the man was dead, there was no doubt. But the damage had already been done.

I pulled Hannah Morgan into my arms and felt her shudder hard as if something larger than either one of us had grabbed her. 'No,' I whispered. 'Don't. Please don't.'

She turned her face up to mine and smiled faintly. There was a small trickle of blood running from the side of her mouth down to her chin, and I could hear the awful rasping sound of an open chest wound. I started to unbutton her blouse but she put her hand on mine. Her eyes were already starting to cloud, even as they moved over my face as if she were taking a look to remember me by.

'Why did you do it?'

I saw her straining to open her mouth and I leaned forward. Then she was gone.

I held Hannah in my arms and cried, Jack whining by my side, until the sky began to lighten in the east. Then I hitched one of the old man's wagons to a couple of mules in the barn, spreading blankets in the bed and laying Hannah and the dead woman in it. The other two women I put on the sorrel and the bay, then drove the wagon with the small girl sitting on the seat beside me. The girl was crying hard and I didn't try to talk to her. Jack rode in the back with his head resting on the blanket that covered Hannah. Martha trotted behind.

I drove all that day until I made the desert creek where I had camped before. It seemed that a lifetime had past since then. Perhaps it had.

The two women made supper and readied the dead woman for burial. They explained to me about her and the old man I'd killed. They had all been kidnapped by the man. Two – Marbeth and the child – had been held in that attic for more than three years. And through their explanation I understood why the child wasn't talking, just crying. I also understood why Hannah Morgan had gone after them. Why she had driven herself so hard to get there. The visions of the child must have eaten at her soul. I touched a hand to her head under the blanket. 'You were right to have gone. But not right to leave without me.'

I dug the graves side by side, figuring the way Hannah liked folks that this would be a treat for her. I dug them deep on a small sandy rise that sloped down on to the creek. I made certain she could see the cat-tails at the water's edge. It was late evening when I finished and I stood and watched cottonwood leaves fluttering down in golden streams from the old trees near the bank, collecting in drifts among the stones near the water. There was a good earthy smell of rotting leaf-mould here and bird calls broke the stillness. Smaller animals I couldn't see were scurrying through the underbrush. There were no longer any of the beautiful swarms of butterflies that I'd seen days before. But that didn't matter. It was still pretty. Hannah would have liked this place. I was certain.

I'd borrowed a comb from the woman called Marbeth and knelt now beside Hannah, carefully loosening the blanket covering her. My breath caught. She looked asleep. And I wanted for a moment to tiptoe away and leave her sleeping like that for ever. Didn't want to put her into the earth. She was every bit as beautiful as that first day I'd seen her. When I could finally move, I reached and touched her lips with the tips of my fingers, then bent and kissed her – the bitter cold of her reminding me of the night I'd spent holding her in my arms. One night for a lifetime. The memory stirred like something living in me.

'Hannah. Why?'

I took her up in my arms again and held her tight and talked to her about the things we would have done. About the little house that Joan and I had built. She'd have liked it. She liked everything. I told her about the Pacific Ocean at eveningtide when we'd have walked together along the sands. The sound of the sea birds, the smell of the spray, the barking of the seals. I shared dreams I wouldn't share with her in life. I talked of everything – talked of nothing. And at the end, I asked her to find my wife and child.

Finished, I combed her hair out and cut a lock, put the little clutch of dried St Johnswort flowers in her hands with her old crucifix, then wrapped her neatly in the blanket and laid her in the ground. Jack was beside himself, standing and staring down into the grave and whining. Martha lay stoically watching. I touched my lips to the lock of hair and felt my chest tightening until I thought I might never get breath again, then I folded her hair into a small scrap of paper I used to sketch a little drawing of her old crucifix. I was feeling desperate at leaving her . . . wanting to remember everything about her. I took a deep breath and held it until it hurt.

Then I heard a sound behind me and turned to see the young

girl standing a few yards away, staring past me to Hannah's grave. Her eyes were red but she had stopped crying.

'I'm sorry about your mother, child.'

'Thank you,' she said, studying the grave. 'She wasn't my mother. But I loved her.'

I could tell she wanted to say something more. I waited and when she didn't, I just wished she would leave so that I could be alone again these last few moments with Hannah. But she didn't. She stood there as if something had been left unsaid.

Slowly, I filled in the grave. Every spadeful seemed to weigh against my heart. When I was finally done, I drove the wooden cross that I'd made back at the barn into the earth at the head of the grave. I knelt and stared at that cross and grave for a long time. Jack had laid down on top of the mound of earth, his head resting on his paws.

I forced myself to stand.

'Mister?'

I turned and looked at the child.

'Who was she?' she asked finally. She sounded ready to cry again.

I cleared my throat. 'Just a woman.'

The child didn't say anything else. She turned and started toward the camp-fire.

I looked back down at the grave. 'Goodbye,' I whispered, the word slicing deep into my soul. I gripped the shovel tighter and turned away. I was headed for the creek.

'I just thought –'

I looked back. The girl was following me, looking solemn and lost.

I wanted to be alone. 'Thought what, child?'

'Nothing.'

Deep purple light was shading the land and she had stopped

and was looking off into the distance as if recalling some distant memory. I felt sorry for her.

'Thought what?' I coaxed.

'I just –' she repeated, stopping as if she wouldn't continue ever again.

'It's OK. Go on and say it.'

'That maybe she was someone else. Someone I'd prayed to.'

I looked at the girl for a long time. Then Jack began to bark. It was his old usual, hell-and-brimstone bark, and given the way he'd taken Hannah's death, it surprised me every bit as much as what the child had just said. I turned and looked.

For ever after, I would always remark to people how odd it was that little things could change a person's life so. Hannah Morgan was still dead in her grave. There were no angels floating in the clouds. No reverberating chorus across the dry landscape. Just a butterfly.

It looked to be the same one – the wandering Cuban – that I'd seen so many years ago. It was fluttering about, landing on Jack's nose, then taking off again as the little dog snapped at it, flitting just above those snapping jaws, landing again, teasing Jack back into doing what he was created for . . . living life like it was meant to be chased hard and barked into submission. I watched that butterfly for a long time. Then I turned to the girl and said, 'I think she was, child. I think she was.'

She smiled at me. And maybe that was when I knew that Hannah was right: that I'd been created for a reason. And I was glad.

EPILOGUE

The old priest sat in the car and watched the house until it was late afternoon. He had found the address in the files of Father Robert Cordova at the archdiocese two days before, carrying it around in his pocket until the urge became too great for him to resist. He moved his eyes slowly over the structure; a typical turn-of-the-century Pasadena home. Large but not particularly glamorous, with its steep roof and vine-covered walls fronted by stands of foxglove and English ivy. Just a solid-looking two-storey Victorian house on a wide, quiet street lined with beautiful old pepper trees. Nothing more. But there seemed to be something more.

He looked down at the seat next to him. The manuscript was sitting in a small cardboard box. Father Mulcahy picked it up and crawled out of the car. His pulse was running faster than usual. 'Slow down,' he told himself. He crossed the street and climbed the brick walkway that led to the front door; hesitated a moment at the bottom of the porch steps; then, clutching the box and papers in both hands, climbed to the large door and knocked.

He glanced around the wide, deep-shaded porch. An old courting swing hung by two chains. Nice large pots held plantings of colourful begonias. There was a tricycle and a pile of toys. Nothing else. The place was neat and clean. The air, even for late winter in Southern California, was warm and fragrant with the smell of early roses.

He was turning to knock again when the front door opened and he found himself staring into the face of a pleasant-looking Latino woman in her early twenties. She was smiling and holding a plump two- or three-year-old boy on her hip. The baby was struggling to get down.

'Good afternoon, Father. May I help you?'

He hesitated, then cleared his throat and returned the young woman's smile and said, 'Yes. I hope you can. I would like to talk with someone about a man who once owned this house.'

'What was his name?'

'Tucker Gibbens. Do you know of him?'

The woman's smile had widened.

'He was my great-great-grandfather. My name is Ruth Espinosa.' She took a welcoming step backwards. 'Come in, please.'

'Richard Mulcahy. From the archdiocese in Los Angeles.'

Without waiting for him to say anything more, she turned and started down a hallway. For a moment, Father Mulcahy stared at the doorway. He could feel a slight sheen of perspiration on his face, his heart was still rushing and he wanted to sit down.

'Father?'

'Yes. I'm coming.'

He followed the woman into a large parlour decorated with old-fashioned mission furniture that had a nice patina of age and comfortable wear. Ruth had placed the baby in a playpen in a corner of the room and motioned now toward a table in the centre.

'Would you like coffee or a coke?' she asked, walking through an open doorway into a large, old-fashioned kitchen.

When he didn't answer, she called, 'Father?'

'Oh, yes. Coffee would be great.'

She returned a few minutes later carrying a plastic tray with sugar, cream, spoons and napkins.

'It'll just take a moment,' she said, smiling again and pulling out a chair for herself.

The house was quiet.

'You're Lucia's child?'

The woman shook her head, her eyes squinting at this priest who seemed to know about her and her family.

'Her great-grandchild.'

'Of course,' he said. 'It was over a hundred years ago.'

They talked for a long time, Ruth reading the final pages of the manuscript and then filling in blanks that he asked about. Curious to know who this woman had been and why her great-great-grandfather had so believed in her, Ruth had, years before, read the family's copy of the manuscript, so she was familiar with it. But nothing in the story had ever convinced her of anything other than the fact that Tucker Gibbens had been in love with Hannah Morgan. She and her husband and baby lived here in the large house, as did two members of the Dunnet family.

'So Tucker Gibbens lived here with your great-grandmother and the Dunnet brothers?'

'Yes. And Olive.'

She sat running the tip of a finger around the rim of her coffee cup. 'He adopted all of the children and brought them here. He never remarried. He worked at the museum of natural history until his death in 1928. We have all kept the house as a tribute to Grandfather Gibbens and –'

She had stopped talking and was staring down into her coffee.

'And her,' he said, finishing the sentence for her.

She looked up and nodded. 'Yes. And her.'

'You seem uncertain about Hannah Morgan.'

'Do I?' she said, pulling her chair in closer under the table and looking slightly flustered for a moment, until she looked up at him. 'It's hard for me to say. Especially to a Catholic priest.' She paused. 'This family owes her a great deal.'

'But you find it hard to believe she was the Virgin Mary?'

Ruth Espinosa nodded.

Some fifteen minutes later, he was standing and ready to leave, having accomplished very little, but glad to have met this bright, energetic young mother and seen the house where Tucker Gibbens had raised the children. He frowned. He had come here for answers and found none. He guessed the events of that week and the woman's true nature would remain for ever a mystery.

Ruth was looking at him as if she felt sympathy. Then his thoughts were suddenly on his dead friend.

'Did Father Cordova ever visit this house after your grand-father's death?'

'There's a room you might like to see, Father.' She walked over and checked her baby, who had gone to sleep in the playpen, then turned and walked to a doorway that led deeper into the house. She waited for the old priest.

'We normally don't let people in it. It was Grandfather Gibbens's rule. We still honour it. But you're a Catholic priest.' Ruth paused, then smiled. 'I'm certain he'd agree.'

She turned and went down the hall. She climbed the narrow, carpeted stairs that led to the second floor. She opened a door and felt for the light switch; found it; turned it on and, instantly, blew the old bulb in the overhead lamp.

'Darn,' she muttered, crossing the dark room and pulling back the heavy curtains on two tall windows. The late-afternoon sunlight spilled in over the wooden floors like buckets of yellow water.

'There,' she said, brushing her hands together. 'That will give you some light.'

The room was nice looking with its high ceiling and dark wainscotting on the walls. There were handsome Oriental rugs with reddish and orange tints on the floor, and lining the walls were large floor-to-ceiling bookshelves. In the centre of the room stood a collection of glass-topped boxes such as might be found in a museum.

He walked over and stood looking down at the closet. There was a large revolver, tinged in places with rust. A specimen card contained the typewritten words: 'Tucker Gibbens's revolver.' Below it were a pair of hand manacles and a card reading: 'Used in the arrest of Altar Ramon, Wilbur Lessing and John Husker.' The old priest's eyes moved slowly over the room. It was part study, part shrine.

It was all here: all of the things that Tucker Gibbens or Hannah Morgan had carried that week. The old priest turned and looked at the young woman.

'May I stay for a while?'

She smiled. 'Of course. I have to get dinner ready. When you're done, just come down the stairs to the kitchen.' She turned and left.

In the dusky shadows of this old room were the icons and memorabilia. Oh that she had been who Tucker Gibbens had believed, the old priest said silently. He stood staring down at the black mass of wool, the brass knitting needles and the small eyeglasses in their open carrying case. He shook his head. She had at least been a wonderful woman. That was something worthwhile in this world. But it wasn't enough to build one's faith on as Father Cordova had.

Father Mulcahy stopped and stared hard for a long time. It was a drawing. The drawing that Tucker Gibbens had made on a small piece of paper at the woman's gravesite. The drawing of Hannah Morgan's crucifix – the crucifix that Gibbens had buried with her in that desert grave in Utah. He wondered if it could ever be located, that grave. It might contain the final answer he so desperately sought. He squinted hard through the glass at the drawing.

The old minister had been right. The letters were ancient Greek. But no scholar in languages, Father Mulcahy had no clue what the faint lettering stood for, had to accept – for the time being – Father Cordova's translation. According to the old man, the letters read: 'God-bearer.' The term had been used for centuries to describe the Virgin. Even though he didn't believe Cordova's explanation, he still felt funny staring down at this small inked cross. Felt as if somehow, in some small way, he had been given a piece of the answer. But that was silly. He knew no more than he had before.

There was a large chair in the centre of the room and he moved to it and sat down. He was feeling tired and alone. He knew that Tucker Gibbens and Father Cordova must have felt this same way at times in this room. He could envision both men sitting in this same chair, talking and praying to Hannah Morgan. Both believing in her absolutely. Was that why Father Cordova had killed himself? Had he realized at the last that Hannah Morgan was not the Virgin, just a woman like any other?

Father Mulcahy rubbed his face in his hands and wished to God that he could believe again. Perhaps in Hannah Morgan – but at least in something bigger than himself. He shut his eyes and leaned his head back.

Father Mulcahy had no idea how long he sat that way before

357

he opened his eyes. Long enough for the light to shift in the room, the rays of the evening sun climbing higher up the wall in front of him.

He saw her when he opened his eyes. She was as beautiful as Tucker Gibbens had written. She was wearing her long blue dress and standing and looking down on him with that same half-smile that Gibbens had mentioned so often in the manuscript.

The old priest got up from the chair and walked closer. The large oil painting had been hanging in deep shadows until the climbing rays of the sun had reached it. It was magnificent. A fitting tribute for a madonna . . . for womankind. He stared into those eyes. He could almost hear Gibbens describing them to the artist, working with him until they were just right. Could it be? He wondered. Could he be staring into the face of the Virgin?

His eyes moving slowly over her lovely features, Father Mulcahy suddenly knew the answer to Robert Cordova's death – seeing Hannah Morgan, he had felt that he had seen part of God's face and was determined to see the rest of it. At all costs.

Was he wrong?

Father Mulcahy stood and began to pace. God, he wished he knew. He looked up at the painting. 'Who are you? Tell me. I've waited so long. Please.'

The two young priests arrived before the paramedics. Their parish house was only a mile from the home and Ruth Espinosa had called them moments after she'd dialled 911.

She stood behind them now, watching as they knelt on either side of Father Mulcahy, the sound of the siren wailing in the distance outside the window. The faintness of it made it seem desolate and lonely in the house and she clutched her child a little tighter.

There was no question that the old priest was dead. She knew it the moment she'd come into the room and seen him in the odd position. She watched as the two priests eased his body back on to the floor. She could see a small round circle of perspiration on the wall where his head had been pressed. He had been on his knees, tipped forward, his head hard against the wall, his hands clasped in prayer. They were still clasped, the priests trying to get them apart.

Ruth felt badly for him, wished that he could have found whatever he'd been searching for in this woman whom her great-great-grandfather had loved so dearly. But there was nothing to find, she told herself. Nothing but dreams and promises of things that never were or ever would be. Nothing more.

She watched as the young men worked at straightening the old man's fingers on one hand, the other hand still clinched tight.

'Did you know him well?' one asked.

'Not at all,' she said, shaking her head. 'He had just come to visit. He was curious about my great-great-grandfather and a woman he knew.' She watched as the man struggled with the clinched fist, then turned and stared out the window, listening to the growing sound of the approaching siren, sadness stealing over her once again. When she turned back, the priest was just prying the hand open and she thought she glimpsed something in it, a flash of something bright. She stepped closer.

'Isn't that crazy?' the young priest said.

Ruth was standing over the younger man and Father Mulcahy, the hand fully open now, her eyes on the colourful object: a butterfly. The creature lay still, seemingly paralysed from the pressure of the old man's hand.

'It's beautiful,' one of the priests said, placing it gently on his open palm.

Ruth stared at the slow rise and fall of the creature's thorax as it fought for breath, mesmerized by the movements. Then she thought she saw something else move out of the side of her eye and she turned her head slightly and squinted. What she saw wasn't movement so much as a sense of movement. She focused harder. Yes. The muscles on the old man's face seemed to be tensing, then Father Mulcahy was slowly arching his neck, pushing the back of his head hard against the floor in a convulsive-like movement, his shoulders beginning to writhe.

'He's not dead. He's not dead!' she cried.

The old man was uttering small, half-swallowed sounds and pushing his breath out hard, as if he hadn't any use for it any longer, then his eyes popped open and he lay staring up blindly at the ceiling, sweat beading over his face.

'You're OK,' one of the priests told him.

Ruth was no longer listening. She was concentrating on the butterfly. It had recovered, taken flight, then returned to land on the forehead of Father Mulcahy and was slowly opening and shutting its wings as if fanning him. The young priests were trying to shoo it away. But each time they reached for it, the butterfly would rise fluttering into the air over their heads, only to return to the old man each time they left it alone.

Father Mulcahy was watching it . . . his mouth opening and shutting as if he were drowning in the air.

Ruth Espinosa knew what the old man was feeling. She stood staring down at the lovely creature, remembering what her grandfather had written and finding it hard herself to catch her breath . . .